This book
belongs to
Sandy Johnson

BUTTERFLY

BUTTERFLY

Kathryn Harvey

A NOVEL

VILLARD BOOKS

New York   1988

Published in the United States by Villard Books,
a division of Random House Inc., New York, and
simultaneously in Canada by Random House of Canada Limited, Toronto.

This is a work of fiction. Any resemblance to real
people or events is purely coincidental.

Library of Congress Cataloging-in-Publication Data

Harvey, Kathryn.
Butterfly.
I. Title.
PS3558.A7185B88   1988   813'.54   88-40143
ISBN 0-394-57177-0

Manufactured in the United States of America

24689753

FIRST EDITION

To my fellow player in The Game,
Annie Draper
(You draw the "all night long" card. . . .)

ACKNOWLEDGMENTS

I would like to say thanks to Anne Samstag, Joyce Wallach, and Mitchell Maher for their very valuable help.

An extra-special thank-you goes to
Shawn Wilds and Dr. Ted Brannen.

BUTTERFLY

Prologue

IT COULD HAVE BEEN any island in any green sea in the world. A white villa stood at the top of a sheer cliff, overlooking aquamarine depths and crashing waves. An eighty-foot yacht rode at anchor, its crew in smart uniforms, keeping the boat ready for the whim of the man and woman up on the cliff. There was an exotic swimming pool behind the white villa; a woman swam in it, reveling in the pure air and silence of her retreat. A feast had been set out under a gently flapping canopy: bowls of iced caviar, chilled lobster and crab, fruit frosted in sugar, cheeses imported from all over the globe, four kinds of wine standing in coolers. No one waited in attendance. The two lovers wanted to be alone.

She got out of the marble pool, climbing up the curved white steps and going between two Corinthian pillars to where chaise longues covered in plush velour towels waited in the sun.

She moved languidly. She felt hot and sweet and ready for sex.

She didn't remove her bathing suit. He would do that for her. Instead she stretched out in the heat and settled her eyes upon the television set that stood in the shade of the striped canopy. It was on. It was always on. She was waiting for something.

A moment later he emerged from the house, the shimmering water of the pool reflected in the lenses of his Ray-

3

Bans. His long white bathrobe was open; he was naked underneath. She gazed at him as he walked slowly toward her. He was tall and lithe, with sinewy muscles and strong thighs; he walked with the stride of an Olympic gold medalist.

He came alongside her chaise longue. She reached up with a lazy hand. The waves of heat rising mirage-like from the white walls of the villa seemed to melt her bones. She stirred on the thick towel, relishing the sensation of its creamy plush pile against her bare skin.

He knelt beside her. She felt strong hands lightly touch her legs. He toyed with the string of her bathing suit. He kissed the inside of her thighs.

But when his hand traveled up, his fingers exploring beneath the Spandex, she suddenly stopped him.

He looked at her, trying to read her expression behind her enormous sunglasses. He saw that her gaze was fixed on the television set.

He looked at the screen. And here it was at last, the thing she had been waiting for—a news broadcast from the other side of the earth, via satellite.

It was showing two funerals. One was in Houston, the other in Beverly Hills. Funerals important enough to be broadcast globally.

She put her hand gently on his head, and stroked him almost absentmindedly as she stared at the solemn processions—one backdropped by California palm trees with people arriving in stretch limos, the hearse white because they were burying a woman; the other beneath a hard Texas sun, attended by men in Stetsons who lifted the coffin of a man from the black hearse. For the moment, she wasn't on this craggy, remote island and about to experience a sublime sexual idyll. She was back . . . back there, at the beginning of the incredible road that had terminated at last in the two funerals taking place on the same day, fifteen hundred miles apart. . . .

January

1

DR. LINDA MARKUS WAS SITTING at the dressing table, her arm raised, about to brush her hair, when she heard a sound.

Her hand froze. On her wrist there was a gold chain from which a charm—a butterfly—was suspended. As she sat suddenly still, listening to the night, the butterfly trembled on its delicate chain, glinting in the lamplight.

She searched the bedroom reflected behind her in the mirror. Nothing appeared to be out of the ordinary. There was the king-size bed on its dais; the satin canopy hangings and mattress ruffle, all a delicate peach color. On the bed lay her white hospital coat, her blouse and skirt, the medical bag she had tossed down after a tiring day in surgery. Italian leather shoes lay on the carpet next to the tan pool of her panty hose.

She listened. But all was silent.

She resumed brushing her hair.

It was difficult to relax. There was so much to think about, so much demanding her attention: that patient in the Intensive Care Unit; the meeting of the Surgical Review Board in the morning; the speech she had yet to write for the annual County Medical Association dinner.

And then, most puzzling, the phone calls she was getting from that TV producer Barry Greene—rather insistent, and not a medical problem, his messages said. She had yet to find time to return his calls.

There was that sound again! A sly, sort of surreptitious

sound, as if someone were outside, trying to get in, trying not to be heard. . . .

Slowly lowering her hairbrush and placing it among the cosmetics and perfumes on the vanity table, Dr. Markus drew in a breath, held it, and turned around.

She stared at the closed drapes. Had the sound come from the other side of the windows?

Dear God, were the windows locked?

She trembled. She stared at the heavy velvet drapes. Her pulse started to race.

Minutes seemed to pass. The ornate Louis XV clock over the marble fireplace ticked, ticked, ticked.

The drapes moved.

The window was open!

Linda caught her breath.

A cold breeze seemed to flood the room as the drapes began to part. A shadow fell across the champagne carpet.

Linda shot to her feet and without thinking ran to the dressing room. Pulling the door shut behind herself, she was plunged into darkness; she groped along the wall for the secret drawer.

There was supposed to be a revolver in it.

Finding the drawer, Linda frantically pulled it open and reached inside. The cold metal felt obscene in her hand; it was long and hard and heavy. Would it fire? Was it even loaded?

Returning to the door of the dressing room she pressed her ear to it and listened. Subtle sounds crept through the spacious bedroom: the creak of a lead-paned window, the whisper of disturbed drapes, the soft hush of rubber-soled shoes on the carpet.

He was in there. He was in the bedroom.

Linda swallowed hard and tightened her grip on the gun. What did she think she was going to do with it? Shoot him, for God's sake? She started to shake. Her heart was pounding.

What if he had a gun too?

She listened. She could hear him moving about. She reached down, grasped the doorknob, and inched the door open. At first she saw only an empty room. Then—

There he was. At the far wall, moving aside a painting and contemplating the combination lock of the small safe.

She studied him. Her trained physician's eye saw beneath the tightly fitted black turtleneck sweater and pants the body of a man who kept himself in shape. She couldn't guess his age—a black knitted ski mask covered his face and hair—but he was wiry. Finely shaped buttocks and thighs moved beneath black fabric.

Linda didn't move, she didn't breathe, as she watched him expertly open the safe and reach inside.

Then he turned suddenly, as if he had felt her watching him. He stared at the dressing room door; she saw two dark eyes peer warily through the ski mask; a grim mouth and square jaw were outlined in black knit.

She backed away from the door, holding the gun at arm's length with her trembling hands. The single beam of light that spilled into the tiny room caught on the shivering platinum butterfly that hung from her wrist; it shot silvery reflections over the camisole and nylon slip she was wearing.

She inched back as far as she could and then stood her ground, watching the door, her finger on the trigger.

The door swung slightly at first, as if he were testing it. Then it swung all the way open and his black silhouette stood against the softly lighted bedroom.

He looked down at the gun, then at her face. Although his features were masked, Linda sensed uncertainty about him, thought she detected indecision flicker in his dark eyes.

He took another step toward her, coming into the dressing room. Then another step, and another.

"No closer," she said.

"I'm unarmed," he said. His voice was surprisingly gentle and refined, the distinguished voice of a stage actor. He had spoken only two words and yet in them she had heard a trace of—vulnerability.

"Get out," she said.

He continued to stare at her. There were only a few feet between them now; Linda could see the curve of biceps beneath the tight sweater, the calm rise and fall of his chest.

"I mean it," she said, aiming. "I'll shoot if you don't get out."

Black eyes in a hidden face studied her. When he spoke again there was a trace of incredulousness in his tone, as if he had just discovered something. "You're beautiful," he said.

"Please—"

He took another step closer. "I'm sorry," he said. "I had no idea I was intruding into a *lady's* house."

Her voice came out in a whisper: "Stop."

He looked down at the necklace in his hand, the thing he had just taken out of the wall safe. It was a long rope of pearls, knotted at the end.

"I have no right to take this," the intruder said, lifting it up. "It belongs to you. It belongs *on* you."

Unable to move, Dr. Markus stared up into dark eyes as black-gloved hands lifted the necklace over her head, slipped it under her hair, and brought it to rest on her bare chest, just above the lace of her camisole.

The night silence seemed to intensify as the thief slowly removed his gloves, keeping his eyes locked on hers, then took the pearl-knot in his hands and adjusted it so that it lay between her breasts.

At his touch, Linda caught her breath.

"I hadn't meant to frighten you," he said in a quiet, intimate tone. His masked face was inches from hers. Black eyes were framed by black lashes and the black knit of his mask. She could see his mouth, the thin straight lips and white teeth. He bent his head and said more quietly, "I had no right to frighten you."

"Please," she whispered. "Don't—"

He raised a hand and touched her shoulder. She felt the strap of her camisole start to slide down. "If you truly want me to go," he said, "I will."

Linda stared up into his gaze. As the two straps of her camisole fell from her shoulders, her arms lowered and the gun dropped to the thick carpet. His hands moved as slowly and expertly as when they had opened the wall safe, feeling her feverish skin, seeming to savor the way she trembled.

When lace and satin came away from her breasts, Linda closed her eyes.

"I have never met a woman as beautiful as you," he said. His hands gently explored her. He knew where to touch, where to pause, where to hold her. "Tell me to leave," he said again, bending his head so that his mouth was nearly upon hers. "Tell me," he said.

"No," she breathed. "Don't go. . . ."

When his lips touched hers, Linda felt a shock go through her body. Suddenly she wanted this man, desperately. Here and now.

He drew her into his arms. She felt the coarse knit of his sweater against her naked breasts. His hands stroked her back, then went lower, sliding under the elastic waistband of her slip. Linda could hardly breathe. His kisses smothered her. His tongue filled her mouth. Her thighs pressed urgently against him; she felt his hardness.

Is it possible? she wondered in desperation. Is it possible that, after all these years, finally, with this stranger I could—

And then a sound broke the silence. It was a rude, insistent bleat, coming from the bedroom.

He brought his head up. "What's that?"

"My beeper. Damn!"

Linda pushed past him, ran to her purse, grabbed the little box and silenced it. "I have to make a phone call. Is that telephone real?" she asked, pointing to the boudoir-style instrument on the nightstand. "Can I call out on it?"

He came to stand in the doorway of the dressing room, folding his arms and leaning against the doorframe. "Just pick it up. The girl will give you an outside line."

As she dialed a number Linda glanced at him, at the gorgeous body in black, and felt her irritation rise. She had taken a gamble; she had had no other choice. The odds had been that she would be able to snatch a couple of hours of peace before having to go back to the hospital, but the odds had turned against her. "His pressure's dropped," the Intensive Care nurse now told her over the phone. "Dr. Cane thinks he's got a bleeder."

11

"Okay. Get him back up to surgery. Tell Cane to open him up. I'm in Beverly Hills. It'll take me about twenty minutes to get there."

She hung up, having made the call without once saying her name—the ICU nurses knew Linda's voice—and turned to the stranger in the ski mask. "Sorry," she said, hastily removing the pearl necklace and reaching for her clothes. "Can't be helped."

"Hey, it's okay. I'm sorry, too."

She looked at him. She couldn't see his face, but his voice sounded genuinely sorry. But she knew it was an act. He was paid to humor her.

After she was dressed, she grabbed her hospital coat and medical bag and hurried to the door. Linda paused to smile at him, a little sadly, thinking about what might have been. Then she reached into her purse, pulled out a hundred-dollar bill, and laid it on the table by the door. He would have gotten it afterward. It wasn't his fault that they were interrupted.

"But I didn't do anything," he said quietly.

"Make it up to me next time."

Linda stepped out into a corridor that could have belonged to an elegant, tastefully discreet hotel. She hurried along, past closed doors, and checked her watch. She really shouldn't have risked coming to Butterfly this afternoon, not with a patient in ICU. But she had been looking forward for weeks to coming here, had already put it off several times because of medical emergencies.

When she turned the corner, Linda was met by an attendant, a young woman in black skirt and white blouse with a butterfly embroidered in gold thread on the pocket. "Is everything all right, madam?" she asked. The attendant did not know Dr. Markus's name; all of Butterfly's members were anonymous.

"I've been called away."

"Was the companion all right?"

They reached the elevator. "He was perfect. I'd like to reschedule. But I'll have to call."

"Very well, madam. Good afternoon."

When the doors whispered closed, Linda quickly removed

the black harlequin mask from her face and folded it into her purse. She rubbed her cheeks, in case it had left any lines there.

The elevator brought Dr. Markus down to the street level and opened upon the brass-and-mahogany elegance of Fanelli, one of Beverly Hills' most prestigious men's clothing stores. She hurried through to the glass doors that opened onto Rodeo Drive and stepped into the glare of a sharp January afternoon. Linda put on her oversized sunglasses and signaled to the parking valet. It was a beautifully clear Southern California day— a citrus-grove kind of a day, Linda thought, and wished she had someone special to share it with.

But there was no one, and there probably never would be. She had come to accept that now, by age thirty-eight and after two failed marriages and numerous unsuccessful relationships.

Although, she thought as she looked up at the plain, unassuming façade of Butterfly, although there in fact was someone to share such a spectacular day with . . . but she had to be at the hospital, and he had other women to see.

The valet brought her red Ferrari around, she tipped him generously and joined the rushing traffic on Wilshire Boulevard. Opening her windows and letting the crisp wind blow through her blond hair, Linda felt herself smile, and then laugh. "I'll be back," she said out loud to the monstrous Beverly Hills traffic. "Come hell or high water, Butterfly. I'll be back!"

2

THE FIRST TIME JAMIE SWAM naked in Miss Highland's pool he had thought she wasn't home. He had pulled himself out and was shaking himself off in the crisp morning sun when he glanced up and saw her standing at one of the second-floor windows, staring down at him. It had startled him. Then he had gotten scared. The wealthy Beverly Highland could see to it that he never worked in Southern California, or anywhere else, ever again.

But, to his surprise, she had not moved from the window. She hadn't shouted at him or called the security guards that protected her enormous Beverly Hills estate. In fact, there had been no visible reaction. She had merely stood there, her hand resting on the drapery, her eyes fastened on him. Suddenly very worried that Beverly Hills cops were going to arrive any second and take him away, Jamie had hastily pulled on his jeans and got to work cleaning the pool. Every so often he had looked up and found her still there.

He'd finished in record time and driven off in his truck, spending the next few days in agony, waiting to be called on the carpet for swimming in a client's pool—*bare-assed naked* at that! But, curiously, no reprimand ever came.

The second time he swam in her pool he did it on a reckless dare with himself. He figured she was home—the Rolls-Royce Silver Cloud that everyone knew was her favorite car was in its garage. And he'd seen the chauffeur working on the Excalibur. Wondering if she would come to her window again, he had dived in with a great announcing splash.

When he emerged a few minutes later, naked and dripping, he saw her up there, watching him.

And again, strangely, no reaction.

This morning was his third time. He had pushed the buzzer at the wrought-iron gate and identified himself to the security guard. Then he had driven his pool-maintenance truck down the long drive and around to the back, where he would spend the better part of the morning cleaning Miss Highland's enormous Italianate swimming pool. With the equipment and chemicals all ready, he paused and squinted up at the house. She was already there, at the window.

He nearly waved, but didn't. Instead, he stood with his hands on his hips, surveying the blue-green shimmering water, as if making up his mind. He was thinking: She wants me to do this.

Although she was a personality constantly in the limelight, a favorite subject of the media, very little was actually known about the reclusive Miss Highland. She lived all alone in one of the biggest mansions in Beverly Hills, surrounded herself with a staff of secretaries, consultants, and hangers-on, jetted frequently from coast to coast in a private Lear, counted top politicians and movie stars among her friends, gave *the* parties of every season, and had the most elegant pool of all the ones on Jamie's ritzy route. But she was something of a mystery. At least, Jamie thought now as he started to unzip his jeans, she was a mystery to everyone else. But not to him. He decided he had figured her out.

Beverly Highland was known for her staunch morality. She was one of the biggest supporters of the founder of the Moral Decency movement, Reverend what's-his-name, the television evangelist. Everyone thought of the chaste Miss Highland as a regular Miss Prim and Proper, a pursed-mouthed disapprover of all fun things. But she had a dirty little secret, Jamie decided. She got her kicks from watching young men swim naked in her pool.

Well, he figured, what the heck. If he got her horny enough, maybe she would invite him in for a romp among her dollar bills. He knew delivery boys who had gold Rolex watches because they serviced these old Beverly Hills dames.

He got his zipper down, then he very slowly, teasingly pulled his jeans down. He paused for a moment on the edge of the pool, giving her a good look at the body he was so proud of, that he worked so hard to keep in shape, and then he dived in. Smoothly, cleanly, like a hot knife going through warm butter. He torpedoed under the water the length of the pool and surfaced at the other end, where his golden head emerged into the bright sunlight. Then he did his laps. Casually, lazily, shooting out each long arm and scooping the water back behind himself, effortlessly, back and forth, back and forth, finally rolling over on his back to let the water run off him and make his tanned skin glisten.

When he pulled himself out, not even breathless, he stretched his arms over his head and shook the water off. Knowing that she was watching him was a turn-on for Jamie. He felt himself get hard, which pleased him because it made his cock bigger. Then he pulled on his jeans and got down to the business of cleaning the pool.

He glanced up a few minutes later and saw that she was gone.

Beverly let go of the drape and turned away from the window. She had found out his name. Jamie.

Then she put him out of her mind.

Her office was very businesslike. Contrasting with the rest of the house, which was lavishly designed for luxury and elegance, Beverly Highland's workplace was practical and no-nonsense. There were two large desks—hers and her private secretary's—mahogany file cabinets, a Macintosh Plus computer, and a Canon copier. Maggie, her energetic secretary, had not yet reported for work. There were letters to be dictated, guest lists to go over, requests for charitable donations to wade through, and invitations to consider to see which Beverly would accept, which she would decline. Beverly Highland held board directorships for several large corporations, sat on the Board of Trustees of American Women for International Understanding, was the chairperson of the cultural resources committee for the Los Angeles Chamber of Commerce, and served on the President's Committee for the Arts and Humanities. There was also personal bookkeeping, which her accountant would attend to, and three press releases to be written, which her publicist would see to. Beverly's staff also included two social secretaries and a public relations liaison.

Resuming her place at her desk, Beverly poured some herbal tea from the silver pot into a Sèvres cup. The aroma of its spice filled the morning air. She didn't add sugar and had nibbled on only one of the delicate lemon biscuits set on a plate. At fifty-one, Beverly Highland was very careful about her diet.

She looked at the calendar on her desk; it was set in an antique gold frame, a gift from a publisher who very much wanted to publish her life story.

There was a date on it, circled in red: June 11.

It was the day Beverly Highland lived for. The day the Republican Convention opened in Los Angeles. Everything she did, every step she took, every breath she drew, was solely for that day.

Never, she was certain, had a presidential hopeful enjoyed such a determined supporter as did the man who had founded Good News Ministries, the billion-dollar TV evangelical empire. When he had announced last year that he was thinking of running for America's highest office, Beverly had been ecstatic. It was the fulfillment of a dream, that he would make such a decision. And now that he had, and now that they were hurtling full steam toward the June primaries, Beverly's anxiousness grew every day—he *had* to make it.

And with her connections and millions, she was going to see to it that he did.

Sipping the cinnamon-spiced tea, she gazed at the photo of him that sat on her desk in its pewter frame. He had signed it, and added, "Praise the Lord." His charismatic smile beamed out at her.

The Reverend had met Beverly Highland only superficially, at fund-raising dinners and heavily publicized political events. He knew very little about her, but she knew him, intimately. She had watched his *Good News Hour* almost every day for years, missing only once when she was in the hospital for a hysterectomy that had involved complications. During her rocky convalescence, she had had a VCR installed in her private room so that she could watch tapes of his sermons, and it was those *Good News Hour*s, she told the press upon her discharge from the hospital, that had urged Beverly through a speedy recovery. Watching him on the screen, she had told the reporters, and listening to his dynamic voice had filled her soul with the power and strength to get up out of that bed and get back to work.

She had written and told him as much, including in the letter a check for one million dollars.

She gazed at the calendar. June 11.

Good News Ministries was the largest "electronic church" in the United States. It broadcasted daily over eleven hundred TV stations, published a weekly "magazine of power," owned a recording company, two airlines, most of Houston, and raked in millions of dollars monthly. It was estimated that nearly 90 percent of the population of the South watched or listened to the *Good News Hour* at least once a week; the actual church membership figures for the entire nation were impossible to count.

There was no doubt about it, the Reverend was a powerful man.

And he emphasized moral decency.

Setting her cup on its saucer, Beverly got up from her desk and found herself walking back to the window. She was wearing a flowing caftan; its yards of pale blue silk whispered against her bare legs. With her hand on the drape, she looked down at the magnificent terraced garden that fell away from her hilltop house. It was such a beautifully, skillfully landscaped setting that one wouldn't guess that the hectic Beverly Hills business and shopping district lay not too far away, awakening for a day of commerce and traffic.

Her gaze went down to the pool.

His name was Jamie, her secretary had reported.

Beverly watched him as he guided the pool sweep through the lime-green water. His back was damp with sweat; sunlight played on the tanned muscles. His long blond hair, drying from his swim, fell down to his shoulders Viking-like. And the jeans were too tight. She wondered how he could even move in them. He had the kind of rear end that girls seemed to go for these days—round and saucy.

"Sorry!" came a breathless voice behind her. "Got stuck on the San Diego Freeway! *Again!*"

Beverly turned to see her secretary, Maggie, come hurrying in, a purse slung over her shoulder, her arms full of papers, one hand clutching an attaché case.

"No rush," Beverly said with a smile. "We have a few minutes yet."

"I swear it's a conspiracy," Maggie mumbled as she reached for the telephone console. Punching the button for the kitchen, she said, "Every morning the traffic gets worse and worse. I would swear that I am seeing the same stalled cars blocking the same lanes— Hi, kitchen? This is Maggie. Send up some coffee, would you please? And a chocolate Danish. Thanks." Maggie Kern, at forty-six, was plump and intended to stay that way.

As she shuffled papers on the desk and continued to mutter about a conspiracy on the part of the bus company to get people to ride the bus—"The same cars stalled every day, I swear it, just to tie up the freeway"—Beverly looked down again at the young, blond pool-maintenance man.

"Ah!" Maggie said when the coffee and Danish arrived. She clicked on the TV set; Beverly immediately turned away from the window and went to the velvet sofa. The two women sat, both shoeless, staring at the screen.

They watched the *Good News Hour* every day before starting work. Even when Beverly had to travel and they were flying over the country in her private jet, or when they were in a hotel room in another city, they always spent the first hour of the day watching the Reverend.

Prostitution and pornography were his main targets, but he had also produced a shockingly graphic antiabortion film. He organized raids on adult movie theaters, sent Bibles and zealous young preachers into the darkness of Forty-second Street, Hollywood Boulevard, and Polk, and, like Beverly Highland, had been instrumental in getting *Playboy* magazine off the stands in convenience stores.

If elected president, he had promised, he was going to clean up America.

The guitars and the Good News Singers belted out a lively hymn, and then he appeared, marching onto the set and literally shouting to his TV audience, "Brothers and sisters, I have Good News for you!"

There was no doubt about it, the man was positively magnetic. He *breathed* power, like some fire-breathing dragon. One felt his heat come right through the glass of the TV screen. His voltaic spirit seemed to pour out from his energetic body. It was no mystery why the Reverend was so popular, even among nonbelievers. He was a salesman, pure and simple. A newsman had once commented wryly that GN's electrifying founder could sell kangaroos to the Australians. But what the Reverend sold was God. God, and decency.

And the main target of today's sermonic attack was a magazine called *Beefcake*, supposedly a magazine for women but which, because of its photographs of nude men in seductive poses, was reported to be a favorite among gays. "I take my Good News today from Paul's letter to the Romans," the Reverend shouted out across America. "And Paul said that because men are such fools, God has given them over to do the filthy things their hearts desire, and they do shameful things with each other. Because of what men do, God has given them over to shameful passions. *Even the women pervert the natural use of their sex into unnatural practices.*"

"Brothers and sisters!" he boomed as he marched across the studio set with an enormous stride. "It pains my heart to have to admit this, but there exist in our beautiful country today houses of sin and corruption. Evil nests where Satan spawns his minions. Where women sell their bodies and men go in lust and sin. It is such places that undermine the strength of our magnificent country. How can America continue to be the world's number one power, the leader to which all the nations of the earth eventually turn, if we tolerate such evil practices in our midst? If men go to houses of prostitution, then what becomes of the blessed married state? If women sell their bodies, then how can our children grow up pure and knowing God's Word?"

The Reverend shook a finger heavenward and hastily mopped his sweating brow with a white handkerchief. "I say we must *bring down* these houses of sin and corruption! We must seek them out wherever they are and cause them to topple! We'll carry the torches of righteousness and put them to their corrupt walls and watch them burn, like Satan's own hellfires!"

"Amen," Beverly Highland said.

"Amen," said Maggie.

When the show was over, they sat for a few moments in silence. Then Beverly sighed and said, "We'd better get to work. The convention is only six months away. There's so much to be done."

While her secretary went to the desk and picked up the day's agenda Beverly Highland went again to the window and looked out.

She was just in time to see the pool-maintenance truck departing down the long drive.

3

HAVING SEX WITH A STRANGER was nothing new to Trudie Stein. It was how she usually spent her Saturday nights. However, having sex with a stranger under these peculiar circumstances, she decided as she gazed up at the butterfly logo over the door, was definitely new.

And it excited her beyond belief.

As she accepted the claim check from the parking valet and heard him pull away from the curb in her electric-blue Corvette, Trudie felt a sudden, unexpected jolt of fear.

But what was there to be afraid of? After all, her cousin Alexis had been coming here for weeks now, Alexis who had gone on and on to Trudie about the fantastic wonders of this place. *"Where you can act out any fantasy you want,"* Alexis had said. And then there was Dr. Linda Markus, for whom Trudie had designed and built a sun deck and spa at her beach house—Dr. Markus had been a member of Butterfly, according to Alexis, for even longer. In fact, it was Linda Markus who had recommended Trudie's cousin for membership, the two being very close friends since medical school. And so now here was Trudie, thirty years old and searching for something, standing on the sidewalk of Rodeo Drive, on the threshold of having her most desired fantasy come true. Thanks, really, to Dr. Markus.

That was how Butterfly operated, Alexis had explained. Since it was a small, private "club," each member was allowed to bring in one other person. Dr. Markus had chosen her best friend, Alexis, and Alexis had decided to recommend her cousin Trudie. Two weeks ago, just after Christmas, Trudie had come here for an interview and orientation with the director. Three days ago she had received her special bracelet, and now she, too, was a full-fledged member with all the rights and privileges that Butterfly offered.

Trudie turned up the collar of her coat and squinted at the building in the cold January glare.

What Butterfly offered . . .

"I tell you, Trude," her cousin had said, "Butterfly has done wonders for me already. It's helping me to find myself, to sort myself out. Perhaps it can rescue you, too."

Rescue. Trudie certainly hoped so. The endless and demeaning cycle of one-night stands with men who never called back, or who proved to be disappointments in the light of dawn, had Trudie Stein on a winding track leading to nowhere. And she desperately wanted to go *somewhere*—with *someone*.

Well, that first step had to be taken.

So she took it, right through the glass doors of Fanelli, the posh Beverly Hills men's store with the enigmatic butterfly on its plain façade. Trudie was familiar with the store; she had come here years ago and purchased a Loire Valley work shirt for her boyfriend, and he had turned around and given it to *his* boyfriend. The store was elegant in a brass-and-mahogany way, and was at the moment crowded with customers returning or exchanging holiday gifts.

Trudie paused a moment to calm her racing heart. She recognized a few of the faces in the crowd: there was the movie director whose swimming pool she had designed and built; there was that famous rock idol Mickey Shannon, trying to look inconspicuous; and over by Toiletries, Trudie recognized Beverly Highland, the famous society hostess.

For an instant Trudie wondered if *she* was a member of the secret operation upstairs. But everyone knew what a staunch supporter of Good News Ministries Beverly Highland was, and what an exemplary, moral life she led. Besides, Trudie saw that the telltale butterfly bracelet was absent from her wrist.

Most of the customers in the store, Trudie knew as she pushed her way through, did not know about what went on upstairs. The director had assured her of that. These people were actually here to buy things—very few were like herself, heading for the back of the store and making sure her bracelet could be seen—the bracelet made of delicate gold links and displaying a small butterfly charm.

She finally reached the back, where live mannequins modeled fashions for seated customers. This part of the shop was overseen by special staff members, women in black skirts and white blouses with butterflies embroidered over the pockets. These, Trudie knew, were separate from the staff that worked the rest of the store. Only these knew where the private elevator led.

Trudie had seen male models before. In fact, a few of the guys who subcontracted for her worked as models on the side. Perpetually suntanned, sinewy from hard labor, and usually with golden locks, they tended to look as good in silk blazers and gray flannel slacks as in dusty jeans and T-shirts. But Butterfly's models, Trudie had always thought, could have put her he-men to shame. And now she knew why, the *real* reason why they looked so good. It had nothing to do with modeling clothes.

Trudie took a seat, declined an offer of tea or Perrier, and watched the fashion show that was a daily feature of the classy Fanelli.

Spellbound, she kept her eye on the doorway to the models' dressing room. The men came out one by one and slowly passed among the seated customers, the majority of whom were women. The models sported a variety of fashions, from leather bomber jackets to Savile Row pajamas, and the men themselves covered a range of types, in age and physique and manner. *Something for everyone,* Trudie thought as her excitement mounted.

The brass ship's clock on the wall ticked and the men came out of the hidden dressing room, strolled about, smiled, posed, and disappeared again. Customers got up and left, more came in and filled the seats. Most left with purchases under their arms (but none, Trudie saw, stepped into that special elevator at the back of the store).

As she looked the men over—the one with the Arnold Schwarzenegger physique in the fisherman's pullover, the short wiry Asian in kung-fu lounge wear—Trudie became aware of two other women who had sat there for as long as she had. Her eye went to their wrists. They wore identical butterfly bracelets.

And then she saw him.

He was silver-haired and distinguished-looking, maybe in his sixties, and modeling an exquisite black cashmere topcoat. Trudie was suddenly breathless. He was *gorgeous*.

Him. She would choose him.

But now that the actual moment had arrived, the time for her fantasy to begin, Trudie felt suddenly shy, inexplicably reluctant. *I've been burned so many times. . . .*

To look at her, one would assume that Trudie Stein was a smashing success in relationships with men: she was a tall, good-looking blonde who wore trendy clothes, moussed her hair into a stylish shag, and drove thirty thousand dollars' worth of car. When on a jobsite, she wore shorts with braless tank tops that showed off her tanned, athletic body, and she bossed as many as twenty men at a time. The problem was, too many of them saw her as just another ditsy blonde, a wealthy, brainless pushover who couldn't possibly make it on her own in the tough construction business, and who therefore needed a "man around."

As she watched the attractive silver-haired model disappear into the dressing room, Trudie allowed herself to recall a painful memory that she normally fought back into the darker corners of her mind.

It was the memory of a night over a year ago. Pool season was starting to wind down—Trudie's company had its busiest time during spring and summer, when most pools were built. That particular November, as the final details were being seen to—waterfalls made to run, spas turned on, landscaping installed and inspections made—Greg Olson, her masonry subcontractor, a man with whom she had exchanged friendly flirtations for several months, had finally come on strong. "Work will be slowing down soon, Trudie," he had said in that drawl she had come to like. "We won't have business conflicts standing in our way. What do you say we go out for a drink?"

Well, Greg Olson had money in his own right, drove an Allante, could have any woman he wanted, and didn't seem pressed to prove his machismo, as so many of the other guys did. So Trudie had decided he was safe; she lowered her defenses. And it had gone well—at first. Dinner and dancing at a restaurant on San Vicente in West L.A. Afterward, a sultry evening drive along the Pacific Coast Highway. And then— they had parked! Like a couple of horny teenagers.

Trudie had loved it. The whole scene was so deliciously juvenile that there had been a kind of endearing innocence to it. As a consequence, she had succumbed sooner than she had planned. Afterward, brushing sand off their clothes as they climbed the bluff back up to where they had parked the car, Greg had said, "Boy, you were good down there. You sure had us fooled!"

"What do you mean?" she had asked as she had gotten into the car, already knowing the answer, fearing it, not wanting to hear it, suddenly wishing she hadn't come out with Greg Olson tonight, that she had listened to her goddamned instincts when they had whispered: Watch out. He's up to something.

"We all thought you were a lesbian. Some of the guys even have a bet riding on it."

When the pool season resumed again, Trudie found herself a new masonry subcontractor. She also instituted a new iron-clad rule for herself: No more going out with guys from the job.

Which left only the Saturday-night pickups, strangers in singles bars who turned out to be hasty lovers, selfish lovers, insecure lovers, and guys who just had to say "Was it good for you?" afterward.

He came out again, the silver-haired model, and her heart jumped.

This time he was wearing a leather trench coat and a white silk scarf around his neck. When he walked past her, Trudie thought he gave her a special smile. She glanced over at the other two women: one was already gone; the other was writing something down on a piece of paper and handing it to an attendant.

Trudie quickly opened her purse and took out a small notepad. She was suddenly anxious, and suddenly afraid that he was already taken. Why was she wasting so much time sitting here!

Her hand shook as she wrote. This was unbelievable! It was *fantastic!*

"What do you do at Butterfly?" she had asked her cousin Alexis.

"Anything you can think of, Trude. They're very accommodating."

"Well, like what about Linda Markus? What does she do when she goes there?" And Alexis had said, "Linda likes costumes. She also prefers to have both her and the man wearing masks."

Masks! Trudie thought as she nervously handed the slip of paper to the attendant. And what was it going to be like with *her* silver-haired lover? Would he really be able to fulfill the fantasy she had requested, would she really go upstairs and find everything there, exactly as she had just written it on the notepaper?

Trudie didn't have long to wait. She sat twisting her hands as the minutes seemed to stretch by—Trudie Stein who was usually so cool, so smooth when it came to casual sex—and prayed that the other woman hadn't beaten her to the silver-haired model. Then the attendant reappeared, murmured, "Come this way, please," and Trudie found herself following the woman into the private elevator.

She had agonized for hours over her appearance for tonight's special "date." Over the years, building up her pool business, fighting to make a go of it in a male-dominated field, and giving orders to tough construction types on jobsites, Trudie had had to learn to suppress her natural femininity and adopt a crusty, aggressive style. If she didn't, none of the guys who worked for her would take her seriously, and the jobs would never get done. And she knew that, as a consequence, she came across as a pushy broad with a chip on her shoulder, out to prove she was just as good as any man.

On the job she tried to "neuter" herself with shorts and tank tops (the breasts she couldn't help), but when she put away her clipboard and blueprints and got ready for a night on the town, Trudie reverted to her instincts for the ultrafeminine. For this first evening at Butterfly she had bought a special outfit: an upholstery-fabric skirt that went down to her ankles,

a blouse of bright blue silk, and silver earrin‚
Trudie knew she was walking femininity wi
construction work gone.

The attendant led her down a quiet hall, past
and finally to the room at the end where the so‚ ‚attendant said, "If you will just go in here, please."

Trudie did.

And the door closed behind her, leaving her alone in a
small, intimate dining room tastefully furnished with French
provincial sofa and chairs, shelves filled with books, thick
carpeting, and a table already set with white linen, china, crystal, and candles. There was a bottle of champagne chilling in
a silver bucket; the subdued lights softly illuminated a crystal
ashtray, a single rose in a bud vase. Muted music came from
unseen speakers.

Trudie couldn't believe how nervous she was. Trudie
Stein, who had been taught by her father to be always in control
of a situation, to be the one in command. Even on her Saturday-
night prowls, when she met and drove home with strangers,
she was the one calling the shots. With not a ripple of anxiety
or self-doubt.

Now she found herself wondering, briefly, *What on earth
am I doing here!*

But hadn't her father taught her always to reach for the
stars, to spin the dreams of her heart's desire? Hadn't he taught
her everything about the construction business, taking her on
jobsites when she was a little girl, hammering into his only
child a sense of self-worth, of identity, of independence? Hadn't
her parents argued on this one issue, Sophie wanting her daughter to follow tradition and find a husband and be a good wife
and mother, Sam insisting that the world was changing, that
times were changing and that his daughter was going to be
anything she wanted to be? Sam Stein, the fairest, most honest
man to walk the face of the earth, in Trudie's mind, had taught
her, right up to the day of his tragic and untimely death, to
dream, and to make those dreams come true.

Well, wasn't that what she was doing here at Butterfly?
Searching for, as her cousin had put it, a *rescue!* Perhaps, Trudie hoped now as she heard footsteps coming down the hall,

she would find answers within these walls, perhaps she would discover what it was she was searching for, find out what it was that drove her out of her apartment on Saturday nights and seemed to compel her to take up with strangers in decidedly unsatisfying and sometimes disastrous encounters. Trudie was here for more than just the sex—that she could get anywhere. She was here hoping to find solutions.

There was another door on the other side of the room. It opened now and he entered. Trudie couldn't believe it—he was even better-looking in this softly lit, intimate setting. He was impeccably dressed. Trudie recognized that the jacket he wore was a Pierre Cardin of black wool, and it fitted him to a T. Gray slacks, pearl-gray silk shirt and burgundy tie. And the man himself: tall and slender, with confidence in the set of his shoulders. He could be the chief executive officer of a large corporation, she thought, or the chancellor of a major university.

He came up to her and said in a quiet, refined voice, "I am so pleased you could come tonight. Dinner won't be for a while yet. Won't you sit down?"

He touched her elbow and led her to the blue velvet love seat. "Would you like a drink?" he asked, walking to the wet bar.

"White wine, please," she said, amazed at how shy her voice sounded.

He came back with a long-stemmed glass for her and a tumbler of brown liquid for himself. He took a seat in a wing chair, settling with the ease and familiarity of being in his own house, and set his drink aside, untasted.

Trudie looked down at her wine. She suddenly felt self-conscious under his gray-eyed gaze. She was surprised to find that she had no idea what to say, what to do next. After all, this was different from a Saturday-night pickup. She was *paying* for this one!

"I am reading the most interesting book," he said, reaching for the book that lay on the small table by his chair. He held it out for her to see. "Perhaps you have read it?"

Trudie looked at the title. Yes, she had read it.

"What did you think of it?" he asked.

"It was all right. Not as good as his earlier works, though."

"How so?"

"Uh, well . . ." Trudie took a sip of her wine, to stall for time. To collect herself.

What was wrong with her? In all her years with her father, one of their favorite pastimes had been to get into heated discussions over books and theories. He had taught her the art and trickery of debate, and she had gotten so good at it that in the year before his death she had usually won.

Trudie suddenly realized what was wrong. *She was out of practice.* Eight years of pool lingo and "What's your sign?" in pickup bars had rusted her skills. Now her silver-haired companion was inviting her to give it a try.

It was just what she had asked for. What she had written on the piece of notepaper downstairs.

"I think he's reaching this time," she said, referring to the book's author. "His earlier works were based on concrete theories and careful study. But this one seems fabricated. You have to bear in mind that his last book came out ten years ago. Since then, nothing. When I read that one there, I couldn't shake the feeling that the author woke up one morning and realized he was fading into oblivion. It's as if he gathered all his friends together and said, 'Hey! I need a new pop-science idea. Anybody got any suggestions?' "

He laughed softly. "You might be right, although I haven't finished reading it. I'll reserve judgment until the jury is in."

"What's your name?" Trudie asked suddenly. "What should I call you?"

"What would you like to call me?"

"Thomas," she said. "You look like a Thomas."

He sipped his drink and said, "You know, even though I haven't finished this book, I believe I must challenge you on what you said about this author's work. You claim that his earlier works are based on solid theories. What about his first book? An obvious contrivance if ever I saw one."

Trudie raised her eyebrows. "But it was his *first!* And it was written in the sixties. He was young and naive, testing his wings, so to speak. Give him the benefit of the doubt, at least."

"It seems to me that you're not giving him that same benefit of the doubt with this book."

"You haven't read it all the way through. Wait until you get to Chapter Ten. His whole argument collapses there."

"I've read Chapter Ten and I disagree, because when you examine carefully the underlying structure of his thesis—"

The debate got into full swing. Growing in confidence now, Trudie kicked off her shoes and drew her legs up under her. Thomas refilled her wine and continued to challenge her ideas. And then there came a discreet knock at the door and a waiter entered with a room-service cart. Trudie didn't feel like eating. She was too keyed up, too involved in the discussion. She and Thomas continued their argument while the waiter presented the fresh spinach and mushroom salad and then tossed it. Trudie attacked Thomas's conclusions as the sour cream and caviar were spooned onto jellied consommé; he drove her back into a defensive corner while the basil chicken and small red rosemary potatoes were served. They completely ignored the custard dessert; they let their coffee go cold. Trudie's pool-green eyes flashed as she scored a point; her voice rose when a win went to him. She talked fast, often interrupting him. She leaned on her folded arms, toyed with her dangling earrings in agitation, grew increasingly more animated with each barrier he threw in her path.

She became acutely aware of *him*. The faint scent of English Leather, the glint of his gold Rolex, his finely manicured fingernails. Class, every inch of him. A far cry from jeans and hardhats and sexist paternalism. Thomas *listened* to what she said, and he gave her credit where it was due. He had removed his jacket and loosened his tie. He was inclined across the table toward her, just as intense and deeply committed to the debate as she. Trudie felt her heart race faster; she grew giddy. She was suddenly high. And very turned on.

"You have your facts wrong," he said.

"I do not! If there's one subject I know better than anyone else, it's this. You have to read Whittington to fully understand—"

"Whittington is on the fringe."

Trudie jumped up out of her chair. "That happens to be an *opinion*, Thomas, not a fact."

She walked away from him, whipped around and strode back. She caught a glimpse of herself in the mirror: her cheeks were flushed, her eyes were bright and feverish. God, but she was turned on. She suddenly realized she wanted this man more than she had ever wanted any man, and decided that if he just touched her she would catch on fire.

And then Thomas was on his feet and reaching for her. He cut off her sentence with a hard kiss, and the debate was all over and Trudie was whispering, "Oh my God, hurry, *hurry!*"

They made love on the rich carpet. When Trudie cried out in orgasm she thought she would die—she had never experienced a climax so intense, so utterly shattering. And when it was over and she lay for a while in his arms, she marveled at the evening she had just spent, and realized that this had been the best sex she had had in a long time, possibly in her whole life. As Thomas held her and caressed and kissed her, Trudie could hardly believe it had truly happened, that it was *real*.

And then a question came into her mind. She wanted to ask Thomas, but didn't want to break the spell. So she asked only herself, and she didn't have the answer.

Who was behind this magical operation in the rooms above Fanelli's men's shop? Who thought of it? Who had started it? Who ran it? *Who, in fact, was Butterfly?*

4

New Mexico, 1952

RACHEL'S EARLIEST CHILDHOOD MEMORY was of waking up in the middle of the night and hearing her mother screaming. She remembered crawling out of the crib—she might even have still been in diapers—and toddling down the hall to another room. The door was ajar. She knew Mummy and Daddy were in there. She could recall walking in and seeing her mother, naked, on her hands and knees on the bed, and Daddy, pushing her from behind, with his tummy it looked like, while Rachel's mother was crying and begging him to stop.

It wasn't until Rachel was fourteen years old that she learned what it was they had been doing.

Two mysteries surrounded Rachel Dwyer's birth. She had been unaware of the existence of either until one scorching day when she was ten years old and, having been left alone in the trailer because her parents had gone down to the local roadside tavern, Rachel had gotten bored.

Boredom leads to restlessness, and restlessness can breed curiosity, which in turn can lead to discovery. Sometimes, unwanted discoveries. As in the case of the battered old King Edward cigar box, which Rachel found wedged under the kitchen sink behind cleansers and rags.

At ten, Rachel was a precocious child—not well educated (her jobless, itinerant father saw to that) but bright. She could read beyond her age level—a self-taught skill born of loneliness and the desperation to escape from a squalid life into the fantasy life of books—and she had a sharp eye. In a glance she saw that the cigar box had not been randomly shoved back in the moldy recess, but had been placed there by a careful hand. Clearly, to Rachel's richly imaginative mind, a treasure box.

She opened it.

Among the baffling collection of ribbons, faded birthday cards, a ring, and movie-ticket stubs were two items that perplexed the ten-year-old. One was a photograph; the other was an official-looking document.

Being able to read so well, she learned in seconds that the document was a marriage license. Her parents' names were printed on it, and there was a town listed that Rachel had never heard of—Bakersfield, California. But the date made her think hard.

The certificate said her mother and father were married on July 14, 1940.

And yet Rachel knew she had been born in 1938.

She was two years old when they got married. That could mean only one thing: that he wasn't her real Daddy!

This pleased her so much that she didn't give the photograph the scrutiny it deserved, for if she had, she might, in her youthful wisdom, have seen something disturbingly familiar about the tired-looking young woman in the hospital bed, a newborn baby cradled in each arm.

It wasn't until later that night—as Rachel lay perfectly still under her blankets on the sofa, which was where she slept in the trailer, waiting for her father to snore himself to sleep (she always tried to be as invisible as possible whenever he was around, especially when he was drunk)—that she started thinking about the photograph.

And then it hit her.

Although she looked much younger, the woman was Rachel's mother.

But who were the two babies?

Well past midnight, as the thin-shelled trailer grew cold and the silence of the desert drew close, Rachel crept from her bed, got hold of the flashlight they used whenever the electricity was cut off—which was often—and retrieved the cigar box, which she had carefully replaced earlier that day. She studied the babies in the picture. There was no doubt about it. One of them looked almost exactly like the one of herself, which her mother kept in her wallet.

Rachel frowned. If this was a picture of herself when she was born, then—who was the other baby?

She bided her time. Rachel's mother was not always an easy woman to approach. If she wasn't drunk or having one of her "sick" mornings, she was over at the trailer-park office listening to Arthur Godfrey on the radio. But there were times when Mrs. Dwyer *was* available, usually when Rachel's father was gone on one of his sudden absences. During these spells Rachel's mother didn't seem to need to add the bourbon to her coffee; she would wash and curl her hair, clean up the trailer and talk about planting geraniums in the dust outside. On such days Rachel actually heard her mother hum, saw the lines vanish from her face, watched her go around in an ironed dress and listened to her laugh with the neighbors. It was on a day just like that when Rachel went up to her mother, who was hanging clothes on the line and singing "Prisoner of Love" with wooden pins in her mouth, and asked her startling question.

The child was too honest for her own good, Mrs. Dwyer often thought. Where had Rachel gotten such a streak for speaking the truth? Like today, just blurting out that she had found the hidden cigar box and had gone through the contents. Really, you couldn't spank a child for such honesty, even if she was confessing to snooping. "Am I illegitimate, Mommy?" she asked, referring to the discrepancy in the dates between her birth and her parents' wedding.

"Where *do* you learn words like that, honey?" Mrs. Dwyer asked as she ran her hand through the child's brown hair. "It's all them books you read. Never known a youngun to read the way you do." Then she knelt in the dust and took her daughter gently by the shoulders. "No, honey. You ain't illegitimate. It don't matter when your father and I got married. All that matters is that we did. You're Rachel Dwyer. He gave you a last name."

"But . . ." Rachel's lower lip trembled. She had so hoped to hear something else from her mother. "You mean he's my real daddy?"

"Of course he is, honey!"

"I kinda thought, you know, because you got married later, that I musta had another daddy."

"I know, honey," the mother said gently, taking the child's pain into herself and sharing it. "But he is your daddy. We had you before we thought about getting married. He's not the settling-down type, you know. He likes to be free. But I told him he had a responsibility to me and his baby. There was a war on and we thought he was gonna get drafted. So he married me."

"Did Daddy go to war, Mommy?" Rachel didn't exactly know what "war" was, but she had heard enough of other people's talk to know that to have been in it was some sort of honor. Maybe there *was* something to love about her daddy, after all.

But Rachel's mother said with a sigh, "No, darling. Your daddy didn't pass the medical. Something wrong with his lungs, they said. That's what makes him so angry sometimes, you see. That all the other men went, but he didn't."

Then Rachel asked about the *other* baby, and a shadow swept over her mother's face, even though there wasn't a spot of cloud in the vast sky. "That other baby died, honey," she said so softly that she could hardly be heard over the dry desert wind. "She was your twin sister. But she died a few days after you were born. She had a weak heart."

After that, books took away the pain and disappointment; they always did. Books closed bad doors and opened good ones. Rachel couldn't remember when she had read her first book; she couldn't recall a time she had never been reading. It was her mother who had come home one day with some borrowed Dick and Jane books and taught her daughter to read; Rachel knew almost nothing of formal schooling. There was a brief time in Lancaster, California—another barren desert—when she had sat in first- or second-grade classes. Not always as the object of derision as she was in some schools—at least in the Mojave there were other children like herself. But there had been that one terrible spell when her father had managed to get himself a job in a service station and they'd lived in a rented house for a while and Rachel had gone to a real school. The kids there had made fun of her bare feet and too-short dresses. Feeling sorry for the child who never brought a lunch pail and never seemed to have money for the school cafeteria, a teacher had shared a lunch with her one day. But the humiliation of it, even in one so young, had made Rachel throw up. The teacher had gotten mad, as if she had done it on purpose, and hadn't shared after that.

But Rachel hadn't been long at that school. Her dad had lost the new job as usual and spent the next year on welfare checks, cursing the government and picking fights in bars with any guy in uniform.

It was Rachel's greatest skill, and her gift—reading. She could never understand why folks made such a big deal of it. After all, when you get pleasure from something, you keep at it and so naturally you get good at it. And pleasure was what books gave her, just about the only pleasure her childhood ever knew. With each new strange town they moved into, with each new neighborhood and new faces, with each new fear of the new place, with each prayer that Daddy would keep *this* job and let them live in this town long enough for her to make friends, with each drunken homecoming and the ranting about the motherfuckers that got him fired and the inevitable abuse of her mother—the screams and begging from the bedroom—with each new desperation and disappointment and deepening of her loneliness and alienation from the rest of the world, Rachel escaped into a book.

Sometimes she and her mother read together. They would sit in the little trailer and take turns reading pages out loud. "Education's like gold," her mother would always say. "I want better for you than I ever had, Rachel. I want you to make something of yourself, and be happy." But mother and daughter read not just for education but also for escape; they helped each other along the road of fantasy so that, for a while, both could forget.

But there was another reason why Rachel ran from reality. She discovered it quite by accident on the day she turned eleven.

She was brushing her hair in the mirror in the dingy room of a motel where they were temporarily living, in a town they were just passing through. Her mother had gotten a job as a maid at this motel, and while her father went "job hunting" in the bleached little town somewhere between Phoenix and Albuquerque, Rachel was once again left on her own.

She was trying her hair in different styles, with the aid of a movie magazine, when it suddenly struck her: *She wasn't pretty*. In fact, she realized in dismay, she was downright homely.

The popular pinups of the day were Betty Grable and Veronica Lake—Rachel held their magazine photos up beside her face and tried to see what exactly was wrong. The list, it seemed to her eleven-year-old mind, was endless. Thick eyebrows, ironing-board straight hair, slightly recessive chin, and—worst of all—an impossible nose.

As if that discovery weren't painful enough, as if she didn't already know it, her father, in a booze haze one night after a trying day of "job hunting," remarked, "Christ, that kid's getting ugly."

Bones in children shift and deceive all through childhood. It is not until preadolescence that the facial features decide to find their place and settle down. From age six Rachel's face had been one of those usual kid blurs—she looked like any haunter of playgrounds. But at eleven she was entering the readying stage, and her face, on cue, was taking its final form.

The nose, strangely, was hawkish; it would have looked good on a boy. In fact, on a man, it would have made him look aggressively handsome. On a woman, unfortunately, even more so on a little girl, it looked grossly out of place. And Rachel knew it.

She watched herself for the next few months, hoping and praying that it was only a phase and that nature would correct its mistake. But the more she watched, the more she realized that this was the way things were going to be from now on, and therefore the more she started to avoid her own reflection. Which was why, when they passed the winter in Gallup, New Mexico, and a kindly neighbor lady, taking pity on Mrs. Dwyer and her homely daughter, had offered to give them both Toni home perms, Rachel had protested so loudly that the lady had been offended and avoided the Dwyers after that.

But Rachel's mother understood, and tried from then on, in her awkward, unpracticed way, to reassure the girl and give her the love she so obviously, so desperately hungered for.

The sad fact was, Mrs. Dwyer was caught in a trap of alcohol and abuse. To please her impossible-to-please husband, she went with him to taverns, shared cheap bottles brought home, and allowed him to keep her down. Mrs. Dwyer's episodes of loving her daughter were sporadic, unpredictable, and often off target.

But there *were* people who did know how to show love, and upon whom Rachel could shower her natural gift for intense loving—people who lived in books.

She would read anything she could get her hands on. Sometimes it was outdated movie magazines, or a *Life* or a *Post* thrown away. Rarely were they juvenile books. But she did read Nancy Drew, all of whose detective adventures Rachel devoured. The local library was her gateway to her fantasy world, and nearly every place, no matter how small and shabby, had a library. Even the trailer park they lived in when she was ten. It was miles from any real town and was just a kind of neglected collection of gas station, general store, and tavern. But the office of the trailer park had a shelf of books. When people moved, they left behind their well-thumbed books so that folks moving in could trade *their* old ones in for new ones. It was the invention of Mrs. Simons, the old lady who ran the park, and Rachel quickly went through the rack.

Lonely and uncertain, unpretty and starved for affection, Rachel placed her shy hand into the outstretched hands of faceless authors and escaped into the exciting world of make-believe. She shared the adventures of Frank Slaughter and Frank Yerby; she walked ancient highways with Mika Waltari and Lew Wallace; she experienced rapture and innocent love with Pearl Buck; she explored the stars with Asimov and Heinlein. There was nothing Rachel would not read; every book offered its own avenues of escape, its own rewards and comforts and joys. Altogether, they created the fantasy world that sustained her and kept her heart clean and trusting. Arthur Clark's spacemen were good and bold and valorous; for Rachel Dwyer, they, not flesh-and-blood men, were the only ones she would ever love.

Strangely, however, although she perforce read many adult novels, Rachel nonetheless remained curiously naive and unworldly. It was as if, she decided in later years, her mind, when encountering anything that smacked of reality or came too close to home, would automatically edit it out. Rachel was nine when she read *Forever Amber*, but if quizzed about it later, she would have been unable to explain the exact cause of Amber's downfall. It was enough for Rachel that Amber lived in a romantic age, wore old-fashioned gowns, and was wooed by dashing men. The other elements—out-of-wedlock pregnancy, disgrace, and abandonment—were completely missed by Rachel.

Which was why, she later supposed, that at fourteen she

was still very innocent, vulnerable and unprepared for what life was about to deliver.

It was raining. One of those suddenly-come-and-suddenly-go desert storms. The inside of the trailer was filled with a terrible racket.

This was a different trailer from the one the Dwyers had rented when Rachel was ten; they had lived in five others since then. But it was different only in that sense. Otherwise it looked exactly like all the rest: cramped, dingy, listing slightly to one side, haunted by the smells and disappointments of previous transient occupants.

Her dad had been out drinking all day. Rachel prayed that the downpour would keep him out all night. In the glow of a dim, flickering bulb, she was deeply involved in *The Martian Chronicles*. She was desperately in love with Captain Wilder, and was wishing herself clear across the sky, on the bank of an ancient Martian canal. Her mother had gone down the highway to the motel, where, in the manager's office, a new Philco television set brought the *Texaco Star Theater* to the far-flung citizens of the Southwest desert.

After three hours of eye strain, Rachel was forced to lay the book aside. She had cramps and her stomach was hurting. "It's what we women have to go through, honey," her mother had explained as gently as possible the year before, when Rachel's period had started. Having missed the sixth and seventh grades in school, Rachel had not had the benefit of what they called feminine hygiene education. The bleeding had alarmed her; Mrs. Dwyer had found her daughter crying one day, declaring that she was dying. But then Mrs. Dwyer had brought out her box of pads, shown Rachel how to wear one, and then had tried, awkwardly, to explain what it was all about. "Pain seems to be our lot, honey. Women get used to pain. We have it all our lives. And having babies is the worst pain of all. That's why I never had any more, after you."

"Why?" Rachel had asked in all innocence. "Why do we have to have pain?"

"I don't know. Something about it in the Bible, I seem to recall. Punishment, I guess, for what Eve did."

"What did Eve do?"

"Why, she led Adam into sin, honey. He was pure, and she made him impure. We women have been paying for it ever since."

Mrs. Dwyer had then haltingly gone on to draw the connection between menstruation and making babies, but hadn't done a good enough job, being rather ignorant herself of the female body and its workings. And so Rachel had come away from the private talk having learned little.

On this rainy night, as she laid aside her book to fetch a couple of aspirins, she secretly, guiltily hoped that her mother would be kept at the motel because of the storm. That way, Rachel could read all through the night, and burn the precious electricity they could ill afford.

When she went into the cramped little kitchenette, she realized she was hungry. The cupboards were rather bare, as usual. But there was some ground chuck in the icebox. If Mrs. Dwyer was a plain, hard-used woman who looked like any of the desperate itinerants that crossed the Southwest desert, she was possessed of one gift that set her apart. She made fantastic hamburgers. The recipe was from an old woman for whom she had kept house as a teenager. "The secret to making good-tasting food," the old lady had said, "is in the spices." Mrs. Dwyer had learned to give life to hamburger with tarragon and thyme, a dash of rosemary, a mention of paprika. Over the years she had so perfected her spice recipe that she could no longer pass it on to others or write the formula down. It was something she did as naturally as breathing. And wherever the Dwyers roamed, folks always raved about Mrs. Dwyer's hamburgers.

The art had been passed on to her daughter. And Rachel's mouth began to water now as she thought of sinking her teeth into a juicy, spicy hamburger with ketchup and a slathering of mustard.

While the patties sizzled in the pan she continued to read the Martian saga under the dim stove light. A few minutes later, as "the moon held and froze" Captain Wilder and his crew in a deserted Martian city, Rachel heard the sound of a car approaching the trailer.

Thinking it was her mother, she thought, Ma is going to be cold and wet. I'll boil water and we'll have some tea. But then, thinking it might be her father, being driven home by some barfly acquaintance, Rachel was filled with dread.

He hated her books. *Resented* them. And she didn't know why. "It's because of his own lack of education," her mother had explained one night when he had thrown an armload of library books out the window. "He never went beyond the fifth grade. He's embarrassed by that. He says it's what keeps him from holding down a job. To see you read like that, so easily and all, well . . ."

Rachel never understood her father's animosity toward her. On occasion, she would look up from what she was doing—the dishes, mending, fixing dinner—and she would find him studying her with a dark, unreadable expression. He'd have a can of beer in his hand, or, on days when the government check came, a tumbler of bourbon. She would find his rheumy eyes watching her, and she would feel, inexplicably, a chill run through her.

He was her father and yet, curiously, he was a stranger.

They had lived together for fourteen years, but she didn't know him. She had cooked dinner for him, washed his clothes, heard him urinate in the bathroom, and he remained as unknowable to her as any stranger on the highway. According to the novels, she was supposed to be his "little girl," but he didn't seem to notice her. He came and went like some mysterious boarder, waking with a groan and a curse, and setting off for who knew where, while her mother spent the day anxiously looking at the clock and glancing through the curtains.

It was, in fact, only two years ago, when Rachel was twelve years old, that she realized her mother was afraid of him. Not that this should have come as a surprise. What Rachel remembered witnessing when she was only a little thing in diapers continued to occur with sickening regularity. The sound of his shoes over the cheap floor, the slamming of the bedroom door, which would shake the whole trailer, and then her mother, softly pleading, ineffectually, because then the slaps would come, and finally the sobbing. The next morning, there would

41

be bruises on Mrs. Dwyer's face; he would stomp out and maybe not come back for three or four days. And Rachel would observe it all with wide, uncomprehending eyes, and suffer it silently, because that was what her mother did, never once thinking that the situation could be changed, because her mother also did not seem to entertain such a thought. If her mother didn't fight him, neither would Rachel.

But then—he had never laid a hand on Rachel.

She stood now, frozen by the stove and listening to the car engine harmonize with the driving rain. A door slammed. Someone shouted good night. Wheels slid in the mud and the motor grinded away. Footsteps on the wooden steps. Finally, the door handle jiggling.

Rachel found herself suddenly afraid. Was it because of the storm? Or was it because she had cramps, because she was so *female* at the moment and therefore vulnerable? She backed up against the tiny kitchen counter and watched the door, her heart pounding.

She already knew it wasn't her mother, home from the motel.

The door flung open and she caught her breath. Dave Dwyer swayed for a moment on the threshold, then he sort of fell in, closing the door behind himself. He didn't look at Rachel, didn't seem to notice she was there. Dripping wet like some shaggy dog, he made his way to a cupboard, pulled out a bottle, and retreated to the torn Naugahyde sofa.

When he kicked one of her books aside, Rachel said, "Don't touch that!" And instantly regretted it.

His red eyes finally focused on her. "Wassat?"

"It's . . . a library book. If I return it . . . damaged, I have to pay for it."

"Pay for it! What do you know about money!" he boomed. "You're nothing but a fucking parasite! If it weren't for me you'd starve. Why don't you go out and get a job, a grown girl like you."

She was terrified into speechlessness.

He narrowed his eyes, as if seeing her for the first time. "How old *are* you anyway?"

"You should know, Daddy."

" 'You should know, Daddy,' " he mimicked. "HOW OLD ARE YOU?"

"F-fourteen."

His eyebrows shot up. "Izzat so?" He looked her up and down. Rachel was painfully aware of the shorts she was wearing, of her bare legs, of the Peter Pan blouse with a button missing.

"You gotta boyfriend, Rachel?" he asked, surprising her.

Boyfriend! How was she supposed to meet boys, cooped up in this trailer all day? Besides, boys and their pimples couldn't compare with highwaymen and Roman centurions.

For some reason, her silence angered him. Or perhaps it was her fear. The way showing fear sometimes made dogs get all riled up.

He got to his feet; she inched back along the counter.

"Heck of a thing," he growled. "A girl afraid of her own father."

She tried to manufacture some courage, for show. "Y-you don't intimidate me."

"Intimidate!" he said with a laugh. "Hoo! Listen to her. Always using big words! You like big words, don't you, little girl?"

She continued to back away.

He kept coming.

"Christ, you're ugly. Look at you!"

"Please, Daddy. Don't—"

"Don't you daddy me! How I could have spawned such an ugly bitch like you is beyond me!"

He was close now, looming, smelling of liquor, unsteady on his feet. "What a namby-pamby bitch you are. Just like your mother. She's such a doormat I could puke! And where *is* my loving wife tonight? Why isn't she here to wait on me, to serve my every need. God, you women make me sick!"

He reached for her. The first time he missed. She jumped back; his fingers brushed her arm. But he was steadier than she thought. The second time he went for her he guessed her move and caught her, painfully, by the wrist. "Whyncha use some more big words, huh? It turns me on to hear you use them. Better'n talking dirty."

"DADDY!" She tried to wrench free. He caught her by the other wrist and spun her around.

The rain came down on the tin roof of the trailer. It sounded like machine-gun fire, or a thousand hailstorms. Then thunder cracked and the trailer shook. It also shook when David Dwyer spun his daughter around and, holding both wrists behind her back with one hand, tugged at her shorts with the other.

"You like big words, bitch? You liked to use 'em before we got married. Remember that? Remember how you tried to humiliate me in front of our friends? You with your college edyu-cation!"

"No, Daddy!" she cried. Rachel struggled. But he held her fast. She felt her shorts tear beneath his powerful fist. He wrenched them down around her thighs.

"Remember the first time I did this, huh?" he shouted. "That night when you told me we couldn't have no more kids. When you blamed me for getting rid of the other baby? Christ, you bitch, we kept the wrong one! Rachel's ugly. WE GOT RID OF THE WRONG ONE! Well, if you don't want no more babies, I can take care of that. And here's a new word to add to your impressive vocab-yulary. Sodomy! How do you like that one?"

Pain.

Rachel screamed.

The door flew open and rain rushed in. Thunder cracked just as a second sound filled the night—a kind of soft splitting sound, like a watermelon hitting the pavement. And then her father let go of her wrists; he dropped away from her, and the pain slipped out of her body.

Instinctively, Rachel fell forward and groped for her shorts. She stumbled, sobbing, toward the narrow bedroom door, blindly, not thinking, aware only of the pain he had inflicted, a pain worse than cramps or having babies or even, she knew, than dying.

He had done it to her. *He had done it to her.*

When hands reached again for her, Rachel fought like a crazed cat. But when she heard her mother's voice saying, "No, honey! It's me!" she went limp.

There seemed to Rachel to be a moment of soothing darkness, and then she opened her eyes and found herself on the sofa, her mother gently washing her. On the kitchen floor, sprawled against the lower cabinets, was her father.

"Is he dead?" Rachel said.

"No, honey. He ain't dead. I hit him with the frying pan. But he's still alive."

Rachel began to cry, softly and bitterly, with her face buried in her arms. "Why did he do it, Ma? *Why did he do that to me?*"

Mrs. Dwyer couldn't speak at first. She gathered up the towels and basin of water and said, "You'll heal. After a few days, it won't give you no trouble."

Rachel looked up, her face streaked with tears. "You let him do this to you! All the time!"

"I have no choice, honey. I have to let him."

"And have *you* healed?"

Mrs. Dwyer turned at the kitchen sink and looked at her daughter. Suddenly, the dreaming fourteen-year-old had the eyes of an adult. "You don't understand, honey. There's things between a husband and wife that—"

"If he were my husband," Rachel sobbed. "I'd kill him."

"Don't say that, honey. You just don't know."

Rachel tried to sit up but found it painful. "Why do you stay with him? He's a monster."

"No, he ain't. In his way, he loves me. He's just hurtin' inside. There's things that happened in the past, long before you were born—"

"He said you gave the other baby away. What did he mean by that?"

Mrs. Dwyer turned pale. "Dear God," she whispered. "Did he tell you that?"

"Ma, I have a right to know."

Mrs. Dwyer gazed at her daughter for a moment, listening to the rain abate outside as the storm moved on; she came to some private decision, then joined Rachel on the sofa.

"Honey," she said softly, taking her daughter's hands in hers. "When I went to the hospital to have you, we were broke. We didn't have a dime. There was a depression on, and your

Dad, well, you've got to realize, he was a good man . . . once. So anyway, there we were with twin babies, and no money to pay the hospital bills. So one day a man came to the hospital. He said he was a lawyer. And he said he knew of a nice couple who wanted real bad to adopt a little girl. They would pay a thousand dollars, he said."

Rachel stared at her mother.

Mrs. Dwyer cast a nervous glance at the unconscious man on the kitchen floor, then went quietly on. "I was against it. But your dad talked me into it, saying we needed the money and that the baby would go to a good home. If we turned the lawyer down, he said, we'd have two babies and no money, and what sort of a home could we give them? He kept after me, honey, until I gave in. I've prayed to God every day since that I made the right decision. I like to think, Rachel, that your sister is living in some nice big house and going to parties—"

"You—you *sold* my sister?"

"Don't say it like that, Rachel. You can't possibly understand. And anyway"—she looked again at her unconscious husband—"you've gotta get away from here now. You can't stay here anymore."

Rachel wanted to protest, but she knew her mother was right. With the shock starting to wear off, Rachel began to cry.

Mrs. Dwyer took her daughter into a clumsy embrace. "Now, listen to me, honey. You've got to be strong and brave. You've got to get away from here. Tonight. And get as far away as you can. I've managed to put away a few dollars that your father don't know about. Enough to keep you for a while if you're careful. Go to California. Go to Bakersfield. You can stay at the YWCA there. It doesn't cost much and they'll take care of you. But don't tell them you're only fourteen, 'cause they'll tell the police. Now, here's the address of a woman I used to know. She owns a beauty parlor. You tell her you're Naomi Burgess's daughter"—she folded a piece of paper into Rachel's purse—"and she'll give you a job. You'll be okay. You're a smart girl. Now, there's a bus that comes through town at midnight. You gotta be on it."

"But you're coming with me!"

"No, I can't. I have to stay with him."

"And put up with his brutality?"

"Rachel," she said quietly, "I love him."

"How can you?"

"You're too young to understand now, honey. But some-day, when you're a grown woman, you'll fall in love and then you'll understand what it's all about."

Rachel sat silently for a long time, feeling her pain, her humiliation, and staring at the man who had done it to her.

"You've got to go," her mother said with new urgency. "He'll be coming around soon."

Rachel regarded her with grave eyes. "What will he do to you, Ma?"

"Don't worry about me, I can handle him."

Rachel thought for another moment, then said, "Do you suppose she looks like me? My sister?"

Mrs. Dwyer gave her daughter a surprised look. "I don't know, honey."

"We're twins."

"Well, there's two kinds of twins. There's the ones they call fraternal, and then the ones they call identical. I don't know why, but one kind, the twins don't necessarily look alike. I don't know which you two were."

"I hope she's pretty," Rachel said softly. "And not ugly like me. And you know something else, Ma? I'm going to look for her."

"Oh—" Mrs. Dwyer suddenly felt panic. "Why would you want to do that!"

"Because she's my sister. And if she knows she was sold, then she might be comforted to know why."

Seeing the hunger and loneliness in her daughter's eyes, Mrs. Dwyer softened. She knew of Rachel's desperate need to love someone, to belong to someone. She herself had felt that every day of her life.

"You were born in Hollywood, California, Rachel. I don't know, maybe she's still there. I'll tell you everything I know about the adoption. But it ain't much. Now—you've got to get out of here."

Fifteen minutes later, with her father still lying on the

47

floor, Rachel stood at the door with a battered suitcase in her hand. There was a P&O sticker on it, but that was someone else's memento. All Rachel was going away with was the photo of her mother with the two babies, a few scraps of souvenirs she had collected in her childhood, and *The Martian Chronicles*, a stolen library book.

Both of their eyes held pain; it was as if Rachel and her mother looked into the same mirror. The storm had passed, the night was calm. Fourteen-year-old Rachel had no idea where she was going, but she said now, "I'll be back, Ma. I'll find my sister and we'll come back for you. We'll leave Dad, and the three of us'll be a family. I'll take care of you, Ma. You'll never have to put up with—" She looked down at the lifeless body of the man who had never meant anything to her. "—with *that* again."

Mrs. Dwyer hugged her daughter and watched her, through eyes filled with tears, as she trudged all alone through the mud toward the distant highway.

5

THE DRESS, THOUGH BEAUTIFUL, was uncomfortable. It pushed her breasts together and forced them upward, and cinched her waist in so tightly that she could hardly breathe. Nonetheless, Dr. Linda Markus liked the look of herself in the full-length mirror. A "belle" from the past. Fragile, dainty, an object to be worshiped.

My God, she thought. *Women really felt like this, once.*

Walking away from the mirror, she looked around the bedroom. It was like something from a dream. The satin draperies, the magnificent bed covered in a thick satin quilt with matching satin canopy cover—all the color of peaches. The plush carpet, the delicate gilt furniture, the sweet paintings on the walls, and vases of fresh flowers. All very feminine, all very romantic.

Actually, it was the same room she had been in just the week before, when her "rendezvous" with the cat burglar had been interrupted by a phone call from the hospital. She had been trying ever since then to reschedule her appointment here at Butterfly. But complications had intervened. First, she had been unavailable. And then *he* had been unavailable.

It was strange. Linda had experienced a momentary twinge of jealousy to learn that she could not be with him on a particular night. For the first time in her months of attending Butterfly, Linda Markus had pondered the reality of her companion servicing other members. And, for the first time, she had felt possessive of him. Intellectually, she had told herself: *He's a hired lover. He takes care of other women.* But, emotionally, Linda was surprised to find herself thinking: *He's mine. He belongs to me.*

She had been with this particular companion only three times. Before that there had been a variety of them—none of them satisfying, none of them able to help. And then she had met "him." That was on the night of her Venetian fantasy. The early citizens of Venice used to wear masks when parading in St. Mark's Square. She had gotten the idea after seeing the movie *Amadeus*. A man, all in black—with a black cloak and wearing a black mask—had stolen into her room and made exquisite love to her.

It was the closest Linda had ever come to having an orgasm.

So she had requested him again.

He was the Highwayman the second time, from the poem. Dashing, forceful, but tender also, stealing into her room, catching her at her needlework, and making love to her. That time, too, she had come very close to that sexual brink which she had never experienced in her life. And so, the third time, when she had called Butterfly and made the arrangements, she had requested the same companion, and that time requested that he be a burglar.

But the session had been cut short by her beeper. Tonight he was supposed to appear in the form of a Confederate officer of the Civil War—at least, a man in a Confederate officer's uniform, and masked, as if he were at a costume ball.

No matter what the circumstance, Linda insisted that her men be masked. She did not want to see her lover's face. Nor could they see hers. The mask was in place now, protecting her identity.

She glanced at her wrist, then remembered that she had removed her watch. For tonight's fantasy she had decided to play it to the fullest. After removing all her modern clothes and putting on the costume laid out for her, Linda had put her things in the dressing room and closed the door. Closing that door had symbolized a sealing off of the modern age. By denying all the accoutrements of Today—her purse, watch, beeper, panty hose—she could more easily step into Yesterday.

Which was necessary for the experiment to work.

From experience, Linda knew that the companion could appear at any moment. Especially in these historical scenarios. Some club members, she knew, didn't want to bother with stage props and costumes. They just asked for a particular model, took a room, and got down to the sex without any theatrical buildup. Others, like herself, enjoyed—*needed*—the drama and make-believe.

To cure her, she hoped, of her problem.

That was why Linda was here, at Butterfly, instead of at the hospital or reading medical journals or working on her speech for the County Medical Association dinner. Normally, Linda's life revolved around her work; she left herself very little time for social or recreational activities. But coming to Butterfly really wasn't for pleasure; she was here to find help for her problem. But as a physician treating herself she had a difficult time detaching herself from professional curiosity, which was necessary in order for the therapy to work, and therefore for her problem to be cured.

Pacing the plush carpet, her crinoline swishing about her, the soft lights of the chandelier casting a dreamy incandescence over the objects in the room, Linda tried to force herself into the role. But she could not.

How many members a day does he see? she wondered. (*We are all* members *here, the director had told Linda during her orientation. Not clients or customers, but members. And our men are* companions.) How many times, after all, can a man, no matter how young and virile, get it up in one day? How many times can he *satisfy* a woman?

He doesn't have to ejaculate each time, she told herself.

She tried to stop such thoughts. They served no useful purpose. She was here to be made love to, not to analyze the physiological logistics of men. Linda had to keep reminding herself to leave her scientist's curiosity and medical thinking outside the door. Otherwise, the experiment would not work.

Footsteps in the hall!

She turned and stared at the door. The doorknob started to turn.

And all of a sudden Dr. Linda Markus was breathless. She forgot everything. All thoughts fled her mind as she watched the golden doorknob slowly turn, as she pictured the hand that might be turning it, the man who owned that hand, those tight muscles, that square jaw, and that deep, refined voice.

That first time with him—whoever he was—she had almost, almost . . .

The door swung slowly open. She drew in her breath.

The first thing she saw were the polished boots, then a long arm in a gray sleeve with yellow embroidery. Finally, a masked face beneath a gray Confederate general's hat. And— a soft, genteel voice, saying, "Howdy, ma'am."

She held herself perfectly still. *They must hire professional actors*, she heard her mind say. *He's so good at it.*

Then: *Damnit, Linda. Get into the fantasy!*

But too many years of medical training had left her with an analytical mind. Fantasies were difficult for her. She could never divorce herself from the keenly dissecting mind medical school had given her.

My God, he's beautiful.

"Ah hope Ah'm not disturbin' you, ma'am," came his soft voice as he touched the brim of his gray felt hat. And then, just when she expected him to walk over and kiss her hand or do something rehearsed like that, he surprised her. "Do you suppose a gentleman might help himself to a drink?" he asked.

Linda, nonplussed, looked around. *Was he supposed to say that?* "There's a liquor cart over there, I think . . ."

He strode over to it and lifted a decanter filled with amber liquid. After having a drink from a crystal glass, he turned and regarded her through the eye holes of his mask.

Black eyes surrounded by black lashes in a black mask.

She felt her pulse race.

"Have we met before, ma'am?" he asked softly.

"I . . ." He actually had her tongue-tied!

"I'm lookin' for a friend of mine. Charlotte's her name. Do you perchance know her?"

Linda was taken aback.

The heady perfume of roses filled the air. The light from the various candles around the room seemed to move and shift and undulate. Linda felt herself become engulfed by the romantic ambience.

But it's all staged!

Nonetheless, she felt herself start to succumb. And she was glad. She wanted the magic to work. . . .

Those flashing black eyes weren't searching for a woman named Charlotte. They were there for her, for Linda Markus, who had asked for this man, and who was already starting to feel possessive of him.

"I don't know what I'm supposed to say next. I mean . . . who's Charlotte?"

His smile lifted his mask slightly.

This time, unlike the time he wore the ski mask, she could see the lower half of his face. And . . . he was *handsome.*

"Then Ah must be in the wrong house."

Linda was confused. Had they put her in the wrong room? But no . . . this was definitely the companion she had asked for. Then what—?

He came toward her, his crystal glass in his hand. "But then," he said quietly, "maybe Ah don't mind not findin' Charlotte."

He came and stood close to her. Linda looked up at him. How could she have forgotten how tall he was? And then she was struck by a familiar scent. Only faintly—a hint of men's cologne. He had worn it the previous times. What was it called? She seemed to know it. . . .

His hand came up to her cheek. Long fingers traced the contours of her face, touched her lips, caressed her eyelids.

There was nothing hurried in him; his manner seemed languid, almost lazy, as if they had all night.

"May a gentleman introduce himself to a lady?" he asked softly. "My name is Beau."

He bent his head and touched his lips very lightly to hers.

Linda sighed. It was so perfect. No names, no faces, no wondering what he was going to think later, no having to explain about her problem, the thing that had killed two marriages and always brought new relationships to an abrupt halt. He wasn't allowed to wonder or ask. He simply had to do what he was paid to do. And send her home cured.

She kissed him back.

"Beau" took his time. Slowly, he removed his gray officer's tunic, and then the linen shirt. The sight of his athletic torso, even though she had seen it twice before, did not fail to make Linda catch her breath. Not too much muscle, just enough to warn of strength. Not too tanned. There was nothing overdone about this beautiful man. Not even his kisses, his exploring touch, as though this were their first time together. How often, on first or second dates, with men who had looked deceptively considerate, had Linda had to suffer the urgent, devouring kisses, the rush to get her panties off, the premature battering with an erection when she wasn't ready.

She felt Beau's erection. She felt it through yards of lace and satin, and through the wool of his Confederate trousers. How much more delicious that was! Delaying the mystery, building up the anticipation. Not rushing her. The things this man could teach other men.

But then, all of a sudden, he became urgent. The timing was perfect, it was exactly when she wanted him to start to hurry, now that her own excitement was rising. Her breath came short; she clung to him, with her arms, her mouth. She felt his fingers work the buttons at the back of her dress. The satin bodice came down, but she was still hidden beneath lace and cotton, ribbons and stays. Beau knew how to undo these as well, swiftly and expertly, kissing her all the while, holding her against him, pressing into her.

And then she wore only her petticoats. Lifting her suddenly, he carried her to the bed and laid her gently down. The kisses continued, on her face, her neck, her breasts. When she groaned, he lingered there, on her nipples, making her body arch, making her gasp, finally, *"Now . . ."*

He removed his boots and trousers. But when he reached for the drawstring of her petticoats, she stopped him.

So he lay on top of her, kissing, stroking, bringing her to a peak. When his hand slid down between her legs, she brought it back up, wordlessly. When he entered her, modestly, not touching her, just enough to guide himself in, he didn't bury his face in her neck, but stayed up on his elbows, so that he looked down at her, through the black mask. Linda was caught in those dark, intense eyes. As they rocked together, joined in body, she was held by that gaze.

"Come," she whispered. "Beau, please come."

But he moved slowly, in a dreamy oceanic rhythm. Linda locked her arms around his neck; she curled her legs around his thighs. "Come!" she whispered. "Please. Hurry!"

She thought she saw a flicker of perplexity in the masked eyes. Then suddenly his body changed. He moved fast now, rapidly. He closed his eyes. He concentrated.

"Yes!" she said hoarsely. *"Yes!"*

Finally he shuddered and groaned and pulled her so hard against him that, for a moment, Linda couldn't breathe.

"Did you have an orgasm?" the analyst asked as Linda paced the carpet.

"You know I didn't. Damn." She stopped and looked at Dr. Virginia Raymond, who was sitting in a wicker chair, silhouetted against the breathtaking backdrop of Los Angeles. "It's the same every time," Linda went on. "The lovemaking is fantastic. But I hold myself back. I can't help it. No matter what he does, how exciting it feels to me, I don't respond internally. I go through the motions. I talk, I move, I tell him what I want. And then . . . nothing. And when it's over I feel the resentment come back."

"Resentment toward whom or what?" asked Dr. Raymond.

Linda smiled at the psychiatrist. "I don't really know. Maybe the doctors that performed so many operations on me when I was little. Or the pot of scalding water that caused the trauma. My mother maybe. All the men who won't stay with me long enough to help me cure my frigidity. *The world*, I suppose." She stopped at the floor-to-ceiling window and looked out. It was January, a breathtaking day in Southern California. The ocean, pearly and blue, stood in the distance, with bright green palm trees and frothy clouds to complete a perfect picture. On the street down below there was an enormous billboard. It displayed the familiar face of the man who had founded the Moral Decency movement. Linda had seen his *Good News Hour* a few times. There was no doubt about it, the Reverend was a charismatic speaker. She wouldn't have believed that a Fundamentalist Christian could gain such a wide following. The popularity polls showed that the Reverend had a good chance of winning the Republican nomination at the convention in June.

She turned away from the window and went to a wicker sofa, where she settled down into tangerine cushions. Dr. Raymond's office was peaceful, a gardenlike haven in the middle of hectic Century City. Linda had been coming here for almost ten years.

"I want so badly to share my life with someone," Linda said quietly, "I don't like living alone. I would like a husband and children. I tried so hard to make those two marriages work, you know. I really tried."

Dr. Raymond nodded. Dr. Linda Markus had started coming to her when her first marriage was failing. Linda's husband had claimed not to have been able to tolerate her late hours at the hospital, or being called away on emergencies. "He says that just once he'd like to see a movie all the way through!" Linda had said back then. But both she and Dr. Raymond knew the real reason for his wanting the divorce. It had nothing to do with doctor's hours. The reason was Linda's frigidity.

And then, four years later, her second husband had echoed those same words, declaring that he had gotten tired of Linda's beeper cutting into their social (and sometimes love) life. And again, Linda and her analyst knew the real reason for his wanting to get away.

That second marriage had lasted a mere eleven months.

Since then, Dr. Raymond had heard from Linda about brief encounters, all of them unsuccessful, until finally Linda had given up.

Linda looked at her watch. When she had returned the TV producer's call and had found that Barry Greene's office was in the same building as her analyst's, Linda had made an appointment with him to precede her regular weekly session with Dr. Raymond.

"He says he has a job for me," Linda had said earlier in the hour. "A job! As if I weren't overloaded enough as it was!"

"But you are going to take it anyway?" Virginia Raymond had asked.

"I was flattered that he wanted me. And it *is* such a glamorous notion: to work on a studio set, telling movie stars how to act like doctors. I told him in all honesty that I'd never watched his show, but friends tell me that *Five North* is one of TV's biggest hits. And he wants me to be the technical adviser. I thought it might be challenging."

"Even though you already can't fit anything else into your schedule."

Then they had gotten down to Linda's problem. "You know why I fill my life with so much, Virginia," she said softly. "It keeps me from having to go home to that lonely house, where I am constantly reminded that I am thirty-eight years old and want a family more than anything. But, to have a family I need a husband, and to get a husband I have to work on my damn bedroom problem. Listen—" Linda moved to the edge of the sofa and looked earnestly at the psychiatrist. "I want so badly to cure myself and I want so badly to be normal that you would think the cure would come easily!"

Linda stood up and paced again. "I can't go on living like this, Virginia, making the hospital my entire life, just so I can ignore the fact that I am *alone*. That's why I decided it was time to do something about it, to face up to my problem and try to remedy it. So, when my friend Georgia told me about this club called Butterfly, and how it was helping *her*, I decided to give it a try."

"And has it helped at all?"

"I'm not sure. I can't seem to get totally into the fantasy.

I think that if I could just achieve that—if I could just be someone else for just a little while—then maybe I could cast off this stigma once and for all."

"And you think the fantasy will help?"

"I thought that if I could be someone else I could get over my sexual block. Maybe as Marie Antoinette I won't be dysfunctional in bed! I don't know. But the problem is, I'm so used to being in charge and in control of every situation that I can't seem to let go and allow the fantasy to take over."

She turned away from the window and regarded her analyst. Virginia Raymond had been trying for years to help Linda with her problem—a problem caused by a childhood accident and therefore not purely psychological—and she had supported Linda in her decision to join Butterfly.

"It might be dangerous," she had advised. "You might not find what you're looking for."

But Linda had said, "I'm willing to take that risk. Challenges don't frighten me."

"What do you think of the masks?" Linda asked now. "Will they help?"

"As I told you before, Linda, if you can't relax you will never enjoy sex. Wearing masks allows you that necessary relaxation. They permit you to enjoy whatever psychodrama you invent, whether it's with a burglar or a Confederate officer. The mask suppresses *you*, Dr. Linda Markus, and allows another self to take over. You're afraid of sex, Linda, or rather you're afraid of rejection during sex, because of the scars. Getting rid of the fear is one of the most important steps toward enjoying sex."

"But will it work?"

"You have to give it time. And you have to learn to relax."

Linda fell silent. She was already mentally sketching out the next scenario—with her masked lover.

6

El Paso, West Texas: 1952

RACHEL EYED THE PLATTER of doughnuts hungrily. From what she could see through the glass, there were the glazed kind, a few dusted with powdered sugar, some thickly coated with chocolate and nuts, buttermilk twists, and, her favorite kind, the fat round sugary ones stuffed with red jam. She had been in El Paso for two days now, and hadn't eaten since she got off the Greyhound bus. If it hadn't been for someone stealing her purse, not only would she be eating right now but she would be back on the bus and heading in the right direction— toward California.

But she was broke and all alone in a strange town, tired, hungry, and dirty, without the faintest idea of where to turn to next.

Out of the corner of her eye she watched the man behind the counter. He was deep-frying burritos and serving up huge plates of refried beans. The last place she had tried to spend the night the proprietor had physically tossed her into the street. But this Texas border town that looked across the Rio Grande into Mexico was a dangerous place for a fourteen-year-old girl all on her own. Rachel had tried to keep on the move during the day, going through the Mexican bazaars, where tourists bought José Cuervo tequila and crepe-paper flowers, wishing she had a few pesos to buy some tortillas and beans, and resting occasionally in Catholic churches, where Mexican and Indian women prayed with black shawls over their heads. Now it was night and the tourists were safely in their hotels and Rachel was trying to be as invisible as possible in the smoky café, hoping they would leave her alone and let her sit at the table all night, out of the cold wind, reading her book. Even though she hadn't bought anything to eat. Not even a cup of coffee.

It would never occur to Rachel to order food and eat it

without being able to pay for it, and face the consequences afterward. Her innate honesty prevented that.

It was midnight, and the noisy café seemed to be a gathering place for insomniacs. Most of them looked unsavory and desperate, which was also why Rachel tried to be as small and unnoticeable as possible, hunched behind a plastic palm tree, her face wedged between her fists, her eyes firmly riveted to the pages of her book. She was coming to the end of *The Martian Chronicles*, to the last story, "The Million Year Picnic," and then she wouldn't even have the book as consolation.

She thought about her mother. A lot. Rachel had cried on the bus, all the way from Albuquerque, and several times had nearly jumped off to run back home. But she knew her mother was right. He had done it to her once. There was no reason he wouldn't do it to her again.

If only she hadn't gotten on the wrong bus! But Rachel had been so distraught, crying nearly all the time, that it wasn't until they pulled into El Paso, Texas, that she had realized her mistake. She was supposed to be going to California! And then she had gotten off the bus to get something to eat, only to find her purse missing. All her money, and the address of the woman who owned the beauty parlor in Bakersfield! She didn't even have a dime to call her mother.

She looked up and saw a stranger eyeing her from the counter. He wore a leather jacket and had a pockmarked face. And she didn't like the way he was looking at her.

Rachel tried to concentrate on her book. Ray Bradbury had written: "Mother was slender and soft, with a woven plait of spun-gold hair over her head in a tiara. . . ." And Rachel began to cry.

"Hey, girlie, whatsa matter?"

Startled, she looked up. Leather-jacket was standing over her, leering down. Rachel suddenly felt small and defenseless.

"Wachoo doin' out so late, little girl?" he said, grinning. "You need some company?"

She gulped back her tears. "N-no, thank you. I'm all right."

"Yeah. I can see that." He pulled out a chair and sat down. "Howdya like to have some fun with me?"

He smelled strongly of beer.

Rachel looked frantically past him, hoping to catch the eye of the man behind the counter. But the man wasn't there, just a few sleepy customers hunched over coffee mugs.

"C'mon," he said, impatience creeping into his voice. "My place ain't far. You and me can have a good time. I got some friends would like you, too."

Rachel's heart thumped; she felt trapped.

"You must be starved, skinny little thing like you. I got food at my place."

"N-no thank you."

"I'll bet yer running away. That's against the law, y'know. I call the cops, they'd arrest you."

Her eyes flew open.

He took hold of her wrist. His grip was hot, moist. "C'mon. I promise you we'll have fun."

"No! I'm . . . I'm waiting for someone!"

"Yeah? Who?"

"M-my boyfriend."

"Boyfriend! You?" He laughed up at the ceiling. "Listen, girlie, I seen some dogs before, but you take the prize. You got a boyfriend, then I'm the Pope."

"Excuse me, Your Holiness," came a voice from behind.

Rachel looked up. A slender young man with almost-reddish hair was smiling faintly down at Leather-jacket. "That happens to be my girl's wrist you've got your hand on."

There was an instant of charged silence, then Leather-jacket jumped up, said, "Hey," with his hands outspread, and hurried out.

"He won't be back," said the friendly stranger. "You okay?"

Tears filled Rachel's eyes. She wanted her mother so badly.

"Hey," he said, sitting down. "Come on now. Shoot, it can't be as bad as all that, can it?"

Something in his voice, something tender in his eyes, stopped her tears and made her take a better look at him. Rachel wasn't good at judging adults' ages, but he looked like the trailer park manager's son, who was nineteen. But he was better-looking than the manager's son. He was *handsome*, in fact. And he had a dazzling smile.

"What's a pretty little thing like you doing out this late on her own?" he asked.

And Rachel fell in love.

"You know," he was saying fifteen minutes later over tacos and enchiladas and bottles of orange Nehi, "I used to always say that running away never solved anything. But shoot, in your case, I think you did the right thing."

True to her nature, because she knew no other way to be, Rachel had poured out her whole story, the stranger nodding occasionally in sympathy.

Now he shook his head and said, "You poor thing."

His name was Danny Mackay and he was on his way to San Antonio. She knew he was a Texan because of the way he would end a sentence going up, as if it were a question. Things like, "I'm on my way home?" and "I been in California a year?"

He lit up a Camel and said, "Just got discharged from the Army. Fort Ord, out in California. Shoot, didn't see no reason to be stayin' there. So I come home to Texas. You wanna come along?" he said as he paid the bill. "Along the way, we might could figure out a solution to your problem."

But Rachel was no longer worried about her situation. Danny Mackay was the kindest person she had ever met, and he had said he would take care of her. And she believed him.

They stopped at a motel off the highway and made love. It wasn't spectacular—in fact, if Rachel had been more experienced, she would have found him to be a very disappointing lover—but Rachel didn't know or care. Nor did she care about the loss of her virginity at age fourteen. She was filled with hope, with the happiness of having been held in someone's arms, of having been comforted by the warmth of another human being, of having experienced her first kisses while being told she was pretty. Never mind what went on down there, or that it hurt (not as bad as what her father had done, however, because she sensed that this was a natural pain, part of what women were expected to bear). All Rachel Dwyer, deliriously happy for the first time in her life, cared about was that she finally had someone to love.

The next day they crossed the Rio Grande and drove down into a Mexican border town, and there Rachel experienced another first.

She got drunk.

She also experienced a new kind of pain.

"Hold still, darlin'," she vaguely heard Danny's voice saying. She was scared, but not too much, because for one thing she was drunk nearly to unconsciousness, and for another she sensed in her stupor that she was doing something for Danny. He had brought her to this strange room above a *cantina*, had given instructions to the fattest Mexican woman Rachel had ever seen, and now sat holding her hand while a white-hot pain seared the inside of her thigh.

He told her the next morning that she had passed out and that he had carried her back to the motel. He was worried about her now, solicitous of her discomfort—he had even gotten her some aspirin for the pain.

"I'm proud of you, darlin'. Some women don't take it well."

She went into the bathroom to see what had been done to her, and received a shock. There, on the inside of her right thigh, just inches from her private place, was a tattoo.

A little butterfly.

And it was so realistic, so lifelike that one might swear it had fluttered down to that pale flesh and now quivered there.

"What do you think?" Danny said from the doorway.

"It hurts."

"That'll go away."

She looked up at him. "Why, Danny? Why did you do it to me?"

He came in and pulled her into his arms. Kissing the top of her head, he said, "Because I want you to belong to me. And this is my way of making you all mine."

Words like that she couldn't resist. Pain or no pain, violation of her body notwithstanding, Rachel had never wanted anything more in her life than to belong to somebody. And if that's what the butterfly meant, then she was glad it was there.

They arrived in San Antonio the next day.

Rachel had sat proudly and happily next to Danny in the old Ford, watching the Texas terrain gradually change from desert to lush farmland, the long stretch of highway cutting through flat expanses of caliche, a whitish clay type of soil that nothing could grow in, and tracts of low mesquite and huisache. And finally Hill Country, where there were mesquite trees instead of bushes, and where, Danny explained, there was now a cow to every five acres instead of fifty acres. The desolation gradually gave way to settlement—filling stations, ranches, old Mexican adobe dwellings—and Rachel hoped that now that they were at their final destination, wedding bells were the next order of the day.

She loved to watch Danny while he drove. The more she looked at him, the more handsome he got, it seemed to Rachel. His nose was slightly crooked and a scar made his mouth uneven—the outcome, he had explained, of a fight—but she thought these tiny flaws only made him more attractive. He had very thick hair, almost-red, and it fell over his forehead in a single curl. His green eyes were lazy and seemed to be only half open most of the time, and he had a kind of playfully sly way of looking sideways at her. But his body was tense and wiry, and he was always in motion. Whether toying with a cigarette or drumming a beat on the steering wheel, Danny was never still. Rachel sensed an intensity about him, as if he were charged with too much energy and was looking for a place to expel it. And whenever he turned those languorous eyes on her, and lifted one side of his mouth in a smile, she felt a jolt go through her. Danny Mackay was *magic*.

No longer did she dream of searching for her sister in California; she had a new dream now.

"Yessir," he said as he switched the car radio to a station that was playing Gospel music. "I'm going to make something of myself. I'm going to be a big man someday, someone to reckon with!"

She smiled and hugged his arm.

"I'm looking forward to meeting your folks, Danny."

"Ain't got no folks," he said.

The city of San Antonio sat at the edge of the Mexican badlands, and to Rachel it was like entering old Spain. She was dizzy with excitement as Danny guided the old Ford past beautiful old missions and Mexican plazas, and down streets with names like Soledad, Nueva, and Flores. The Wild West was still here for the romantic-minded Rachel, in street names like Houston and Crockett. They drove past dilapidated Spanish-style houses, and big homes that looked like Southern mansions, and ordinary storefronts that reminded her of small towns in Arizona and New Mexico. When they turned a corner and there was the Alamo, it took her breath away. Rachel had read a book about the siege of the Alamo, about the small group of brave men fighting for Texan independence, dashing tragic heroes like James Bowie and Davy Crockett.

And to think that she was going to live here with Danny!

He finally pulled the car up in front of what looked to Rachel like an old farmhouse. It seemed to squat on the edge of arid chaparral and was surrounded by giant prickly pear gone wild. On what used to be the lawn was a rusting pickup truck, raised on blocks and without wheels. Out back she saw lines and lines of washing. Danny told Rachel to wait, and went up the steps. He knocked once, and was let inside.

Danny was gone longer than she had expected, so she decided to read. She had closed her book in the café in El Paso and hadn't opened it in the days since. She remembered that she was just three pages from the end. Father had promised to show Mother and the boys some real Martians.

Twisting around, she opened her suitcase on the backseat and rummaged through her few things. The book wasn't there.

Danny was back a few minutes later. "My friend says we can bed down here for a few days, until we find a place of our own. What's the matter?"

"I've lost my book!"

"We'll get you another."

It was a sad little house; Rachel sensed it the minute she walked through the front door. The first thing that struck her was the pungent smell of dirty diapers. The second was the drab woman at the ironing board, listening to the same Gospel hour Danny had had on in the car. She barely acknowledged Rachel. A brief glance up from her steamy work, a weak smile, a return to the monotony. Rachel saw a long rack of freshly ironed shirts and dresses, and realized that the woman must take in laundry. From somewhere at the back of the house came the unmistakable swishing rhythm of a washing machine.

There was a young man about Danny's age, with limp blond hair and hands shoved into the back pockets of his pants. He said his name was Bonner Purvis, and he led the two of them through a dining room where Rachel saw uncleared breakfast dishes on the table. Remnants of hotcakes and congealed white ham fat lay soaking in syrup; a fly sat on the uncovered butter.

They were taken to a bedroom that had an iron bed with no sheets on it, the mattress stained and sagging, a picture of Jesus on the wall over the head. "Used to be old Tom's room," Danny's friend explained cryptically.

"Shoot, Bonner," Danny said, and when he put a possessive arm around Rachel and said, "It'll do us just fine, won't it, sweetheart?" she beamed like a sunrise and thought the room was a palace.

They slept in it for two weeks, on borrowed blankets; and they dozed off each night and awoke each morning to the constant beat of the tired old washing machine.

He left her there alone every day, but Rachel didn't mind. Unlike her father, he really was out looking for work. She didn't know what Bonner did; the two were pretty secretive about where they went, but she had no doubt that soon she and Danny would be in their own place. And she knew exactly what she was going to do. First thing, she'd put up yellow curtains. Then she'd get some geranium seeds and plant them by the front door to let folks know they had come to a friendly house. She'd get a cookbook, too. Not that Danny and Bonner complained about her cooking. They came home and wolfed down her special spicy hamburgers and then left again for the evening. Bonner's mother said what a blessing Rachel was, to free her from the kitchen and let her get caught up on her ironing.

A van came three times a week, bringing great big bags of dirty laundry and carting away the clean. And three times a week Bonner took the money from his mother.

Danny made love to Rachel every night. She got so used to it that she thought nothing of it anymore, especially because it didn't take long. The tattoo had healed (the other wound had healed, too, as her mother had said it would), and she loved the way he fell asleep right after with his arms around her.

The only cloud to spoil what Rachel thought was really a happy time was that she couldn't reach her mother.

It was a long way from San Antonio to Albuquerque, but she had persuaded Danny to let her make a phone call to the trailer park. Rachel had been devastated to be told by the manager that the Dwyers had moved and she didn't know where they had gone.

Rachel decided she would figure something out; she'd find them again, someday. And then, as Mrs. Danny Mackay, she would be able take care of her mother properly.

And then Danny came home one night with good news. "Pack your things, darlin'," he declared. "I'm taking you out of here."

"Danny!" she said, laughing. "Where are we going?"

"You'll see. It's a surprise."

They stopped on the way for burritos and beans and then headed out of the center of town, away from the river, eventually turning onto streets where there were bars and girls loitering in doorways and an awful lot of men, Rachel noticed, in uniforms. "Two air force bases up ahead," Danny said as he steered the Ford onto a dark street. "Kelly and Lackland. The flyboys come here for some fun."

Danny slowed the car at the end of the street, where the pavement gave way to dirt, and to fields beyond. Rachel stared out at the strangest sight she had ever seen. Right here, at the end of a street where all the businesses were dark and closed up for the night, stood a brightly lit, castlelike house with rounded turrets, huge bay windows, and gingerbread work all around. There were lights on in all the windows, so she could see that the house was bright yellow with white trim. There were a lot of cars parked in the dirt compound that was shielded by a prickly-pear barrier, and honky-tonk music poured from the open doorway.

Danny carefully maneuvered the Ford along the side and around back. He paused to light up a Camel, then said, "C'mon, Rachel."

They entered through a screened-in porch and walked into a brightly lit kitchen, where the savory smell of roast pork hung in the air. Rachel saw a black woman standing at the counter rolling dough; there was an enormous bowl of freshly sliced peaches waiting to be put into a pie. The kitchen was hot from the oven, and it was huge. Rachel had never seen such a large kitchen.

"Howdy," the woman said in a friendly way, looking up from her work and smiling.

Danny told Rachel to sit down and wait, he'd be right back.

She watched him go, the door swinging open and letting in some music and what sounded like a cowboy yelp, then she looked uncertainly around the kitchen.

"Lordy," said the black woman, wiping her hands on a white apron. "If you ain't the skinniest thing I ever did see! You must be hungry. Now you sit down there. No sense in not eatin' while you're waitin'."

Rachel did as she was told, and was soon sitting before a large wedge of warm apple pie with a scoop of vanilla ice cream on it and a cold glass of milk.

"I'm Eulalie," the woman said, returning to her pie-making. "Who might you be?"

"Rachel."

"That's a pretty name. Where you from, child?"

The ice cream was melting all over the warm pie. Rachel put the fork down and used a spoon to scoop it all up. "New Mexico," she said.

"Hi, honey," said a woman who suddenly appeared in the doorway.

Rachel stared at her. She had never seen so much makeup on a face before, and Rachel decided the woman must be rich to afford it. She was fat, too, which meant she ate well.

"Stand up. Let me look at ya."

"Where's Danny?"

"Talkin' to a coupla old friends. You're skinnier than he let on." She came all the way in and stared at Rachel's face. In the past few weeks Danny had made Rachel forget her homeliness, but this woman's scrutiny brought back all of Rachel's old self-consciousness.

"Stand still. I ain't gonna eat you. Hmmm. How old are you?"

"Fourteen."

"You got your periods yet?"

"I . . . I, uh . . ."

" 'Sall right. I'll check with Danny."

As if he had been listening on the other side of the door, Danny came in. "So what do you think?" he said to the woman.

"Sorta homely, ain't she?"

Danny grinned. "Rachel has hidden charms."

Going to his side and taking possession of his arm, Rachel said, "Danny, can we go now?"

"Well, I'm afraid we can't do that. You see, Hazel's an old friend of mine and she's very generously offered to take you in and let you work for her. I don't want her to think we're ungrateful."

Rachel blinked up at him. "Work for her?" She looked at the black woman, who was pounding that dough as if she were all alone in the kitchen and angry somehow. "What kind of work, Danny?"

"Just doing what Hazel here tells you to do."

"You mean maid work? Is this a boardinghouse, Danny?"

"It'll be all right. Shoot, you'll even like it, I'll bet."

"Like what? What are you making me do, Danny?"

Now he grew grave. His voice came on like a minister's and he put on a stern-father expression. "Well, the hard truth of the matter, darlin', is that we're flat broke and I can't find a job. We can't impose on Bonner and his mother any longer, so one of us has to work. Hazel has agreed to let you work for her here. Even though you are underage and she's already got all the girls she needs. It won't be for too long, sugar. I promise. Then we'll move into our own place, just like you wanted."

"But . . ." She glanced at the woman in the doorway, who was inspecting her fingernails with a bored expression. "What do I have to do?"

"You just be nice to her customers, is all. Kind of like a, well, hostess."

"Danny, no—"

"It's real easy. The easiest way to make money as far as I know. You just lie back and let the customer do all the work."

"Oh God, Danny. No!"

His grip tightened on her shoulders. "Now listen. I've worked my butt off trying to get a job, but it's no go. So now you're going to have to pitch in. You don't want to be a parasite off me, do you?"

Suddenly she heard her father's voice saying, *You parasite.*

"Danny," she sobbed. "Please don't make me—"

"Now listen, Rachel. You're used to sex by now. You know there's nothing to it. You just take Hazel's customers up to your room, and lie back, just like you did for me."

She was crying in earnest now.

He gave Hazel an exasperated look. She shrugged and said, "The young ones always cry at first. She'll get over it."

"Damnit, Rachel. I'm supposed to meet Bonner and already I'm late. Now, stop being such a baby. If this is what you're really like, then you can just forget about us. I'll just go out and get myself a girl who really cares about me."

"Danny! *I* care!"

"If you did you wouldn't be throwin' such a hissy fit over nothing. For Christ's sake. You'll have a place to live, regular meals, and a salary. Of course, Hazel will turn your pay over to me to put into our nest egg. But I'll give you an allowance. You can buy yourself some pretty clothes."

"I don't want clothes, Danny!" she cried, tears streaming down her cheeks. "All I want is you!"

"Well, I don't want you, not if you're going to be a selfish bitch!" He pushed her away and turned his back on her.

"Danny!" she screamed. "Don't leave me! I can't live without you!"

"Make up your mind, honey," Hazel said quietly. "You ain't got but one choice. You let your man down, and he walks outa your life."

Rachel gaped at her. She hiccuped and choked back the sobs. Her chest heaved; she ran her hand under her runny nose. For a moment, Rachel looked far younger than fourteen. She looked like a little girl.

When Hazel suddenly nodded in satisfaction, as if something had pleased her, Rachel ran to Danny, flung her arms around him and sobbed against his rigid back. "Don't leave me!" she cried. "I'll do anything you say, Danny! Just don't leave me!"

He turned around, smiling. "That's my baby," he said. He took her in his arms and kissed her. Then he said, "I know it's hard for you, in a new town and all. So I tell you what. I'll come back on Tuesday and take you to see the Alamo. Would you like that?"

She nodded and clung to him.

"Okay, I gotta go now. Me and Bonner have something on. Hazel here will take care of you."

"But Danny . . ." Rachel whispered. "With . . . with *other men*?"

He touched the end of her nose. "I'll tell you a secret. The easiest way to get through it is to close your eyes and pretend it's me doing it to you. Will you remember that?"

Rachel stared up into his compelling gaze, into those lazy, deceptive eyes that seemed to have some sort of power over her, and she felt herself nod.

"I'll see you Tuesday. We'll make a special day of it, just you and me. We'll go into Little Laredo and we'll eat the best tortillas and beans you've ever tasted. How's 'at?"

He kissed her again and left.

Rachel was aware of little of what happened next. A young Mexican girl named Carmelita appeared and took Rachel upstairs, explaining that they were to be roommates. She showed Rachel the bathroom and showed her how to insert the sponge that Hazel demanded all her girls wear, and then she was left alone.

The knock on the door, a few minutes later, was so discreet that it sounded ludicrously out of place here, even to Rachel. She heard herself say, "Come in," and stared at the man who shyly entered.

He gave her a nervous smile and began automatically to take his clothes off. When he was naked (years later she would still recall those spindly legs, the limp penis), he said, "Don't you want to get undressed?"

Rachel moved in a dreamlike way. The blouse and pedal pushers, the cotton underwear, torn in places. Then she remembered what Danny had told her. She lay back, stared up at the ceiling, and opened her legs.

The customer was considerate enough to turn out the light, and then she felt the bed dip.

She closed her eyes. A tear tumbled to her pillow. *Danny,* her heart cried. *Danny . . .*

7

WHEN THE JUDGE SAID, "I find for the defendant, Mickey Shannon," the plaintiff shot from his chair and shouted, "You won't get away with this, you little shit!"

And all hell broke loose in the courtroom.

Mickey Shannon, the famous rock star, was angry and coiled to spring. But Jessica Franklin laid a hand on his arm, keeping him seated. She kept him in his chair while the judge banged his gavel for order in the court. Then, making sure the hotheaded young Mickey wasn't going to jump up and go for the guy who had just called him a shit, Jessica rose and, in the midst of the pandemonium, called out in a voice that rang over the crowded courtroom: "Your Honor, I request an immediate restraining order, keeping Mr. Walker away from my client."

The plaintiff's counsel stood up and shouted, "Your Honor, I object!"

The photographers and reporters jammed into the courtroom were having a field day. This was one of those delicious celebrity trials that made for sensational headlines. But while internal dissension seemed to be breaking up the plaintiff's team—with lawyer and client locked in murmured but heated argument—Jessica Franklin had her side under control. Which was a miracle, considering what a quick temper everyone knew Mickey Shannon had.

She had learned to control him, in their seven years as attorney and client. Mickey had been a struggling unknown actor when Jessica, fresh out of law school, had hung out her shingle on the Sunset Strip. He had come through her door, a humble and confused young man who had been shafted by an unscrupulous screen agent. She had succeeded in getting Mickey's money back from the agent, and since then she had advised him through contracts and salary disputes, had stayed by him when he couldn't pay her, and had ultimately given him the introduction that had led him, finally, to stardom. When his songs hit the charts and Mickey achieved almost overnight fame, he had not left Jessica for one of the glitzy, hotshot firms over in Century City, where all the big stars had their agents and attorneys. Mickey Shannon was steadfastly loyal to the struggling young lawyer who had taken him on when no one else in Hollywood would give him the time of day. And now, on this crisp January morning, he was reaping the rewards of that loyalty.

When Les Walker, notorious photographer of celebrities, had hounded Mickey just once too often, provoking Mickey into ripping the camera out of his hands and smashing it on the sidewalk, the film pulled out and exposed, Walker had sued the rock star for interference with his livelihood and for damages to replace his equipment. Walker was also asking for five million dollars in punitive damages.

Mickey, frantic, had gone to Jessica, and she had calmly told him there was nothing to worry about. They were going to countersue. She had then gone on to defend her client successfully in a crowded courtroom, using for his defense a dramatic rendition of the excesses to which the photographer had gone—following Mickey Shannon dangerously close on the freeway, blocking his parked car, maliciously hounding him every minute of the day—so that Mickey was now demanding restitution for the mental anguish caused by the hazardous situations the photographer had placed him in.

And the judge had found in *his* favor.

When the commotion died down and the courtroom was quiet, the judge issued a temporary restraining order against Mr. Walker and set a calendar date for a hearing to determine why it should not, in fact, be a *permanent* restraining order. Mickey Shannon, handsome rock idol of millions of girls, threw his arms around his attorney and planted a kiss right on her mouth.

They had won.

Out on the courtroom steps, Jessica and her client were immediately surrounded by reporters and TV cameras and crews. She made a rather flamboyant statement, her face glowing with victory, her voice strong and triumphant, while the people from the press made note of the fact that Jessica Franklin, Mickey Shannon's "powerhouse attorney, a dynamo in the courtroom, petite and feminine, was conservatively dressed in a tailored suit with a briefcase that matched her handbag and shoes. . . ."

Jessica would have liked to join the celebration luncheon at Spago, but her schedule was too full. Picking up her husband at the airport was top priority, and after that, back to the office to do some dictation, then a much needed visit with her best friend, Trudie.

It was upon this last that Jessica now settled her thoughts as she sped along the San Diego Freeway in her commodore-blue Fleetwood Cadillac. Trudie, who had something mysterious to tell her. Something about a butterfly. "You absolutely *must* work me into your schedule somehow!" Trudie had said on the phone last night. She had spoken breathlessly, with barely contained excitement. "I want to tell you about Butterfly. You just won't believe it!"

And that was all. Typical of Trudie, to be so theatrical and secretive. To lend drama to what was probably going to turn out to be a very mundane item. But that was one of the things Jessica loved about Trudie—the way she exaggerated, the way she injected so much *life* into things. Trudie's passion for living had been responsible for saving Jessica's life years ago. It was part of what bound the two women so closely together.

To Jessica's dismay, she arrived late at the airport. John was already at the baggage carousel, claiming his suitcases. He greeted her with "Hello, darling" and a kiss on the cheek.

John Franklin was a good-looking man. Appearing to be older than forty because of his salt-and-pepper hair, he kept himself in shape by running five miles a day and playing handball three times a week. Brooks Brothers dressed him in three-piece executive suits, and his natural arrogant bearing made people take notice of him. On the flight from Rome, Jessica had no doubt he had received special attention from the first-class stewardesses.

When they stepped out of the terminal, he paused to squint and say, "Smoggy again as usual, I see."

Jessica had thought it was a lovely day, but she didn't say anything.

"Why are you late? I told you last night what time my flight was coming in."

"I was in court. The Mickey Shannon case . . ." Her voice trailed off.

John Franklin didn't look at his wife. When the crosswalk light turned green, he strode across without looking right or left. She hurried along at his side. He had that frown on his face, a deep etching of his features that he had perfected over years of sitting at the head of a conference table. Today the look indicated his disapproval of her career. Mickey Shannon, according to John Franklin, was a snot-nosed, drug-using punk who was beneath people like the Franklins. And certainly not worthy client material for Jessica.

When they reached the car in the parking structure, he said, "Why did you come in the Cadillac?"

Jessica didn't know what to say. She should have thought of it that morning before she left the house. But she had had the trial on her mind. John hated her car. While to her it was grand and a symbol of her years of struggle and achievement to make it as a lawyer in the entertainment industry, John thought it merely gaudy. "You know I prefer to ride in the BMW," he said.

"I didn't have time to go home. I came straight from the courthouse."

He got in the passenger seat and turned on the air conditioner, even though the day was wintry-cool.

"How was the trip?" Jessica asked, feeling nervous as she maneuvered the huge car out of a too-narrow space. When she drove alone or with Trudie, it seemed to Jessica that she could run the Cadillac through slalom courses. But with her husband's silent judgment hanging in the air, Jessica was suddenly incapable of driving. "Was it a success?"

He sighed and undid the buttons of his vest. "I kicked Frederickson out and put a new man in charge of operations. We'll see results almost instantly." He smiled dryly. "The man I replaced him with I stole from Telecomm."

Jessica drove for a while in silence, trying for but missing the on-ramp onto the San Diego Freeway North, and having to go around again, while her husband sat at her side saying nothing.

Once they were under way and in the flow of traffic, John finally said, "So what happened with the Shannon case?"

Jessica gripped the steering wheel. She was still feeling the effects of that morning's heady excitement. The thrill of *victory.* "We won."

"Good. Let's hope the little bastard pays the fee he owes you. And speaking of which, did you do what I asked about the gardener?"

Jessica bit her lip. She had forgotten. She had been too busy with the trial to remember to withhold paying the gardener's bill until he paid for the repair of the sprinkler he insisted he had not broken.

"John," she said tentatively. She had something to tell him. She hated to do it, but it was better that he was forewarned. "About the Shannon trial."

"What about it?"

She glanced at her husband's stern, patrician profile. "I'm afraid I'm going to be in the papers again."

"Damnit, Jessica," he said softly. "I wish you would stop calling attention to yourself. Every time you do that, I have to pay. I go into a board meeting and all anyone can talk about is the latest movie actor my wife is representing. Don't you realize it hurts my credibility to have a reputation for being known as Jessica Franklin's *husband?*"

"I'm sorry," she said, and felt a wash of relief to see the Sunset Boulevard off-ramp draw near.

"I'm going to the gym this afternoon. I suppose you have to get back to the office?"

"Yes, I have a lot of paperwork to do. And then I'm meeting Trudie at Kate Mantilini for a late lunch—"

He looked at her. "Better go easy on that, Jess. You look like you're putting on weight again."

When Trudie saw her friend come in off the street and hesitate in the doorway, she jumped up and ran to embrace her. "Congratulations, Jess!" Trudie cried. "It's about time someone put a stop to that bastard Walker!"

Jessica smiled at the customers, who stared at her as she followed Trudie to their table. News of Mickey Shannon's victory that morning had hit the streets and everyone was talking about it. As Jessica sat down with a flourish, breathless and scarlet-cheeked, she heard murmurs of approval from nearby tables. She was in the limelight again and she loved it.

"This will be the one to do it for you!" Trudie said, barely able to sit still for the excitement. "God, I wish I could have been there this morning! They said on the radio that Shannon actually *kissed* you! Right on the mouth!"

Jessica reddened slightly. She prayed that John wouldn't find out about that.

"I'm telling you, Jess," Trudie said, beaming, thrilled and proud of her friend's accomplishment. "You and Fred are going to have to turn down clients after this."

Jessica laughed and tossed her short brown hair. She felt as if she stood on top of the world. "I hope so!"

"What did John say?"

"Well, you know John," Jessica said quietly, toying with her folded napkin.

Trudie saw some of the light dim in her friend's eyes. "He isn't pleased, is he?"

"Well, he's right, you know. The trial did turn into something of a circus. I should have insisted on a more dignified atmosphere."

"You loved every minute of it, and you know it!" Trudie shook her head. "Oh, Jess, when are you going to own up to the fact that you're married to a prick?"

"That's not true. John is a good man—"

"Oh, stop defending the jerk. Come on, let's order, I'm starved."

Kate Mantilini was currently *the* L.A. eatery, where bigwigs and movie types competed for the best tables; men dressed in Members Only and Rive Gauche sat in boxy booths with women wearing rhinestones and moussed hair. Trudie ordered for herself a meat-loaf and Wonder Bread sandwich, to be followed by a hot fudge sundae, while Jessica restricted herself to a plain salad.

As Trudie watched her friend pick at the lettuce she felt her annoyance rise. She had wanted this to be an outrageously sinful celebration of Jessica's courtroom victory. Instead, her friend's meal looked like a punishment. Trudie surmised that John must have mentioned something to Jessica about her weight again.

It was Jessica's main weakness, her irrational fear of getting fat, and Trudie knew that John exploited that fear, turning it into a kind of power over her. Jessica was obsessed with her weight; it was an obsession that had nearly killed her once.

That had been back in their college days at UC Santa Barbara when, thirteen years ago, they had been thrown together as unlikely roommates in the freshman dorm: painfully shy Jessica Mulligan, fresh from the cloisters of an all-girls Catholic school, and Trudie Stein, a brash and sassy San Fernando "Val-Gal" who declared that a *shiksa* must have snuck into her ancestry at some point in the past. They had experienced an almost instant mutual rapport, Jessica having never known anyone as free-spirited and crazy-minded as Trudie, and Trudie almost in awe of Jessica's conventlike unworldliness and innocence. In fact, Trudie had envied Jessica in those early days—twelve years of Catholic schools had turned out an impressively bright and educated young woman, with high grades and appallingly perfect SAT scores to prove it. Trudie, on the other hand, had received a sporadic education, from her father, from the football-rally, party atmosphere of Taft High School. Trudie Stein had been a cheerleader and homecoming queen, and knew how to take a car apart and put it back together as well as any boy could, but she had barely squeaked through with a grade point average that could get her into college. But then, she wasn't going to be a lawyer as Jessica was; Trudie was going to follow in her father's footsteps into the construction business.

It hadn't been until one particular rainy night when finals were drawing near that Trudie had discovered the truth about her brainy, superachieving roommate—that Jessica was literally starving herself to death.

"You're not eating much," Trudie said now as she ate her meat-loaf sandwich. "Aren't you hungry?"

"I'm very hungry. But John is after me to lose weight again."

"Damnit, Jess, there's nothing wrong with your weight. I should have your thighs!"

"No, John's right. I really should watch myself more."

"I think you should just tell him to stuff—"

Jessica smiled. "The last thing I want to do is start something with John. You know I can't bear it whenever he's angry with me. As it is, I work hard to keep the peace."

"He's got you brainwashed into thinking everything's your fault. There are two people in a marriage, in case you hadn't noticed."

"Please, True. Can we drop it? Now, what's the exciting thing you were so anxious to tell me about? On the phone last night you mentioned something about a butterfly."

Trudie absently toyed with one of her long dangly earrings. How to broach the subject of Butterfly? She desperately wanted to get Jessica in as a member, to let her experience that indescribable excitement and satisfaction that couldn't be found in the real world. Having walked away from her silver-haired lover in a mood of intense euphoria, Trudie had decided that, surely, Butterfly could help Jessica.

"Well," Trudie said, "you remember my cousin Alexis?"

"The pediatrician, yes."

"Well, she has a friend, a surgeon, they went to medical school together. Anyway, Alexis's friend got her into a kind of private club, and now Alexis has got me in as a member. . . ." Glancing around to be sure no one overheard, Trudie leaned toward Jessica and, in a lowered voice, recounted her evening in the private rooms above Fanelli.

When she was finished, Jessica laughed and said, "You can't be serious!"

"Dead serious, Jess."

"But—" Now Jessica looked over her shoulder and then lowered her voice. "You mean, it's like a bordello? Where the customers are women, and the men inside are, well—what are they?"

"They're called companions."

"I don't believe it. Right here in Beverly Hills? How can something like that be kept a secret?"

"Well, I'm certainly not going to blab about it to just anyone, and I imagine the other members feel the same way. We'd put ourselves at risk, since it is illegal. And the screening of prospective members is very thorough. No chance of a newspaper reporter or a cop sneaking in."

"But it sounds dangerous. What about disease? What about AIDS?"

"It's safer than a casual Saturday-night pickup. The companions are tested regularly and frequently, and they're required to use condoms."

"But why would you do it, Trudie? *You* certainly shouldn't have to pay for sex. Not with your looks."

"It's not just the sex, Jess, although that's a large part of it." Trudie pushed her plate away and reached for her coffee. "It's more than that. It's the . . . *fantasy* of it. You see, at Butterfly you can live out any fantasy, any scenario you wish. It's like making your dreams become reality, for a little while, at least."

Jessica settled back in her seat, her dark brown eyes betraying interest. Yes, she could see Trudie getting involved in something like this—Trudie had always been a risk-taker, had always liked the challenge, the element of danger. "What exactly did you find there last night that you can't find anywhere else?"

Trudie had to frown at this because she didn't really know the answer. In fact, it had occupied her mind all last night and today, trying to figure out exactly what it was that had made her encounter with the silver-haired companion so intensely satisfying. "He is an excellent lover," she said quietly, her aquamarine eyes growing unfocused. "Very considerate . . . made sure that he was giving me pleasure. But . . ." She ran her hands through her blond shag. There was more to it, but she couldn't put her finger on it. "Maybe it was just the fantasy aspect of it. The knowledge that I didn't know who he was, he didn't know me, we weren't going to exchange phone numbers and pretend that we were going to see each other again." She looked at Jessica and shook her head. "I don't really know, except that when I walked through that door and saw that room, and then *he* came in, it was as if the rest of the world, the real world, no longer existed. It was as if, for a few hours, all my troubles, all my fears, all my disappointments just dissolved away. Leaving me completely free to live out a dream."

The two friends stared at each other for a moment while the busy restaurant bustled around them, then Jessica said softly, "I'm happy for you, then, if that's what it does for you."

Trudie leaned forward. "I want you to experience it, Jess. I want you to know that same happiness."

"Me!" Jessica laughed and shook her short brown hair. "Oh, I could never do that, True."

"Why not?"

"I just couldn't, that's all."

But even as her friend was protesting, Trudie saw the flicker of interest in Jessica's eyes. She knew that a part of her was intrigued by the idea, that Jessica's innate love of a challenge was battling her common sense. That was what made

Jessica Franklin such a good lawyer—she never shied away from a risk, was always ready to take chances.

"I'm married, True. Why on earth would *I* go to Butterfly?"

"You have fantasies, don't you? Just because you're married doesn't mean you no longer dream, does it?"

"No," Jessica said softly, thinking of her secret fantasy, the one she retreated to sometimes late at night when John and the world were silent and asleep and she was troubled or tense or worried about an upcoming trial. It was always the same: a soft-spoken cowboy in a Western bar. She would conjure up the scene and the man to the minutest detail, their conversation, the way he would look at her, his touch, the kiss . . . and usually she would drift off to sleep and the fantasy would become a dream and her sleeping mind would take over and let her live out an hour of ecstasy before she had to face the competitive world again.

But it was only a dream. She could never *really* do it.

Trudie remained silent, sipping her coffee and looking around at the crowd in the restaurant. She wasn't going to press Jessica. Butterfly was something you turned to because you wanted to, *needed* to. And despite outward appearances—a successful career, a handsome, distinguished husband, a beautiful home on Sunset Boulevard—Trudie knew that there was something desperately lacking in her friend's life. Something that Jessica had been wrestling with since she was a child, the thing that had driven her nearly to her death thirteen years ago.

Noticing that little of Jessica's salad had been touched, Trudie felt a twinge of concern. That nightmare of thirteen years ago, when Jessica had suffered from anorexia and would have died of it but for Trudie's quick intervention, Trudie did not want to see repeated. In their years together since, Jessica had fought the phantom that shadowed her day and night, the morbid fear of getting fat, and Trudie had helped her through days of hunger and self-chastisement when a deep-rooted need for approval would threaten to manifest itself in the abuse of her own body. Jessica had starved herself in her first year of college, but after that had managed to keep the anorexia under control. She was slender now, but not too thin, at her proper and healthy weight. But when she looked at herself in the mirror she still seemed to see something no one else saw, and that invisible image terrified her.

"Don't think of it as a brothel, Jess," Trudie said quietly. "Think of it as a place where dreams are kept, where fantasies come to life."

"Is that why it's called Butterfly?"

"I don't know why it's called Butterfly."

"Who are the people who run it?"

"I have no idea."

"Oh, Trudie," Jessica said, slowly shaking her head. "It just sounds too dangerous."

"And going home with a stranger from Peppy's on a Saturday night isn't?"

"I don't do that. I have John."

"No. *John* has *you*. There's a difference."

Jessica looked at her watch and reached for the check.

But Trudie got it first, saying, "This one's on me. Jess, I just want you to think about it, okay? If I were to turn your name in tomorrow, it would still be a couple of weeks before you'd have your butterfly bracelet."

"No," Jessica said as she slung the strap of her purse over her shoulder and pushed her chair back. "It's just not for me, True. You're single. That's different."

They walked to the door together and paused to put on their jackets. It was getting dark out now and cold. Rush hour had brought the traffic in the street to a standstill. "One last thing," Trudie said after they embraced and were about to go their separate ways. "Butterfly has all kinds of rooms upstairs, not just private dining rooms. There are bedrooms, elaborate bathrooms—" She turned her coat collar up to her cheeks. "And a Western bar, complete with sawdust on the floor and Kenny Rogers on the jukebox." She looked at Jessica and smiled. "Just think about it, that's all I ask."

It was all Jessica could think about. Butterfly. And so she arrived at home in such a distracted frame of mind that she did not hear her husband call to her from the den. He came out into the hall and removed his reading glasses. "Honey? Are you okay?"

She turned around. "What? Oh, yes."

He came toward her, his arms open. "It must be cold out. Your face is bright red."

Jessica liked it when John hugged her this way, warm and hard at the same time. The house smelled good; the housekeeper was preparing dinner. Jessica decided to put that silly Butterfly nonsense from her mind.

"How was your visit with Trudie?" he asked as they walked arm in arm into the den.

"It was fine. Just girl talk." Jessica detached herself from him and picked up the mail. The first envelope contained an invitation to a fund-raising party that was being held at Beverly Highland's house.

Jessica and John had been there before; Beverly Highland was always putting on functions to raise money for various charities or to bring people's attention to an important issue. This particular fund-raiser was for the TV evangelist who wanted to run for president.

"I think we should go to it, Jess," John said when he saw what she was reading. "The Reverend's a good man. I would like to see him in the White House."

"Yes," she said absently as she heard John sit down and turn on the television. She was staring down at the invitation but not really looking at it. Beverly Highland was known for her strict morals and fight for public decency. What, Jessica wondered, would she do if she found out about the secret operation above Fanelli?

Butterfly . . .

Where you can act out your dreams.

"It's expensive," Trudie had said. "But you can afford it, Jess. It costs about the same as joining an exclusive country club. Very classy, very discreet. You wear your bracelet in the store and that's how the special attendants spot you. You look the models over, decide which one you would like to be with, write him down on a piece of paper and anything special you might want—like wearing a crinoline or being wooed by Don Juan—and they'll come and get you when it's all ready."

Jessica shook her head and started to go through the rest of the mail when she heard a newscaster on the television mention her name.

She turned around in time to see herself on the courtroom steps, surrounded by reporters and spectators, boasting about her victory against Les Walker. By a curious trick of the camera lens, Jessica actually looked tall. And one could see by her face that she was high on victory. A stranger would look at her and declare that Jessica Franklin was the very personification of self-assurance and self-confidence. And then a photograph was flashed on the screen. Mickey Shannon kissing his attorney in the courtroom.

"Tonight," the newscaster was saying, "Ms. Franklin is no doubt the envy of the millions of teenage girls who have made Mickey Shannon this year's rock superstar—"

The TV was clicked into silence and John stood abruptly, throwing down the remote control. He turned and looked at Jessica. She felt herself go cold. "I can't believe you allowed that to happen," he said. "It is demeaning to both yourself and me."

"John, I—"

He strode from the room.

Jessica went after him. "Wait. I couldn't help it. Mickey took me by surprise. We were just so pleased to have the court find in our favor—"

He turned and faced her. "I did not approve of your taking Shannon on as a client in the first place. Against my strongest objections, Jessica, you continued to represent him. You have exhibited a surprising lack of sound judgment."

"There's nothing wrong with Mickey."

"Oh, for God's sake, look at him. He's a punk rocker, Jessica. And no doubt a drug user."

Mickey doesn't use drugs, she protested silently. *He even does antidrug commercials on TV.*

"If you think this is going to generate business for you and Fred, Jessica, then you are sadly mistaken. All it will do is bring unsavory types into your office, making you look even more ludicrous than you already do."

"Everyone is entitled to legal representation," she said.

"Not by my wife, they aren't. This whole issue has deeply distressed me, Jessica. If you don't mind, I'd rather have dinner alone tonight."

As he started to turn away she caught his arm. "John! Please don't be like this."

"How else do you expect me to be, when I come home to *that*." He pointed to the doorway of the den. "I have a very important meeting tomorrow morning, Jessica, and I shall have the specter of my wife's fiasco hanging over me."

She tried to think of something to say, something to convince him that there was nothing wrong in what happened in the courtroom that morning, that he was all wrong about Mickey Shannon, about the kind of law she practiced. But Jessica couldn't make her voice work. Out of frustration, tears rose in her eyes. "I'm sorry," she murmured. "I hadn't meant for it to get out of hand. You're right, I should have had better judgment in this case. I won't let it happen again. I promise."

He gazed at her for a moment longer, then the rigidity went out of his body. "There's my girl," he said. "Hey, I've been gone a week. Let's not fight, okay?"

She felt a wash of relief, and she laughed.

John put his arms around her and drew her into the comfort of his embrace. "What a silly bit of nonsense anyway," he said as he held her. "Seven years ago Mickey Shannon would have given anything to have his picture taken, and now he goes around smashing photographers' cameras. Arrogant little bastard."

But everyone in the Industry knows what a bastard Les Walker *is!* Jessica wanted to say. *How would you like to have someone hound you day and night and shoot a flash in your face every time you turned around?*

"I tell you what," John said, lifting her face up to kiss her. "Why don't we put dinner on hold for a while and go up to the bedroom?"

It was the way their fights always ended, in bed, with John putting the whole incident behind them—having sex was his way of letting her know he had forgiven her—and Jessica lying in the darkness with a feeling that nothing had been resolved, that the problem still remained. And so, as she usually did at these times, Jessica solaced herself with the comfort of her fantasy: the nameless cowboy in the bar.

And as she walked across that phantom sawdust-covered floor and approached her smiling dream lover, a frightening new thought sprang into her mind: *It no longer has to remain just a fantasy. . . .*

8

San Antonio, Texas: 1952

"YOU SEE?" said Carmelita, holding the paper up for Rachel to look at. "This is how you make eight eights equal a thousand. It's real simple. When you write the numbers down like this, they don't mean nothin'. But when you write them *this* way"—she pointed with her short chewed-down pencil—"five eights in this column, then two, then one—they add up to one thousand."

Rachel stared at the piece of paper, torn out of a cheap dime-store pad, and smiled weakly.

"Aw, you poor thing," Carmelita said, laying aside her pencil and paper and putting an arm around her friend's shoulders. "Don't you worry. He'll be here this time. I just *know* it. Like, I had this dream last night?"

But Rachel stepped out from under the girl's arm and went to the window. It was so grimy she could barely see out. Just enough to make out the cars in the street below. Looking for Danny's Ford to come driving up . . .

She had done this four Tuesdays in a row. It had been that long since Danny had left her in Hazel's house.

"Why doesn't he come, Carmelita? Why doesn't he even phone? It's like he's forgotten me!"

The Mexican girl regarded her roommate with sorrowful eyes. In the month that they had shared a room, the two had become close friends. For one thing, they were the two youngest in the house, Carmelita having just turned fifteen, and for another both lived in the hope of being taken away by the men they loved. *She* hadn't seen Manuel in four months. But she knew he hadn't forgotten her and that he was still in San Antonio. He picked up her pay from Hazel, regularly.

"I don' know, *amiga*. They get busy, men, you know? They got things they gotta do. Hey, maybe he came by an' you were with a customer. Hey? Rachel?"

The girl continued to stare forlornly out the window. She was too thin. If Hazel had complained of skinniness four weeks ago, now the child looked as if she might soon disappear. Not that it hurt business, however. Rachel had discovered that some men liked girls this way. The scrawny arms and legs and the knobby knees made her look far younger than fourteen. Which was why Hazel insisted Rachel wear her hair in two long braids, and forbade lipstick.

If he doesn't come to see me today, she decided, *I'll kill myself.*

"Watch," Carmelita said as she picked up the dime-store tablet and opened it to a fresh piece of paper. "This one will really amaze you!"

Rachel stared down at the pad as her friend's brown hand sketched more numbers on the page. She knew what Carmelita was trying to do—distract her and get her mind off Danny. Rachel knew that Carmelita understood the pain she was suffering; it was a pain they shared. In a world that seemed to have no use for them, the two discarded girls found ways of comforting themselves and each other.

For Carmelita, Rachel had discovered to her surprise that first day a month ago, it was numbers.

Rachel had come down to the kitchen that first morning and found Carmelita sitting at the table with several of the girls, in kimonos or just their underwear, standing around her. Rachel had joined them to see what her new roommate was doing, and she had been amazed, like the rest of them, to see Carmelita do magic tricks with numbers. "I guess I was born with it, you know?" Carmelita had explained to Rachel later over hotcakes and molasses. "My *tía*, my aunt that I lived with, said I played with numbers when other little girls played with dolls. It's something that's in my head, you unnerstand?

I see them inside my mind, the numbers. I *feel* them. Like, I dunno, but I know numbers and what they do."

"You should see her add a column of numbers?" said one of the other girls, talking the way Danny did, her voice going up at the end of the sentence. "We make bets on how fast she can do it? I'll write down maybe twenty numbers four columns wide, and as soon as I've drawn the line underneath, Carmelita here has the total. She beats us every time."

"I would think you could do something with a gift like that," Rachel had said, warming to her new friend. She had not slept; she had spent the night throwing up and wishing Danny would come back for her. But there, in the hard light of morning, in the presence of the other girls who lived in Hazel's house, girls with moon-colored faces and backward-looking eyes, Rachel had realized the harsh truth of her situation. And she had found herself feeling grateful to have a moment to forget about herself. "You could work in an office," she had said to the Mexican girl. "You could be an accountant."

But Carmelita had shaken her head and closed her sketch pad. "I ain't educated. What could I do? I can add columns faster than an adding machine, but I can hardly write my own name. No, *amiga*, the numbers are just fun, a game to make me forget for a while. I'm where I belong. I know that."

And here was Carmelita again, four weeks later, trying to distract her.

But all Rachel could think of was Danny.

The bedroom door opened and Rachel spun around, suddenly hopeful. But it was only Belle, the third girl who completed their tight knot of friendship. She was older—seventeen—and she took care of them. It was Belle who had comforted Rachel through those first nightmarish days, and who had soothed her when she cried as if her heart were going to break. If Rachel and Carmelita were like little girls, Belle was like a grown woman. After three years in Hazel's establishment, she had lived a lifetime.

"Sorry, kiddo," she said. "It's only me. Wish I were Danny. I truly do."

Tuesday mornings were always slow at Hazel's house—dead, in fact. That was when the eighteen girls who lived there

88

got their laundry and mending done, wrote letters (those who knew how to write), or slept all day. In another age Rachel would have spent the time consuming books. Now she waited for Danny.

"Listen," said Belle. "If he doesn't come, do you want to go to the show with me? *High Noon*, Rachel! Down at the Majestic. My treat. I got enough money."

"You already seen that movie six times," Carmelita said, throwing herself down onto one of the two twin beds and inspecting the new coat of Max Factor polish on her nails.

"And I'll see it *sixty* times if I want to. Come on, Rachel. What do you say?"

But Rachel only glumly shook her head.

Belle exchanged a look with Carmelita, then went up to her young friend and, laying a hand on her arm, said quietly, "Maybe his car broke down. That can happen, you know?"

"He's got to come today, Belle. He's just got to."

"And what will you do if he doesn't?"

"I'll run away."

Belle shook her head. "Kiddo, we all dream of runnin' away. But the thing is, we don't get far, not even in our dreams. We got no money, no wheels, and, most important of all, no *protection*. If you ran away, where would you go, what would you do, how would you live? You don't even know where your folks are."

Belle spoke for most of the girls in Hazel's house. The majority had been brought here, or had come here out of desperation, out of need for shelter and protection. The days of hippie communes and youthful hitchhikers on the highways lay far in the future. These girls sold their bodies and dreamed of one day leaving respectably, on a man's arm.

Belle's dream was to go to California. Everyone said she looked just like Susan Hayward; she even had the flaming hair. It was her ambition to get into movies, and in preparation for the day that she was sure would come, she lived inside movie magazines. The walls of her room were covered with pictures from *Photoplay*; she always bought the lipstick the stars wore; tried to imitate their life-style with the bit of money she earned at Hazel's. Nylon gloves were currently in vogue; Belle had a pair that she wore constantly, no matter how badly they made her hands sweat. She had a pink felt skirt with poodles on it, and a tube top for a blouse, just like the one Jane Russell wore with capris. She even had a pair of fake Dior "knock 'em dead" stiletto heels, except that she hadn't yet learned how to walk in them. When the call came, as seventeen-year-old Belle was certain it would, she didn't want Hollywood to catch her unprepared.

That was one of the things that made Rachel so special to her: she had actually been *born* there. When Rachel had first told Belle, she might as well have said she was born on Mars, Belle was that skeptical. But when Rachel had shown Belle her birth certificate—*Mother*: Naomi Burgess; *Baby*: Rachel; *Born at*: Presbyterian Hospital, Hollywood, California—Belle had stared at it as if it were a holy relic.

But there were other reasons for Belle's deep affection for Rachel. There was the girl's unusual honesty—a commodity rarely found around Hazel's house. Rachel could be disarmingly frank, but you always knew she spoke the truth. So when she had told Belle that she thought Belle one of the most beautiful girls she had ever seen, they all knew Rachel meant it. There was also the aura of vulnerability that surrounded the sad little Rachel; it seemed to bring out maternal instincts in even the most hardened girls. If they could no longer care about themselves or about the men who used them, they could care about this waif with the pathetically homely face.

And she made fantastic hamburgers too. Some of the girls were starting to put on weight because of Rachel's magic with hamburger meat. And once she got together with Carmelita, who showed her how to add jalapeño peppers to ordinary french fries, Rachel's fattening dinner was much in demand.

But Rachel's best quality was her storytelling gift.

On slow days, when they were all bored and getting too close to thinking about their miserable lives, there would be Rachel, spinning an incredible tale of adventure in faraway places. The fact that they were not Rachel's own original stories didn't matter. These girls had never read any of the books she had read; each story, no matter how old or classic—*Jane*

Eyre, Pride and Prejudice, Captain Blood—was brand-new to them.

And then, perhaps, they loved her most of all because of her ability still to hope—a flame that had been snuffed out in all but the greenest of them. To see hope glimmer in one so sad meant that there was hope still for them all. And the most hopeful in Hazel's house were Carmelita, who just knew Manuel was going to come back for her someday, and Belle, who dreamed of the Hollywood producer who was going to walk through Hazel's front door, set his eyes on the Susan Hayward look-alike, and take her away from all of this.

They dreamed together, the three of them.

But today, on this fourth Tuesday after Rachel's arrival, the brittle dream was coming dangerously close to being shattered. There had been no Danny on the day he had promised to come, no visit to the Alamo, no burrito dinner in Little Laredo. The way she sat at the window every Tuesday made some of them mad enough to want to see Danny Mackay suffer.

And then: "There he is!" Rachel cried, hands pressed against the window. "It's Danny! Danny's here!"

They ran to the window and looked out. It was indeed he, like a wish materializing right down there on that street. Danny Mackay, his almost-reddish hair catching the morning sun; his white shirt dazzling; black pants perfectly pressed; shoes polished. He was tall and lean and good-looking, and because he had finally come they all forgave him.

Rachel hugged her friends, gave herself a final look in the mirror, and flew down the stairs.

He was already in the kitchen and talking to Hazel, who was saying, "She's doin' okay, but she needs to be told a few things. I've had a few complaints."

"DANNY!"

He opened his arms and she flung herself into them. "Hey!" he said, kissing her and laughing. "What's all this, darlin'?"

"Oh, Danny, Danny." She held him as tightly as her thin arms could, and buried her face in his chest. "Oh, Danny, you came."

"Shoot, darlin'. I told you I would. Look what I brought ya."

She looked at the daisies as if they were diamonds, and took them from him to dance around the room with them. "Oh, Danny! They're beautiful! No one ever gave me flowers before!"

She went to a cupboard and took down three milk glasses. "I'm going to share them with Carmelita and Belle. Is that okay?"

"Sure!" he said, laughing.

"They never get flowers. And daisies, Danny! They're so pretty! Like stalks of sunshine!"

When the little vases were arranged, she turned around and beamed at him. "Oh, Danny," she said again. *"Flowers!"*

"I told you I'd come," he said with a grin. "You didn't doubt me, did you?"

"Well . . ."

"Still want to see the Alamo?"

"Yes! Oh yes! And can we go for burritos?"

"I might be able to arrange that."

"And go down along River Walk and look in the shops?"

He laughed and took her into his arms. "You can have anything your heart desires, darlin'. I just want you to be a good girl, okay?"

"I'll be anything you want, Danny," she murmured against his shirt.

He looked over her head at Hazel, who nodded slightly.

"Say, darlin'," he said. "Before we go out, what do you say we go up to your room and have a little talk?"

She drew back and looked up at him. "What about?"

He mussed her hair and touched the tip of her nose. "Don't be soundin' so fretful. I just want to be alone with you, is all. Hey, it's been a month since we've been together, doncha know?"

She pouted. "I know. I've counted every single hour since I saw you last."

He took his arms away from her and stepped back. "You're not going to scold me now, are you? I don't want no girl who's going to nag me like a wife. Let's go upstairs."

She went, leaving the three little vases of daisies down in the kitchen.

They went into a vacant bedroom and he closed the door, quietly locking it. When he turned to her, he found Rachel sitting on the bed, smiling. "I'm so glad you're here, Danny."

"Listen, Rachel." He came over and sat next to her. "Hazel tells me you've been giving her trouble. I can't have that. She's doin' us a favor, you know?"

Rachel bowed her head. "I know."

"Then why aren't you behavin'? It looks bad for me."

She raised pleading eyes. "Danny, she makes me do terrible things! I get sick every morning! I throw up all the time!"

He frowned. "You're using the sponge she gave you, aren't you?"

"Oh yes," she said impatiently. "It's nothing like that. I'm sick from what I have to do. Some of the customers are, well, just *awful*. They force me to do horrible things with them."

"Look, Rachel," he said softly, laying an arm around her shoulders. "It don't help if you fight it. You have to cooperate. After all, this is a house of pleasure."

"Pleasure!" she cried mournfully. "How can men find pleasure in what we're doing here? I thought that when men and women make love, both of them are supposed to enjoy it."

"Shoot, Rachel. You're not *making love* with anyone. You're getting paid to let these guys fuck you."

She covered her ears with her hands. "Please don't talk like that, Danny. I hate that word. *They* use it, when they're with me. They like to say it while they're doing it. And then I get sick!"

"All right, all right," he said, drawing her against him. "It won't be much longer, Rachel. You'll see."

"Do you have a job yet, Danny?"

"I told you to stop nagging me! Didn't I say I'd take care of you?"

"Yes, but—"

"And didn't I come today? Didn't I bring you flowers? Is this any way to treat me?"

"Oh, Danny! Please don't get mad at me. It's just that I want us to be together all the time."

"You think I don't want it, too? It's not easy finding a job, you know. Life is harder for us guys than it is for you girls. We don't have no one to take care of *us*."

"I'll take care of you, Danny. I promise."

He softened. "I know you will, darlin'. But you've got to do what Hazel tells you to do."

"But it's so awful . . ."

"I tell you what. Why don't you show me what it is you have to do. That'll make it easier for you with the other guys. Just close your eyes and think it's me."

He took hold of her resisting hand and brought it down to his groin. "Come on. Do for me what you do for the customers. Huh? How about it? And then we can go see the Alamo and get burritos. What do you say?"

She fought back the tears. She so badly wanted to tell him that she wanted things to be different for them; she wanted their love to be pure and beautiful; she wanted him to make her forget the nightmare she was living. But he looked at her with those compelling green eyes that were at the same time lazy and intense, and she felt herself fall once again under his spell. As he unzipped his pants and guided her hand inside, and then gently urged her down to her knees, Rachel tried hard not to cry, not to get sick. She just wanted him to love her and take care of her. That was all she wanted in the world.

9

THERE HE WAS. Getting out of his GMC 4X4.

Trudie turned toward him, hands on her hips, mad as hell. "Hey, Bill!" she shouted. " 'Bout time you got here!"

He grinned below aviator sunglasses. Trudie did not doubt that he melted many a feminine heart with that smile. But not today. She was going to let him have it.

He came sauntering up the lawn, just as casual-as-you-like, one of those egotistical types that are aware of their masculine beauty. He waved to the electrical crew now working on the fifth stage of the pool's construction. They all waved back. Most of them were Mexican, but there were a few blond types, shirtless—good ol' boys.

"Hey, Trudie," he called when he was close. "So what's up?"

She was mad and had to control herself. "Bill," she said with her jaw thrust forward. "Why aren't there three return lines on this pool? You know I always have three return lines on my pools. Did you read the work sheet? Didn't you even look at the plot plan?"

"Hey," he said easily, laughing. The January sunshine did things to his hair and he knew it. He paid for that special cut, made sure the waves caught the light just so. It never failed to work magic beneath dance-floor lights. He studied Trudie from behind the dark glasses. Maybe the old charm wasn't going to work in this case. Well, he'd heard she was a ball breaker.

"Just give me a straight answer, Bill." As the plumber for the pool, Bill's work came right after the initial excavation. He had called her two days ago and said he was all done. So she had called for the Gunite to be applied. That particular crew, headed by Sam Brand, a good guy overseeing a good crew, had begun work early this morning, spraying the Gunite into the big scooped hole in the ground. She'd received the call at eight. "Hey, True," Sam had said, "don't you usually have three return lines?"

So she'd gotten on the phone and told Bill to get his ass down here and fast. Why the rush? Because the concrete was hardening and it was going to be hell to cut into it for that third return line.

"Hey," he said now, "why so riled up?"

"Tell me why you didn't install three return lines."

He looked at her appraisingly. Not a bad-looking chick, he thought. She filled out a tank top and a pair of shorts the way no male contractor ever did. And beneath the ballsy façade, he was certain, beat the frustrations of any single female.

95

"I didn't think it was necessary to have three return lines on a pool this size."

"You don't tell me what's necessary. I have three return lines on all my pools because I happen to build the best pools in Southern California! You're to follow my instructions."

Now she was getting to him. Here he was being nice and easygoing, trying to explain the way real work was done, and she comes on like some Sherman tank. These women who try to be men! What True Stein obviously needed was to get laid. "Well, it's done, isn't it?"

"No, it isn't," she said evenly. "I want you to get your crew back down here pronto, and I want to see that third line in there by tomorrow morning."

"Hey listen, honey! Do you know what it means to redo it? It means sawing through concrete!"

"I don't care if it means chipping away at the concrete with your teeth! That third line goes in."

He glared at her. He could tell she was mad by the way her breasts heaved. But he could get mad, too. "No way," he said quietly.

Just as quietly, Trudie said, "All right, then. I have something for you." She picked up a plastic trash bag that was lying by her feet. She opened it up and held it out for his inspection. "Do you see these, Bill?"

Warily he looked in. There must have been eight or ten empty beer cans in the sack. "Yeah . . . So?"

"Sam found them this morning in the trenches. Bill, your guys were drinking on the job."

"Hey, no way—"

"Don't you 'no way' me!"

"Those cans could have come from anyone. Sam's crew, for one—"

"Sam's a born-again Christian, Bill, and you know it. You know he runs a clean crew. He says he found these cans here this morning, and I believe him! That means your guys are responsible."

Bill shifted nervously. "So what does that—"

"*You don't drink on my jobs!* Is that clear?"

He eyed her with caution. His relaxed stance was gone. "So what are you saying, Trudie?"

"What I'm saying, Bill, is that you cut through that concrete and install the third return line. If you don't, I swear I'll see to it that you don't work a single job in this county ever again."

He was silent for a moment, measuring Trudie and the situation. Then he spread out his hands and said, "Hey. So what's the big deal? I'll get my guys on it right away."

"And no more drinking."

"Yeah, yeah, sure." He turned and walked away, muttering something about uptight broads. Trudie turned on her heel and marched away around the deep end of the gray, dry pool. *Butthead,* she thought. *The man's a butt-head.*

She looked at her watch. There were two more excavations to be inspected, and then she had to get over to Jessica's office. The two were going to Butterfly this afternoon. Jessica had an appointment to meet with the director and receive her member's bracelet.

The offices of Franklin and Morton were located on the Sunset Strip—a small Greek temple tucked in between the ostentatious Federal-style offices of doctors, lawyers, and interior decorators. It was High Rent but so was the clientele. Jessica and Fred had been in partnership for seven years, competing with the big established law firms housed in the towers of Century City. Their appeal was that they dealt with clients on a personal, intimate level. They didn't mind that they were known as a "boutique firm." Their client list was still small, but it was growing, thanks to the publicity from the Mickey Shannon trial. All Fred and Jessica needed, they knew, was to win a few more cases like that one and their days of struggling would be over.

Jessica was in her office, facing a scowling man. He was the opposing counsel for a case she was involved in, and he sat drumming his fingers on the leather briefcase in his lap. "Mrs. Franklin," he said, "this happens to be the amount your client asked for."

"Yes, it is, Mr. Hutchinson. Or, rather, I should say, it was. But that was weeks ago, and the agreed date of settlement has passed. We are now demanding a million dollars."

"What!"

Her intercom buzzed. She picked up the phone and said, "I told you to hold all calls." The voice on the other end informed her that Trudie Stein was waiting in the reception area. "Oh yes, thank you. Please offer her a cup of coffee and tell her I'll be with her shortly."

After she hung up, Jessica folded her hands on the desk and said, "Mr. Hutchinson, you know that we are fast approaching the date of trial, and I am sure you are aware that a jury will be very sympathetic to my client. We will win, and the court will award us two million dollars. But my client is willing to accept one million now to avoid the strain and inconvenience of a trial."

He gave her a long, thoughtful look. This was the first time Ron Hutchinson had entered into litigation with Jessica Franklin, and although he wasn't pleased with the way things were going, he admired her tenacity. There were no guarantees that she was going to win, and he *was* offering her a generous settlement: three hundred thousand dollars, signed, sealed and delivered on her desk today. Yet she stubbornly held out for more. He wondered how far she would go to chance losing everything.

"We agreed on three hundred thousand," he said, putting a finger on the cashier's check that lay on her desk and moving it toward her. "Take it now, or we meet in court and you don't get a penny."

"We are asking a million now, Mr. Hutchinson. By the close of business tomorrow."

He could see by her face that she wasn't going to budge. So he took his check back, rose, nodded curtly to her and left the office.

Before joining Trudie, who was waiting to take her to Butterfly, Jessica stopped by her partner's office to report on her meeting with Hutchinson. Fred Morton, prematurely bald, ran his hand over his smooth head and said, "I don't know, Jess. Are you sure we should hold out? After all, we can't be certain that we're going to win in court. Chances are good that we will, but it is still a big gamble."

She smiled. "I'm willing to take that risk, aren't you?"

As Trudie deftly maneuvered her Corvette through the heavy traffic on Sunset, she glanced at her friend and said, "Nervous?"

Jessica laughed. "Intrigued!"

"I'm glad you decided to join."

"Well, I'm not a hundred percent convinced that I need to go to a place like Butterfly, but you've made me curious. I want to get inside and see how it works."

"Believe me, it works wonderfully! I went again last Saturday."

Jessica looked at Trudie. "What did you do this time?"

"I chose the same companion. My intellectual lover. He was so good the first time, I didn't see any reason to change. Apparently a lot of the members request the same man over and over. You develop a sort of relationship, as you would if you were seeing a therapist."

"Therapist! You make it sound like a sex clinic."

"In a way, that's what it is, isn't it?"

Jessica studied Trudie's profile, the expensive shag cut of blond hair, the long silver earrings, the aquamarine eyes. Jessica had always envied Trudie's beauty. "What do you and your intellectual companion do?"

"We argue and then we fuck."

"And you find that satisfying?"

Trudie made a quick lane change and sped off down Beverly Canyon Drive. "I find it *immensely* satisfying. And I couldn't really tell you why, except that it seems as if every man I meet doesn't quite measure up to my expectations. Dates usually leave me feeling unfulfilled. Even after I've gone to bed with a guy, and even if the sex was okay, I still come away feeling it wasn't a *total* experience. Whereas with Thomas, both times were dynamite. Maybe it's the anonymity of the situation—he doesn't know who I am, he doesn't even know my name—or maybe it's because I control the scene. I don't know. And I've been trying to figure out the answer, but it eludes me."

Jessica gazed out the window as they turned onto Rodeo Drive. Exactly what was *she* hoping to find in Butterfly's secret rooms? Why had she decided to join? A lot of it, she knew, had to do with the element of risk about it all—that was why she loved litigation so: nothing was predictable, there were no guarantees, you either won or lost, and each day each new case presented a whole new set of challenges. She perceived Butterfly as being something like that. But there was more to it— ever since Trudie first told her about it Jessica had felt an inexplicable compulsion to become part of Butterfly. Was it because there was, despite Trudie's protests that Butterfly was safe, an element of danger?

"How can I be sure I won't be blackmailed?" she asked as they pulled up in front of Fanelli. "I have to think of my career, my law partner."

"Well, according to my cousin Alexis, who got it from her friend Linda Markus, who got it from the woman who got *her* into Butterfly, this place has been in operation for several years, and in all that time there hasn't been an incident of blackmail or anything even close. After all, how could it happen? The companions have no idea who we are. Our identities are well protected. Only the director has access to the files, and she certainly isn't going to talk."

"Still, the secret of this place is bound to get out sooner or later. Just let the papers get a whiff of it and we're all in deep trouble."

Trudie flashed Jessica a smile and said, "Since when have we ever let *that* stop us from doing something?" Then the parking valet opened her door and she handed him the keys.

The plan was for Trudie to do some shopping downstairs in Fanelli while Jessica went with an attendant into the elevator. While they waited for the attendant to arrive Jessica and Trudie browsed through a rack of expensive coats. Lowering her voice so that no one else could hear, Jessica said, "What does Alexis do when she comes here?"

"My cousin the doctor is in reality a frustrated artist. She goes for wild, outlandish scenarios. Some of them get really elaborate—costumes, props, everything. She's very much into the fantasy thing."

100

"Does *she* request the same companion each time?"

Trudie shook her head. "Alexis is into variety. A different guy each time, a different scene."

Jessica did not deny that the prospect of experiencing sex with another man, an expert, titillated her. She had been a virgin when she married John, and she had not been with anyone else since. She had always supposed her husband was good in bed—she even occasionally had an orgasm—but she really had no way of making any comparison. She also had no way of knowing if she was satisfied or not after sex. She liked it when John made love to her, but there were times when she preferred to be left alone to make dream-love with her fantasy cowboy.

Jessica wondered if Trudie was right, about Butterfly being more than just a place to go for sex. Could a woman find fulfillment and satisfaction in acting out her fantasies? Was this a way of learning to cope, of finding answers possibly, a catharsis that stripped away inhibitions and old phobias and taboos?

But why am *I* here? Jessica wondered finally, as the attendant came up and told her the director would see her now.

And then she thought, *John*, surprising herself. It had something to do with her husband, John.

She was taken upstairs and shown into a room that was tastefully decorated in misty desert tones, with a Navajo rug on the floor, dried plants in Indian pottery, a Georgia O'Keefe print on the wall, and a coffee table on which had been laid out a crystal carafe of white wine, two long-stemmed glasses, and a platter of small sandwiches. As Jessica took a seat she realized she was suddenly nervous.

John came to her mind again, as if he had followed her here, as if he were haunting her.

That would please him, Jessica knew; John liked to think of himself as her guardian, her *conscience*. Well, she had to concede that maybe he was. But she had allowed him to take that job; she had no one to blame but herself. John had come into Jessica's life during a period of stressful transition—from college to law school. In her childhood and teen years her father and the Church had been her conscience and guide. Then she

101

had gone away to college, away from her father's authority, and had eventually lapsed from the Church. When she met John he immediately filled a void in her life. Even in their first days of dating John would tell her what to wear, advise her on whom she should make friends with and whom not, order for her in a restaurant, choose the movies they would see. And Jessica had let him. She had been in love and anxious to please.

But the problem was, once she had her law degree and was out on her own, a professional in her own right, their roles did not change. Only just this morning, before she had left for the office and her meeting with Hutchinson, John had made some critical comment about the way she was dressed. So, to save the peace, she had gone upstairs and changed.

In eight years of marriage she had never defied him.

But she was defying him now, in a most outrageous way, and the sudden realization of that, of knowing why she had really decided to join Butterfly—to secretly break the rules, *John's* rules—made her suddenly giddy.

The director of Butterfly, who did not give Jessica her name, was tall and slender—in her fifties, Jessica judged—and dressed in a tailored suit. She came through the door and greeted her guest with a warm handshake. Then they sat down and got right to business.

Money changed hands—memberships were always paid for in cash—and Jessica was given a butterfly charm on a gold bracelet. The director explained the rules, but Jessica had already heard it all from Trudie. When the director said, "Do you have any questions?" Jessica said, "About the companions. Who are they? How are they recruited?"

"I'm afraid I can't tell you that. We protect their identities as strictly as we do the identities of our members. But please rest assured that they go through a thorough screening, psychologically as well as physically, and that you have nothing to fear from them. I must also add that it is a club rule that members and companions do not fraternize outside Butterfly. Several members have requested a companion to come to their home, or meet them at a hotel. But, for security and safety, we cannot permit that. For this reason we do not allow them to give their real names, or reveal where they live. And we must insist that our members, for their own safety, are as discreet about their own identities."

"Who in here will know me?"

"Only myself and my assistant. The phone number I gave you rings only in this office, and one of us is here at all times. We do keep a file on each member, but the files are coded, and only I and my assistant have access to them. In each file we record a member's personal preferences, or complaints, if you have any. For example, if you don't wish to choose a companion from among the models downstairs—a few of our members are uncomfortable with that process—you simply give us a call and leave the choice of companion to our discretion. Many members request the same companion each time; if that is *your* preference, it would be noted in your file. Also, if you find a companion unsatisfactory in any way, that, too, will be noted in your file and you will not be placed with him a second time. It would be of great help if you could give me an idea of what you would like to see Butterfly provide for you."

How strange it was, Jessica decided, to sit in this room and actually tell this woman, whom she had met only minutes ago, the most secret fantasy of her heart. But she felt curiously safe and unthreatened, even though she was in an unfamiliar setting. It had a lot to do with the director: she had a warm and intimate manner; she was the kind of woman who put people at their ease, invited them to confess their secrets and feel better for it afterward. "Trudie said you have a room here," Jessica found herself saying, "that's been made into a Western bar. . . ."

And there was a model downstairs, he had been wearing a Kenya safari outfit—he was blond and had an interesting face. He resembled the star of a currently popular TV cop show, and, more, he was the image of her fantasy lover. . . .

"Do you wish to begin today?" the director said after Jessica had disclosed the details of her desired scenario.

No, she couldn't begin today. Jessica had to fly to Las Vegas and take depositions from witnesses in an upcoming trial. "Next week," she said. "I'll have to call you."

As Jessica shook hands again with the director and walked to the door, she wondered, *But will I really come back here*

*and visit that Western bar? Will I, for the first time in my life,
let a strange man make love to me?*

But as she stepped into the hall where an attendant was
waiting to escort her to the store downstairs, Jessica knew
suddenly beyond a doubt that she would come back.

She had to.

10

San Antonio, Texas: 1953

WHEN RACHEL ACCIDENTALLY DISCOVERED Danny Mackay's
secret, they had been living in San Antonio for a year. In that
year, she had seen a change come over him, and she had been
wondering if she might be the cause of that change. And then
she stumbled upon the secret.

They were driving to a honky-tonk on the edge of town
to spend one of Rachel's infrequent nights off together. She
had adjusted to seeing Danny sporadically, with his not showing up when he said he would, and then showing up when she
least expected him, but privately she didn't like it. Whenever
they parted, after an evening of fun and lovemaking, Rachel
would be happy for a while. And then the days would roll by
and Danny's absence would get longer and longer and she
would grow depressed and Hazel's customers would complain.
And then there Danny would be, miraculously appearing at
the back door to take her out for enchiladas and a drive.

That was what had happened tonight, after six weeks of
not hearing from him. Rachel had started to grow frantic and
had mentioned something to Hazel about going out to look for
him, when all of a sudden there he was, smiling his half-smile
at her and mesmerizing her with his lazy green eyes. Danny
had a way of casting a spell on Rachel that made her forget
her misery and the long lonely days without him; he could
make her suddenly happy and reaffirm her conviction that
there was nothing in the world she would not do for him.

Rachel didn't know that Danny had that effect on most people and that she was not the first, nor would she be the last, to fall under his magic.

Some of Danny Mackay's charisma was in his nature; he had been born with it. But a lot of it, Rachel had begun to realize in the past year, was practiced. Danny affected a certain way of walking, he struck poses that he knew were flattering. Rachel had even come upon him once standing in front of a mirror, practicing his mischievous sideways look, a kind of sexy-sly look, which he had perfected, that he knew few people could resist. He was also a careful dresser. When she had met Danny in El Paso, he had been neat and clean, but his clothes had been of poor quality. Now he dressed expensively, using the money Rachel earned lying on her back.

But those weren't the only ways in which Danny was changing. And Rachel hadn't been able to put her finger on it until she unwittingly discovered the secret buried in the backseat of his car.

She had said, "I'm cold, Danny," and he didn't say anything. He just sat there in his usual distracted way, drumming his fingers on the steering wheel, his knee going up and down—so like Danny, always moving, full of that curious energy he never seemed to be able to discharge. So Rachel turned around in her seat and reached down for the blanket that lay on the floor behind her. And when she pulled it up, out tumbled his secret hoard.

She said, "What's that?" and Danny, seeing what had happened, suddenly swerved the car to the side of the road, slammed on the brakes, yanked the blanket out of her hand and shouted, "What're you snooping around my things for!"

She stared at him, afraid for the moment that he was going to hit her. Then she said, "I'm sorry. I was cold—"

"Look what you did," he muttered, stretching over the seat to retrieve the scattered books and papers.

"What is it, Danny? What is all that stuff?"

"What does it look like?" he muttered defensively, casting her a guarded look out of the corner of his eye.

"But you don't read, Danny. You don't even *like* books." When Rachel saw the three-ring binder with its bright blue school logo, her eyebrows arched. "Oh, Danny! Are you going to *school?*"

He gave her a suspicious look. "Yeah. What about it?"

"I think it's wonderful!"

He slowly straightened, keeping his eye on her. "You do?"

"It's the most wonderful thing in the world!" She threw her arms around his neck and kissed him. "Why didn't you tell me?"

He withdrew from her and sat back in his seat. He pulled a pack of cigarettes out of his pocket and turned it around and around in his hands. "I wanted it to be a surprise."

"It *is* a surprise, Danny. The best surprise I've ever had. Books are just so wonderful and now here you are, *reading*. What are you learning in school, Danny?"

He looked at her, at the face bright with happiness and the smiling eyes, and he felt his pride start to swell. "I'm learnin' how to make somethin' of myself, Rachel. Don't think I'm gonna be like this forever." He started to speak rapidly; his knee went up and down. The intensity that seemed to drive Danny day and night came close to the surface. Rachel could feel his energy. "I'm going places, Rachel," he said. "I'm tired of living among scum and lowlifes. I'm going to carve me a big chunk of this world and make it mine. And a man can't get anywhere less'n he's educated. So that's what I been doing, going to school, and *learning*."

He spoke with such determination, and there was such light burning in his eyes, that Rachel was speechless. She had never seen him like this, had never felt such electricity. Danny charged the cold night air with his passion; Rachel thought wildly that he could set something on fire simply by touching it. And she was overwhelmed.

"This man here," he said, holding up one of his books. "This man knows what power is, Rachel. And he knows how to get it."

She read the title. *The Prince*, by Machiavelli.

"He lived hundreds of years ago, Rachel, but he knows. The man knows!" Danny slapped the book between his hands. "He says that anybody who relies on luck is a fool, because when his luck changes he'll fail. I'm not gonna rely on luck, Rachel. I'm gonna *make* my way. The power is out there just waiting to be used. And power doesn't fall to ordinary men or stupid men. The power is out there waiting for someone like me to come along and grab it."

Danny fell silent, but his body, tense and charged, could not be still. He turned the cigarette pack over and over in his hands. His foot tapped the floor. His head turned this way and that, his eyes searching. He was thinking about the incident that had set him on this new path.

It had happened just under a year ago, shortly after his return to Texas. He and Bonner and a friend got drunk one night and decided to rob the poor box of a local church. Actually, it had been the third kid's idea, and Danny and Bonner had gone along. On their way out of the church, the three nineteen-year-olds paused to pee on the steps, and the police caught them. Danny and Bonner received sentences while the other boy went free. They were sent to a work farm, while their friend beat the rap because he was the son of the chief of police.

Power, Danny had thought during those first terrible days on the road gang, before he and Bonner managed to escape. That was what power did for you. You spoke and people danced. You lifted a finger and people moved. You controlled the strings, you called the shots. *Power, real power*. It was then, as he sweated under the hot Texas sun and beneath the eye of one mean guard with a rifle, that Danny had made the decision that, someday, he was going to be the one with that power.

He stared through the windshield now and listened once again to the words he had read in Machiavelli's book: *A man who strives after goodness in all that he does will come to ruin; therefore a prince who will survive must learn to be other than good. The man who would be prince must be unencumbered by morals and ethics; he must be part lion and part fox.*

A smile crept slowly into his lips. He felt those words reach deep down inside him and touch a place in his soul that had been hungering. All his restlessness and energy had been waiting for the necessary direction. Now he had it. Danny knew where he was going.

"What do you want to be, Danny?" Rachel said. "What are you studying to be?"

He turned his lazy eyes to her. "Have you ever read this book?"

She shook her head. Rachel had never heard of Machiavelli; she had no idea what was contained in that slender volume.

"Machiavelli says that a wise man follows the paths of great men and imitates them. Alexander followed the example of Achilles, and Caesar imitated Alexander. Because they knew that great men, through their deeds, beget great men." Danny picked up another of his dog-eared textbooks and showed it to her. *Caesar's Conquest of Gaul.*

He smiled and said, "This is what I'm studying to be, Rachel. I'm studying to be a great man."

Rachel was so happy she literally ran up the back steps and flew through the kitchen, letting the door slam behind her.

Danny was getting an education! All on his own, just like that, he had gone and enrolled in night school. And he was *learning!*

Rachel was breathless with joy. She could hardly contain it; she wanted to hug the whole world. Danny had set her on fire with his passion, with his driving ambition. And he had convinced her beyond all doubt that someday he was going to achieve his goal.

He was going to be somebody. And she was going to be right there at his side.

There was a party going on in Hazel's parlor. The girls were celebrating the birthday of one of their steady customers, and the liquor was flowing, the hi-fi blasting out music. Rachel ran up the stairs, anxious to share her good news with Carmelita.

With the exception of Danny, who was really a boyfriend, Carmelita was Rachel's first real friend. Rachel had never before known anyone for a whole year, much less shared a room with someone. A rare and special kind of intimacy, something Rachel had never experienced, had grown between the two girls, binding them closer to each other than to anyone else in Hazel's house. They were such opposites, with Carmelita being so beautiful but illiterate, that they fascinated each other. And they were close in age, but not the exact same age, so that they could joke about it. When Rachel turned fifteen, the two of them were fifteen together for a while, but then Carmelita turned sixteen and she teased Rachel about being a child and Rachel called Carmelita an old woman. Next year Rachel was going to turn sixteen and she planned on teasing her friend and saying that sixteen wasn't such a big deal after all, and then a few weeks later Carmelita would become seventeen and the teasing would begin all over again.

But the most important bond between them was that they dreamed together.

And Rachel's dream looked as if it were going to come true. Danny, *educated!* And so full of ambition! Rachel wouldn't be surprised if he owned his own gas station someday, or maybe had a government job, like working in the post office! He'd make a regular salary and they would buy a house and they could start having children, and it was going to be so wonderful.

She flew into the room she shared with Carmelita and was just about to blurt out her good news when she saw that her friend wasn't there.

Rachel looked around the small room, frowning slightly. She hadn't seen Carmelita at the party downstairs, and she couldn't remember her saying she was going out tonight. Maybe Manuel had come by unexpectedly. . . .

Rachel was about to turn around and go back downstairs when she noticed a light coming from under the bathroom door.

Most of the rooms in Hazel's three-story Victorian house shared tiny bathrooms. These had been installed for the benefit of the guests, not the girls. Rachel and Carmelita were lucky—they had a corner bedroom and therefore had a small lavatory all to themselves. Rachel went up to the door and listened.

She thought she heard running water but couldn't be sure because the music downstairs was booming up through the floor and making the walls vibrate.

Rachel knocked. There was no answer.

Thinking that perhaps Carmelita was in the shower, she knocked louder.

The crowd downstairs started singing. A few drunks whooped and hollered. Rachel had to pound on the door to be heard over the racket. "Carmelita?" she called.

She listened. Then she stepped back and looked at the light streaming under the door. A shadow moved in it. Which meant Carmelita wasn't in the shower. Then why didn't she answer?

"Carmelita?" Rachel called out again, louder.

Pressing her ear to the door, Rachel tried to hear if her friend was okay. There was a brief pause in the music downstairs, and on the other side of the bathroom door Rachel heard the sound of glass shattering.

"Carmelita!" she shouted, suddenly alarmed.

She pounded the door, thought a moment, then tried the knob. Hazel had removed all the locks from all the doors years ago; privacy was a precious commodity in this house.

Opening the door a few inches, Rachel called, "Carmelita? Are you all right?"

"Go away—"

"What's wrong? Are you crying?"

"Just . . . go . . ."

Rachel opened the door all the way and looked in just in time to see her friend, bent over the sink, leaning on it for support, bring a piece of broken glass down on her wrist.

"No!" Rachel said.

A thin ribbon of blood sprang up.

Rachel dashed forward. She grabbed her friend's arm.

"Get out of here!" shouted Carmelita, pushing Rachel away. She switched the shard to her other hand and started to slice her right wrist. Rachel reached for her again, slapped the glass out of her grasp. "Don't do it—"

Carmelita spun around and lashed out. *"Leave me alone!"*

Rachel stared for a split second at her friend's bruised and swollen face, then when Carmelita snatched up the broken glass again and brought it down on her other wrist, Rachel lunged at her.

They struggled. The bathroom was small; as the girls wrestled they banged against the walls and sink. Rachel had hold of Carmelita by the wrists, trying to get her to drop the piece of glass. A shattered liquor bottle lay underfoot, the shards sliced into Rachel's shoes and Carmelita's slippers. *"Please,"* sobbed Carmelita. "Leave me alone—"

"I won't let you do it!" Rachel's hand slipped on Carmelita's bloody arm. She lost her grip for a moment and was pushed back against the wall. But when her friend scrambled for a piece of broken bottle, Rachel grabbed her again and spun her around. They were locked for an instant in an embrace, the two being of equal strength with neither able to overcome the other. Then Carmelita suddenly went limp and began to weep.

Rachel led her to a bed and seized the first thing handy— the sash of her bathrobe—and quickly bound it around the cut wrist. She had difficulty tying it securely, she was shaking so badly. She was frightened and out of breath. "You didn't cut too deep" was all she could think to say. "I don't think you got an artery—"

"Please leave me alone," Carmelita sobbed. "I don't want to live."

Rachel jumped up, ran into the bathroom, kicked the pieces of glass out of the way, and came back to the bed with two towels, one wet and one dry. Carmelita was lying down with an arm flung across her face. She was weeping so bitterly that tears came to Rachel's eyes. Carefully washing first the injured arm, Rachel then sponged smeared blood off Carmelita's face and neck.

Rachel didn't know what to say. She was too stunned, too shaken. Carmelita was wearing only a slip. Rachel saw the fresh bruises, the places where she had been beaten.

"Who—" she finally said. "Who did this to you, Carmelita?"

With the weeping subsiding, Carmelita lifted her arm off her face and stared up at the ceiling. "Manuel," she said.

111

Rachel was shocked. "Manuel! But *why*?"

"He found out I've been holding back some money. You know, the tips. Hazel told him."

"But that money's yours, Carmelita! That's extra. It's like—like a gift from the customers. Manuel has no right to that."

"Yes, he does. I shouldn't have held back. He's good to me. He gives me money whenever I need it."

Rachel gazed down at her friend in disbelief. *He's good to you!*

Carmelita rolled her head on the pillow. She looked at Rachel with lifeless eyes and asked softly, "Why did you stop me?"

"What kind of a question is that? You're my friend, Carmelita. My only friend. I couldn't let you do that to yourself."

"I want to die," the girl said, her chest starting to rise with sobs again. "I don't want to live like this anymore."

Rachel tried to smile. "You have to live, Carmelita. You're only sixteen."

"I'm sixteen and a whore! I can't even read or write! I'm worthless!" She turned over and buried her face in the pillow.

Rachel remained seated on the edge of the bed while her friend wept anew. Then Carmelita's voice came from far away: "Please let me die. If you love me you'll let me die."

A cold pain filled Rachel's chest. The night was suddenly black and empty and sinister. The music booming downstairs sounded discordant; the laughter sounded like mockery. For the first time in a year Rachel felt small and vulnerable and abandoned, and for a moment she felt what Carmelita was feeling. And she, too, thought that maybe dying was the best way out.

But then she remembered her evening with Danny and his wonderful secret and how good she had felt coming home and running up the stairs to tell Carmelita the good news. And suddenly Rachel was full of hope and optimism again, so that she laid a hand on her friend's arm and said, "You have a lot to live for, Carmelita. You don't want to die now. Not for a long time yet."

Carmelita rolled over and glared at Rachel with tear-filled

eyes. "Who are you kidding! We've got nothing to live for! Nobody cares about us! We've got no family, no friends. Even our boyfriends treat us like shit! When are you going to wise up, Rachel! You think this is the first time Manuel did this to me? You think it's the last?"

Rachel bit her lip. Danny might have smacked her around a bit, but he had never hurt her as badly as Manuel had hurt Carmelita. "Listen," she said, "I found out the most wonderful thing tonight. Danny is going to school!"

Carmelita looked away. "So what."

"It means he's going to improve himself. It means we aren't going to be living like this forever! It means he has dreams and ambitions, and with dreams and ambitions you just have to go on to better things."

Carmelita smiled sadly. "You're a dreamer, Rachel. But don't you know dreams ain't real? All they are is dreams, nothing else."

"No they're not. You can *make* them real! Don't you see?"

"That's just wishful thinking."

"For some people, maybe. But dreaming can also show you what you can be. You know my dream, Carmelita. To be Danny's wife and live in a nice house and have children. And it's going to come true, you know it is. What's your dream? Tell me about it."

"No."

"Tell me your dream about the office."

"I don't have no dream."

"You do. You've mentioned it. Please, I want to hear it."

Carmelita stared up at the ceiling. She drew in a deep breath and let it out slowly. Her body trembled. She was close to tears again. "I imagine myself working in a nice office," she said softly. "You know, like Feldman's Realty or the Let's Go Travel Agency. Whenever I walk down the street and pass those places, I look in and I see the girls at their desks, talking on the phone or typing or smiling at customers. And I see myself—"

Carmelita closed her eyes.

"I see myself sitting at one of those desks. There's a carnation on it. Maybe a card from a grateful client, telling me how nice I had been. I have a real fancy typewriter, one of those new electric ones, and everyone calls me Miss Sanchez." Carmelita sighed again.

"What are you wearing?"

"Something real nice. Maybe a skirt with a matching jacket. And *gloves*. And when I walk down the street, men don't whistle at me 'cause I'm respectable. But it's only a dream—"

"And it's a wonderful dream. If you think about it hard enough and step inside it and *live* it, you can make it come true."

Carmelita's head rolled from side to side. "It's just fantasy, Rachel. And fantasy ain't real."

"Listen to me—"

"No! You listen to me!" Carmelita turned eyes full of pain on her friend. "You go around with your head in the clouds, Rachel. Don't you know the score yet, after a year of living at Hazel's? There ain't no way out for any of us!"

"I refuse to believe that."

"How'm I gonna get a job in a office, Rachel! *I can't even read!*" Carmelita started to cry. "I'm sixteen and I can't even write my name!"

"But you're good with numbers, Carmelita, and that's a start."

"That don't help me if I can't read."

Rachel gazed down at her friend, at the beautiful face Manuel had ruined. She listened to the music downstairs and the laughter of the other girls—faked laughter, most of it, because they too had dreams and wanted to be anywhere else but at Hazel's. Rachel watched the anguish in Carmelita's eyes and felt it wash over her, like a cold morning mist. And she tried to think of the words, what to say, to help her.

And then—it came to her.

"Carmelita," Rachel said, suddenly excited, "I've got the answer."

"Leave me alone."

"Listen to me!" Rachel put her hand on Carmelita's shoulder. "You can *learn* to read."

"Are you crazy? Leave me alone! I already told you, I tried

that once. It didn't work. And Manuel got mad. And besides, when have I got the time to go to night school!"

"But you don't have to go to night school! You can learn right here and Manuel will never know."

Carmelita looked at her. "What are you talking about?"

"*I'll* teach you to read."

"You?" Carmelita stared at Rachel for a moment, then she looked away. "It won't work. I'm too old."

Rachel jumped up from the bed and ran to her dresser. Picking up a book, she came back and held it up to Carmelita's face. "Look. Do you see this letter?"

"So?"

"Do you know what that letter is?"

"No."

"It's the letter C. It's the letter your name begins with. And look"—Rachel flipped open pages and pointed to random words—"here it is again. C. And whenever you see it, you make a *k* sound, like in cat. Look here"—she turned pages—"and here. And here. Carmelita, what's this letter?"

She squinted at where Rachel was pointing. "I don't know."

"Sure you do. What is it?"

"A C?"

"C for Carmelita! Now you already know one letter!"

"How many letters are there?"

"Twenty-six."

Carmelita laughed softly and murmured, "*Santa Maria.*"

"You can learn them, I know you can. I'll teach you. We'll have lessons between customers and in the mornings and on our days off. We'll go to the library and I'll show you all the books they have. Carmelita, the library has books on how to become a secretary, how to type, how to do office things! When you know how to read there's nothing you can't do!"

Carmelita stared at the book in Rachel's hands. It was a dog-eared paperback that Rachel had been buried in for the past few days. And Carmelita had been envious—to be able to escape from reality for a while! To be able to read stories, to be able to open a book and *learn* things. Like how to type and how to work in an office and how to be respectable. And Carmelita experienced a sudden rush of hope. She forgot her pain, in her heart and in her wrist, and suddenly wanted to learn all twenty-six letters and put them together to form words and then read books and make her fantasy come true.

"I don't know," she said, uncertain but interested now.

"We can do it, Carmelita. Together! I'll help you!"

"All right," she said softly. "I'll try it. As long as Manuel don't find out."

Rachel reached down and hugged her friend. "Don't worry. It'll be our secret."

Just like Danny's wonderful, wonderful secret.

11

IT IS ONE THING to plan an act of defiance, quite another to carry it out.

As Jessica walked through the busy men's shop toward the rear, where an attendant was to meet her, she felt surprisingly, inexplicably afraid. Outwardly she looked like any young successful career woman, dressed conservatively, with purpose in her stride and confidence in the swing of her short brown hair. But internally Jessica found herself suddenly full of misgivings. She felt as if invisible phantoms tugged at her.

To hold her back. To keep her from stepping into that forbidden elevator.

There was her father, a man who, all through Jessica's childhood, had withheld affection from his children until they earned it through high achievement and special honors, a man for whom she had once starved herself in pursuit of his approval and love. There were the priests of her schools who had ruled over the nuns and therefore over the all-girls student body, distant, formidable men whose word was law and who called all the shots. And there was John, whom she believed she loved but who confused her and frequently filled her with self-doubts. *They* didn't want her to go upstairs to Butterfly's secret rooms.

But didn't Trudie repeatedly say that Jessica needed to be her own woman? That it was time for John to turn over her reins to her? For eight years Jessica had believed she was an individual, even within her marriage, that she maintained an identity separate from her husband's. Her law office, her clients, her days in court proved that. Didn't they? And yet, ever since the specter of Butterfly had crept into her life, taking a place in her mind where it couldn't be shaken free, Jessica had begun to question. And her first question had been: Why *can't* I join? I'm free to do so, aren't I? That was when she had discovered that her autonomy had really been an illusion all these years, that her identity was something John had carved out for her, that she was, after all, not her own woman. And so she had decided to take the first step toward selfhood. Today, Jessica was actually doing something, for the very first time in her life, for which she had not received permission.

"Good afternoon, madam," said the attendant with the butterfly embroidered on her blouse. "Will you come this way, please?"

What would John/her father/the Church do if they found out about this? As the elevator doors began to close behind her, shutting off the bustle of Fanelli and the noise of Rodeo Drive traffic, Jessica gave the phantoms that dogged her a mental shove, cutting them off, leaving them out there, and suddenly she was alone and free and riding up to meet her fantasy.

"What do you do at Butterfly?" she had asked Trudie. "Do you just walk into the room and there he is?"

"You do whatever you want. You have to tell them how you want it to be."

How I want it to be . . .

As she followed the attendant down the carpeted hallway, Jessica looked at the closed doors they passed. No sounds came from any of the rooms; a strange kind of silence hung in the air. Were there women behind those doors right now? she wondered. And what dreams were they acting out?

The attendant came to a stop before a closed door and said, "If you will please go in."

Jessica realized that her heart was racing. The door looked like the door to any hotel room. What on earth was she going to find on the other side?

She opened the door and stepped in.

Right into her fantasy.

It was just as it was in her dream: the sawdust on the floor, the plain tables, the jukebox playing Kenny Rogers, the dim lights, the bar at one end where a lone cowboy stood with one foot on the brass rail, wearing jeans and a Western shirt with his black Stetson pushed back on his head. He was listening to the music and bringing a drink up to his lips.

When the door closed behind Jessica—closing out the attendant, the hallway, Rodeo Drive, and reality—the cowboy looked up. And a slow smile lifted his mouth. "Howdy," he said quietly.

She twisted the strap of her purse. "Hello."

"Can I buy you a drink?"

She looked at the bar. There was a large mirror behind it, making the room look bigger than it was, with liquor bottles lining the shelves. She hesitated for a moment—how her heart was pounding!—then she walked up to the bar and set her purse down. "There doesn't seem to be anyone here."

"No, ma'am. We're all alone. What can I get you?"

She looked at him. He was young, in his twenties, and smiling in a kind of self-conscious way. He slowly removed his hat and ran his hand through his sandy hair.

"White wine, please," she said.

As he went around the bar and reached underneath he said, "What's the weather like? Sure looked to me this morning like it was going to rain."

"No," she said a little breathlessly. She watched his nicely shaped hands set out a wineglass and fill it from a bottle. His shirt was tight across the chest and shoulders and had little pearly buttons. The top ones were undone; she could see his chest. "It's not raining, yet . . ."

"Never could get used to California winters," he said with a smile as he handed her the wineglass. Their fingertips touched. "Where I come from, we'd be knee-deep in snow by now!"

She looked away. She didn't know what to say.

He came from behind the bar and picked up his beer. They stood for a long moment in silence, Jessica trying to avoid looking at their reflections in the mirror, he studying her. Finally he said, "Guess we got the place to ourselves tonight."

She nodded. *How her pulse raced . . .*

Something slow and moody came out of the jukebox and the cowboy said, "Would you like to dance?"

John was the only man she had ever danced with, the only man whose body she had really felt. Hugs with her brothers had always been brief, and she couldn't remember what her father felt like. That was why it was so strange to feel this man's arms go around her, to feel him so near, to feel the warmth of his skin through his shirt. John had a firm body; so did this cowboy. But in different, subtle ways. And he smelled different, too. He guided her over the floor with a very firm step. They barely touched. Jessica didn't look at him but focused on a point above his shoulder. There was decor on the walls, she realized now; Western stuff like stirrups and saddles and old-fashioned signs advertising a shave for five cents. She kept her eyes on the walls, read all the signs, as he slowly turned her around the floor, as the song got sadder and lovelier, as he began to draw her closer to him so that they finally were touching, chest to chest, pelvis to pelvis, and she felt her shyness start to melt away and she allowed her arms to go around his neck and abandoned herself to the fantasy.

How good he felt.

When the song was over they returned to the bar. They talked for a few minutes, about the weather, about things that didn't count, and then Jessica heard herself suddenly asking him what his name was.

"You tell me," he said.

"What?" she said. Then, remembering the club rules, she said, "Lonnie," surprising herself. She vaguely recalled a movie, an endearing cowboy character named Lonnie. It had just sprung into her mind.

"Well, ma'am," he said, "my name's Lonnie, and I was wondering if you'd care to dance with me again."

It was another slow song, and this time Jessica started out

by holding on to him. As the sad country-western ballad carried them around the room, their embrace became tighter, until she was burying her face in his neck and thinking, *This is it. This is really it. . . .*

When his lips finally met hers, it was at exactly the right moment. Jessica was no longer afraid or nervous or shy. John was the only man she had ever kissed; it was as if he had molded her mouth. And now a tongue and lips other than John's were reshaping her mouth, showing her a different way to kiss, a *better* way.

Then he whispered in her ear, "Tell me what you want."

Her eyes flew open. She had no idea what she wanted. John had never asked; he always took the lead in bed and she mutely followed. But now that Lonnie was asking her, Jessica was suddenly excited. She felt her inhibitions falling away like old clothes. She was beginning to feel free, truly free, as if she could fly, as if she were invincible, as if there was nothing she could not do. "Anything," she said deliriously. "I want you to do anything and everything—"

They continued to dance, to sway to the music, clinging to each other, while his hands went up under her blouse and unhooked her bra. He massaged her breasts as he kissed her; she pressed herself against his hardness with a passion she had never before felt. There were no rules here, no conventions, no sins to confess, no husband to disapprove. Jessica was suddenly unfettered; she was free to revel in herself, in her sexuality, in Lonnie.

And then he had her stretched back over a table. He pulled her panties off, pushed her skirt up around her waist, and he entered her, so abruptly and with such force that it took her breath away.

It was happening so quickly. Her head reeled. She felt herself racing to that delicious brink she so infrequently experienced with John, but before she could reach it Lonnie withdrew, and then he was on his knees and making love to her in another, totally new way.

Jessica drove her hands through his hair and cried out.

Then he was inside her again. He reached up under her blouse and half lifted her; he bent forward and pressed his mouth over hers as he rocked her. She clung to him. She wanted to devour him. She felt her body opening wide, wider, until she wanted the moment never to end. And when it did he held her for a long time; they joined the music again and moved dreamily around the floor, exhausted, holding each other up, still kissing, but gently now, tenderly.

Something had happened here tonight, Jessica realized as she prepared to leave. Something more than just one woman's discovery of terrific sex. It was as if, while in the throes of ecstasy, with Lonnie inside her, holding her, she had finally been able to reach down into some deep, secret core of herself and tap a buried spring. Sex with Lonnie had been more than physically gratifying; she had come away from it feeling— emancipated.

As she rode down in the elevator Jessica experienced a strange illusion: she felt as if she were growing tall. She felt inexplicably filled with power, her own power. And she knew that an irrevocable step had been taken, a step that was going to have far-reaching effects.

She had defied John, once. Having done it once, she could do it again.

12

San Antonio, Texas: 1954

WHEN RACHEL TURNED SIXTEEN she was still living in Hazel's house. The girls threw a party for her and invited several of the regular customers. Hazel uncorked the champagne, which didn't fizz, and poured it sparingly into Dixie cups. "Here's to our favorite girl," she said magnanimously, and they all drank. Everyone present agreed that Rachel looked so happy that she positively glowed.

The glow was because she had a secret.

And this was her best birthday ever. When she was a little girl, her birthdays had come and gone, just like ordinary days.

Once, her mother had remembered and had promised Rachel that she would make her special hamburgers that night as a special treat, and Rachel could help with the little jars of spices, and even pinch some into the meat. But Mrs. Dwyer had gone off with her husband to spend the day in the local bar, and by the time they got back late that night, finding Rachel just where they had left her that morning, sitting on the sofa, ready to make hamburgers, they had had a fight and Mrs. Dwyer was already showing a black eye and was in no mood to cook.

But nobody let Rachel down on *this* day.

Not even Danny was going to, for once.

The girls had had a special breakfast and Eulalie had baked an extra-rich chocolate layer cake with mounds of strawberries on top. And a present had been bought with money collected from all the girls: the new *Lord of the Rings* books. Rachel cried with happiness. She had found her family at last.

Those early days of sorrow and throwing up were now but a memory. She had pushed them back to a dark place in her mind where she kept such things. The men went there, too, the ones who continued to use her every night. That part of living in Hazel's house hadn't changed, but Rachel had learned to separate herself from it. When she gave them her body, she kept her soul. They did what they liked to her physically while she retreated into fantasy. And when she awoke the next morning, all would be forgotten and Rachel would join the other girls.

They were her sisters, and she loved them, even Frenchie, the one Negro girl who was so bitter and had such a chip on her shoulder that she was difficult to like. Rachel had not forgotten her mother and her vow to find her someday, but for now the girls in Hazel's house were Rachel's family. They stuck together. They helped one another. Whenever one was in trouble, they all rallied to her aid. If one needed money, a collection was taken. Lipsticks and stockings were freely loaned. A sorrow was shared, a joy celebrated. And if anyone had asked why such a dreary, desperate place such as Hazel's sleazy brothel could have any happiness in it, Hazel herself would have been the first to admit that an awful lot of it had to do with Rachel.

For one thing, Hazel said when asked, how could anyone feel sorry for herself with that homely little thing around? No matter how bad things got for the girls, how low they sank, they still had decent looks—and a few were actual knockouts. But Rachel Dwyer had arrived homely and was growing homelier by the year. Yet it didn't seem to bother her. And that would be the next thing Hazel said that contributed to the congenial atmosphere in the place—if Rachel could be so accepting of the way she had been constructed, well then Hazel supposed that a person could accept just about anything life dished out to them.

And Rachel did things for people. She liked to please people. Like cooking things no one else could quite duplicate, which the girls gobbled up and even the customers were now buying. And like teaching Carmelita to read, which was as big a miracle, Hazel thought, as any ever performed.

But don't think for a minute, Hazel would hasten to add, that Rachel Dwyer was perfect. Far from it. She dreamed too much. She buried her head in books all the time. She sometimes forgot to do the chores assigned to her so that someone else had to cover for her. And the customers, Hazel would sigh, still complained. She was too listless in bed, she didn't participate, she didn't give a customer any encouragement or praise for his performance. When a man shells out five bucks for a woman, he expects a little enthusiasm, a little acting, for God's sake, to make him feel like a man. That certainly wasn't asking so much, was it? But Rachel was obsessed with Danny Mackay; she saved her love only for him. And that wasn't a healthy thing—in any woman.

But what the hell, Hazel thought now as she gave in and opened the second bottle of champagne. Can't begrudge Rachel her bit of happiness. And she certainly did look happy, even if Danny hadn't yet arrived.

Hazel did not know that Rachel was happy because of a secret.

Although Hazel's house had become Rachel's family, and the girls her sisters, and Danny her father/brother/husband, there was still an emptiness in Rachel's love-hungry heart. She wanted a child.

Ever since she could remember, she had thought it would be wonderful to be a mother. Even on that day when Rachel was thirteen and her period had started and her mother had explained about bleeding and pain and babies, and had made childbirth sound so awful, even then Rachel had secretly thought: *No. It's a wonderful thing to have a baby.*

It came out of your own body! You felt it move inside you, you felt it living within you, depending on you, *needing* you, and then when it came out it was so helpless; it cried for you to hold it and it fell asleep in your arms and was just so hungry for all the love you could give it. Someday Rachel was going to have a baby of her own—that was her cherished dream—and when it arrived, she was going to make it the best-loved baby in all the world.

Well, that day was coming sooner than she had expected.

It was not in Rachel's nature to be devious. Just as it had never entered her mind to steal doughnuts when she was starving in El Paso, just as she never held back any of the money the clients gave her, as some of the girls did, it would never have occurred to Rachel to trap Danny with a baby. Other girls, she knew, had done that. They purposely got pregnant so their boyfriends would marry them and take them out of here. Once in a while even a client married one of the girls and took her home. Pregnancy was, for many women, a means of getting rescued. And so it would be for Rachel. But she had not planned it that way.

She really had forgotten to put in the diaphragm the night she slept with Danny.

And that was how she knew it was his baby.

With the clients, she was fastidious about practicing birth control. As much as she desired a baby, she did not want a child by one of these men. She wanted it to be a love child, conceived in love, and loved from the moment it stirred in her womb. And that was exactly what Danny's baby would be. They were going to get married one day—he kept telling her so, and she never let *that* dream die either. And when they did, she would have his children and be the best wife and mother on the face of the earth.

"Listen, honey," Hazel said when the party was over and

the girls drifted back to their routine of waiting, "if Danny don't come tonight, you gotta work."

Rachel pretended not to hear. She was sitting at the table, carefully pressing and folding the wrapping paper her birthday present had come in. She would save it in her special cigar box of mementos, a box similar to the one her mother had kept hidden under the sink.

"Look, just 'cause it's your birthday don't give you no special privileges. Mr. Atkins is in town and he'll be wanting you."

Rachel felt her stomach turn. Mr. Atkins was a traveling Bible salesman and one of the least-liked customers. The girls were glad he had taken a shine to Rachel; it relieved them of the unpleasant task of servicing him. And the reason he liked Rachel was the very fact of her detachment. He liked the way she lay quiet and still. And he liked to cross her arms over her breasts before he started; he asked her to close her eyes. It wasn't hard for Rachel to do, but it still sickened her.

"Danny will be here," she said softly.

"I've heard that one before," Hazel said.

When her employer was gone, Eulalie, standing at a sink full of hot soapy dishwater, muttered, "Lordy, hear that wind blow. Don't I feel a norther comin'! And don't we about need some rain!" She looked at Rachel and said gently, "Don't let that old cow get to you, child. A girl's got a right to be happy on her birthday. And Danny'll be here, God willing and the creek don't rise."

Rachel would not let Hazel dampen her spirits. Danny *would* come tonight. Sure, he had forgotten many times in the past two years, or he had gotten tied up in something he and Bonner were involved in, and then his schoolwork took up so much of his time and energy. But he did love her and he would come for her birthday.

Besides, Rachel told herself with strengthened resolve, now that she was pregnant, she was never going to bed with another man again.

Danny was going to take her away from here. Tonight.

"Hey, kiddo!" came Belle's voice from the doorway. "Great party."

Rachel turned around to see her two friends. She smiled at them. "Thank you for the books."

"Hey, you know?" said Carmelita as she strolled across the kitchen toward the coffeepot. "It ain't easy finding you a book you ain't already read!"

"Are *you* going to read it?" Rachel asked her with a teasing grin.

"*Santa María!* You are a tough teacher!"

A year ago, to the amazement and delight of both, Carmelita had turned out to be a quick study. Rachel had had her reading the alphabet in a week, and Dick and Jane books a month after that. Soon, Carmelita had graduated to grammar school textbooks, and finally to adult novels. It took her a long time, and she often struggled over words, but she was able to get through a library book—she liked historical novels about biblical times and stories about the saints—in about two weeks.

As she poured herself a cup from the ever-brewing pot, adding thick rich cream and three teaspoons of sugar, Carmelita pulled several envelopes out of her fake-silk kimono and waved them at Rachel. "Got six more to send," she said.

Rachel beamed. The first thing her friend had done with her new skill was to write a letter to a crossword-puzzle magazine asking if they could use number puzzles. They had accepted, and she had been paid five dollars for her first puzzle. Now Carmelita was regularly thinking up new ones and sending them in. She was putting money in a bank account now, with her numbers. If only, Rachel thought wistfully, Carmelita had enough self-confidence to leave Hazel and get more schooling. With her natural ability with numbers, and her fantasy of the respectable office job, there was no reason why Carmelita could not make that dream come true.

But unfortunately, like most of the girls in the house, Carmelita had been beaten down and abused into believing she was exactly where she belonged.

The only other girl, besides Rachel, who did not share that view was Belle.

Belle remained firm in her conviction that, with her Susan Hayward looks, she was made for better things, and that this was only a way station. A place to save some money, and bide her time. How she bided her time was following the movies and dreaming. Today she wore a scarf over her head to hide the 125 pins that kept her short curls in place. When the poodle cut became the fashion, Belle got one. Likewise the Capezio shoes and wide plastic belts. With the advent of television, and most particularly with the installation of a set in Hazel's "reception" room, Belle was kept even more currently up to date with the latest styles. Now she followed the examples of Dorothy Kilgallen and Lucy Ricardo. Someday Hollywood was going to call. She didn't want to look like a hick.

Rachel got up and went to the kitchen door. From the reception room came the sound of "Mr. Sandman" on the radio. A few deep voices mingled with high girlish laughter. It was late afternoon and business was starting to pick up. Gently closing the door and leaning with her back against it, she looked at her two friends.

She was going to miss Belle and Carmelita when Danny took her away. Of course, if they found a place in San Antonio, then she could come and visit, and bring the baby and let all the girls ooh and ah over it. Rachel's child would be a lucky child, because it would have so many aunts to love it.

And maybe once in a while she could leave the baby with Danny and go into town with Belle and Carmelita as they usually did, getting on the bus and going to the drugstore to buy movie magazines and Coty face powder. The three liked to spend their Tuesdays sitting at the drugstore counter inventing ice cream concoctions. Rachel's were always the best, with nuts and marshmallow topping and three flavors of ice cream and whipped cream and a cherry on top. Quality girls would sometimes come in, wearing their full skirts with yards of petticoats underneath and being called "ma'am" by the druggist and getting doors opened for them by clean-cut young men. Belle and Carmelita and Rachel would watch the quality girls and secretly yearn for such respectability. Once in a while, if one happened to look her way, Rachel would smile, but she never got a smile in return. No matter how clean and decent she and her two friends tried to look on their Tuesday outings, they could never disguise the fact that they were trash. And quality never mingled with trash. Those other girls with their pert ponytails and talk of dances and football games would whisk past the three at the counter as if they weren't even there.

Standing at the kitchen door, Rachel looked at her two friends and said quietly, "I have something to tell you."

Belle was going through a well-thumbed *Life* magazine. "What is it, kiddo?"

Rachel's heart was thumping, she was so excited. "I'm going to have a baby."

Carmelita spun around. "What!"

"I'm going to have a baby. Isn't it wonderful?"

The two exchanged a glance.

"Well?" Rachel could hardly contain her excitement.

"Does Danny know?" Carmelita asked.

"I'm going to tell him tonight. He's taking me out to dinner. Someplace special down on River Walk. I thought I'd wait till then."

"What are you going to do?" Belle said, laying aside the magazine.

"Do?"

"Yeah, you know," Carmelita said. "What're you gonna do?"

Rachel looked at them, puzzled. "About what?"

The two gave each other a quick look again, and Carmelita came to take Rachel's hand. "Come here, *amiga*," she said quietly. "We gotta talk."

Frowning, Rachel joined her friends at the table. "I thought you'd be happy for me," she said. "What's wrong?"

"What's wrong, kiddo," said Belle, "is that we don't think Danny's gonna like it."

"What?" Rachel laughed. "You must be joking! It's all we ever talk about, how many kids we're going to have! We even know where we're going to buy our house, just as soon as he's finished school and we have enough money saved up."

Belle exchanged a glance with Eulalie at the sink while Carmelita drew circles with her finger on the tabletop. It was beyond them how Rachel, after over two years in Hazel's house, could still be so naive!

Nearly all the girls had "boyfriends"—men who brought them here, came to visit once in a while, and took their money from them. There were many scenarios enacted, a lot of pretense and self-deception, but in their hearts all the girls knew what their men were in reality. Pimps, gigolos, no-goods. Nothing more. They smooth-talked their way through women, lived off them, exploited them, just as Danny did, as Carmelita's Manuel did. They weren't the most ideal of partners, they weren't respectable husbands, which was what the girls would have preferred, but they were, after all, men. And women needed men. For identity, for protection. A woman simply didn't go it alone. A woman without a man had somehow failed, she was an incomplete person, a woman who had been "passed over." A man gave a woman meaning, a place in the scheme of things; even if she was his whore, she belonged to a man, and that was what mattered.

But Rachel carried it too far. She actually believed Danny's fast talk. She blindly overlooked his thousands of shortcomings and saw only the knight in armor who had rescued her in El Paso. Damn, Carmelita and Belle both thought. The poor kid had been so desperate, she would have fallen in love with the first thing that showed her a kindness. A dog, even.

Which, incidentally, was what they both thought Danny Mackay was.

"Well, you're wrong," Rachel said, sad and hurt that her best friends were acting this way. They just didn't know Danny the way she did. He was going to be thrilled with the news.

"You're *what?*" he shouted.

Rachel's joy vanished. "I said I'm pregnant."

He pounded the steering wheel. "I don't fucking believe it. How the hell did it happen?"

She started to wring her hands. "I don't know, Danny. It wasn't on purpose. You know how careful I've been. But, well, that night we were together, I was so happy, I just forgot—"

He stared at her. "Are you trying to tell me that it's *mine?*"

She shrank from him, from the terrible look on his face.

"Shee-yit," he muttered, hitting the steering wheel again. "I don't believe any of this. I just don't. Damn it, Rachel! Just when things were starting to go good for me. School, my plans—" He turned a dark look on her, something she had never seen on his face before. It terrified her. "Okay. So what did you want me to do about it?"

"Do?"

"Yeah. You laid it on me for a reason. What did you expect me to do? Pass out cigars?"

"I thought we'd get married—"

He swung away from her and looked out at the sidewalk. "I don't fucking believe this! Well, we're not getting married, so you can just forget that."

"But, Danny," she pleaded, reaching for him, "I thought we were going to get married sometime. And now, if we don't get married the baby will be illegitimate!"

He turned back around to give her an incredulous look. "You really take the prize, you know that? I mean, you are a real winner! You know I can't get married now. I've got another year of school, and after that I have to start looking for ways to make something of myself. I don't want a wife and kid now for Chris'sake!"

She started to cry. It was turning out all wrong. This wasn't how she had imagined it would be. She had pictured a loving embrace, reassurances that everything was going to be all right, maybe a drive across the border for a quick wedding, and then a little house somewhere, geraniums. . . .

He started the car.

"Where are we going?" she asked, suddenly hopeful and afraid at the same time.

He didn't answer. He just drove the old Ford in smoldering silence. Rachel wanted to sink into the cracked upholstery and disappear. And she couldn't stop the quiet sobbing, which only seemed to make him madder.

To her surprise, they pulled up in front of Bonner's house. There was the ever-present laundry on the lines in back, the sound of the washer going. Rachel hadn't been here in over two years. Now she grasped at the insane hope that he had decided to let her stay with Mrs. Purvis until the baby was born. Yes, she would do it. And she could help the poor old woman with her laundry—

130

"Stay here," he said, and got out.

She watched him go inside. She felt her anxiety mount. Suddenly she felt terribly alone, more alone than on that hungry night in El Paso, more alone that she had ever felt in her life.

He came out a few minutes later, his body stiff, his gestures abrupt. He got back in the car, still not saying anything, threw it into gear, and headed off away from the direction of Hazel's house.

Eulalie's "norther" had hit San Antonio, so that a cold rain was starting to fall. Danny drove like a maniac, speeding down deserted streets, screeching around corners, until he got to a section along the river where locked-up warehouses stood in ominous silence. He stopped the car in front of a run-down brick building and said, "Get out."

"Where are we, Danny?"

"I said get out."

A nameless fear made her cling to the car seat. "What *is* this place, Danny!"

"Just thank your lucky stars I've got connections."

"Connect—" She looked at the old building, at the flight of stairs, the yellow light at the end. "Oh no, Danny!" she cried. "Not that!"

"You can't keep it, Rachel. You've got to get rid of it."

"No!" she screamed, her hands going protectively to her abdomen. "I want my baby! Danny, please! Don't kill my baby!"

He reached inside and pulled her out. Rachel fell to her knees on the wet pavement.

"Make all the noise you want," Danny said, "there's no one here to hear you. And I'm warning you. If you don't go through with this, you'll never see me again."

On her hands and knees in the dirt, she looked up at him. How he towered over her. She had never realized he was so tall.

All of a sudden a voice came into her mind, as loud and clear as if the speaker were standing right there with her. It was her mother's voice, and she was saying, "Someday, when you're a grown woman, you'll fall in love and you'll understand what it's all about. I'll stay by your father no matter what he does to me."

Rachel got to her knees and put her arms around his legs. "Please, Danny," she sobbed. "Don't make me kill my baby. It's all I want in the world. I already love it. And it loves me, I know it does. I want to carry it and keep it safe."

"Come on," he said in something close to a bored tone. "We haven't got all night. We're just lucky he would take you right away. This guy does a brisk business."

She looked up at the windows painted black. "Is he a doctor?" she heard herself ask.

"Does it matter? Look, Rachel. He's done hundreds of girls. And he's doing it for us at a low rate."

She looked at him. "Please, Danny. I'll do anything. I mean it. I'll be good from now on. I'll do whatever Hazel tells me. I'll do anything the customers ask. Just don't . . . make me kill my baby."

He took her by the arm and propelled her out of the street. She barely struggled. This was becoming too much like a nightmare—it couldn't be real. She felt herself being moved along by forces she couldn't fight, up those horrible stairs, through a brown door, and into a room that was filled with storage crates and furniture covered with dusty sheets. She watched Danny go to the opposite door, knock, and then murmur softly. She heard a lock turn, and saw the door open. Sickly yellow light spilled out.

"You caught me just in time, Danny," a male voice said familiarly, as if he and Danny were old friends. "I gotta thing to go to. But for you, I'll make the time. Who is it this time?"

"You don't know this one." He leaned forward and whispered something in the man's ear.

Rachel stared at Danny. *Who is it this time?*

The man stepped back for her to enter. "Take off your skirt and panties and stockings if you got them on. Lie down on that table."

She didn't move.

"Get in here," Danny said.

She looked at him. Those hard green eyes beneath half-closed lids seemed to reach across the room and seize her.

132

Rachel felt his power, that Danny Mackay magnetism, which she had never been able to fight. She did as she was told. While she removed her lower garments, modestly retaining her bra and blouse, she saw the stranger place some long metal objects in a medicinal basin that was filled with a strong-smelling solution. The sheet on the table was clean, and there was a stack of fresh white towels near the foot of it. There was also, it struck her oddly until she understood, a box of Modess napkins.

"Here," the stranger said, handing her a glass of water and two pills. "Take these. They'll kill the pain."

For an instant her eyes met his, and in that instant she saw that he was not an unkind man. He had a gentle sort of face, like a teddy bear's, with apologetic eyes and a stubbly beard. *He's a victim, too*, she thought.

She took the pills and lay back on the table.

"Open your legs," Danny said. "Slide them into these things."

Rachel had never been to a doctor in her life. She didn't understand the stirrups. Danny had to help her while she heard the stranger wash his hands.

"Can you hurry?" Danny said. "I'm late as it is."

"Gotta wait for the narcotic to take effect. Otherwise she'll scream bloody murder."

"Let her. No one can hear."

"Danny," she murmured, reaching up for his hand. "Danny, please don't talk like that. Please don't kill my baby."

"Hey," said the stranger. "Is this being done against her will?"

"Just get on with it, will you?"

"I don't force anyone in this, you know that, Mackay. A girl's gotta come willingly. Otherwise, it's no go."

"I said do it."

"Take her out of here. I won't do an abortion on a girl against her will. Damnit, Mackay, this is a risky enough business! My license is on the line every time I do one of these scrapes! Girls who come willingly keep their mouths shut. How do I know this one won't talk?"

"I can vouch for her. And I'll vouch for something else.

You don't do it, and I'll blab your name all over the street. Then see how long you keep your license."

There was a moment of charged silence. Rachel stared up at the stained ceiling and pictured two stags with their horns locked. For an instant she had hope. She prayed, Please God, let me keep my baby. I'll be good to it for the rest of its life. And I won't be a whore ever again.

Then she heard the stranger say, "Okay."

She kept her eyes fixed on the ceiling, but her eyes filled with tears. "Don't, Danny," she whispered. "Don't do this to me. Let me keep my baby. I'll go away. I promise you'll never have to see me again."

Danny looked down at her. He towered over her, tall and smooth and handsome. The familiar light was in his eyes, a light Rachel knew too well. It meant that he was in control now; neither she nor the abortionist could stand up to him. And then suddenly, in a flash of foresight, Rachel saw Danny as he was going to be in the future. And it frightened her.

Then Rachel felt the fingers of the stranger enter a place where she had felt the fingers of so many strangers. He said, "Hmm. Interesting tattoo. What is it, a butterfly?"

And Danny said, "Just get on with it."

The stranger was right, he was doing it too soon. The narcotic had not yet taken effect when the curette came into contact with the tender lining of her uterus. Rachel screamed so loudly and shrilly that for a moment Danny looked alarmed.

A whirlpool rose up and seemed to swallow her. She became all pain, all agony. It was as if he had thrust a burning torch into her pelvis. *My baby*! her mind screamed. I can't save you! I can't help you!

She started to thrash around on the table. Danny had to lie across her to keep her still. But she was unaware of him. She saw herself being sucked down a long black tunnel; there was the sound of wind rushing past her ears. She thought of all the men who had invaded her body—her father, Danny, Hazel's customers, and now this stranger with his killing instruments.

As she felt the life being dragged from her body, as she felt her soul cry out in this ultimate of violations and degradations—man punishing woman for what was her natural state—as she felt the life within her slowly die, the tiny life, and her own life, she saw a great, dark tide come rolling toward her. It was like a black malevolent sea. And what it was, at last, was hatred. Rachel Dwyer had suddenly discovered hatred. She had also discovered vows. Never again, she promised herself now, as she heard the instruments fall into the pan, and heard rubber gloves snap off the stranger's hand, never again was a man going to enter her body.

And then it was over. It didn't take much. Just a stinging rinse that hurt almost as much as the scraping, and then the stranger was bringing her legs slowly down.

Danny had to carry her to the car; she couldn't walk. Whatever the pills were, they were strong. She was starting to feel a peculiar numbness invade her body. She thought she was floating down the stairs. There was something thick and uncomfortable between her legs; it was for the blood, she knew.

They drove in silence. She felt tears and sobs waiting to be released, but for some reason she couldn't cry. Not now.

When they pulled up in front of Hazel's house, Danny didn't get out of the car. Instead, with the motor running, he turned to her. The look on his face was one of disgust. "Get out," he said. "Go sleep it off."

"Danny," she murmured, "you killed our baby."

"You women make a big deal out of nothing. You should be down on your hands and knees thanking me for getting you out of a mess. How did you think you were going to be able to work, with a big belly? Three more months and Hazel would have thrown you out on your ear. I did you a favor, you ungrateful bitch!"

"I don't understand."

"Just get out, will you? God, I'm sick to death of you. I have been since the first day I brought you here."

"Danny!"

"Where the hell are your brains anyway? Why do you think I even came to visit you once? Because I wanted to? You must be crazy! It was because Hazel called me and told me to get over here and straighten you out. Whenever you got uncooperative, she called me—"

"No! Danny!"

"And all it took was one evening with me and you were singing like a lark again. Pleased the customers no end, until you started to get moody again."

She clamped her hands over her ears. "No! That's not true! You loved me!"

"Christ, do you think I'm blind as well as stupid?" He took hold of her wrists and yanked her hands away from her head. "You're ugly, Rachel! You think I could love someone as ugly as you? Do you think any man could?"

"Please stop—"

"I knew Hazel could use you because she's got customers who have kinky tastes." Danny spoke coldly. His eyes sliced into her when he looked at her. Rachel realized she was seeing him for the first time as he really was. "You made me some good money, kid. With your earnings I was able to go to school and make something of myself. But I don't need you anymore. I have better, surer ways of making money now. You were just a stepping-stone in my life, and now you and I are parting ways."

"Then why didn't you let me keep my baby!"

"Because I'm going places. Look at this face and remember it. Hear this name and remember it, too. Danny Mackay. I'm going to be a big man someday. I'm going to be someone everyone looks up to. I'm going to have the power. And I don't want anything from my past hanging over my head. Years from now, when I've got my millions, I don't want you coming by with our bastard and trying to blackmail me. Now you have nothing on me. I don't even have to say I ever knew you. Now get out of my car."

"You can't mean it!" she sobbed. "You're lying. You loved me. I know you did."

"Love! You were a goddamn freak, Rachel. With your big nose stuck in fairy-tale books all the time. Like that Martian thing you were reading in El Paso. You actually had the nerve to read it the night I first made love to you. As though it was more important to you than I was. So I threw it out!"

She was suddenly silent. She stared at him. "My book?"

she whispered, thinking now of Captain Wilder and how captivated by him she had been.

Captain Wilder would never have murdered her baby.

"Rachel," he said, sounding tired. "Will you please get out now?"

"Yes," she said dully. "I'll get out. But before I do, I want to tell you something. Just now, you mentioned the first night you made love to me. You know what, Danny? I was fourteen and a virgin then. Since then I've been with hundreds of men. And you know something? You're a lousy lay, Danny."

He slapped her so hard across the face that her forehead banged against the dashboard.

When she slowly raised her head, there was blood trickling down her face. "You think you've seen the last of me, Danny Mackay. But you haven't. Someday I'm going to make you pay for what you've done."

His scarred mouth lifted in a one-sided smile. "And just how do *you* think you are going to get back at *me?*"

"You said you're a man who's going places. Well, I'm a woman who's going places. Someday, I'll be rich and powerful, too. Only I'll be richer and more powerful than you."

He threw back his head and laughed. "Is that right? And how are you going to make your millions? As a hooker? Listen, sweetheart, with your looks, you'll never get out of Hazel's house. You'll be here giving blow jobs until the day you die. Now—" He reached across, opened the door and gave her a shove. "Get out!"

She fell sprawling into the street. As he slammed the door and put the car into gear Rachel took one long last look at him, memorizing his face, scorching the name of Danny Mackay onto her heart. *Remember my name,* he had said.

She would. And another thing, about what she was going to be doing until the day she died—it wasn't going to be working for Hazel. It was going to be living for one thing, and one thing only: to get revenge on Danny Mackay.

February

13

"WILL YOU BE MY MOMMY?" the little girl asked as she tried to put her arms around Linda's neck.

Taking hold of the poor little bandaged arms, Dr. Linda Markus tucked them back under the blankets and said, "You have a very nice daddy to take care of you. Don't you love your daddy?"

"Yes . . ." The six-year-old face produced an adult frown. "But I wish I had a mommy, too."

Linda smiled, stroked the child's hair—what was left of it after the fire—and got up from the bed. "I'll come by and see you tomorrow, how's that?"

The scarred mouth lifted in a smile. "Okie dokie," the little girl said.

Back at the nurses' station, Linda jotted some notes on the child's chart. Standing next to her, flipping through nursing-care-plan cards, the head nurse said, "How's she doing, Doctor?"

"Her skin grafts are taking very well. I think she'll be able to go to the general ward next week."

"I sure hope so. We need the bed."

Dr. Markus looked out of place in the Children's Burn Unit of St. Catherine's Hospital. Even though she had borrowed a white lab coat to put over her evening gown while she made rounds, her hair was piled up in an elegant fashion and sprinkled with baby's breath, her earrings caught the antiseptic lights, and a stethoscope shared neck space with a diamond necklace. Linda was on her way to a party in Beverly Hills with Barry Greene, the television producer. She had swung by the hospital to take one last look at her kids before checking out for the night.

"Dr. Cane will be taking my calls," she told the nurse. "But I doubt anything will come up."

The nurse smiled an insider's smile. "Nothing ever does when you hand your beeper over to someone else. But as soon at it's yours again, *bang.* I'll tell you one thing, Doctor. I've been called out of some pretty interesting situations."

Thinking of Butterfly and her interrupted rendezvous with the cat burglar, Linda laughed and said, "We must compare notes sometime!"

Hospital work done, she returned the lab coat to the visitors' rack, folded her stethoscope into her evening bag, and took the elevator down to the lobby, where Barry Greene paced impatiently.

He is a good-looking man, Linda thought. In his fifties and looking trim and fit in his tuxedo, Barry Greene was also witty and generous, and gifted with a rich sense of humor. Linda knew that she could be attracted to him if she let down her defenses. But she had to hold back, fearing that a possible sexual relationship with Barry might end in disappointment.

"Hospitals!" he said as they went through the front doors and out into the night. "I hate them!"

Linda laughed. "*You* say that? The creator and producer of the hottest medical show ever to hit television?"

"What can I say? I'm a masochist."

Linda climbed into the backseat of the limo while the chauffeur held the door open, and when Barry was seated beside her, helping himself to a drink from the small bar, she couldn't help glancing up at the windows of the fourth floor—the Children's Burn Unit.

Will you be my mommy?

God knows I would like to be, Linda thought as the limo pulled out onto the Pacific Coast Highway. But making babies involves sex, and sex happens to be a problem for me.

142

She watched the dark ocean spread away to the starry horizon and thought again about Butterfly.

About her companion.

Last week he was a Confederate officer. Next Wednesday night he would be someone else yet again—someone so extra special and exciting that Linda couldn't wait for that evening to arrive. It was going to be a fantasy so wonderful and unique, and she was going to try so hard to give herself up to it that she dared to believe it might even work.

"You're far away," Barry said next to her.

Startled, she looked at him. Then she smiled. "Just thinking about my kids. Those poor burn victims. No one can know what it's like to be burned until they've gone through it themselves. Those kids need extra-special care."

"And I'm sure you give it to them."

"Yes," she said, looking into Barry Greene's smile.

He was a good-looking man, and it was refreshing for Linda to be out with someone who wasn't medically connected. Also, she liked to be with people who, like herself, were in charge, had power. Her large circle of friends was composed of men and women who had strength, and Barry Greene was indisputably one of the most power-wielding she had ever met. This was their first date; she wondered if he would ask her out again, and if she would accept.

The house on the hill was so lit up it looked like the Parthenon waiting for tourists. Beverly Highland was known for giving fabulous parties; no one ever turned down her invitations. As a result, the stream of cars now entering between the massive-wrought iron gates stretched from Sunset Boulevard and the entire length of Beverly Canyon Road all the way up to Highland House. Barry's limo joined the parade, and it was fifteen minutes before he and Linda were climbing the front steps of the mansion.

Maids greeted the arriving guests, taking coats and wraps, and giving the ladies small corsages of winter roses. The main bulk of the party was being held in the terraced garden at the rear where, under a striped awning, a New Age band played

Kitaro and Vangelis. Under a magnificent canopy a feast was set out: long tables groaned beneath the weight of enormous honeyed hams, rare beef roasts, glistening prime ribs, each with a white-coated chef in attendance, carving knife ready. As Linda emerged through the French doors and into the cool night air, she could see fantastically arranged salads, fabulous ice sculptures, chafing dishes keeping delicious morsels hot. Maids circulated among the crowd with platters of hors d'oeuvres: Emperor grapes stuffed with blue cheese, Norwegian flatbread spread with green-pepper jelly, shrimp, oysters, cheeses, fancy eggs—feasts in themselves before one could even make it to the dining tent. Most of Beverly Highland's parties were fund-raisers, and tonight's was no exception. This one was to raise campaign money for the founder and chairman of Good News Ministries, a famous TV evangelist who was hoping to be a candidate in this year's presidential election. Expecting to run on the Moral Decency ticket, the charismatic Reverend was way ahead of the others in the popularity polls and appeared to stand a good chance of winning the Republican nomination in June. And with so many people willing to pay five hundred dollars for the privilege of tasting the arts of Miss Highland's famous kitchen and hobnobbing with celebrities, tonight's gala, Linda had no doubt, should generate a sizable campaign donation.

In Miss Highland the Reverend had no small backer. Everyone knew that campaigns required money, lots of it; and the pre-primary caucuses currently going on in states all over the country were showing evidence of a great deal of financial backing for the Reverend. If he did win the nomination in June, then he would owe a good part of it to the vigorous support of Beverly Highland.

Linda did not know the socialite well; they had met only briefly at various charity events. But then Linda had heard that no one really knew Beverly Highland well. When not in the limelight, she was something of a recluse, unmarried and un-attached, although her name was frequently linked in gossip columns with those of senators and corporate heads.

Linda spotted the beautiful Beverly moving among her guests on the extravagant terrace that was said to have been patterned after the one at Versailles. From where Linda stood, the woman didn't look fifty-one. Her platinum hair was pulled back to emphasize the beauty and strength of her profile, and she wore a simple long black gown with a black mink wrap because of the chilly February evening.

Leaving Barry with a movie director friend he had been trying to get to see for the past few weeks, Linda strolled out onto the patio and through the crowd.

The names made up a stellar list. Movie stars, of course, and no doubt a heavy helping of people in the Industry who were movers but whose faces were publicly unknown. And there were the politicians, a few bigwigs from UCLA, the chief of surgery from Linda's own hospital, two notorious plastic surgeons, and various hangers-on. At least five hundred people, Linda estimated, all fawning over the gracious Miss Highland, who sailed among them as if, even in a gale wind, not a hair would escape her immaculate, if old-fashioned, French twist.

Linda was about to descend into the crowd when one of the circulating waiters passed in front of her, bearing a silver tray with champagne glasses. Linda looked at him, briefly wondering where she had seen him before, and when it came to her, she was frozen to the spot.

He was a companion at Butterfly.

A year ago, when she had first become a member, Linda's initial sessions were with unmasked men. The idea of going even further with anonymity than the safeguards the club already provided had entered her mind on her third "date," when it occurred to her that she might accidentally encounter one of these companions in the outside world—in the emergency room, for example, and she his doctor! All sessions since had been conducted with masks. But this young man with the surfer tan had been that third companion. And here he was, serving drinks at Beverly Highland's party.

Linda watched him. He turned slightly, glanced her way, smiled at the other guests, passed out the champagne, then looked her way again. For an instant their eyes met. Then he turned and continued serving, with not a flicker of recognition on his face.

"Our men practice the utmost discretion," the director of

Butterfly had assured Linda during her interview over a year ago. "You need not fear that your identity will be found out, or that you will find yourself in an embarrassing situation."

As she watched him wend his way through the evening gowns and tuxedos Linda thought again of her own special companion at Butterfly, her masked lover, and the elaborate fantasy she was going to orchestrate next Wednesday night. If it worked and she was cured at last, as Dr. Raymond, her analyst, seemed to believe could happen, then Linda could be free to enter into a relationship with someone like the attractive Barry Greene, enter into it wholeheartedly and without fear.

She looked for Barry now and found him deep in conversation with a man and a woman. By the look on his face, she judged money was being discussed. She decided to get something to eat.

Helping herself to the baked oysters in mignonette sauce and accepting a fluted glass filled with Cristal champagne, Linda retired to a chair at poolside, where she sat among quiet conversations and serious eaters.

She watched the surfer-waiter. He wore a short red jacket and tight black pants. His blond hair curled over the collar of his starched white shirt. He moved among the crowd with the grace and ease of a cat. Linda saw more than one woman regard him with an appreciative eye.

She recalled her one occasion in bed with him, and it got her to thinking once again about her masked companion. The director had assured her that it was not uncommon for a member of Butterfly to request the same man over and over again. Very few members, in fact, opted for weekly variety. After all, a safe and unthreatening relationship could be established, comfortable and sexually satisfying, with no strings attached.

How nice it would be, Linda thought wistfully, to have a relationship like that with someone real, have children with him, grow old with him, and look forward to their nights together in bed. She didn't blame her two ex-husbands for wanting out of the marriages. Linda knew she was guilty of making up excuses—a headache, early surgery in the morning, exhaustion after an all-night emergency—and that wasn't fair to them.

The evening wore on. The crowd shifted and moved like a restless sea. People made contacts, avoided contacts, strutted and preened, or remained reasonably hidden, like Dr. Linda Markus, whose mind was elsewhere. She accepted a cheese puff from a passing tray, and a taste of the salmon mousse, but smilingly refused the rich desserts and liqueurs. As she was sipping Kenya coffee and watching Barry Greene move from contact to contact, Linda wondered again if there would be a second date. So far she and Barry had met professionally, at the studio, going over the weekly TV scripts of *Five North*. And then he had asked her if she would like to accompany him to this party, and after some hesitation and a little fear, she had accepted.

The music suddenly died down and Linda saw Beverly Highland step up on the small stage occupied by the band and raise her arms for silence. It was amazing that so many people could be so quiet. As soon as all talking and music stopped, it seemed that the city of Beverly Hills was a deserted place. Not a sound reached the hilltop retreat.

Beverly spoke in a poised, assured way, explaining why the Reverend had not been able to attend tonight's party—he was at the hospital bedside of his younger child, who had just undergone an emergency appendectomy—and then she went on to outline the platform of the Reverend's campaign, assuring her guests that they were supporting one of the worthiest causes in the nation at the moment. "We are going to clean up our cities," she said. "With this man as president, and with the backing of Good News Ministries, we will sweep smut from the face of America."

There was applause and the music started again. Barry materialized at Linda's side, apologizing for abandoning her, assuring her that had not been his intention, and when they climbed into his Rolls-Royce a little while later and he asked if she would like to come to his place for a nightcap, Linda declined, pleading an early-morning surgery schedule.

"Another rousing success, Bev," Maggie Kern said as she followed her employer up the enormous winding staircase.

The last of the guests had gone; the musicians were packing up and the cleaning crew was working silently around the grounds under the watchful eye of the estate's security team. The two women went into Beverly's bedroom suite, where a French maid was drawing down the satin sheets and laying out a silk-and-lace nightgown. In the enormous all-marble bathroom another French maid was running her mistress's nightly hot bath, filling the air with the perfume of exotic oils.

Maggie kicked off her shoes and padded across the thick carpet to a small table where late-night refreshments had been set out. Pouring two glasses of chilled Perrier, she handed one to Beverly and then sank wearily into a chair upholstered in pale blue silk.

"Yes, it was a good turnout," Beverly said as she handed her black mink wrap to the maid. Then she went to the table and selected a carrot stick from the platter of freshly cut raw vegetables. She hadn't eaten all evening.

Maggie hadn't eaten either, having been busy overseeing the smooth operation of the party, but, unlike her employer who assiduously watched her weight, Maggie helped herself generously to the bagels, lox, and cream cheese.

"And in three weeks," Beverly said as she walked to the window to look out at the cold February night, "the New Hampshire primary."

Maggie looked up at her and, for an instant, their eyes met and held. Then Beverly returned to staring out the window.

They were both feeling the pressure of racing against time.

The forty-six-year-old secretary regarded her employer for a long moment. She could see in Beverly's slender body a rigidity that betrayed the tension and anxiety she must be feeling. It had been growing in her, in both of them, ever since the Reverend had announced the possibility of his running for president. Maggie could not remember a time, in her twenty years of being Beverly's personal secretary, when the Reverend was not under Beverly's careful scrutiny. She had never missed a *Good News Hour*; she knew his every movement. And now that he was aspiring to the White House, Beverly was aspiring right along with him.

In fact, it had become an obsession.

And where will it all lead to? Maggie wondered as she set down her empty plate and retrieved her shoes.

Before leaving the bedroom, she paused again to look at her employer. Beverly had that trancelike faraway look about her. Maggie knew there was no need to bother to say good night—Beverly wouldn't hear. Then Maggie looked at the calendar on the desk, and the date, circled in red. June 11. It was so close now, so close. . . .

Some minutes later Beverly bestirred herself, dismissed the maids, locked the door, and walked slowly around the room, the chilled glass of Perrier in her hand.

Yes, it had been a successful party. Beverly had raised a lot of new votes for the Reverend. A drop in the bucket, of course, for the billion-dollar-rich GN ministries, which already had a following of a million people strong. She had raised the votes for him, as another stepping-stone in his rise to power.

There was nothing Beverly Highland would not do to get him to the very top. She had dedicated herself to that end. And this party was just another step on the ladder she so anxiously climbed. June 11—now less than five months away. While the polls looked good for the Reverend and predicted a respectable showing of voters, he was still not the shoo-in. Two other Republican favorites still outstripped him. If he was going to get that nomination in June, Beverly was going to have to step up her campaign. Nothing, absolutely nothing, must get in the way of her ambition.

She sat on the edge of the bed and picked up the gold-framed photograph that stood on her desk. His handsome, compelling smile reached out to her from behind the glass. The photo was signed; he had added "Praise the Lord." Beverly was fifty-one years old, and if it took another fifty-one years, she was determined to reach her goal.

The top. The very top. With the Reverend Danny Mackay.

14

New Mexico: 1954

Danny Mackay, Danny Mackay, the train wheels on the track seemed to whisper. *Danny Mackay, Danny Mackay . . .*

When the whistle blew, Rachel awoke with a start. She experienced a moment of confusion—where was she?—then, remembering, shifted uncomfortably in her seat and looked out the window.

Desert. As far as the eye could see.

She had passed this way once before, nearly two and a half years ago, but the Rachel Dwyer who now headed west away from Texas toward Albuquerque was a far cry from the frightened fourteen-year-old who had gotten on the wrong Greyhound bus. That skinny little girl had had no idea where she was going. But sixteen-year-old Rachel, the woman who had already lived a lifetime, knew exactly where she was going.

To see that, someday, Danny Mackay paid for his crime.

When a wave of pain came over her, she clenched her stomach and held her breath. When it subsided, she looked at her watch. It had been only two hours since her last pill. It didn't seem to have had any effect. The pain was getting worse. And so, she realized in alarm, was the bleeding.

Glancing around at the few other passengers in the train car—thank God most of them were dozing in their seats—she got up and very carefully made her way down to the rest room at the end. There, her alarm turned to horror when she saw the amount of blood she was losing.

She was in fact hemorrhaging.

Fighting panic, she looked at her watch again. The train would be pulling into Albuquerque in less than an hour. She would get off and find a drugstore. Then she would try to find her mother.

That was the first plan Rachel had made when she left

San Antonio—to find her mother. Even though she knew her parents had left the trailer park two years ago, Rachel suspected they must still be somewhere nearby. When Dave Dwyer pulled up stakes and moved, he never went far, just into the next little town that had a bar. Rachel was hoping they were still in New Mexico. Her mother would take care of her.

Beyond that, Rachel's plans were vague, the only specific one being a long-range plan. Danny Mackay . . .

After taking another morphine tablet, she made her way back to her seat and collapsed into it. The pills had come from Carmelita, who herself had once had an abortion.

Carmelita . . .

Rachel closed her eyes and pictured the pretty olive face of her friend. Yesterday morning Rachel had awakened in her bed to find that face looking down at her, the big brown eyes full of sadness. "I'm sorry, amiga," the Mexican girl had said, "but Hazel sent me up here to get you packed. She said you gotta leave. Here's your wages."

Still in a fog from her ordeal of the night before, Rachel had not quite understood. "Where . . ." she had whispered, almost too weak to talk. "Where am I going?"

"That's up to you, amiga. You just gotta get out of here. Otherwise, she says she's gonna throw you out. And she will. I seen her do it once."

Then the fog had started to lift. "You mean Hazel's throwing me out?"

Tears glistened in Carmelita's eyes. "She says she don't want no troublemakers in her house."

But Rachel knew Hazel's real reason for kicking her out. Danny must have told her to do it.

Belle and Carmelita helped her gather her few things together with tears streaming down their cheeks. They gave her what money they could and then they went with her by bus to the train station, where they hugged and cried some more.

"I wish I could go with you, amiga," Carmelita had said. "But I just can't leave Manuel, you know. . . ."

"It's all right," Rachel had said. "I understand." And she did. Only too well.

"But listen," Carmelita said, holding tight to Rachel's arm, "you ever need me, you just call and I'll come running. You hear me? You ever in trouble, or you need money or *anything*, you give Carmelita a call. You promise?"

Rachel had promised, adding, "And the same goes for you. If *you* ever need *me*, just send word and I'll be there."

Rachel stared out at the passing desert landscape and wondered why it wasn't in focus. She closed her eyes and waited for the pain to pass. She felt ill, desperately ill. So she did what she always did when her body was in an unpleasant circumstance, she removed her mind from it and concentrated on something that pleased her. San Antonio came into her thoughts, a city she had grown to love. She recalled now the plazas and cathedrals, the peppery Mexican dinners eaten in the homely cottages of Little Laredo, evenings along the River Walk, where spotlights hidden beneath bushes illuminated the new flagstone walks along the San Antonio, the arched footbridges and the gondolas on the water where soldiers made love to their girlfriends. Danny had once taken her on a boat ride on the river, beneath the lights and the romantic moon. . . .

A sudden stabbing pain in her abdomen brought her upright. Clasping herself, doubled over, she threw away the past and summoned up the future. From now on, she was going to concentrate on what was going to be, not on what had already been.

First she would find her mother, Rachel vowed as more waves of pain were starting to come. Then, after she had healed and had her strength back, she would go on to Hollywood, and look for her twin sister. . . .

The morphine was not working. She felt as if she were on fire. She was burning with thirst. Thinking of the water dispenser at the end of the car, Rachel struggled to her feet. Strangely, her seat was wet.

The train lurched and she lost her footing. Then she thought she heard someone scream, or was it the train whistle again?

A face appeared above her, fuzzy at first, then coming into focus. The mouth was smiling, but the eyes were not. The eyes were full of concern. "How are you feeling?" the stranger asked.

Feeling?

Rachel tried to think. Feeling. *Pain.* Yes, there had been pain. A little while ago. But it seemed to have gone away now. In fact, her body felt strangely numb. She was lying on her back. And the train was still. Had they stopped?

"Where am I?" she said.

"You're in a hospital. You collapsed on the train as it was coming into the station. Don't you remember?"

"No . . ."

The stranger sat down on the edge of the bed and studied Rachel's face. "How old are you?" he asked.

"Sixteen."

He looked surprised. What did he think she was? Older? Younger?

"Am I in"—she swallowed with a dry throat—"Albuquerque?"

"Yes. Your ticket said you were getting off here. Was someone going to meet you? Is there anyone we can call?"

She thought a moment, then wanted to cry. "No. There's no one. Are you a doctor?"

"Yes."

"What happened to me?"

His voice grew grave. "You lost a lot of blood, but you'll be all right now. You'll have to stay here for a few days, but you will be all right."

"I feel so funny."

"It's because you've just come out of surgery."

"*Surgery!*"

"Don't worry," he said gently. "You're out of danger now."

The doctor came back a few days later to say good-bye to Rachel as she was preparing to leave the hospital. Finally, reluctantly, he said, "I'm sorry, Rachel," sounding genuinely sorry, "but whoever worked on you did a butcher's job. I'm afraid . . ." He faced her squarely. "I'm afraid you'll never be able to have children."

■ ■ ■

It had taken her five days to get well, and when she left the hospital she went straight to the trailer park that had been her last New Mexico address.

It was winter and snow lay on the ground. A cold wind cut through her sweater as she stood staring at the dingy little trailer where she had passed the last day of her childhood. Then she went to the office to make inquiries.

This was a new manager—such people, too, tended to move on. But the woman had received the park's history from her predecessor, a woman like herself, given to lurid gossip. "The Dwyers?" she said. "Yeah. I heard of 'em. 'Bout two years ago it was, I guess. She murdered him, you know."

Rachel stood in the chilly office while the winter wind shook the thin walls. "Murdered him?" Rachel said.

"Yeah. A real pair they were, from what I heard. He got drunk one night and she bashed him over the head with a frying pan. But that wasn't what killed him. From what I heard, he recovered from that, although she had clearly intended to do him in then! No, she finished the job a week later with a carving knife."

It was as if the biting New Mexico wind had gotten through her skin and was freezing her bones. Rachel felt numb, as if she were on the morphine again. "What happened to her after that?"

"Beats me. She disappeared. The police searched for her but she had long gone."

What was it, Ma? Rachel thought as she headed back to the train station. What was it he did that finally drove you over the edge? Had you reached your limit at last, just as I did with Danny? We're a pair, aren't we, Ma?

As Rachel bought her ticket for Los Angeles, the end of the line, she thought with resolve: I'll find you, Ma. Just as I'm going to find my sister, I'll find you. And then I'll take care of you and we'll be a family again.

It was a hot November day and smog hung heavy in the Southern California air. The impressive Union Station terminal reminded her of San Antonio, with its classic Spanish style. She hurried through it and out into the famous sunshine.

Palm trees, everywhere.

At a taxi stand she asked the way to Hollywood and was told which bus would get her there. Rachel counted out her change, and sat on the bus bench, ready. It arrived an hour an a half later. An hour after that she was stepping down to the sidewalk, and her first thought was: Hollywood isn't at all how I imagined it.

Of course, she had been listening to Belle, who was an "expert." Rachel didn't see any big houses or swimming pools or women in mink coats. Just rows of tired-looking old stores, coffee shops that looked like rocket ships, and an endless chain of motor court apartments. The first thing she did was get herself a room at a very plain little motel, paying a week in advance—using nearly all the money she had left after paying the Albuquerque hospital bill—then she went out for something to eat. Hamburger and strawberry malted. It was her first meal on her own.

In the coffee shop, she asked if they had a job they could give her. Sure, the manager said. Any experience as a waitress? No? Sorry.

By the fourth coffee shop, Rachel had learned to lie. She found the manager, and told him she was an experienced waitress who wanted work. He seemed to study her face for far too long, then he said no.

As she hit the sidewalk again Rachel wondered what he had seen that had made him reject her? Was it her homeliness? Or the fact that he hadn't believed her when she said she was eighteen?

After walking three more miles in the heat and being turned down four more times, Rachel went back to the motel and drifted off into a deep, dreamless sleep.

She awoke the next morning to a ferocious hunger, but restricted herself to coffee. Then, striking off in the opposite direction from the one she had taken yesterday, she hit the pavement once again.

Like a ghost, her dear friend Carmelita walked with her. Rachel took comfort in her imagined presence, listened to her encouraging chatter, and several times caught herself answering her out loud. If only they could have left Hazel's together!

155

Rachel saw that Hollywood was a sort of characterless sprawl that went on forever, its palm trees hanging limp in the haze, its people rushing by with vacant faces. And everywhere the same peculiar restaurants: shaped like dogs, like hot dogs, like sombreros, with waitresses who wore phony cowgirl uniforms, or sped about on roller skates, or had outsized handkerchiefs pinned to their blouses. And everywhere the answer was the same: Not hiring.

As she walked beneath the gay lights of Grauman's Chinese Theater and paused to watch tourists stand in the cement footsteps of movie stars, Rachel felt loneliness and despair come over her. But she fought it back. She had to keep going. If not for herself, or for her mother, then for achieving her goal. When her spirits flagged, she thought of Danny Mackay. When her stomach growled with hunger, when her feet raised giant blisters from walking, when creeps on the back streets said lewd things to her, when she heard the people in the next room having a fight and she wanted to run away from this terrible Hollywood, Rachel would think of Danny Mackay. And it would keep her going.

On the third day she decided to start looking for her sister.

"I can only tell you two things," her mother had said. "You were born at Presbyterian Hospital. And the lawyer's name was Hyman Levi."

So Rachel went through the phone book in her motel room. There were a few Hyman Levis in the Los Angeles area. But only one was listed as the name of a law firm. She dialed the number and got a secretary. She asked to make an appointment.

"What is it regarding?" the secretary asked.

"It's confidential."

Rachel was told to come in that afternoon at three.

Because it was such an important occasion, she pulled out her nicest blouse and skirt, smoothed them as best she could, and got dressed. Then she went to sit on a bus bench for the inevitable hour.

Miraculously, she got to Levi's office on Western Avenue right on time.

It wasn't a spectacular office, not like the ones she had seen on television. But you could tell it had been here for a long time. She wondered if her sister's file was in that very file cabinet over there behind the secretary. The thought of it made her heart race. She wished Carmelita and Belle were sitting on the Naugahyde sofa with her.

Mr. Levi was momentarily delayed, she was told, so Rachel got up and paced. The secretary kept looking at her. Rachel knew she looked awfully young to be seeing a lawyer on her own. She hoped she wouldn't get thrown out. All she wanted was her sister's address. Rachel knew what would happen after that. They would have an incredible reunion; they would catch up on the sixteen years since they were separated; and then her sister, no doubt being rich, would insist that Rachel move in with her family and they would be true sisters at last.

Rachel came to a halt before a framed diploma hanging on the wall. Hyman Levi, it declared, had graduated from the Stanford University School of Law in 1947.

Seven years ago.

Rachel stared dumbly. Hyman Levi didn't even become a lawyer until nine years after she was born.

He was the wrong man.

"I'm sorry," she mumbled to the secretary, "I've made a mistake—"

Rachel hurried out the door and let it slam behind her.

The secretary was still looking perplexed when, a moment later, a man came through the same door. "Sorry I'm late, Dora," he said, looking around the reception area. "Where's my three o'clock appointment?"

Dora shrugged. "She was here, Mr. Levi. And then just suddenly ran out. She was only a kid, though. Maybe it was some kind of a prank."

He smiled and headed for the inner office. At his door he turned and said, "Has my father called in yet?"

"He's still in court."

"When he does check in with you, would you tell him I have six new adoption cases I'd like to review with him?"

"Certainly, Mr. Levi," she said, as Hyman Levi, Jr., went through the door of the office he shared with his father.

. . .

Rachel lay for a long time on the motel bed, sobbing her heart out. She had so counted on finding her sister. Now there was no hope. Her mother gone, her sister beyond reach—now she was truly alone in the world.

Then, forcing herself to think of Danny, she got up, changed her clothes, washed her face, and hit the pavement again.

In a couple of days her rent would be up and she'd be out on the street. She needed a job. Fast.

Hollywood at night, at casual glance, looked glamorous. But closer scrutiny revealed the stains. As Rachel walked along the busy street her heart went out to the prostitutes who hovered in doorways or leaned against lampposts. My sisters, she thought. My only true sisters.

She went into five more coffee shops and was turned down in all five. At least in one the manager was honest enough to say she was too young. "Need a work permit," he said. "You ain't eighteen."

Tired and hungry, she came to the intersection of two heavily trafficked streets. Young women loitered hopefully on all four corners. Rachel looked up at the lighted street signs. Highland Avenue and Beverly Canyon Road. Pretty hifalutin names, she thought, for such a seedy district.

She watched the prostitutes, the men driving slowly by in cars, shopping.

It was a story as old as the rocks in the hills: women sold it and men bought it. Why was it never the other way around?

Maybe it was because of lack of opportunity, Rachel decided. And social stigma. Girls were brought up differently from boys. Girls were supposed to go to their marriage beds as virgins, boys were expected to be experienced. And then for how many centuries had girls been taught that "good" girls didn't actively seek sex, that it was more "feminine" to wait and be pursued. Promiscuity, it seemed to sixteen-year-old Rachel, was the jealously guarded privilege of men. She thought of women down through the centuries, oppressed by men. From novels she had learned that her sisters in previous generations had been kept subjugated by constant pregnancy.

Supposedly, a woman burdened with babies and a belly had no interest in sex. And therefore would not "stray."

But what if, Rachel found herself wondering now, women could be as free as men to enjoy sex? What if the fear of pregnancy was removed? Would they become sexual aggressors? Would they go out and seek it? And if men had it for sale, would women buy it?

Rachel noticed that there were young male prostitutes on the street as well, but they, too, she knew, were for the men.

She turned and looked up at the sign over the window of an unremarkable little diner. TONY'S ROYAL BURGERS, it said in rather grandiose characters. She looked inside. Three people sat at the counter. The booths were empty.

There wasn't a hope, she knew, that they would hire her—they didn't even look as if they could afford to pay their electric bill—but she had to keep trying, keep going. *Danny Mackay, Danny Mackay . . .*

There was a tired-looking blonde at the cash register, filing her nails. She didn't look up when Rachel said, "I'd like to see the owner, please."

A jerked thumb in the direction of what was probably the kitchen sent Rachel walking down the length of the little diner. This time she wouldn't lie about her age, Rachel decided, feeling as tired as the blonde. Lying didn't seem to pay.

She pushed through the door into the tiniest kitchen she had ever seen. A short, balding man in a greasy white apron stood at a table making hamburger patties. Rachel cleared her throat. He looked up. "Yeah? Whaddya want?"

"Are you Tony?"

"Naw. Tony died four years ago. I couldn't afford to have the sign repainted. What can I do for you?"

"I need a job."

He looked at her. The simplicity of her words, the way she had spoken them, made him put down the hamburger meat and wipe his hands on his apron. "What kind of job?"

"Anything."

"You ever done waitressing?"

"No."

"How old are you?"

"Sixteen."

He looked her up and down. God, but she was skinny. And those clothes! The Salvation Army would reject them. Pathetic little kid. "Where do you live, honey?"

"At the Wheel-in Motel."

He made a face. "That rat bag. Hey, it's two miles from here. You walk it?"

She held up one of her feet. There was a hole filled with cardboard in the center of her shoe.

He shook his head. "Listen, honey. You're too young. I can't hire you. I'd get in trouble with the law. You should be in school, you know?"

"I'm hungry," she said quietly. "And I have no money."

"Where's your folks?"

"I don't have any."

"No family at all?"

"No."

He raised his eyebrows. Fleetingly, a vision of the girls in the street went through his mind. How many similar stories were out there?

"You can't work the front," he said thoughtfully. "Cops come in here at lunchtime. Can you do dishes?"

"Yes," she said so quickly, so hopefully, that it stung his cynical heart.

"Listen, honey," he said coming up to her and glancing through the round window in the door that led to the restaurant. "Me 'n' my wife own and operate this place. That's her at the cash register. We don't got but two waitresses. And I do all the cooking. But . . ." He rubbed his chin. "Sometimes we get a rush on—"

"Please."

"I'll give you the job as long as you stay back here and keep outa trouble—"

"I promise," she said softly.

Eddie noticed that there was a strange sort of intensity about her. She looked as if she had never smiled. He also saw, close up, an alarmingly adult look in her eyes—it was more than adult, it was like an aged wisdom, as if a very old and traveled soul had come to rest in this thin young body.

"Now, the pay ain't much," he said slowly, marveling at his sudden fit of generosity. Eddie hadn't had a moment of weakness like this in twenty years of struggling to make a go of it. "But it'll buy you something a little cleaner than the Wheel-in. I got a sister who runs a decent boardinghouse on Cherokee, other side of Sunset."

"I'll work hard for you," she said quietly. "And I'll never give you any trouble."

Eddie looked into the intense brown eyes and saw something that almost frightened him. Whatever had happened to this girl, whatever scars or nightmares held her together so tightly, he decided he would never want to be her enemy.

"We gotta deal, then," he said and stuck out his greasy hand. "I'm Eddie. That's Laverne, my wife."

She didn't give him her hand. She didn't want to touch anyone. But she managed a small smile and said, "Hello, Eddie."

"What's your name, kid?"

She started to say "Rachel Dwyer," but stopped herself. Tonight she was starting on a new road to a new life. It called for a new name. Suddenly, the two street signs on the corner outside sprang into her mind. "Beverly," she said. "My name is Beverly Highland. . . ."

15

ALTHOUGH A darkness darker than night surrounded her, Alexis knew where she was.

In a bedroom. In Butterfly.

And she was in bed, lying naked between cool satin sheets. They felt like water on her bare skin, as if she were floating in a pool of delicious sensation; they were creamy and silky, like solid opalescence. She thought of mother-of-pearl. If she turned on the light, she knew what color the sheets would be: a liquid green shimmering into shades of aquamarine, with oily illusions of rose and violet, changing with each movement of her body.

And there was a faint perfume in the air—the fragrance of freshly cut gardenias. She pictured the white blossoms that drifted in water in a silver bowl across the room, delicate and white-petaled, like softened stars in the black night. Their aroma swirled around her and filled her lungs, making her feel giddy and light-headed as if she were inhaling some exotic forbidden opium.

And there was a kind of perfume in her ears as well, the soft notes of a harp, barely heard, coming from hidden speakers but sounding as if clouds had produced it.

She felt languid, carefree. Timeless.

When someone entered the bedroom, she sensed it only. No light spilled in as the door opened briefly and then closed. Whoever was invading her banquet of sensations had stepped from darkness to darkness. She sensed the presence of the intruder in the room. The perfumed air seemed slightly displaced. She thought she heard the kiss of bare feet on the plush carpet. And then she felt the invading presence come near to the bed and stand over her, softly breathing.

She knew who it was. It was *he*.

She lay perfectly still. Her heart speeded its rhythm; her flesh shivered as her senses became suddenly heightened. She could almost smell him. The scent reminded her of almonds.

When the sheet was drawn slowly away from her body, she closed her eyes. She felt cool air whisper across her naked breasts. And then a hand, warm and tentative, fluttered over her skin, like a butterfly exploring a flower. He felt her breasts, touched her nipples, made her moan.

He sat on the bed. She felt his nearness. His hands slid up behind her back as he brought his mouth down on her breasts. He made exquisite love to her there, for what seemed an eternity, until she drove her fingers into his hair and brought his face up to hers.

His kiss made her dizzy.

He was bearded. It excited her all the more.

God, could he kiss.

She wanted to stay there forever, feasting on his mouth, his tongue, but when he laid his firm body alongside hers, then she wanted other things, urgent things. She took his erection into her hands. His breathing grew rapid. She moved on the bed, gliding on the satin as if swimming, changing direction. And she feasted on him down there as well, while he continued his delicious kisses on her belly and inside her thighs.

Suddenly he drew back and pulled her up to him. They kissed sitting up, face-to-face in the darkness, his one hand twisted into her hair, the other feeling her breast. She still had hold of him, but gently now, so as not to bring him to completion too soon. She let him withhold himself so that their lovemaking could go on and on.

He gently turned her over onto her stomach and lay on top of her, entering her that way, slowly, agonizingly slowly, with his hands up under her breasts.

She came almost immediately.

Then he turned her onto her back and began kissing her anew. She wrapped her arms around his neck and clung to him. He coaxed her legs apart and teased her with his fingers, exploring. She didn't speak—they never spoke; but she told him with her body what she wanted. She put her hand over his and guided his finger inside her. He was kissing her almost into madness, holding her so tightly to his hard, sweating body that she could barely breathe.

And then he took his hand away, lay on top of her, and was inside her again, vigorously this time. She clutched the sheets at her sides. She arched her neck, pressed her head back into the pillow. He was so hard. . . .

When she came a second time her heart felt as if it had almost stopped.

And then he withdrew from her, took his chest away from her breast, and, for a moment, she floated all alone in space. But then he had hold of her again, his strong hands on her thighs while he resumed his kissing, his exploration with his tongue. She curled her legs around his neck and felt herself drown in a sea of hot sensation.

She shuddered and cried out.

Then she reached for him and took command. No more holding back, her body said to him. Do it now, hard, quickly, *quickly. . . .*

But even then, when it was for him, he didn't forget her. As his body rocked in the ancient rhythm, he brought his hand down and touched the small place that, for now, was her core. His finger moved in cadence with his body, until he finally came, and she came with him, at the same time.

When Alexis awoke a little while later, he was gone, the smell of him in the sheets, the lingering warmth and dampness of his lovemaking the only evidence that he had been there at all.

16

San Antonio, Texas: 1955

THE FIRST NAME on Danny's secret "hit" list was Simon Waddell—*Doctor* Simon Waddell.

There were six other names on the list: the sergeant at Ford Ord who had put Danny on report for fighting, which had led to the stockade and ultimately to a dishonorable discharge; a schoolteacher who had once whipped Danny with a strap in front of the whole class; a girl his own age who had once laughed at him because he had a tear in the seat of his pants; and so on—men and women who had touched Danny's life at some point in his twenty-two years and who had done something to him that needed to be paid back. No one crossed Danny Mackay and got away with it.

Dr. Simon Waddell didn't know about the list, didn't even know Danny Mackay existed. But he was the man Danny most wanted to get even with. And Danny knew where to find him.

Danny smiled at his reflection in the mirror as he pulled down a perfect curl and combed it over his forehead. It always took Danny an hour to get dressed: he was meticulous down to the last detail. No threads hanging, no buttons missing, no crease out of place. He might not be rich yet, but he had the look, and the power—that wasn't yet his either, but it too was in the carefully cultivated look.

You're a dynamite-looking dude, Danny said to his image. *You son of a West Texas sharecropper!*

He whistled as he smoothed back the sides of his head and made sure there wasn't a hair out of place. Danny was in a cocksure mood this morning; he had graduated from night school yesterday. With honors. Now he was a man with a diploma and the sure knowledge of where he was going.

As he picked up the cuff links that lay on the dresser and fastened them to his starched cuffs, he gazed at the battered book that also lay on the dresser. It was Danny's bible; it went with him wherever he went. He had memorized it.

The only sure way to possess a conquered city, Machiavelli had written, *is by destroying it.* Danny carried that lesson one step further: You can totally possess anything only by destroying it—whether a city, an object, or a human being.

And there were cities and objects and human beings Danny definitely wanted to possess.

But first he had to find his road. The goal he already knew—to be the man with the power; now all he had to do was discover the way to get there.

He whistled as he finished dressing. He tapped his foot and moved his head this way and that. In three years Danny had become charged with even more restless energy. He could not be still for a moment. Strangers who met him sensed a vaguely disquieting edge in the handsome young man with the sly, compelling eyes. He seemed at times to be relaxed, in the laziness of his gaze and the drawl with which he spoke, but he was hyperactive, and looked like a young man constantly flirting with the brink. Danny liked this look, he maintained it, because he knew it made him appear unpredictable, a man to be wary of. It also gave him power over people.

Before he left his room he paused to give himself one last sideways smile in the mirror. The world was out there waiting for him. No more supplying girls and booze to the horny flyboys at Lackland Air Force Base. No more penny-ante jobs like driving trucks or selling encyclopedias door to door. It was time to get moving.

"Remember my name," he had said to that stupid bitch Rachel a year ago, the night he threw her out of his car. "Danny Mackay. A man the whole world is going to know."

And, he added now as he walked out into the warm evening, *a man the world is going to learn to fear.*

He drove to Hazel's, where a few of the girls, in kimonos or baby doll pajamas, were lounging around the TV set watching Milton Berle. Two sat with customers, making phony sweet talk. Hazel was serving bad liquor at cutthroat prices, and handing out Eulalie's thick ham sandwiches at two bits apiece. Pulling out his Camels, he lit one and went through the back door into the kitchen. Eulalie was there listening to *Davy Crockett* on the radio and cleaning up after a supper of crunchy-crusted roast pork, mashed potatoes and gravy, and hot peach pie. Sometimes Danny would come around mornings, and there would be thick slabs of bacon sizzling in a pan, with slices of tomato frying along with it in the grease. One thing about Hazel—you couldn't say she didn't feed her girls right.

"Howdy there, Eulalie," he said as he sauntered to the fridge and got himself an ice-cold grape Nehi.

"It's a hot one tonight, Mr. Danny," she said, wiping her face as she whipped the dough for her famous pound cake. By midnight, along with the blackberry wine, it would all be gone. Men had more than one appetite that needed feeding, old Eulalie knew. "Been eatin' dust all day."

He pulled out a chair, turned it around, swung one leg over it and sat on it backward, leaning on the cane back and thumbing through the *San Antonio Light* that lay on the table. "What do you think of these here niggers in Alabama, Eulalie?" he said, shaking his head. "Trying to ride white folks' buses."

"Won't nothin' but bad come of it, Mr. Danny. Folks gotta know their place. There's your black coloreds at the bottom, and then your light coloreds, and then your trash and finally your quality on top. That's the way it always was, the way it always was meant to be."

Danny didn't listen to her. He knew which category she placed him in: trash. As far as Eulalie was concerned, quality had never once set foot across Hazel's well-worn threshold.

There had been a time when Danny never read a paper or bothered with the news. But that had been before he had gone back to school. Now the makeup of the world and what made it turn were the focus of his interest. Studying his target and knowing his competition better than they knew themselves was what was going to make Danny rise above his mean beginnings.

Born in 1933, Danny Mackay was one of seven children of a transient sharecropper and his sickly wife. Danny had never known anything but poverty, from his earliest memory of nights when they took their beds outside, hoping to catch a breeze, to reporting for duty at Fort Ord, California. He and his brothers and sisters always went barefoot and wore overalls with no shirts. They never even had a real comb for their hair, but used a curry comb, the kind used on animals. When they walked together, into the nearest small town or to the local grammar school, the Mackay kids always walked with their heads down because they knew they weren't as good as the other kids. And they moved—Lord, how they moved. It was the Great Depression and, like thousands of other families on the roam for jobs, Augustus Mackay dragged his ragtag brood across Oklahoma, Arkansas, down into Texas and eventually into the Hill Country, where he found temporary jobs on share-cropping farms. They would live in clapboard shacks with gaps between the siding boards and no electricity, and the outhouse was just a hole in the ground. If Augustus Mackay failed to produce a good crop, the landowner would call the sheriff and have the family evicted, and they'd move on like before, heads down, beaten.

Danny didn't grow up on the Hardy boys and Jack London, like the quality boys of the middle class; he was fed on pulp magazines. And his sisters weren't expected to be educated at all, so they developed animal instincts and learned to make their way on those, which was how they came to be referred to as "those dirty girls."

His only prized possession as a boy was a nigger-shooter,

which he'd made out of a forked stick and two pieces of rubber from an old inner tube. He'd take himself far away from the squalor and hopelessness and spend hours taking potshots at birds with it, using pebbles. He learned that by being a loner he was in a class by himself, that he had no one above him to look down on him, that he had no peers to judge him. In his solitary world there was no such thing as trash or quality, no remembering how to act around your betters. There was just the endless Texas sky and the eternally blowing wind and a bewildered little boy. In all those lonely years, however, there had been one other person in Danny Mackay's life.

And he loved her with a ferocity that was close to obsession.

"You help yourself to some of that there pie, Mr. Danny," Eulalie said as she put the pound cake in the oven. "Them apples was so sweet I didn't have to put no sugar in."

Danny helped himself to a large wedge. In all of San Antonio he knew of no woman who made pie like old Eulalie did.

Someone started to sing "The Yellow Rose of Texas" on the radio while Danny read about Eisenhower's heart attack.

Not that he cared about the president's health. What Danny cared about, was totally absorbed and fascinated with, was the presidency. Now *there* was real power. In the right hands the power of the presidency could become something almost unimaginable. And Danny saw himself as that man.

The song intruded upon his thoughts.

It wasn't a sad song, but the reference to a Texas rose made Danny put down the newspaper and gaze at the wall, a forkful of pie forgotten in his hand.

He had called *her* that. His Texas rose.

When had he first noticed it, that his mother was the most beautiful woman in the world? At what age had he looked up from the bare kitchen table and seen her for the first time, suddenly no longer just his ma but a delicate, fading flower, like a rose among dandelions? He had a dim memory of sitting in a cold shack, the boards rattling all around them, the two younguns crying in their box, the three older ones huddled beneath a patchwork quilt, trying to get warm. And his ma bent over a stove that barely worked, stirring something, her face illuminated in a peculiar kind of glow. Of course, it wouldn't be until years later that he learned that her frailty and bewitching luminosity were due to tuberculosis, and that her cheeks flamed not with health but with fever. But by then Danny Mackay would be so desperately in love with her that he saw only the beauty in which she walked.

Lord, she had a way about her. It was as if a kind of pride burned flamelike and so steadily deep within her soul that no amount of Texas dust and heat and wind could blow it out. She took pain silently, she suffered hunger without complaining, she accepted charity with dignity, and she taught her son to find worth within himself, and not to walk with his head bowed. "You've got to make something of yourself, son," she used to say in her soft-spoken way. "Your pa can't read and that's why we're poor. But I want better for you and the little uns. I know you hate school, but it's what's going to get you ahead in life. When you're educated, no one can call you trash." No matter what chore she was at, if it was mending their clothes or fixing a meal of sowbelly, black-eyed peas, and molasses, she did it with a kind of nobility, young Danny thought as he watched her long, slender hands and the delicate curve of her neck. She didn't hold to the belief that one was either quality or trash. "All people are the children of God, Danny," she would say in her gentle, melodious voice. "It's what you do with yourself that counts."

It was for her that Danny ever attended school, going barefoot the many miles to sit in a stifling hot classroom and being the butt of other boys' pranks. He suffered education for her, he stayed out of trouble for her, he dreamed for her. One day, he vowed with almost every breath he took, he was going to make something of himself and come back and take her away from the failed and useless Augustus and set her up in a house complete with a garden and colored help.

Danny didn't know anything about New Deals in those days, or government schemes to bring medical care to the depressed rural areas. He didn't know that the doctors who came out in their Chevrolets were paid a subsidy by an agency called the FSA and that Danny and his family were a statistic.

All he knew was that there was nothing those men in their black suits and stethoscopes could do for his mother, and that once Augustus Mackay couldn't even pay his small share of the doctor's fee they stopped coming, and so his mother had to turn to local healers for the traditional "nanny tea" and bleeding. That didn't help either.

It was snowing the night she lay dying, and Danny was all alone with her.

The younguns were all asleep and tucked in the giant iron bed that was pushed against the wall, where yellow newspaper had been plastered over the gaps. Pa and the two older ones that were left (Becky had run off with a farm-equipment salesman) had gone the three miles to the landowner's house in the hope of talking him into letting them stay through the winter. His wife was sick, Augustus would be telling the man, and the children had nothing to eat. It was no time to be putting their possessions in the wagon and moving on.

Danny was scared that night. He'd never known such fear. She lay on the other bed, coughing, her skin burning hot.

He had sat by her side, holding her feverish hand, listening to the "blue norther" come down from the Panhandle to remind folks that there was in fact something worse than hellfire. Young Danny had sat and squeezed her hand and begged her not to die and prayed to a dimly conceived God, who couldn't seem to hear a boy's plea over the wind.

That was when he decided to give up on God and take matters into his own hands. "Just goin' out for a few minutes, Ma," he had murmured to her. Then he had struck out into the frigid night, running as fast as he could down the snow-covered road. He reached the doctor's house an hour later; it stood at the edge of town like a glowing Christmas ornament on a white counterpane. The windows were lit and music was coming out. Danny ran to the door, fell exhausted against it, and knocked with the last of his strength.

Dr. Simon Waddell came to the door himself, his generous belly spread with a dinner napkin. "What is it?" he said, peering down at the ragamuffin.

"Ma's terrible sick!" Danny had blurted, wishing he could go inside, into the warmth and music and good smells of food.

"I'm sorry, son," Dr. Waddell said, "but there's nothing I can do for her."

"You gotta come!" Danny cried.

"You go on home now," the doctor said, closing the door. *"She needs your help!"*

As the door closed in his face Danny heard the man say to an unseen occupant in the house, "Sorry I ever left New Orleans—"

Danny went out of his mind. He continued to pound on the door and call Dr. Waddell's name. Then he raced around the house, trying to open windows, peering through gaps in curtains. He pounded on the back door, then came back to the front.

He gasped for breath and the frosty air seemed to cut his lungs. His hands and feet were numb; his face throbbed with the cold. He slumped down on the front step and started to cry. Then, from inside the house, he heard a bell ringing. Danny ran around and looked through a window. Dr. Waddell was on the telephone. Danny pressed his ear to the glass. He heard the doctor telling Reverend Joshua Billings that he would be right over. "Keep her warm until I get there," the doctor said. "It doesn't sound serious. But I'll take a look anyway."

Danny stood with his back pressed against the house as he watched the doctor hurry out into the night, wrapping a muffler around his neck; he climbed into his black Chevrolet with his medical bag in hand. As the car disappeared into the snowy blackness Danny felt the winter storm enter his body and gather in the pit of his stomach. It was as if a ball of ice had settled down there, and it caused him tremendous pain.

Simon Waddell, he thought as he plunged through the snow in the direction of home. *Simon Waddell,* Danny's mind said over and over as he stumbled in the drifts and sobbed and tried to fly back to his dying mother. And in his anger that grew with each icy step he took, the twelve-year-old mind called up another name, *Reverend Joshua Billings,* because he had taken the doctor away, and it was then, as Danny finally drew near to the shack and found a last scrap of strength to get him to the door, that the list of special names was started. Names never to be forgotten.

He sat at his mother's side, weeping and wringing his hands, feeling utterly defenseless and powerless, until, sometime around dawn, she came out of her delirium, looked at her handsome son for a brief lucid moment, ran her hand over his almost-reddish hair and said, "Grow up to *be* somethin', Danny." And then she died.

He had gone mad with rage and grief, and hadn't been found until days later, his nigger-shooter worn out from the vengeance he had taken upon innocent nature. Augustus Mackay hadn't been able to control his son after that, no matter how many razor stroppings he resorted to. When the sweet soul of Danny's ma had left her body, something black and malevolent had flown into his. He was twelve at the time—a grown man.

The song ended and Danny focused back in on Hazel's hot kitchen, where he was surrounded by baking smells and girlish laughter coming through the open door. From where he sat he could see down the hall into Hazel's parlor, where men were mingling among the whores and taking their pick of them.

On the night of Mary Mackay's death a strange and complex love/hate relationship with the memory of his mother had been born in Danny. He had worshiped her and she had let him down. So Danny had grown up knowing two things for certain: that no woman in the world was ever going to measure up to his beautiful ma, and that, just like his ma, all women were going to let him down.

"You okay, Mr. Danny? Somethin' wrong with that pie?"

He looked at Eulalie, her sweating face like polished ebony. By her own scale of human worth, she had placed herself at the very bottom of the ladder. She was "black colored."

Well, he thought as he finished the pie and pushed away from the table while reaching for his Camels, if this old nigger-woman was doomed to be fixed forever at the bottom rung, Danny Mackay was most definitely not going to stay white trash.

Someday, quality was going to have him in their living rooms and expect him to bed their daughters. He'd show his ma, he'd show them all, that Danny Mackay was a man going places.

The San Antonio night was so hot that it was like driving through soup. Danny and Bonner Purvis talked for a while about going to the pictures, but the theater would be hot and unless it was a John Wayne movie or you had a girl in the back row, going to the pictures was no fun.

Bonner Purvis was a year younger than Danny and he still had pimples. He had been rejected by the army because of flat feet, and that was why he sold bad liquor and "dirty" girls to the flyboys, out of spite. Bonner was a walking irony: ever since he was very little he'd had a cruel streak in him that no amount of beatings from his pa could drive out of him, but he also possessed the most angelic face ever to grace a man. Men and women alike would stare when Bonner Purvis walked by; he was pure Angel Gabriel, they told themselves, with that limp blond hair like silk off an ear of corn, and those blue eyes, and the dimpled chin. His smile, they all declared, could charm the warts off a hog, and he had nice hands, too, kind of like a woman's. Although his reputation was known in this part of San Antonio—everyone knew what he had done to poor old Fred MacMurphy's dog—folks still couldn't completely dislike Bonner Purvis, he was just so *nice*-looking. Which was why the flyboys trusted him and gave him good money when they didn't have to.

But, like Danny, Bonner had outgrown small-time schemes. He was restless. San Antonio was suddenly too small, and he was getting ambitious.

Anyway, it was a hot night and they had nowhere in mind to go, so they got themselves a bottle of Jack Daniel's and headed off out of town in Bonner's old pickup. They were thinking of visiting one of the border towns, where you could get a Mexican whore for a dollar.

But along the highway they came upon a sight that made Bonner jam on his brakes. "Well, well, Danny. Looky there, will you?"

Danny, having just taken a swig of the sour mash, ran his hand across his mouth and gazed out the open window of the pickup. There, about a hundred yards off the road, in the middle of a big field, was an enormous tent, all glowing and looking like a birthday cake against the black Texas night. There were a lot of cars parked around it, and hundreds of people, it seemed to the two San Antonio boys—quite a mixture of Mexicans, colored and poor whites, they saw—all streaming into the tent while an unseen organ piped out "When the Saints Go Marching In."

"Well, I'll be," Danny said under his breath.

"You ever been to a revival meetin'?" Bonner asked, already reaching for the door handle. "My ma took me to a couple when I was young. A real show they are!"

"Let's take a look."

They sat in the back on a bench that creaked and threatened to collapse under the weight of so many people. The tent was packed to its canvas walls, with people standing all around the sides and back, fanning themselves, their clothes dark with sweat and filling the tent with the smell of unwashed humans at midsummer.

The Reverend had the magnificent name of Billy Bob Magdalene, and he wore an ice-cream-white suit with a black string tie and he spewed fire and brimstone over his perspiring congregation.

It wasn't a remarkable meeting, as far as tent revivals went. But Billy Bob Magdalene knew his business, he knew that in order to get the people to part with their money he first had to put the scare of eternal hellfire into them and then convince them that with his intervention the Lord might spare them. "God can be bribed" was the subliminal message. And it worked. By the end of the evening, Billy Bob Magdalene had those people clapping and rocking and so scared out of their heads for all the sins they'd committed that when the baskets came around, in went the dollars and the pesos and the hope that Billy Bob Magdalene did indeed have some influence with God.

It was during the collection that Danny got his brilliant idea.

The place was in absolute chaos, what with Sister Hallie pounding away on the organ and Brother Bud leading the congregation in "Rock of Ages" and a few Pentecostals rolling in the aisles and jabbering in tongues. So Danny got up, removed his cowboy hat, and nonchalantly passed it down the row. When Bonner saw what he was up to, he too removed his hat and went across the aisle, passing down the next row. They didn't risk being too greedy, in case they were spotted. But with so many people standing up and waving their arms and running up to Billy Bob Magdalene to be blessed, well, no one would notice the two boys slipping out of the tent with their hats pressed to their chests.

"Whoo-ee!" shouted Bonner as they ran to the pickup. "Bet you we got fifty dollars easy!"

Danny whooped and hollered as he flung the door open and threw himself inside. He dumped the contents of the hat onto the seat and started counting as Bonner put the truck into gear and began to grind back to the highway.

When they heard the explosion and felt the truck suddenly rock, they wondered what they'd hit. When the second explosion made the front end of the pickup dip and they realized their tires were being shot out, Bonner cried "Jesus Christ!" and dived under the dashboard.

Danny stared ahead in fright as, through the settling of dust and grit, a figure came into the beams of the headlights. It was Billy Bob Magdalene, and he was aiming a shotgun right at Danny's head.

"Awright, boys," he drawled. "C'mon outa that there truck. Nice and slow like."

Danny was too startled to move and Bonner had peed in his pants.

"Step down, I said! What do I have to do to get you two pecker-heads to hear me?"

Slowly and shakily the two boys got out of the truck and looked down the barrel of the Reverend's shotgun, their arms raised.

Billy Bob Magdalene took a long look at Danny's face. And then, when he saw Bonner's pants, he lowered the gun, shook his head and said, "Shee-yit. You two come on back with me to my office."

His office turned out to be a battered bus with lettering

on the side that said, BILLY BOB MAGDALENE BRINGS JESUS. It was hot and fetid inside, thick with the smell of sweat and whiskey. As the boys climbed in ahead of Billy Bob Magdalene and his shotgun they saw the crowd start to stream out of the tent to the tune of "Amazing Grace."

"Shoot," Billy Bob Magdalene said, setting aside his gun. "You two pissants are the poorest excuses for small-time crooks I ever did see! Siddown, the both of you."

"Listen, Mr. Magdalene," Bonner began. "We'll give the money back. We was only foolin' you."

The Reverend heaved a sigh of boredom and eased himself into a chair that groaned. He opened the bottom drawer of the desk that was wedged behind the driver's seat and produced a bottle of whiskey. But he poured a glass only for himself.

"You two pudknockers sure think you're smart, don't you?" he said after draining the glass in one gulp. "Don't you know that's the *oldest* scam since the serpent sold the apple to Eve? You think we didn't spot you two the minute you come into the tent? An audience fulla wetbacks and niggers and poor white trash, and here come two lusty young bucks just thirsting for mischief. You let me down, boys. I kinda hoped you'd be more original than the rest."

Bonner and Danny shifted self-consciously.

"Here's what I got to offer you," Billy Bob Magdalene said after downing a second glass. "How'd you two like a job?"

"Job?" they said together.

"Yeah. Workin' in my show. I need a coupla shills in the audience. Since Sister Lucy and Brother Abner ran off together last month, my nightly take's fallen off. You two know what a shill is?"

They shook their heads.

So Reverend Billy Bob Magdalene explained how his operation worked. And while he talked he opened a basket and took out some sandwiches—thick roast beef with mustard and tomatoes—and some cold fried chicken and chunks of angel food cake. Which he did share with the boys and which they devoured hungrily. But the whiskey he never offered.

"I'm in the protection racket," Reverend Billy Bob Magdalene said. "First I remind folks that God is so angry with them that He's got it on His calendar to squash them soon's He can get around to it. Then I kind of hint that I got some special *in* with the Lord, like I got His ear. And then I sort of let it slip that for a small sum I might just whisper a few words in God's ear in their defense. It never fails. They come into my tent as scared-shit sinners, and they leave feeling fully insured."

He picked a drumstick clean, threw it out the open window and refilled his glass. "Now, here's how I work it. I go on ahead of this here bus and come into town quiet-like, where I make a deal with the local ministers. For half of my take, they agree to close their own churches and urge folks to come to my tent. That way everyone's happy. I get paid, the ministers get paid, and the folks have a brief reprieve from God's wrath."

Wishing he had a cold Nehi to wash down the sandwich, Danny said, "Where do we come into this?"

"I need some plants in my audience, to kinda get things rolling. It's a good practice to have one shill for about every twenty-five people. When I give a certain prearranged signal, you start the folks to clapping. When I give another signal, you stand up and shout Hallelujah. By the time the plate comes around, you've gotten them so worked up they literally empty their pockets." Billy Bob Magdalene sat back and belched loudly. "So, what do you boys think?"

"What's our cut?"

"Your cut?" Billy Bob Magdalene threw back his head and roared with laughter. "Hell's bells, son! Your cut is that I don't turn you over to the sheriff for what you done tonight! *After* I shoot your balls off."

He fell silent then, picking his teeth and measuring the two boys. He was thinking how the ladies always put more into the collection plate when they thought there was the possibility of being personally brought to Jesus by good-looking young studs like these. Nothin' like young Texas manhood to bring the ladies to the Lord, he thought.

"Five percent of the take," he said. "Split between you. Plus, you ride in this bus and get your meals free. I got a circuit that goes clear into Louisiana and Oklahoma. The possibilities, sons, are boundless. Whaddya say?"

Bonner looked at Danny and the two exchanged a smile.

That morning, she had fed them fried ham with buttermilk biscuits. Now she was putting great bowls of chili in front of them, along with corn bread and ice-cold milk. Danny smiled his special smile, looked her up and down with his lazy green eyes, and said softly, "Boy hidey, ma'am. Ain't no one can make chili like a fine Texas woman. And that's a fact!"

He looked across the table and winked at Bonner. They had both had her last night—all three of them together in the same bed.

Soon after joining Billy Bob Magdalene on his preaching circuit, the two boys from San Antonio had discovered that a lot of these isolated farm wives were starved for a bit of excitement. With husbands too tired from working the fields all day, or too Bible-strict to vary from the missionary way, many wives found an outlet in these handsome young men who could be coaxed into doing anything. Last night this young wife of a cotton farmer who was away in Abilene had wanted Danny and Bonner inside her at the same time. It was a first for Danny, and he decided he liked it.

Besides, there was a ten-dollar bill on their plates for each of them the next morning.

"It's too bad you-all can't stay awhile longer," she said, bringing a fresh pitcher of cold milk.

Danny rocked back on his chair and gave her his smoothest smile. This farm wife was doubly talented; not only was she a hellcat in bed, she put out a table spread that was nearly as good as old Eulalie's had been.

Soon after joining up with Billy Bob Magdalene a year ago and after a quick visit to Bonner's house to gather their things and leave without saying good-bye to Mrs. Purvis, the two friends had discovered that they had no need of sleeping in that smelly old bus with Sister Hallie and Brother Bud and the Reverend. Every town they rode into, there was a competition to see who would have the honor of feeding and bedding down the boys for the night. The Reverend didn't mind, when he saw which way the wind was blowing. It was just as he thought: handsome young bucks like these, full of piss and vinegar, were the best draw he had ever had.

Almost at once his nightly takes went up. What with Danny and Bonner moving up and down the aisles, smiling their heart-melting smiles and urging people to praise the Lord, folks just seemed to part with their money easier.

And then one night outside of Austin with Billy Bob Magdalene down sick with something he ate, Danny decided to give the preaching business a try, and discovered that he was miles better than the Reverend. His natural energies and magnetism rolled out over the heads of the congregation and they were his within minutes. He strutted his stuff on the stage, gave them sex and charisma and hellfire, and that night their take was the biggest it had ever been. Afterward, Danny had had his pick from the mob of women seeking private counsel in the bus.

It was right around then that Bonner had suggested that maybe they didn't need Sister Hallie or Brother Bud. After all, nearly every town church had an organ, and nearly every town organist was female. And as it was considered an honor to play at Billy Bob Magdalene's revivals, there was no thought of payment. The boys had been able to persuade Billy Bob Magdalene to abandon old Hallie and Bud in Shreveport once they showed him on paper how much greater their three takes would be without the other two.

Still, it wasn't enough. As he ran his bread around his bowl and said "Yes, ma'am" to a slice of apple pie, Danny got to thinking again. It had been on his mind a lot lately, the fact that they weren't realizing their full potential.

Every night, in every town, it was the same thing. Billy Bob Magdalene shooting fire and brimstone over the heads of the terrified congregation, then handsome Bonner and Danny moving smoothly among them to take the money. The problem was, they just weren't special.

In fact, they were pretty much like any revival troupe traveling the South. A few times Danny had gone on over to other meetings to see what they were doing. He'd seen a scantily clad "virgin" writhing with snakes, a seven-year-old preacher in a miniature white tuxedo, people being faith-healed out of their wheelchairs, total-immersion baptism, and so on. Everybody, it seemed to him, had a gimmick. And that's just what he and Bonner needed in order to get ahead. Otherwise, they were just another dime-a-dozen act.

Not that Danny complained. It had been a smart move to join up with Billy Bob Magdalene. It got him out of San Antonio and away from the flyboys and whores; it got him on the road and moving and seeing what the world was like; it gave him new beds and new bed partners almost every night; and it fed him and kept him in money until he came up with plans for his future.

Because one thing was for certain, Danny wasn't going to do this for the rest of his life. Just look at Billy Bob Magdalene. Fifty, if he was a day. And a whiskey-toting nobody who was going to die in mediocrity. Not so for Danny Mackay. He had finally tasted the power of controlling a crowd, of manipulating them, of making them dance to his tune. And having once tasted such power, he wanted to experience it again.

"I'm afraid we can't stay on, ma'am," he said now as he pushed his empty pie plate away. "The Reverend says we have to be in Texarkana by nightfall."

"A pity," she said.

He looked at her behind in the tight print dress—the most perfect teardrop ass he had ever seen. Just thinking about last night started getting him excited again.

When he looked across at Bonner, Danny saw that his friend was thinking the same thing.

They grinned at each other.

Hell, they'd done it before, hadn't they? Gotten Billy Bob Magdalene so stinking drunk that they had to stay over? Like that time those two twins had nearly sucked them dry in Wichita Falls. Danny had been sore for a week afterward, but it had been worth it, to get Billy Bob Magdalene so skunked that he'd slept for three days while Danny and Bonner enjoyed the Macfee sisters.

After they thanked the farm wife and left through the

kitchen door, Danny murmured to Bonner, "What say we go into town and buy ol' Billy Bob a bottle?"

It was around about midnight, as the three of them lay naked and sweating and intertwined on her bed, that the idea came to Danny.

We don't need Billy Bob Magdalene anymore.

The boys bided their time and waited until it was the dead of summer and they were on a lonely stretch of highway. Waves of heat shimmered up from the baking asphalt; pools of fake mirage water lay like melted silver out on the desert. Nothing but mesquite scrub for miles, and prickly pear, the scourge of West Texas. They were tuned into a station that was playing "Heartbreak Hotel" by that new country-western singer named Elvis Presley. And Reverend Billy Bob Magdalene was nursing another hangover.

He hadn't been doing well these last couple of months. His health seemed to be declining rapidly. He didn't know what he would have done without the two boys, who were so concerned about his health and so good to him by always buying him a bottle.

"Hey," said Bonner from the back of the bus. "What do you all know about this town Odessa? You been there before, Billy Bob?"

But the Reverend was too busy cradling his head. Once again, he wouldn't be preaching tonight. Danny would be doing it. But that was all right. Although Billy Bob Magdalene wouldn't admit it to the boys, Danny was a better hellfire preacher than he was. And just so darned good-looking, flashing that sly, sexy smile at the audience. Couldn't deny it—the boy brought in the greenbacks.

"Hey," said Danny all of a sudden. "You feel that?"

"Feel what?" said Bonner.

"I don't know. . . ." Danny frowned and gripped the steering wheel. "Something doesn't feel right."

"Might could be a tire," said Bonner, coming forward and leaning down to peer between his friend and the Reverend at the endless stretch of highway before them. They hadn't seen another car in hours.

"Better check it," Danny said, slowly easing the old bus over to the side.

"You stay there, Billy Bob," Bonner said when they got out. "It's way too hot out here for you."

But when he saw them standing there lighting up Camels and shaking their heads at the front wheel, Billy Bob just had to get out and see what was wrong.

And he found out just exactly what was wrong as soon as the boys climbed back into the bus, saying they were getting the jack and some tools, and started up the engine instead and drove away.

Bonner and Danny watched him in their rearview mirror, a small, bewildered figure growing smaller as they sped away. A shirtless, hatless, half-drunk old man with no water in the middle of a merciless desert.

"Whoo-ee!" shouted Bonner.

"We're on our way now, boy!" cried Danny as he pressed down on the accelerator and sped on down the highway in their BILLY BOB MAGDALENE BRINGS JESUS bus toward what he knew were going to be better things.

17

Hollywood, California: 1957

RACHEL HAD LIVED as Beverly Highland for three years, serving up Eddie's Royal Burgers and living in the respectable boardinghouse on Cherokee, before she came to the realization that in order to make a new life for herself changing her name hadn't been enough. She had to change her face as well.

Not that any of her new friends, by word or deed, reminded her of her homeliness. They saw through the unfortunate arrangement of flesh and bone and saw the gentle spirit of the quiet girl who had appeared from nowhere one night, who had stayed with them loyally ever since, who didn't talk much, whose background was a mystery, and who, above all, in three short years, had turned Eddie's diner into a success.

People now stood three-deep waiting for seats at the counter; Laverne kept a reservation book for the booths. And these days the sound of hammers and chisels filled the air around the clock as a work crew knocked down walls and expanded the diner into the shop next door, which used to be a dry cleaner's.

The day Beverly had shown up for work, three years ago, to mop the floors, wash dishes, and scrub pots, Eddie had given her a free lunch, and she had startled him by saying quietly, "This isn't a very good hamburger." He wasn't used to her honesty yet—he wasn't used to honesty in anybody—so he had said indignantly, "You don't like my cooking, eat somewhere else."

But instead of apologizing or keeping her mouth shut, the girl had persisted by saying softly, "I know what your hamburgers need." And she had had the audacity to get up from the counter, go into the kitchen, take his prepared patties out of the refrigerator and *mess* with them. Eddie had been a combination of mad and ready to fire her, but curious also, when he saw her hand fly along the spice rack, pulling down tins and jars, her fingers working swiftly, her face set in concentration. Ten minutes later, when he was biting into a revised hamburger, his taste buds had told him this was his lucky day. He used cheap hamburger meat, but the girl's secret spices made it taste like expensive steak, and then when Beverly had also let him in on the secret of adding chopped jalapeños to his fries, the rest became history.

Eddie fed the spiced-up burgers to the cops, prostitutes, and out-of-work actors who were his regular customers, and got rave reviews. Then, at Beverly's suggestion, he shaved ten cents off the price, did away with plates, wrapped the burgers in waxed paper, and customer response was phenomenal. The word went up and down the street, and people started coming. Pretty soon, not only locals came to feast on Royal Burgers in the plain, unassuming diner, but people drove in from Santa Monica, Pasadena, and even next-door Beverly Hills to see what the noise was all about. They went away satisfied, and told their friends. Then Eddie got the idea of having a To Go window, and soon did a thriving sidewalk business. People drove up, purchased Royal Burgers by the bag, and took off for the beach or mountains or desert to enjoy them. Word spread, and spread.

So now Eddie was expanding into the shop next door, having bought out their lease, and was thinking of opening up another Royal Burger diner in the rapidly growing San Fernando Valley.

He owed it all to Beverly Highland. But she didn't capitalize on his praise as another girl might, demanding money or credit for his success. She just told him she was pleased, in that maddeningly reserved way of hers, not smiling but being sincere nonetheless when she said she was happy for him. And although Eddie often wondered about her, about her past, which she refused to talk about, about the silence she seemed to live in, about her standoffishness and the fact that she would never go to his and Laverne's house for dinner, and the way she shied away from making close friends, the way she wouldn't let anyone touch her—and although he *was* curious about her name, which was coincidentally that of the intersection outside his diner—Eddie never pressed her. She was quiet and diligent and loyal, and had not, in three years, missed a day of work or made any demands on him. There was nothing, absolutely nothing, in this world he would not do for her.

"A *vacation?*" he said. "Are you out of your mind? We can't handle the load as it is! I have to interview new waitresses, Laverne has to keep all three eyes on that shiftless work crew, and some magazine is coming to do a story on us. And you want a vacation?"

Beverly was used to Eddie's bombast. It came and went like L.A.'s Santa Ana winds—hot and fast and unpleasant, but transitory and unsubstantial, leaving little behind it except dust.

"I haven't had a vacation in three years," she said quietly.

"So who has?" He turned away from the grill and eyed her.

She was not "little" Beverly anymore, he noticed. Three

years of his cooking had fleshed out those sticks and bones—
that, plus nature. Beverly had curves now, and just the right
amount of roundness in the right places. He caught many a
customer giving her the twice-over. Too bad about her face.

"So where you gonna go, on this vacation?"

"Just . . . away," she said in her usual cryptic way. Getting
information out of Beverly, Eddie had learned in three years,
was like getting sex from Laverne. You might as well forget
it.

"For how long?"

"Three months."

He dropped his spatula.

The girl had moxie. No doubt about it.

"Sorry, kid," he said. "Can't afford to do without you for
that long."

"Would you rather do without me forever?"

Now, that stopped him. In all the time they'd been together Eddie had never known Beverly to so much as question
his orders. She was dutiful and obedient and never complained.
To hear a challenge in that soft-spoken voice was like a dec-
laration of war from anyone else.

He gazed into those enigmatic brown eyes, eyes that
locked away secrets—some of them terrible, he suspected—
and thought for a long moment. Then he realized: it must be
something she just had to do.

"Starting when?" he said finally.

"I don't know yet. But I'll tell you when I do know."

"We'll miss you, kid," he said quietly.

He thought she was going to hug him then. But of course
she didn't. Even though there were times when he thought
Beverly was going to do something impulsive like that, do
something that any other person in the same circumstance
would do, she always held herself back. She never touched
anyone, and never let anyone touch her.

"Thanks, Eddie," she said, and went back to work making
up her secret spice mix.

The first doctors she went to were general practitioners
who unanimously said there was nothing that could be done.

Then she made appointments with surgeons and suffered their close scrutiny of her face, only to be told the same thing. "The nose, maybe," they all agreed. "But you'll always have that chin." She learned that only a specialist could help her. So she went painstakingly through the telephone book and began visiting plastic surgeons. Few were interested once she said she had no money and no insurance; one suggested he might work on her face if she worked on him in payment.

Beauty, it seemed to Beverly, or even just passing looks, was the privilege of the moneyed.

But she would not be daunted. Sitting in front of her mirror in Eddie's sister's boardinghouse and staring at her face, she would recall one of the last things Danny Mackay had said to her: "You're a stupid, ugly bitch, Rachel."

Well, she had already changed part of that sentence—her name. Surely it would be a simple matter to change the rest.

But eight weeks of searching—of riding L.A.'s every-two-hours buses to the far-flung offices of doctors who ended up shaking their heads, and of repeatedly telling Eddie that her vacation would start soon—produced no results. She was no closer than the day she had started her quest. Still, this did not discourage the determined Beverly. The more elusive her goal and the harder she had to fight to reach it, the more each new day strengthened her resolve.

She *was* going to change her face.

And then one morning early in May, when the weather was cool-warm and the smog hadn't yet started to collect for its summer siege, Beverly was standing at the chopping block, mixing her secret spices for Eddie's Royal Burgers and listening to the radio. The news was all about Eisenhower sending paratroopers into Little Rock, the Russians launching something called Sputnik, and a pilot named John Glenn breaking a speed record in a jet. "And now for the local news," the announcer said. As Beverly was about to add the tarragon, basil, and sage to her chopped scallions, a report came on about a famous movie star being in a spectacular car accident on the Pasadena Freeway, and rushed to Queen of Angels Hospital. "Dr. Seymour Wiseman, chief physician on the case, told KFWB News that while Miss Binford sustained serious facial injuries, she has been stabilized and is off the critical list. Miss Binford, who won an Oscar for her stunning performance in *Desperate Roses* last year, will require extensive reconstructive surgery, said Dr. Wiseman, who is a plastic surgeon. And now for the sports. Here's news! The Brooklyn Dodgers are moving to Los Angeles—"

But Beverly didn't hear the rest. She was already going through the phone book.

Seymour Wiseman, she discovered, had an office in Beverly Hills, a town that—despite its proximity to Hollywood and despite the fact that Beverly Canyon Road, the street the diner was on, wound around and eventually found itself snaking up into the Hills above famed Sunset Boulevard—Beverly had never visited.

She called for an appointment. She was given one two months away—Dr. Wiseman was very much in demand.

Then she went up to Eddie, who was filling out his order for beef, and said, "I'll be starting my vacation on July the eighth." She was that certain Dr. Wiseman would take her.

Beverly had never seen a doctor's office like this one before. The furniture of polished leather and delicate tables with dainty wrought-iron legs, with modern art on the walls, and magazines she had only seen in drugstores but could never afford to buy. The receptionist didn't look like a nurse; she didn't wear a uniform but was all dressed up. And the only other patient in the waiting room was a woman wearing a mink coat. In July.

Beverly filled out a form asking for medical history—*Parents*: dead; *Pregnancies*: none—and sat down to wait.

An hour and a half later she was called.

No scary examining room for Dr. Wiseman's patients. Beverly was taken into a comfortable office that was, in contrast to the impeccable waiting room, surprisingly messy. Stacks of medical journals covered a desk; all sorts of knickknacks and mementos were placed haphazardly on bookshelves—little doctors made out of nuts and bolts, ceramic figurines of surgeons standing at operating tables, "Thank You" carved out of redwood, and so on. Little extra gifts from grateful patients.

Beverly was just wondering what little extra gift she could give him when he came into the office.

"Now then, Miss Highland," he said, sitting at his desk. "I see on this form you've filled out that you want to me 'fix your face,' as you put it. What exactly would you like me to do?"

"I want you to change my face."

He looked at her. She sat rigidly in the chair, her back ramrod-straight, hands clasped tightly in her lap. There was an intensity about her that made him curious. She looked so . . . *serious* for one so young. Had her unfortunate homeliness made her short life so miserable that she was angry at the world? "What exactly don't you like about your face?"

"Do you see anything in it to like?"

"You have very pretty eyes."

"Can you help me?"

"I think so. There is a small operation I can do to pin your ears back, and I can transplant some cartilage into your chin. Your nose might require more than one operation—"

"I have no money," she said quietly. "And no insurance."

His smile faded. The look on his face said, Then why are you here?

"Dr. Wiseman," she said softly. "I'm homely and I'm poor. I need help and I have nowhere else to turn. You're a famous doctor. You operate on movie stars. You don't need my money. But you have a God-given skill in your hands that I don't think someone as nice as you is going to keep from someone as desperate as me, just because I have no money."

Seymour Wiseman very carefully removed his glasses and wiped them on his white lab coat. When he put them back on, he crossed his arms, gave Beverly a skewering look and said, "Young lady, are you hustling me, or are you really as naive as all that? Did you honestly think you could come in here and ask me to operate on you for *free*?"

"No, sir," she said, a little of the San Antonio accent creeping out. "I have never asked for anything for free in my life. What I want, I work for. And I'll work for you, Dr. Wiseman. I've got to work for Eddie, because I owe him that, but

I'll work for you, too. For as long as you say. Just please fix my face."

He gave her a thoughtful look. "Are you a nurse?"

"No."

"Can you type?"

"No."

"Do you know medical terminology?"

"No."

"Do you have a high school diploma?"

"No."

His look turned to one of incredulousness. "What *can* you do?"

"Anything that needs to be done. I sweep floors and wash dishes—"

"We don't have dishes in this office, young lady, and a cleaning service does our floors. How old are you?"

"Nineteen."

"Do your parents know you're here?"

"My parents are dead."

He frowned slightly. "I see. Who takes care of you, then?"

"No one. I've been on my own since I was fourteen."

"Are you from the South?"

"I was in Texas for a while."

"How did you live?"

"I worked for a woman named Hazel."

"What did you do?"

"Hazel owned a whorehouse. That's where I lived for three years. I was one of her girls." She added softly, "My boyfriend Danny put me in there."

A silence filled the office then. A silence that seemed to admit every sound from the outside and magnify it: the cars down below on Rodeo Drive, high heels click-clacking by, a distant siren. Seymour Wiseman removed his glasses again and wiped them even though they didn't need to be. He suddenly found himself remembering something—an incident in the past that he hadn't thought about in years, hadn't *allowed* himself to think about in years. What was it about this strange young girl that had triggered the unwanted memory? He looked at her eyes—yes, her only redeeming feature—and saw the flame of a very strong and determined soul burning brightly. He thought of Texas whorehouses and boyfriends named Danny who victimized homely girls who have no parents to watch out for them.

Then he said, "I have a daughter your age."

He put her in a private hospital that evening and started the very next morning on her nose. The cartilage to build up her chin he borrowed from her seventh rib; her ears he would do last.

On the first morning of surgery, as Beverly lay on the operating table, a nurse asked her to lift her hips so that she could slide the conductor plate under her—it was for the electric cautery, she said. And in so doing, the nurse noticed the tattoo on the inside of Beverly's thigh. "How pretty," the nurse said. "It's a butterfly, isn't it?"

Dr. Wiseman, coming into the room with upraised wet hands, water running off his elbows, took a look and said, "I can remove that for you if you would like, Beverly."

But she said, "No." It was her daily reminder of Danny Mackay.

The surgery hurt, but Beverly stoically withstood it. All through the injections of local anesthetic, the sound of a rasp sawing away at the bones in her nose, the taste of blood running down the back of her throat, the feel of sutures going in, coming out, all through the days and nights of loneliness in the hospital with no one coming to visit, no flowers to cheer up her room, the endless chain of starched women with starched smiles ministering to her body, and through the long hours on the operating table and the long hours of waiting for the end, of looking at her swollen, bruised face in the mirror, the bandages and caked blood—through the entire ten-week ordeal—Beverly thought of only one thing: her ambition to make something of herself. And someday, when she was ready, to meet up again with Danny Mackay.

When Dr. Wiseman was finished, Beverly saw that he had almost completely erased the face Danny had so despised, the ugliness that Hazel's kinkier customers preferred, the face that had so enraged her father. In its place, he had put the face of a stranger.

"What do you think?" he asked on her final day in the hospital when the last of the bandages and sutures came off.

Beverly wasn't sure. Actually, she looked ghastly. The bruises had melted down to greeny-yellow blotches, there were angry red lines where silk thread had sewn up the cuts, and she was still puffy. Nonetheless, there was some evidence there. . . . The nose was definitely smaller, the chin no longer recessed, and the ears stayed respectably back against her skull.

"Don't worry," Dr. Wiseman said, putting a fatherly hand on her shoulder. "The bruising will disappear soon and the swelling will go down. The scars will vanish, and the sun will give you some good color. Now let me give you some advice. Pluck your eyebrows and do something with your hair. You'll look like a movie star, guaranteed."

She checked into a motel in West L.A. and visited Dr. Wiseman three more times after that. Finally, the face he had promised her did appear, and when she saw him for the last time, she arrived prepared to pay him.

"I earn ninety dollars a month at Eddie's diner," she said. "I can send you five dollars every two weeks. You tell me when you want me to come in and I'll be here, Dr. Wiseman. I'll do anything that needs doing around this office. I'll come in on weekends if you want—"

But he held up a hand. "Beverly, to quote yourself, I don't need your money. I am, as you accused, terribly rich. Don't ask me why I operated on you—your case was very routine and not at all a medical challenge. I had other things to do and you were an inconvenience. But I'll tell you one thing. Twenty years ago a younger Seymour Wiseman had a modest medical practice on a nice residential street in Berlin. He didn't think much of money in those days. In fact, he didn't like people who worshiped it. And then a terrible day came"—his eyes misted behind the little round glasses—"a day in which soldiers came and took his neighbors, his best friends away. Then that young Dr. Wiseman, terrified because he knew he was next, heard about a way to get out of Germany, so long as he had the money. So Dr. Wiseman got the money, and was able

191

to get his family out of Germany and into America. All of his friends, however, died in Nazi ovens. Do you know what I am talking about?"

"Yes," she whispered.

He sighed. "Anyway, it happened a long time ago and in a world that no longer exists. But ever since then, I have placed all my faith in money. I worship money, Beverly. I always will. And if you're smart, you'll listen to what I say. Money is power, Beverly. Money is the key to freedom. Money allows you to do all the things you want to do. Can you understand that?"

She nodded.

"However," he hastened to add, when he saw how intensely she agreed with him, when he saw secret visions burning darkly in her eyes, "just once in a long while, Beverly, let yourself do something purely for charity, purely because it will be a tonic for your soul, and you'll be able to live with yourself. Do you understand?"

"Yes."

He regarded her for a long moment. She made him sad. It made him want to weep to see one so young already set on the road of hatred and vengeance, for that was surely what he saw burning so feverishly in her eyes. And that was what it was about this strange girl that had triggered the unwanted memories the day he had met her. She had reminded him of himself, of a bitter, grieving young Seymour Wiseman on his way to a new world while the corpses of his friends and loved ones burned in Nazi ovens.

He stood and held out his hand. But, of course, she didn't take it. That was where he and she differed: at least Seymour had learned to touch again, and to love. He could only pray that whatever wounds tormented this poor girl would someday heal and she would forgive but not necessarily forget, and allow herself to live once again. "We'll say good-bye now, Beverly. You don't need me anymore, and I have to get back to my rich patients. Promise me you will come back and visit me someday. And tell me what you have done and where you have gone with your beautiful new face."

• • •

192

Beverly got off the bus on Highland Avenue and went into the first beauty shop she saw. She was there for six hours and gave the beautician all the money she had, which included her bus fare the rest of the way home. So she walked it, suitcase in hand, down the familiar streets of Hollywood to Eddie's diner.

He was in the kitchen frantically frying up hamburgers when she walked in. "Hey!" he said. "No customers allowed back here!"

"It's me, Eddie," she said.

"Me, who?"

"Me, Beverly. I'm back."

He frowned. He stared at the beautiful face with the pretty nose and delicate chin, at the finely arched eyebrows and platinum hair stretched back into one of the new stylish French twists. Then he looked down at the familiar battered brown suitcase with the P&O sticker on it, and he dropped his spatula.

18

JESSICA SCREAMED when she scored a direct hit.

Then, seeing the stunned look on John's face, she turned and started to run. But the snow was too deep and her clothing too cumbersome for her to make a good getaway; John was on her in an instant, pulling her down and pinning her arms over her head.

"You won't get away with that!" he shouted as he straddled her and scooped up snow with his free hand.

She shrieked and struggled. But he was too strong for her. As he rubbed snow in her face he said, "Say 'uncle'! Come on, Jess, say 'uncle'!"

She tried to fight him, but finally she had to cry *"Uncle!"* and then he released her. But as soon as she rolled away from him, she scrambled in the snow, hastily packed a ball between her gloved hands, and threw it at him, scoring another direct hit. Before he could strike back, Jessica was on her feet and running, laughing, looking over her shoulder and sticking out her tongue at him.

John, also laughing, ran after her. This time, when he caught her, he swung her around, pulled her into his arms and kissed her.

She slumped against him, exhausted, breathless, and happy.

"Come on, honey" he said, holding her. "Bonnie and Ray will wonder what's taking us so long."

Jessica didn't care. She knew that the other couple had returned to the condo an hour ago and were waiting for the Franklins, but the walk back from the ski slope had been so invigorating that Jessica hadn't been able to resist starting a snowball fight.

She hadn't wanted to come to Mammoth for the weekend and share a condo with John's business partner and his wife—she had too much work waiting on her desk. But now she was glad she had given in. This was what they needed: a weekend of escape.

They stamped the snow off their boots and delivered themselves into the cozy warmth of the house. A fire was blazing, and Ray and Bonnie were sitting in front of it, playing Scrabble.

"Ooh!" said Jessica, shedding her parka and mittens. "Is that mulled wine I smell?"

"It's on the stove," said Bonnie. "Help yourself."

As Jessica started to head for the kitchen John said, "Why don't you go upstairs and change first?"

She started to protest—she desperately wanted to get something hot inside her—but instead she said, "Okay," and headed for the stairs.

While she slipped into a soft velour caftan she heard the rumble of laughter down below. Bonnie and Ray prided themselves on being expert Scrabble players. It wasn't a game Jessica particularly enjoyed, but John liked it, so she was resigned to spending the evening playing it. Before leaving the bedroom, she paused to look at herself in the mirror. Her cheeks were flushed, her dark brown eyes bright with happiness. John had made love to her that morning, before they had headed out with their skis. And it had been very nice. She knew he would do it again tonight.

A mug of hot wine was already waiting for her when she joined the others. As John handed it to her he gave the emerald-green caftan a critical look.

"What's wrong?" she asked, looking down at herself and talking quietly so that the others didn't hear.

"When did you buy that?"

"Last week. I thought it would be comfortable after a day in the snow. Don't you like it?"

"Green isn't your color, honey. You know that. Anyway, come on. Bonnie and Ray are waiting for us to start a new game with them."

They sat on the carpet and played on a low coffee table. As they took turns laying tiles out on the board, the four talked amiably, drinking their wine and enjoying the fire. Jessica didn't say much; Bonnie and Ray were John's friends, and she hardly knew them.

"I tell you, John," Ray said as he played four tiles and scored thirty points, "I can sell this place today for *three times* what I paid for it. You can't buy anything in Mammoth anymore for what Bonnie and I paid for this place a few years ago. I get offers all the time. But we would never sell, would we, Bon?"

Bonnie turned to Jessica. "How did you do out there today?"

Jessica was only now learning to ski. She wasn't sure yet that she liked it. Before she could reply, John patted her hand and said, "I think Jess had better go back to the beginners' slope. You sure took a tumble today, honey."

"I tell you," said Ray, playing and scoring high again, "skiing isn't for everyone. I got my first skis when I was seven. Can't even remember what it was like not to know how to do it!"

Jessica said quietly, "I would imagine it's easier for a child to learn it than an adult. Kids don't have the fears we do."

"Honey," said John. "Look what you just did. Why didn't you play the Double Word square? You had a perfect opportunity. You don't gain anything by the move you just made."

Yes I do, she thought. *Now I've blocked Bonnie from playing on Triple Word and I haven't placed my "u" out where whoever has the "q" can score on it.*

"Jessica," said Bonnie, "what's Mickey Shannon really like?"

Jessica glanced at John and then at the game board. "He's a nice person."

"My sixth-grade girls are absolutely mad about him. When I told the class that I was spending the weekend with Mickey Shannon's lawyer, they went positively crazy. I promised them I would ask you if you could get his autograph for the class."

"Jessica is trying to avoid notoriety," said John. "She isn't Mickey Shannon's publicity agent."

"Well, I just thought—" Bonnie looked for a place to put her "q" and saw that the only "u" on the board was unplayable. "I mean, what's an autograph?"

"I don't mind doing it," Jessica began.

John said, "Don't you see, honey, what getting Mickey Shannon's autograph would do to your image? It lacks dignity."

She looked at her husband. "Yes, you're right," she said. "Besides, Bonnie, he's on tour right now. . . ."

The fire roared and crackled; sparks flew up the chimney. Jessica won the game, outdistancing Ray by twenty points.

When the tiles were spread out and turned over again, she said, "I don't really feel like playing this anymore. How about cards?"

John cast her a look. "You're outvoted, honey. Why don't you go upstairs and take a nap?"

"But I'm not tired."

"Well, you look tired. And you did take a nasty tumble on the slope today. Come on"—he took her hand—"I'll go up with you."

Upstairs in the bedroom John took her in his arms and kissed her on the forehead. "I'll wake you for dinner," he said quietly.

"We played Scrabble for six hours last night," she said, drawing away. "There are other games. Why can't we take a break from it?"

"Because this is their house and they were kind enough to invite us. Besides, you won. Why are you complaining?"

"I'm not complaining, John—"

He patted her arm. "You take a nap and you'll feel better. There's my girl."

As she watched him go, she thought, *I'm not your little girl.*

When the rumble of laughter rose from below, Jessica went to the bed and sat on it. She was beginning to think she had been right in the first place, in not wanting to come here. She didn't care for Bonnie and Ray, didn't like skiing, hated Scrabble, and was worried about all the work piling up on her desk. She also felt, despite the company downstairs, lonely.

She looked at the phone, thought a moment, then dialed Trudie's number.

"Hi!" came a voice on the other end of the line. "You've reached Gertrude Stein. No kidding, that's really my name. I'm away from the house right now, buying dog food for my three hungry, vicious Doberman watchdogs, but if you leave your name and number—"

Jessica hung up. She hadn't really expected to reach Trudie. This was, after all, Saturday night. So she stretched out on the bed, pulled the quilt up over her and listened to the muffled conversation down by the fire. She closed her eyes. She pictured Lonnie.

In the two weeks since that incredible night in Butterfly's Western bar, Jessica had been able to think of little else. Her fantasy had come true, it had actually taken form and been real. It had left her high for a while, but then the elation had worn off and she had found herself thinking: *Now that my cowboy is no longer a fantasy but reality, I don't have a fantasy anymore.*

She realized that she had entered into some sort of bargain and had paid an unexpected price. It had been an unanticipated trade-off: her fantasy for reality. It was difficult to fantasize about him now, knowing that he was really there, that she could see him in the flesh, be with him anytime she wanted.

But . . . was that what Jessica wanted? To visit a male

whore every time she felt lonely or angry or in the mood for sex? Was that going to solve any problems? Or was it only going to compound them?

Compound them, yes . . .

In the two weeks since her evening with Lonnie, Jessica had found herself unfulfilled after having sex with John. And that wasn't fair to him. He had no idea he was being compared with a stud skilled in the art of making love. The realization of it had made her feel guilty, and so, wanting to make it up to him, Jessica had responded warmly to John that morning, surprising him a little with her uncharacteristic enthusiasm. And the sex had ended up being good.

She drifted off to sleep and was awakened two hours later by John telling her that dinner was ready. They ate French bread and cheese fondue in front of the fire, and decided to have another round of Scrabble. Jessica begged off, despite John's displeased look, saying she had a book she couldn't put down.

So she waited for John in bed, lying awake while the game went on downstairs, wondering if she should join them, if she was being unfair to him. But when he did finally come quietly into the bedroom Jessica decided she would make it up to him.

He climbed under the covers and she reached for him. He kissed her on the cheek, said, "I'm tired, honey," and rolled over.

While her answering machine was taking phone messages Trudie was surveying the Saturday-night crowd at Peppy's, a popular nightclub on Robertson Boulevard. With her was her cousin Alexis, the pediatrician friend of Dr. Linda Markus.

Alexis had come out for an evening of drinking and people-watching, but had no intention of going home with a stranger as Trudie intended. For Alexis, Butterfly served her sexual needs, until she found someone she wanted to settle down with. Ever since medical school, she had never had much luck in places like this, even though she was pretty in a dark Eastern European way, and had a nice personality. The reason was her profession: Alexis had discovered that, for some unfathomable reason, men were turned off by a woman doctor. Perhaps she was a threat to them, she decided, or possibly her intimate knowledge of human anatomy made them vaguely uncomfortable. Whatever the reason, Alexis rarely got far with someone at a pickup place. Usually, once she told them what she did for a living, the interest cooled.

But she liked going out with her cousin anyway because Trudie was a lot of fun. And a refreshing change from going out with other doctors, with whom the conversation invariably turned to medicine.

What amazed Alexis tonight was that Trudie seemed to be so urgently on the prowl. Why, she wondered, was she doing this when she could go to Butterfly and be a lot better off?

What Alexis didn't know, and what Trudie herself didn't even really know, was that Trudie was looking for something. She was looking for a way to re-create her Butterfly fantasy with a real man. Her evenings with "Thomas" were wonderful, but she knew they were only interludes bought with cash. He wasn't real, their relationship wasn't real. Trudie wanted to re-create that magic in real life, to find that same spell with a flesh-and-blood man to whom she could pledge herself and thereby put an end to the search. But the problem was, Trudie had not yet figured out just what it was about her evenings with Thomas that made them unique. She had been with a few pickups since starting at Butterfly, but none had generated that special "spark." If only she knew what it was that was lacking, what it was she was seeking. . . .

Trudie could have had her pick of any guy in the place. With her looks and personality, the game was all hers. Men, it seemed to Trudie, never had any problems deciding whom to go home with, or what to do with her once they got there. It also seemed to Trudie, she thought now as she smoked a Virginia Slims and stared at a guy who was leaning against a pillar staring back at her, that single men didn't seem to have any of the problems single women did. She didn't see them as searchers, as seekers for a permanent relationship. As far as she could discern, men were out for quick sex and that was all.

There were so many things that hung women up that men seemed to be free of. As she caught sight of an appallingly thin woman out on the dance floor, Trudie recalled her college days with Jessica when, in the middle of the night, she would waken and hear girls in the bathroom throwing up. Those same girls would be stuffing themselves in the dining room the next day— riders on a carousel of bingeing and starving. Just as Jessica had done. But only women, Trudie noticed, suffered from bulimia and anorexia. How come men never did?

The man leaning against the pillar now slowly straightened and started to walk across the crowded dance floor toward her. He and Trudie had been looking each other over for the past hour, and apparently she had passed some sort of visual test. He, too, had passed a test. Trudie liked his looks. He reminded her in a way of Bill the pool plumber, whom she had shouted at last month and who had been frosty with her ever since. It was too bad, too, because Bill was a good-looking, sexy guy. Certainly in another time, another incarnation, Trudie decided, she and Bill might actually have been able to make contact. But her position as the contractor who hired him for jobs placed them both outside the normal man/woman relationship.

"Hi," said the stranger when he reached her table.

Trudie smiled up at him. He was tall, with an interesting way of filling out a shirt. He wore wire-rimmed glasses, the kind hippies wore back in the sixties, and it gave him an interesting, intellectual look. College grad, she speculated. Certainly the academic type.

"Hi," she said, and offered him a seat.

He sat down, turned to Trudie and said, "So—should I call you or nudge you tomorrow morning?"

The electric-blue Corvette sped down Wilshire Boulevard, squeaking through yellow lights and making zigzag lane changes. Trudie had the top down so that her hair and Alexis's blew in the wind. The signal ahead turned red; she slammed on the brakes and came to a cursing halt.

Alexis looked at her cousin, and the angry profile, and said, "There was a time when you would have gone home with him."

"Is that *all* men can ever talk about? I am so tired of the same old phony come-on lines!"

"You go to pickup bars, you get phony lines."

Trudie slumped in her bucket seat and shook her head. "I'm thirty years old, Alexis. I want to find a guy to spend the rest of my life with. But I don't want just any man. He has to be . . . oh, I don't know."

"He has to be like your Butterfly companion?"

"I guess. I don't even know what I want anymore."

A car pulled up next to them and waited for the signal to change. Trudie glanced at it—it was a white Rolls-Royce Silver Cloud, the late-fifties classic kind. The windows were darkly tinted; even the chauffeur was unseen. "Nice car," said Alexis.

The light turned green and Trudie stepped on the gas. "Probably owned by some rock star!" she said into the wind and they sped away.

The Rolls moved sedately through the intersection and turned into the driveway of a tall glass-and-brick building. Most of the building's windows were dark, except for a few lights coming from the twentieth floor. The Silver Cloud stopped in front of the subterranean entrance and the chauffeur got out to open the passenger door. Beverly Highland stepped out, turned up the collar of her fur coat, and hurried into the deserted building.

On the twentieth floor she went through the large oak doors of Highland Enterprises, Inc., and went directly to the inner offices.

"Hi," said the woman who was already there, waiting for her.

"Sorry I'm late," said Beverly, shedding her coat and hanging it up. "I had to take a call from the coastal commissioner. I'll be needing to testify again. What have you got there?"

The woman held out a sheaf of papers.

Beverly took them. "New members?" she asked.

"New *companions*," said the director of Butterfly.

"We might have to think about expanding," Beverly murmured as she quickly looked through the papers. Then she set them aside and gave her friend a serious look. "He took the

201

money," she said. "Danny took the five hundred thousand and invited me out to his Texas ranch. I was able to get out of it again, but sooner or later I'm going to have to meet him face-to-face. He's anxious to thank me in person for all my support of his campaign. Anyway, it's time to put the next phase of our plan into motion. Tell the others that I want to meet with you all one week from tonight, just before the New Hampshire primary."

"All right."

"Worried?" Beverly said.

"I don't know."

"Don't be. Danny may be powerful, but I'm more powerful. Nothing can go wrong. I promise you that."

The two women looked at each other. They each knew what the other was thinking. That, after thirty-five years, Beverly was going to have her revenge at last. On June 11, the day Danny Mackay was going to wish he had never been born.

19

Hollywood, California: 1960

"SEX IS WHAT SELLS TODAY, you know that, Bev?"

She didn't hear him. She was too busy struggling with the diner's incomprehensible accounting books. It was times like this when Beverly thought of Carmelita. A girl born with a phenomenal talent, forced to bury it along with the rest of her dreams. Carmelita, who had stopped answering Beverly's letters two years ago.

"Hey, Bev. Who's the sexiest actor you can think of?"

"I don't know," she said without looking up from her accounting.

Roy Madison scowled over the top of his *Variety* and said, "I'm serious, Bev. Come on now, who's the sexiest man on the screen today?"

Beverly put down her pencil and looked up from her stool

at the end of the counter. Roy was sitting at his usual corner table, the one nearest the pay phone, with the latest copies of *Variety*, *Casting Call*, and *Hollywood Reporter* spread out before him. And as usual he wore clean but carefully patched clothes, sat with his chair situated so that he could frequently check his looks in the shine of the jukebox, and nursed a cold cup of coffee bought two hours ago (he never bought anything to eat—Roy was so broke he couldn't even afford Eddie's) while he checked out the opportunities. A typical out-of-work actor.

"I really don't know, Roy. I don't go to movies."

"What about Paul Newman?"

It was the morning lull—between the breakfast and lunch rushes—there were only a few customers at other tables. Even Highland Avenue out front seemed quiet this morning. "Why do you want to know, Roy?"

"I'm thinking of changing my image maybe. Making myself sexier."

She gave this some serious thought. Although Beverly rarely gave consideration to men in general and had not found them appealing for six years, she was observant enough to know that there was nothing wrong with Roy Madison's image. He was really quite good-looking, in a plastic screen-idol kind of way. Eddie often remarked what a shame it was that with his looks Roy wasn't getting more acting jobs. But the problem was, he was a small unknown fish competing in an ocean full of barracudas. He'd landed a few nonspeaking bit parts here and there—once even on *Bonanza*, in color—but it wasn't enough to launch him. He held down part-time jobs, quitting them when he was briefly flush, scrounging again when he was broke. Like today. It had been over a month since his agent had returned any of his calls.

"I don't think there's anything wrong with your image, Roy."

"The last casting director I saw told me I look too much like Fabian. Is that true, Bev?"

She watched the way he observed himself in his reflection on the jukebox, turning his head this way and that, patting his perfect pompadour, and she had to agree: he did look too much like Fabian.

"If I could land just one good part, you know? A *speaking* part. Show them my real stuff. But you can't get a speaking part if you don't have a SAG card. And you don't qualify for a SAG card if you haven't ever done a speaking part. Shit, Bev. Just once, *just once*, I'd like people to see what I can really do."

"You will, Roy," she said softly. "The opportunity will come for you someday."

"Yeah," he snorted. "Like it came for Eddie." Roy had been coming to the diner for eight years now; he remembered Tony's Royal Burgers when it was a second-rate joint with nothing but hookers, cops, and unemployed actors like himself eating Eddie's rancid burgers. And now? Well, Eddie drove a brand-new Edsel, he was that successful.

Consistency was the secret of Eddie's success. He now owned six Royal Burger outlets and guaranteed his customers that when they bought a burger at the Pasadena store, it would be of the same quality and taste as the one they had enjoyed last week at the Santa Monica store. Chain hamburger stands were a very new concept; Eddie was familiar with White Tower and White Castle back East, but the West Coast, with the exception of a few relatively unknown chains, such as the one started by the McDonald brothers out in godforsaken San Bernardino, knew no such phenomenon. Eddie, in the six years since Beverly had spiced up his burgers, had discovered to his surprise what it was the public wanted these days: fast service and standardized food at low prices. He was getting rich on his Royal diners, even though the burgers still came wrapped in paper and you could buy them by the bag at ten cents apiece. The diner's motto was "Millions of people have eaten Royal Burgers," and it was written on every Royal Burger sign, just beneath the distinctive, familiar golden crown.

The mailman came in just then, his big postal sack slung over his shoulder. "Hi, Beverly," he said, handing her a small stack of envelopes.

"Hello, Mr. Johnson," she said as she took the mail from him.

He watched her carefully inspect each piece. He knew she was looking for something, but he didn't know what. Fred

Johnson liked looking at the pretty young Beverly Highland. He'd been on this beat for nearly twenty years, and in all that time had never once set eyes on a sight as refreshing as the girl who ran Eddie's diner. He'd once even thought of getting up the courage to ask her out, bowling maybe, but then had gotten the lowdown one day from Eddie: Beverly didn't date. She didn't have a boyfriend; in fact, she didn't seem to have any friends to speak of. What was she like? Fred had asked Eddie. But Eddie had had to admit that although she'd been working for him for six years now, he still knew about as much about her as he did the first night she had come into the store asking for a job.

Fred watched her hands shuffle the envelopes—long and slender and pretty they were. Like the girl herself. She amazed him. No matter how busy the diner got—and lately that was pretty busy—Beverly never had a hair out of place. She was always calm, quiet, and under control. Her uniform was always pressed with never a spot on it; she never raised her voice or got harried with the rush. She made him think of lemonade on hot days, or picnics under shade trees.

She sighed and laid the bills and notices aside. Fred decided that whatever it was she so diligently searched for every day, it still hadn't come. It suddenly occurred to him that if he knew what it was Beverly was looking for, he'd move heaven and earth to get it for her.

But not even Fred Johnson with his mid-life ardor could arrange that. What Beverly looked for in the mail every day was an answer to an advertisement she had placed in newspapers all over the country. "Naomi Burgess Dwyer," the announcement under Personals read: "Contact your daughter Rachel at 1718 Highland Ave, Hollywood, Ca." In four years there had been no reply.

"Can I get you something, Mr. Johnson? A Coke or something?"

She was like that. Always thoughtful and considerate. Since Fred stopped in at several doughnut shops and delicatessens on his mail route, he had plenty of opportunities to eat. But he never refused Beverly. He liked to watch her stand at the soda dispenser and fill the big paper cup. He liked to take it from her hand and say, "Thanks, you're an angel," and watch the way she blushed sometimes. That was what attracted old Fred to the unblemished young Beverly. Her innocence. You could tell just by watching her that she hadn't so much as ever been kissed.

After the mailman had left with his usual free drink, Beverly closed the accounting books and slid them under the cash register. Ever since Eddie got semirich, his wife, Laverne, had quit working at the diner and Beverly had taken over her job as manager of the store, and was still trying to make sense of Laverne's cryptic bookkeeping. It was for that reason that Carmelita sprang up frequently these days into Beverly's mind.

On that terrible night six years ago, when, as Rachel Dwyer, she had boarded the train heading for California, Beverly had vowed she would never set foot in Texas again.

But time, she found, does help you heal. Having lived since then in the company of kind and decent people, Beverly's bitterness toward Hazel had been tempered. From the perspective of the years and the miles, and Beverly's safe and respectable life, not to mention the security of savings in the bank, she was able to look back without feeling the old rage boil up inside her. She was able to recall her two years at Hazel's, and her friendship with Carmelita, with fondness, nostalgically almost, and lately found herself wondering more and more what had become of Carmelita, why she had stopped answering Beverly's letters.

But a trip to Texas was out of the question right now. Eddie was so busy planning new sites for future stores, and redesigning the diner to make it more efficient, more accommodating of cars, for example, that he left the running of the small company to Beverly. Not that she minded. It kept her busy from morning till night. It kept the loneliness at bay; it gave her an excuse not to spend time with the friends she had made in the diner. Being busy allowed her to concentrate on the only important thing in her life: revenge against Danny Mackay.

A young woman came into the diner and ordered two barbecued burgers to go. She carried a small child on her hip, and when Beverly took her money at the cash register, she said, "How old's your little girl?"

"She's nearly two," the proud young mother said. "Ain't you, Cindy?"

Beverly gazed wistfully at the child. Her own baby, if it had lived, would be five years old now. "Here," she said, handing the baby a peppermint candy cane.

"Say thank you, Cindy," the young mother said, and Beverly watched them leave.

Roy got up from his table, dropped a dime in the jukebox and paused to look at himself as Marty Robbins started to sing "El Paso."

"I don't know, Bev," Roy Madison said, sauntering up to the counter and throwing one lanky leg over a stool. "I work hard to look good. They just don't seem to want me."

She studied him with a serious expression. She wished he wouldn't keep playing that song on the jukebox. Outside the South, country music wasn't fashionable. She was glad of that, because it reminded her of things she didn't want to be reminded of. "Maybe you should change your looks, Roy."

He gave her a startled look. No one had ever said *that* to him before.

"What's wrong with my looks?"

"You were just saying you were thinking of changing."

He frowned. Yes, but Roy had said that because he had been fishing for compliments, not insults. Obviously no one had ever taught Beverly tact. He looked at her. Beverly's face was always so open. She never acted coy, or teased, or winked, or even smiled, hardly. She took life very seriously and, if asked, gave her most honest answer.

Which meant she really *did* think he should change his looks.

"Holy cow," he murmured, worried now.

But she came around from behind the counter and sat down next to him. "You've been told more than once that you look just like Fabian," she said quietly. "Maybe that's why no one will hire you. They already have Fabian. What they don't have is Roy Madison."

She had him interested now. No one, not his mother, his sisters, his string of roommates, his casual boyfriends, had ever suggested he should look any different from the way he did right now. Well, maybe this was just the advice he needed. "Yeah, but what *is* Roy Madison?" he asked, surveying his reflection in the mirror behind the counter.

Beverly studied him. "I don't know, Roy. Did you go to college?"

"No."

"You look like a college boy. You look like Bobby Rydell or Ricky Nelson."

"What's wrong with that?"

"It's too slick."

"Slick?"

"It's a dishonest look, if you aren't really like that." She frowned slightly. "You look like a man with something to hide."

"Hide?" He laughed a little nervously. "Me?"

"Don't wear your hair like that."

Roy brought his hand up protectively. "Hey, I work hard to get it just like this."

"I know. And it looks that way. It's not natural, Roy. It's not honest."

He looked at his reflection. How can a hairdo be dishonest? "What do you suggest I do to it?"

"Just be natural. Just be yourself. You aren't like any of those other boys. You have your own style. You shouldn't try to force yourself to adopt someone else's."

"But their style sells! It's what girls think is sexy these days."

"There are different kinds of sexy, Roy," she said quietly. "Some men weren't meant to have their hair combed like that. It makes them look phony."

He laughed. "What makes you an expert on men all of a sudden?" As far as anyone at the diner knew, Beverly hadn't gone out on a date in her life.

"Don't put all that grease on your hair," she said.

"It'll stick out all over if I don't!"

Beverly continued to study him in all seriousness. Well,

he had brought it up. If he hadn't wanted an answer, he shouldn't have asked. The mellow voice of Marty Robbins filled the little diner, bringing with it visions of mesquite and cactus, of Texas longhorns and steak barbecues, of tortillas and hot nights and dust and the moonlight on the San Antonio.

"Where are you from, Roy?"

That caught him off guard. Beverly Highland never asked a personal question. "South Dakota."

"Be natural. Be yourself. Don't try to look sophisticated, because you're not."

"And just how do I go about doing that?"

"You don't do anything. Leave your hair natural. Let the wind do the styling. Use baby shampoo and towel it dry. And let it grow over your ears a bit, it will soften the lines of your face."

Beverly looked up at the clock then and stood up. "I'm going home for a few minutes, Roy. Will you tell Louie to watch the store?"

As he watched her hang up her apron and pull on her sweater to leave, Roy looked at himself one last time in the jukebox chrome. *Baby* shampoo!

With the salary Eddie was paying her these days, Beverly could afford a car. But she didn't want to spend her money on a car, so she sat at bus stops and purchased monthly MTA passes. And even though she had long since moved out of Eddie's sister's boardinghouse—it was too noisy—Beverly had not moved into an extravagant apartment. She had chosen a modest little building of sixteen units off Cahuenga, behind Hollywood Boulevard. It was white stucco with the usual palm trees, and there was a tiny pool that wasn't worth jumping into. She could take the bus straight down Highland and be home in twenty minutes. Beverly had a more important use for her money. Every week she banked her paycheck. She doled out a small living allowance to herself, clipped coupons when she could, bought clothes at discount, and ate free at the diner. The dollars were slowly adding up. She was patient; someday she was going to be rich. And when she was, she was going to find Danny Mackay.

She got there just as Ann Hastings, her neighbor, was pulling mail from the box.

"Hi!" said the exuberant Ann. "Wow, a ton of Christmas cards. Over half of them from my mother's friends. Why does she do that, give my address out?"

Beverly smiled and proceeded up the steps. Beverly Highland, Ann noticed, rarely checked her mailbox. It was as if she knew there was never going to be anything in there.

"Haven't seen you for a while," Ann said, following her up the steps, clutching her brace of holiday envelopes.

"We've been busy at the diner. And Eddie's in Covina, looking for a site for a new store."

As Beverly put her key in the door to unlock it Ann came and leaned against the wall. "You know, I told my Dad all about Eddie's burgers. He said you could sell the recipe and make a bundle."

"Eddie's received offers to buy his secret recipe. But he doesn't want to sell." No one except Beverly and Eddie knew that it was really her recipe. And when he had been approached by someone wanting to buy the recipe and market it, Eddie had consulted with Beverly. But she had said, "Your hamburgers are special. If the recipe is available to everyone, then they'll stop coming to your diner." He had thought that good advice and so declined to sell.

"Yeah," Ann said, not making moves to leave when Beverly went inside. "I've had Royal Burgers. They're real good."

Beverly didn't close the door in the girl's face. She knew that Ann Hastings was lonely, and that whenever she could she would seize upon a neighbor and trap him or her into conversation. Beverly had seen some of the rude brush-offs Ann had gotten.

So she said now, "Would you like some iced tea?" And Ann jumped at the invitation.

It was just a one-room apartment, with a sofa-bed and a kitchen nook. But it had a nice sunny exposure facing the Hollywood Hills, and Beverly liked it. She had fixed it up with curtains and pillows from Pic 'n Save and that was all. Living for the future as she did, Beverly was content to make sacrifices now. It was also for the future that she practiced strict self-discipline. The first two years of working at Eddie's had put pounds on her frame. She had taken them off and kept them off. She ate modestly, just enough to sustain herself, and didn't allow herself to develop any expensive or addictive tastes. She neither smoked nor drank, nor went to movies. She didn't buy herself any luxuries; she didn't pamper herself. Discipline and hard work were the touchstones of Beverly Highland's simple life. All calculated to get her to the day when she would meet up again with Danny.

She had two exceptions to this rule: The first was her hair, which needed to be touched up every week so that the platinum looked natural. She did this to keep Rachel Dwyer buried, totally and forever. The second exception was books. Beverly spent money on books. But these were no longer mainly novels; they were nonfiction books from which she learned about success, about how to get ahead—stories of real men and women who, through guts, risk-taking, determination, and an instinct for what people want, made it to the top. Her current book was *Be My Guest*, by Conrad Hilton.

"How come you're home at this hour?" Beverly asked Ann out of kindness. There was nothing at all wrong with Ann Hastings except perhaps that she was too eager to be everyone's friend. Twenty-two years old, a little overweight and not terribly attractive, Ann tended to overcompensate by generating a personality that many found intrusive. But Beverly remembered what it was like to want to be accepted.

"I quit my job this morning."

Beverly looked at her. "Oh, I'm sorry."

"Yeah, so am I. My dad's going to kill me. And my mother's going to say I told you so."

Beverly knew Ann's story; anyone who crossed her path heard her story. The only child of overindulgent and overprotective parents in the Valley, Ann was trying to break away from them by going it on her own. With a degree in art from Valley State College, she had recently gotten a position at the Broadway department store on Hollywood and Vine as a window dresser. It was a decent job, but the problem was, Ann was very creative and desperately wanted some artistic freedom.

"I came up with this great concept for doing the windows this year," she said enthusiastically. "What do you think: Christmas in the movies!"

"I like it."

"Each window would be a scene from a movie—like *White Christmas* or *It's a Wonderful Life*. Even *Ben Hur*. I thought, I would make each window like a movie set, with costumes and everything. I've got a friend down at Western Costume, you know."

Beverly knew. Ann Hastings had "friends" everywhere.

"But my supervisor said no. Just Santa and his elves this year. So I lost my cool and said something I shouldn't have. I just got mad, Beverly. I can't stand being restricted, you know?"

"What are you going to do?"

She glumly stirred sugar into her tea. "I don't know. Diplomas in art don't exactly rake in the job offers. My mother wants me to move back in with them and pursue a master's degree. I can't live with them anymore, Beverly! They suffocate me!"

Beverly wouldn't know anything about that. She'd never been suffocated with love. "We lost a waitress last night," she said, "and I was going to start interviewing. Would you like to work for Eddie?"

Ann thought about it. Clearly, it didn't appeal.

"Free meals," Beverly added.

"I'll do it."

There wasn't anything to say after that, except speculate on what it was going to be like having the Kennedys in the White House. Ann asked Beverly if she had read Errol Flynn's *My Wicked, Wicked Ways* yet, and Beverly said simply, "I might get to it if I have time." How a movie star spent his time on bearskin rugs did not interest Beverly. But one man's climb up the ladder of financial success did. *"To accomplish big things . . ."* Conrad Hilton had written, *"you must first dream big dreams."* And dreaming was something Beverly had done all her life.

It was too priceless an opportunity to avoid going to her

own empty, lonely apartment, and such a treat to sit at someone else's table for a change, as if they were old friends, that
Ann was in no hurry to leave. And Beverly didn't mind. As
she watched Ann's pudgy hands sort through the stack of mail
she had received Beverly wondered if she should try writing
yet another letter to Belle and Carmelita. Her last one, two
years ago, had come back marked, "Moved—No Forwarding
Address."

"Oh, no," Ann groaned.

"What's the matter?"

Ann waved a letter in the air. "My cousin again! Jeepers,
I wish she'd leave me alone. My cousin is on the rich side of
the family. They have a house in the hills, and they're very
snobbish. Every year my cousin throws this massive Christmas
dance, and every year my mother forces me to go."

"Don't you like parties?"

"Oh, the dance is all right, it's just that all the other girls
my cousin invites arrive with escorts. *I* go with my parents. I
told my mother last year that I wasn't going to go anymore,
and we had a big fight. 'It'll upset your Auntie Fee,' she said.
'And make us look bad.' My mother just doesn't understand.
I'm twenty-two, Beverly, and I don't have a boyfriend."

"Neither do I."

Ann stared. She looked at the enviably slender body and
perfect platinum hair and gorgeous face and did not believe
her.

"It's true," Beverly said. "I don't have a boyfriend. If I was
invited to a dance, I'd have to go alone."

"How about that. . . ." Ann said slowly. Then, remembering the letter, she said, "But I have to go to this one and
I'll just die walking in with my parents. I swear Janet—that's
my cousin—does it just to humiliate me! We've been rivals
for years. Ever since we got a swimming pool before she did."

"Can't you find someone to go with you? Surely you must
know someone who might be willing to go, just to do you a
favor."

But Ann sadly shook her head. "I tried that when I was
nineteen. The guys I asked all thought I was on the make, as

if going to one dance with me meant we were engaged or
something. It scared them off. Well, this has certainly turned
out to be a doubleheader of a day!"

"You want me to *what?*" Roy Madison said that afternoon
during the brief postlunch lull.

Beverly was sitting at his table, sharing a plate of jalapeño
french fries that were on the house. She ate three; Roy polished
off the rest. "I was wondering if you would take a friend of
mine to a Christmas dance."

"Who?"

"One of my neighbors in my apartment building."

"Why can't she get her own date? Is she ugly?"

"She's a very nice girl."

Roy looked down at his hands. This was by no means the
first time someone had tried to set him up with a blind date.
His mother and sisters were doing it all the time. Because he
couldn't possibly tell them they were wasting their time, that
he just wasn't interested in girls—they didn't know about his
boyfriends—he usually had to suffer through evenings with
girls anxious to get engagement rings. He hated it.

"I'm sorry, Bev. I just don't think I want to."

"Is it because you're homosexual?"

Roy snapped his head up so sharply that his neck made a
sound. He couldn't speak at first. Then he said, "Holy shit,
Bev. What are you talking about? How do *you* know about . . .
that kind of thing?"

Ironically, she had first met homosexual men at Hazel's.
They went there to try to get themselves straightened out.
Once in a while a young man would come afflicted with doubts
and would buy a woman to prove to himself he was a real
man. They all ended up talking, believing that their words fell
on sympathetic ears. After all, prostitutes were just as persecuted as homosexuals were. And so Beverly had heard nearly
every story.

"Listen, Roy," Beverly went on in her quiet, serious way,
"Ann Hastings isn't looking for a boyfriend. This is just a
fantasy. That's all it is. And we need you to help her live it
out."

All Roy Madison could do was sit and stare at the ever-perplexing Beverly. Just when you thought you had her all figured out, she pulled something like this. "How did you know?" he asked quietly, looking around. "I mean, does it *show*?"

"I don't think anyone else suspects, Roy."

"Then how did *you* know?"

"Roy, Ann Hastings is lonely and unhappy," Beverly said, avoiding his question the way she sometimes did when she didn't want to tell the truth and couldn't tell a lie. "The party is a family affair, and she desperately wants to show off in front of a certain cousin. With you at her side she'd cause a sensation."

His eyes flickered to the polished chrome of the jukebox. "You think so?"

"You're an actor, Roy. Think of this as a part."

"Hey," he said slowly, a smile spreading across his face. "Not a bad thought."

"Then you'll do it?"

"Wait a minute. What's in it for me?"

"What do you mean?"

"Well, this girl gets to put one over on her friends and relatives, what do I get out of it? I mean, if she wants to hire me to play a part, then I think she should pay me."

"Pay you?"

"Yeah. Why not? I'm an actor, aren't I? And you're hiring me to act, aren't you?"

Beverly studied him. Actually, she thought, why not? For her money, Ann would be escorted by the best-looking man at the dance, she would no doubt be the envy of her Fabian-loving friends, and she would get Roy's undivided attention because there was no danger of his flirting with other girls.

"All right," she said. "You'll be paid."

Roy was a success.

Ann didn't need much persuasion to get her to agree to the thirty dollars. Once she took one look at Roy, when she started as a waitress at the diner the next day, the deal was sealed. And when he arrived at her apartment dressed to the

215

hilt, holding out an orchid corsage and driving Eddie's new Edsel, Ann decided it would have been worth a *hundred* dollars.

But the capper came at the party. Her snobbish Uncle Al had hired valets to park cars up and down the street, and even had a local band to play variations of the twist. The girls wore showy beaded crop tops and tight skirts, or Jackie Kennedy A-lines with bubble hairdos and stylish pointed-toed shoes. Ann had done her best in a simple Empire dress with the required long gloves. Janet Hastings greeted her cousin and was about to make a remark on the wonderfully slimming lines of the dress when she set eyes on the hunk Ann had arrived with.

He was like nothing she or any of her friends had ever seen before. While all their escorts wore black suits with white shirts and narrow ties, their hair slicked with Wildroot cream-oil into perfect pompadours, Ann's date wore chinos and a bulky cable-knit fisherman's sweater, and his dusty blond hair just sort of fell naturally, over his forehead and the top of his shirt collar, giving him a kind of shy, vulnerable look that melted almost every feminine heart at the dance. By evening's end, most of the girls were clustering around the intriguing Roy and trying to catch his eye. But he only had eyes, to their great astonishment, for the chubby Ann, which caused some of the guys at the party to wonder what it was she had to snare such a boyfriend like Roy. By the time she left she had given her phone number to four of them.

One morning a few days later Roy came into the crowded diner and ordered two Royals with extra cheese. Beverly was making a fuss over a customer's baby, tickling it and holding it up in the air, so he put "El Paso" on the jukebox and that got her attention. It always did.

"Guess what!" he said, coming up to her. "Remember that director I met at Ann's cousin's party? The one who said he liked my style and gave me his card? What do you think, Bev? He's offered me a part in a commercial."

"That's wonderful, Roy."

216

"Here," he said, reaching into his back pocket and pulling out his wallet. "This is for you."

Beverly looked down at the ten-dollar bill. "What's this for?"

"It's your cut. That thirty was the easiest money I've ever made. And I might get a job out of it, to boot. I owe you for it, Bev."

"You don't owe me anything, Roy. I just wanted Ann to be happy."

"Well, I owe you for my new look as well. Saw my agent yesterday. Her eyes nearly popped out of her head when I walked into her office. She says she thinks she might have something for me. So I owe you, Bev." He pressed the bill into her palm. She kept it.

Beverly went back to the cash register, where people were lined up to pay for their burgers. She felt the ten-dollar bill in her hand. It was going into the bank that afternoon.

20

"CODE TRAUMA MAJOR! Code trauma major!" came the voice over the public-address system.

Linda Markus, about to step into the shower, snapped her head up and looked at the speaker on the wall.

"Dr. Markus to Emergency!" the voice said. "Dr. Markus to Emergency!"

She picked up the phone, dialed the ER, and said, "I'm on my way."

After quickly pulling her surgical greens back on, Linda ran out of the on-call room, where she had hoped to take a shower and grab something to eat, and raced down the hall. She didn't bother with the elevator but flew down the fire stairs that delivered her, moments later, to the service entrance of the Emergency Room.

She found chaos. Nurses and technicians were hurrying about, rooms and beds were being readied, three residents in white lab coats came flying in, plus one surgeon in a jogging suit. Linda went straight to the emergency department's radio room. On the receiver she heard the wail of a siren and the voice of a paramedic shouting, "We've got four patients! Multiple stab wounds!"

"Oh my God," she said. "A gang fight!" She picked up the microphone and had to shout into it. "This is Dr. Markus. Can you triage?"

"Three are stabilized, Doctor. But the fourth sustained a stab wound to the left chest. Blood is spurting, pulse weak and thready, pupils dilated, eyes rolled back . . ."

"Get an airway down him! Apply pressure pants!" Linda looked at the nurse who had been monitoring the call. Their eyes met for an instant, then the nurse said into the microphone, "Estimated time of arrival?"

"Seven minutes."

"Damn," whispered Linda. "Can you get an intravenous started?"

"Negative, Doctor. The veins are all collapsed and his jugular's empty, and— Oh shit!"

"What is it?"

"No pulse!"

Linda and the nurse stared at the radio as they listened to the whine of the ambulance siren and the rapid exchange between the two paramedics. "Commencing CPR!" one of them finally shouted.

Linda dashed from the radio room and literally ran into the head nurse. "Get set up for a thoracotomy," Linda said. "I'm going to open his chest."

Six minutes later she heard the sound of the siren outside and heard the voice over the radio shout, "We're at your door!"

A team rushed outside and began receiving the stretchers just as three police cars came screeching up. Linda was snapping on her sterile gloves when she heard the thunder of feet down the hall and the head nurse saying, "Chest wound in here."

Linda's scrub nurse had set up the room for an emergency

thoracotomy: the sterile table was laid out with chest-opening knives and rib spreaders, long instruments, piles of sponges. The team hadn't had time to do a full scrub: they stood in whatever clothes they had been wearing when the call came; only their gloved hands were sterile.

The unconscious young man was hastily moved to the operating table; the anesthetist began at once to monitor his airway. While two pale-faced residents proceeded to cut into the veins in the boy's wrists and ankles, a technician stood ready with IV lines, bottles of saline and units of blood. Linda moved just behind the nurse, who literally poured a bottle of skin antiseptic over the chest; she cut an incision from the boy's breastbone down the side and to the back. As soon as the ribs were spread open, blood began pouring out.

Linda reached inside and took hold of his heart. It was empty.

She looked at the boy's face. He couldn't have been more than fourteen or fifteen years old.

He's so young, she thought as she desperately squeezed and released the heart. *Please don't let him die. . . .*

The room fell silent. Six grim-faced people watched Dr. Markus as she kept up the cardiac massage, her arm bloodied up to the elbow, a film of perspiration on her forehead. *Come on*, she pleaded. *Come on, live!*

"Might as well pronounce him, Doctor," the anesthetist said.

She ignored him. She closed her eyes. Half bent over the unconscious youth, her back aching, Linda kept up her relentless massage.

"His brain's been without oxygen for too long—" the anesthetist began.

"Wait," she said. "I think . . ."

Linda felt a slight movement in her hand. And then she felt the heart begin to swell.

She turned to the head nurse. "Is OR ready to take him?"

"The heart team said they're standing by."

"Tell them he has a lacerated left ventricle. I'll run a suture. . . ."

●   ●   ●

219

Two hours later she was sitting in the doctors' lounge of the surgical suite. Old Dr. Cane was dictating orders over the phone, and two surgeons dozed in chairs.

"Linda, you look awful."

She looked up from the patient's chart she was writing in, gave Dr. Mendoza a withering look, and said, "Thanks."

"Hey, no. I mean it, my friend. You look terrible. You're working too hard."

She sighed, closed the chart and settled back into the comfort of the Naugahyde sofa. The large color TV was tuned in to the six o'clock news; she stared at the screen without really seeing it.

"Well, José," she said wearily, "I *am* working too hard. This is my seventh straight day on ER call."

He winced. They all hated taking ER call. That messy business was usually relegated to residents and doctors new to the staff. "How come, my friend?" he asked. "Don't tell me you need the money!"

No, Linda didn't need the money. But she couldn't tell this handsome orthopedic surgeon with a social life that read like *People* magazine just what her needs were. Namely, that she needed to stay away from the loneliness that was haunting her house on the beach.

It seemed to lie in wait for her every night, that cold loneliness, hovering just on the other side of her salt-weathered front door ready to engulf her the minute she walked in and turned on the lights. It would rush at her in the same way the sounds of the eternal waves rushed at her, and she'd find herself standing in the entryway, among her driftwood and sea-gull sculptures, unable to move.

How could she tell this man, who had girlfriends galore and who went to parties every night, that she was afraid of her own house?

Emergency Room call gave her an excuse to stay at the hospital and sleep in one of the on-call rooms. It gave her something to do, kept her busy, worked her mind to the point of exhaustion, so that she couldn't think about anything else. Because St. Catherine's was located near the beach and on the

Pacific Coast Highway, the Emergency Room of the enormous medical complex handled more than a normal share of car accidents, surfing mishaps, muggings, and knifings. Linda was kept on her toes, examining, diagnosing, suturing, taking patients up to surgery. She drank copious amounts of strong black coffee, ate stale Danishes from vending machines, and was losing weight. The OR greens hung on her.

She felt José Mendoza studying her, but she ignored him. When he had first come to St. Catherine's three years ago, a hotshot sawbones whose patient list included famous athletes and movie stars, José had put the make on the single and somewhat aloof Dr. Markus. She had rebuffed him in a firm but friendly way. She had been a puzzle to him then, and she was a puzzle to him now. Linda wasn't married, he knew, and not dating anyone, according to the hyperactive hospital grapevine. All she did, it seemed, was work.

"Can I give you some advice, my friend?" he said.

She looked at him. José Mendoza was one of those men whose sexuality was enhanced by the drab, tacky operating-room duds. That, plus his sparky Latino charm, and it was no wonder that most of the nursing staff was in love with him.

"Well!" drawled old Dr. Cane. "Would you look at that?"

Linda and José turned to the TV.

The screen showed Danny Mackay coming out of the residence of a former president of the United States. A man who, to everyone's surprise, had just endorsed Danny Mackay as a presidential candidate. Danny was smiling and waving to the cameras, his arm around his wife's waist, a mob of reporters around them. It was the image of a man determined to make it into the White House.

"Would you look at that," said old Dr. Cane. "Who would've thought Mackay would have gotten *his* backing? That's sure to give the other runners in the race something to think about!"

"Think he'll get the nomination in June?" José asked.

Dr. Cane got up from the desk and headed for the locker room. "Wouldn't surprise me a bit. The man's practically becoming a national idol."

"He is a smart man, too," Dr. Mendoza said softly. "He's doing everything except coming out and calling himself the next John Kennedy."

They stared at the TV for a few minutes. Finally, the other two doctors left the lounge, and José and Linda were alone. He got up, turned off the TV, and looked at Linda. "How is your patient? The young gangster?"

"He's comatose, but liver and kidney functions are restored. I think he'll be all right."

José Mendoza regarded the woman on the sofa for a thoughtful moment, then he drew up the chair from the dictating desk and sat in front of her, elbows on knees. "May I talk to you, my friend?" he said quietly.

She smiled and reached up for the green paper bonnet that covered her hair. It felt good to take it off and let the cool climate-controlled air blow over her perspiring forehead. She had put the bonnet on early that morning for surgery and hadn't removed it since. "What do you want to talk about?" she said, wadding up the hat and tossing it into the waste basket.

"Why are you driving yourself so, my friend?"

She looked at him. Earnest and sincere eyes were gazing at her. "Why does any of us?" she asked quietly. "With me it's work. You drive yourself, too, in a different way."

He nodded solemnly. "I do not dispute that. The last time I was in my house was last weekend, when I needed my tennis racket. But at least my madness is recreational. You, my friend, are filling up your hours with work. This is not good for you."

She started to rise, but he stayed her gently with a hand. "Let me give you some advice," he said. "I have seen this before, what you are doing. Some people work themselves to death in order to forget something; others are trying to fill their lives with something. Others yet are running from something. But I tell you, my friend, this is no solution."

"And which are you?" she asked quietly.

He leaned away from her and gazed at the wall. "I was married once, back in the old country. But she died. And when she went out of my life, the light went out of my life. So now I surround myself with friends and I go to parties every night." His eyes came back to Linda. "But as I said, it is no solution."

222

She returned his gaze. Through the closed door came sounds of a busy surgical suite: gurneys rolling by, nurses calling orders, a voice paging softly over the PA system. Linda thought of Barry Greene. He had called again, asking her out. She had hesitated, wanting to go. But in the end she had declined, knowing that it could not lead to the bedroom. At least not yet. Not until she had worked out her problem, with Butterfly's help.

"Why don't you let me take you out to dinner," José Mendoza said. "We can talk about it."

She looked into his sincere dark eyes and smiled. "I'll be all right, José," she said quietly. "Thanks for caring."

Puzzled, he watched her go.

21

Texas: 1963

"Manuel nearly killed me this time! You've gotta help me, Rachel!"

The words in Carmelita's desperate letter echoed over and over in Beverly's mind as she sped along the highway in her blue Corvair, crossing from New Mexico into Texas, with the Tornadoes singing "Telstar" on the radio.

It had been five years since Carmelita's letters had stopped coming. And then all of a sudden, last week, an envelope had come to the diner, addressed to Rachel Dwyer. "We had a bad fight," Carmelita had written. "Manuel tried to kill me. I can't live like this any more, Rachel. You and I once promised to help each other if we were in trouble. I hope this letter gets to you because I'm in real trouble now."

Beverly had left the diner in the care of Ann Hastings and was now once again speeding across the vastness of Texas. For the first time in nine years.

Change was in the air. She could feel it. The world seemed to be moving faster and faster. The Russians had sent a man into space, everyone was dancing the twist, and bomb shelters were a national obsession. It seemed to Beverly that the world had arrived at a brink, as if the way of life that America had known for so long was about to alter suddenly, drastically, forever.

If asked to be specific, she would not have been able to do so. It was simply something she felt but could not see or touch. There were the signs for everyone to see: riots were increasing among oppressed Southern Negroes; folk singers were emerging from the Beatnik fringe and gaining public popularity; even the movies were changing, with everyone going mad for spies and secret agents. And Beverly seemed to see it all, as she gazed out at the flat Texas desert, against the formidable backdrop of a mushroom cloud.

Was that what was causing the change? The Bomb? The ever-increasing threat from across the ocean?

What, she wondered as "Telstar" ended and the Beach Boys launched into "Surfin' U.S.A.," had happened to the innocent, insular way of life of the last decade? And if this was only a threshold, as her intuition was whispering, then what lay beyond?

Whatever it was, whatever kind of future lay just over the horizon, Beverly knew one thing for certain: that she was going to be rich.

Earlier this year Eddie had rewarded Beverly with 10 percent interest in his company. With fourteen Royal Burger stands raking in profits, Beverly was beginning to receive handsome dividends. And when she had decided that her savings account wasn't growing as fast as she would like, she had taken Eddie's advice and bought one of the new tract houses out in Encino. She didn't live in it; she rented it out to a family. Already the value of the house was going up; the San Fernando Valley was undergoing a building boom. So she withdrew more of her savings and put down payments on two more little houses, renting them immediately. The three Valley houses were, at this moment, as she was whisking across the Pecos River, bringing in a positive cash flow. Beverly planned next to raise her sights to the new houses in the Tarzana hills, which were being built with views and swimming pools. They were selling for twenty thousand now; in ten years, Eddie guaranteed, they would be worth ten times that much.

However, Beverly continued to be careful with her money. When Eddie had tried to urge her into buying securities and bonds, she had held fast to her bank account. She could see that the San Fernando Valley was a boomtown; her own common sense told her that those investments were going to grow. But she shied away from the chancier gambles that Eddie and Laverne were getting into. And, by the same token, while Eddie and his wife had moved into a fancy new home, Beverly continued to live in the tiny apartment on Cherokee. Every dollar that she put away was a dollar for the future.

The blue Corvair that she now drove through the town of Sonora had not been new when Beverly bought it, and she had gotten it out of necessity rather than for convenience. As the regional manager for Royal Burgers, she was required to travel around Southern California and check up on the stores. Royal Burgers were up to fifteen cents apiece now; jalapeño fries, twelve cents. Quality control was essential for continued success. And Beverly wanted very much to be successful.

On this warm November morning, Beverly followed the same route to San Antonio that she and Danny had taken eleven years earlier. She was following it on purpose. The journey was like a bitter tonic. Each mile she covered injected new strength into her soul. As the west fell behind her and the Hill Country of Central Texas drew nearer she felt her body become invigorated with purpose. She saw familiar landmarks, she filled her eyes with sights that had thrilled an ignorant fourteen-year-old Rachel Dwyer, in love with Danny Mackay, racing toward her destruction. Beverly clutched the steering wheel and forced herself to remember those days of long ago; she kept the memory alive, she kept the anger and taste for revenge alive. *"You said you're a man who's going places,"* she had said to Danny the night he had thrown her out of his car. *"Well . . . I'll be richer and more powerful than you."*

The Beach Boys faded as a radio commercial came on. And then the San Antonio deejay reported the local news. "President John Kennedy, on a mission to smooth over a bitter fight between a Democratic bloc led by Governor John Connally

225

and a liberal coalition headed by Senator Ralph Yarborough, has arrived in Houston today as part of a nonpolitical tour of Texas. The president was met by cheering crowds as he drove by in his custom-made blue Lincoln limousine. He had requested that the protective plastic bubble be removed from the car so that he could stand and wave as he rode by. His wife, Jacqueline, is accompanying him on the tour, which will terminate in Dallas at the end of the week."

The landscape changed. The desert grew into mountains, farmland appeared. San Antonio, just up ahead.

Beverly sat for a long time in front of Hazel's house.

She hadn't driven directly here. She had first gone down the street where Bonner Purvis's house had stood and had found children playing in the yard, a dog barking on the front porch. What had become of them, Danny's strange angel-faced friend and his poor toiling mother? Then Beverly had gone down the street where a certain dismal brick building had once stood, where she had been forced to surrender her unborn baby nine years ago. But there was a new apartment building standing in its place, green stucco with flowerpots in the windows. Nonetheless, the memory remained alive. Bonner and his mother might be long gone, but the smell of dirty laundry and the creak of the iron bed where Danny used her every night were still alive in her mind. And the abortionist might no longer be here, but the flight of stairs with the light bulb at the end—it was all still here.

Beverly started up the motor. San Antonio was not the terminus of her long drive; Carmelita no longer lived here. The desperate letter had come from Dallas. Beverly was only passing through this town full of memories. She knew she would never need to pass this way again.

There were 270 miles between San Antonio and Dallas, so Beverly found an inexpensive motel along the highway and spent the night trying to figure out just how she was going to go about looking for Carmelita.

There had been no return address on the envelope. Out of fear, or perhaps having written the note in haste, Carmelita

had failed to say where she was living. On a slim hope, Beverly
looked her up in the telephone directory. She found one Carmelita Sanchez listed. Beverly dialed the phone but found she
had the wrong woman. All that was left to do was get to Dallas
and try to find her friend somehow. Nine years ago they had
made a promise to each other, and Beverly never forgot a
promise.

She arrived in Dallas on a Wednesday evening with two
fervent hopes: that she had come in time to save Carmelita,
and that she could persuade her friend to go back to Hollywood
with her.

After driving around for a while, and deciding on the most
likely locations where she would find her old friend—if, as she
suspected, Carmelita was still a prostitute—Beverly checked
into the Bar-None Hotel in one of the older sections of town,
not far from the red-light district. She wasted no time. As soon
as her suitcase was safely locked in her dingy room, she struck
out in search of Carmelita.

There was only one way, she had decided, to go about
looking for her. Beverly had to put the word out and hope that
some sort of grapevine would reach her old friend. Many of
the women in the streets looked upon the young blonde with
suspicion. Was she a cop? some of them asked. Others wanted
to know why she was looking for Carmelita. The majority said
simply that they had never heard of Carmelita Sanchez and
turned away. But Beverly persisted. She told each one of them
that she was staying at the Bar-None, and that she would wait
there for Carmelita. For the first time in nine years, Beverly
gave out her real name: "Please tell her Rachel Dwyer is looking for her."

It was a long and uncertain wait. Early on Thursday morning Beverly took a seat in the dark, shabby lobby of the Bar-
None, in an easy chair that faced the main entrance. She didn't
move except to go to the bathroom and to fetch a ham sandwich from the coffee shop next door. People came and went—
drifters, elderly residents on pensions, young people on their
own, a newlywed couple having a fight, two spinster ladies in
old-fashioned dresses. None paid much attention to the quiet
girl who sat with her feet firmly together, her hands in her lap,

her face set toward the door. The Bar-None was a place where you paid your bill and minded your own business.

She set out again that night, walking streets that other clean-cut middle-class girls avoided, but which held no terror for Rachel Dwyer. The hookers and their boyfriends stared at the girl as she walked past, wondered what she was doing there, asked themselves if she was looking for trouble. The way she walked up to them as if they were ordinary people on an ordinary street, and just spoke up asking about a whore as if she were asking for the time of day, surprised them. They didn't know that the soft-spoken girl was actually a sister, from long ago.

Still no cooperation, no information. She returned to the Bar-None tired and hungry. But undefeated. Beverly was determined; she was also patient. She would find Carmelita.

She was back in the easy chair on Friday morning, nursing a Styrofoam cup of coffee and listening to the news broadcast on the radio behind the registration desk. "President Kennedy gave a speech this morning," the announcer said, "to the Chamber of Commerce of Fort Worth. He and Mrs. Kennedy are now aboard Air Force One and are scheduled to land at Dallas's Love Field at eleven-forty. From there, the President and the First Lady will take a ten-mile ride in a motorcade through Dallas, where already crowds are lining the streets to greet them."

Beverly sat up. Someone was standing uncertainly in the doorway, looking around the lobby. A young woman.

Carmelita.

Their eyes met across the dim room. Then Beverly rose to her feet while Carmelita came slowly forward, a frown on her pretty face. As she drew near, Beverly felt a lump gather in her throat. The memories that rushed back!

Carmelita stopped a few feet away. "You the one been asking around for me?" she said.

Beverly nodded.

"My friends said you told them Rachel was here. Where is she?"

"She's right here, Carmelita," Beverly said softly. "Don't you recognize me? *I'm* Rachel."

Carmelita tilted her head. A look of puzzlement swept across her face. "You're not Rachel."

"Oh yes. I'm Rachel," Beverly said. "From Hazel's house in San Antonio. We last saw each other nine years ago, when you put me on the train for California. And we made a promise to send out a call if we ever needed help. You remember."

Carmelita narrowed her eyes. "You funnin' me? You ain't Rachel!"

"I am. I taught you to read. And you used to invent number puzzles. You and Belle and I, we were a threesome."

"Rachel?" Carmelita whispered, still uncertain.

"I have a tattoo on the inside of my thigh. A butterfly."

Carmelita's dark brown eyes flew open. "The butterfly!" she cried. "Holy mother of God! Rachel!"

She threw her arms around Beverly, laughing and crying at the same time, and the two embraced.

"I don't believe it," Carmelita said, wiping her eyes. "Rachel, you came. Just like you said you would. But . . . you're so beautiful now! What happened?"

"I want to tell you all about it. But first, Carmelita, are you all right? How badly did Manuel hurt you? Your letter—"

Carmelita looked around the lobby and said quietly, "Can we go somewhere for coffee?"

They went to a small roadside restaurant where the drivers of petroleum and cattle rigs devoured crunchy fried chicken and biscuits with honey. Carmelita polished off a plate of barbecued ribs and hot corn on the cob while Beverly picked at a salad and a cup of black coffee. Carmelita was reluctant to talk about Manuel, so Beverly told her old friend everything that had happened to her in the time that had passed since they stopped exchanging letters. When Beverly spoke about her plastic surgery, Carmelita studied her face with undisguised curiosity.

When she was done, Beverly said, "But what about you? Why did you leave Hazel's?"

"Oh, Manuel, you know, he got into trouble with the cops. We left real quick-like. In the middle of the night, you know. I called Hazel when we got to Dallas, told her where I was. I told her to forward my mail. She didn't. And I had some checks coming from puzzle magazines! The bitch."

"Why did you stop answering my letters?"

Carmelita washed off her fingers in her water glass and wiped them with a paper napkin. "It was like this, *amiga*. You and I, we wrote letters to each other for a couple of years. It was okay then, at first. We were still friends. But then, I started seein' how our worlds were drifting apart. There you were, living respectable with a job and everything, and me, I was still a hooker. It didn't seem right anymore—me still writing to you."

"But we still are friends, Carmelita," Beverly said softly. "Tell me what happened."

Carmelita twisted the paper napkin in her hands. She spoke quietly, from behind the curtain of long black hair that fell down the sides of her face. "He really scared me this time. We had a fight. Manuel's got this other girl. He says he can't be a one-woman man. I caught him with her and I got jealous. I hit him. He pulled out a knife—"

Carmelita raised deep brown eyes, eyes that Beverly remembered from years ago, full of the same pain and confusion, and shame. "You wouldn't believe it, it was his girlfriend who saved me. She jumped in and stopped him. He was aiming for my heart, but the knife went in here," she put her hand below her rib cage. "I spent a week in the hospital. The police came and talked to me. They scared me. They made me think he was going to come after me and kill me. So I asked a nurse for some paper and I wrote you that letter."

"I came the instant I got it."

Carmelita averted her gaze. "I wasn't even sure you would get it. I didn't know you were still working at that diner. I wish now I hadn't sent it."

"Why?"

Carmelita was beginning to feel self-conscious and uncomfortable. In the past hour she had come to realize that Rachel had changed in too many ways. She was respectable now, and clean. Rachel was quality now, Carmelita realized as she watched customers start to leave the restaurant in a hurry, while she herself was still trash. Even Rachel's name wasn't the same anymore. She was Beverly Highland. New name and new face. This was not a woman she had anything in common with. Carmelita suddenly realized she was sitting with a stranger.

"Hey, where's everyone going?" Carmelita said. She looked at her watch. It was nearly one o'clock. Then she remembered: The president's motorcade was due to pass by soon.

"Carmelita," Beverly said, "come back with me."

"Where?"

"To California. Come back with me and start a new life."

Carmelita gave her an astonished look. "You mean leave Texas?"

"Yes."

"Oh no."

Beverly's voice grew soft. "Carmelita, are you happy?"

The girl shrugged. "Who is?"

"You can be, if you come back with me. I can give you a good job. You can go to school. You would like California."

Carmelita shook her head.

Beverly laid a hand on her friend's arm and said, "Remember how we used to dream together? You wanted to go to school and then get a job in an office somewhere, with a typewriter and a telephone. You can do that if you come with me. Carmelita, in California fantasies can come true!"

Something rose up behind Carmelita's Spanish eyes, something Beverly had seen long ago on rare occasions. It was the look of someone seeing a vision, or a dream, or trying to imagine something. What Carmelita was experiencing was a brief hope, or the brief *possibility* of hope. And it *had* happened before, when she had learned to read her first words, when she had sold her first number puzzle to a magazine. There had been a split-second taste of hope, of dreaming for a better life, and it had shone in her dark eyes. But then it had quickly faded, just as it did now, because Carmelita was unused to hoping and dreaming, she was too long habituated to accepting the terrible lot that was her life. Hope was simply a skill she had never perfected.

"It's too late for me, *amiga*," she said, looking down at the shredded napkin in her hands. "I could never leave."

"Why not?"

"I'm too old. I'm twenty-five. And there's Manuel . . ."

"But you can't love him!"

Love? Manuel? Maybe once, years ago. Now he was just the man who protected her, who took her money and told her what to do. He was good to her when he felt like it, and he punished her when she deserved it. She couldn't leave Manuel. He made all her decisions for her, he even told her what to wear. She had been with him since she was thirteen years old. He was the other part of herself.

Carmelita rarely examined her life, she rarely thought about her own existence at all. She lived day by day, taking men up to her tiny room and selling her body in a kind of futureless void. After all, what was there to think about? Manuel did all the thinking for her. Like last night, when she told him she was pregnant again. All he said was "I gotta guy who'll get rid of it for you." Despite the criminal nature of her life, Carmelita Sanchez was a devout Catholic and she went to confession every week. Now she was going to have a really big sin to confess again—another abortion. But that was Manuel's decision. It would never occur to Carmelita to think for herself, to challenge his wish, to stand up to him and say, "No more abortions. I'm keeping this baby."

The two fell silent, Carmelita because she suddenly didn't know why she was here, Beverly because she so badly wanted to find the words that would persuade her friend to come away with her.

"Hey, listen," Carmelita said, rising, "I gotta go, you know? Manuel, he'll be wondering where I am."

As Beverly eased her Corvair through the traffic congestion near Stemmons Freeway, she said, "If you're afraid that Manuel will find you in California, you don't have to worry. He never will. You can change your name. Remember how you used to say you wished your name was Carmen? You can change your identity just like I did."

Carmelita cast her a nervous glance. Actually, that was a very real danger—Manuel coming after her. But that wasn't the only reason she wouldn't leave him. Girls like her, well, they just didn't give up the life and try to go straight. It just wasn't done.

There was something else Beverly wanted to say—that in a few years Carmelita was going to start losing her youth and her looks and Manuel was going to abandon her for someone younger, and then she was going to be completely on her own, a worn-out whore whom nobody wanted—but she knew Carmelita was already aware of that. She and Beverly had been aware of it nine years ago, when they were only sixteen.

The traffic was terrible. As Beverly inched her car past the Texas School Book Depository she searched for a way out. All of Dallas, it seemed, had turned out to greet the President.

She got stuck in the intersection of Elm and Houston. Cross-traffic blocked the way; she was penned in on all sides. Behind her a bus practically nudged her bumper, the driver leaning on his horn.

Carmelita cursed in Spanish, then said, "He can see we can't go nowhere! Why honk at us?"

Suddenly there was a brief opening in the traffic and Beverly pressed her foot down. The Corvair shot forward and the gap closed behind her, leaving the bus and its angry driver stuck like a dinosaur in tar.

Beverly immediately swerved down a side street and was able to get away from the crowds trying to glimpse the president. "I have to get back to Hollywood," she said to Carmelita on their way to the Bar-None. "I'll be checking out tonight. If you should change your mind about coming with me, I'll be there until six o'clock."

But Carmelita knew she wasn't going anywhere.

Danny Mackay pounded the bus horn and tried to nudge the blue Corvair out of his way. From what he could see, the blonde driving it wasn't looking for opportunities. She just sat there yakking with her friend while the cross-traffic continued to stream in front of her.

Finally there was an opening. He leaned on the horn and shouted, "Hey! Come on! Move!" And the little Corvair shot forward and disappeared down a side street.

"Man," said Bonner Purvis in the seat next to him, "don't this beat all?"

"Shoot, just 'cause old Jack Kennedy's come to town."

Danny anxiously tapped his foot and tried to find a way out of this mess. He hadn't come to Dallas to see the President. He was here to conduct important business.

Even though it wasn't too warm a day—just in the seventies—Danny was getting hot under the collar. Actually, he felt as if he were getting hot under the skin, he was that restless. Seven years they'd been at it. Seven years since dumping old Billy Bob Magdalene in the desert and taking off in his bus, and in that time Danny had made more money than he had ever dreamed possible. Although he spent a lot of the take from his nightly tent revivals on fancy women and hotels, he regularly put enough away to get him started on the glory road. Danny was in Dallas to see about buying some property, to take a look around and start making those contacts that were going to ease him up the ladder of success. He was thirty years old and he had money in the bank—it was time to start thinking less about preaching and more about ways to achieve his personal ambition.

The energy that had charged him back in San Antonio was driving him still. Danny's fame as a charismatic preacher had spread all over Texas; his meetings were so big they had to be held outdoors, there wasn't a tent large enough to contain them. People liked the agitated young preacher who could never sit still. Danny was forever in motion, fidgeting, moving his head this way and that; even when he sat back and talked in his slow drawl and gave that lazy-eyed look, one sensed the tension gathering within him.

He felt the power building in him again, the electricity just bursting to get out. Preaching wasn't enough anymore. *Texas* wasn't big enough. Danny wanted to *own* things; he wanted to control things. So he was in Dallas today to see a man about an office building, and maybe some apartments. Danny was property-hungry, and now he was financially able to start acquiring.

The sign on the side of the bus read DANNY MACKAY BRINGS

JESUS. It wasn't the same bus he stole from Billy Bob. This was a big shiny new model complete with bedroom, bathroom, and kitchen inside. Danny didn't as a rule drive the bus himself; that was Bonner's job. Danny had a white-and-chrome Lincoln Continental for his personal use. But since he had decided to sell the bus and settle down in Dallas, he was driving it to the buyer himself. In a way, Danny was going to miss the big sleek vehicle. He'd had some good times in it. But he wasn't going to stay here forever. And he had put a small bust of Napoleon on the dashboard to remind him of that. Power was his goal, and the tent circuit had merely been a stepping-stone.

"Look down there," Bonner said, pointing.

They were on the triple overpass. Down below, on Main Street, they saw the President's twelve-car motorcade. Sister Sue, one of the girls currently traveling with Danny, looked out a window in the back and squealed, "It's Jackie! Look, Marcia. There's Jackie."

"Shee-yit," muttered Danny as he braked at a stop sign and reached for his Camels. He admired and envied the Kennedys, knew exactly what made people go ga-ga over them, and expected to wield that kind of power someday.

Crack!

"What was that?" said Bonner.

Crack! Crack!

"Car backfiring," Danny said.

"Oh my God!" screamed Sister Sue. "Oh my God!"

"What—" Danny turned around and looked down. The President's limousine had stopped. Jackie was leaning over her husband; Governor Connally was strangely slumped in his wife's arms.

And then chaos broke loose. Suddenly, people were running, falling to the ground; a Secret Service agent was shouting at Lyndon Johnson's car, "Get down! Get down!" Jackie was up on her hands and knees, crawling over the back of the car.

And then the President's car was roaring off, the Secret Service car immediately behind with an agent standing up holding a submachine gun.

Danny stared in disbelief as the cars swept beneath the

underpass, and then, seconds later, when he saw them suddenly appear on the freeway, just up ahead, he said, "Holy shit!" and threw the bus into gear.

"Jesus, Danny!" cried Bonner, holding on tight. "The President's been shot!"

Sue and Marcia began to scream in the backseat.

Danny wasn't thinking; he had no idea what he was doing or why. He just raced after the two cars, slowing to sixty when they slowed to sixty, veering off Stemmons Freeway in close pursuit and down Industrial and Harry Hines boulevards.

When he saw the tan thirteen-story hospital up ahead, he realized what they were doing. The President's car raced up to the emergency entrance, and within seconds the two unconscious men were being placed on stretchers.

Danny brought the bus to an abrupt halt, sending his three companions vaulting forward. He flew out, knocking Bonner out of the way. "Hey!" Danny shouted, running. "What happened?"

But Secret Service agents stopped him; cops on motorcycles pushed him back. He stood and stared. Jackie was still clinging to her husband. There was blood on her skirt and legs. Danny saw her go through the double doors with the stretcher, and the agents took up positions immediately behind.

"What is it, Danny?" Bonner said breathlessly, running up. "Is he alive? Who shot him? *Danny!*"

"Oh God," Danny groaned. "I don't know. Christ, I don't know!"

More cars were pulling up to Parkland Hospital now. People were running up the sidewalk, some were shouting, some were crying, some walked like zombies in stone-dead silence. The police kept them away from the building. Reporters rushed through the double doors; a television news crew was setting up on the lawn as quickly as they could. There was a station wagon there now, from one of the big Dallas radio stations. People milled around helplessly, looking for guidance.

The President had been shot. The world had come to an end.

Danny looked around himself in shock. He saw a Negro woman kneeling on the grass, tears streaming down her cheeks. She was beating her breast and wailing. Others stood staring at the hospital, holding hands, their faces white, stunned. Danny saw Sue and Marcia stumble down from the bus, clutching each other. And the news crews were trying to get some answers.

How badly hurt was the President?

The crowd was growing. People were drawn to the hospital in order to be near their fallen leader. To Danny the chaotic scene looked like an anthill that had been kicked. There was no direction, no cohesion in this mob of panic-stricken Texans.

And then, all of a sudden, he saw it.

His place in history.

"Hey," he said. "Hey!" He ran to the bus and hauled himself up onto the dented hood. "Brothers and sisters in Christ," he cried with his arms outspread. "Join me in prayer for our beloved president."

Just like that, Danny had them. Here was someone saying something at last, here was someone standing out from the crowd, like a beacon, a man with the voice of authority, a man suddenly saying words they wanted to hear—familiar, comforting words—and they converged on him like bees on honey.

Danny looked down at the bewildered, hopeful faces and he knew what he had to do. They were like children, he thought. Lost little children. They were asking for someone to take them by the hand. They were asking to be led.

"I do not know what is going on inside that there building, my brothers and sisters," his voice rang out over their heads. "But I do know that the man who lies on that hospital stretcher is in desperate need of our prayers. We have to lift our voices up to God and let him know that we don't want Him to take John Fitzgerald Kennedy to His bosom today. We have to pour out our love and our need to God so that He sees how worthy we are."

"Amen!" someone shouted.

"We know who the world's going to blame for what happened today!" Danny cried. "They're going to blame Texas! But Texas didn't shoot our beloved president. The Devil did! It was the sin and corruption running rampant in our world today that shot John Kennedy! If that blessed man in there

237

dies"—he flung an arm toward the emergency entrance—"then it will be our sinfulness and godlessness that killed him!"

"Amen, brother!" shouted Bonner.

Danny was getting warmed up now, just as he did in his tent revivals. Once he got the heat started, there was no stopping him. He felt the power take over, he thought he was going to burst with it. His body felt as if it were soaring above the crowd; his voice rolled out and the words just came and came.

He dropped to his knees and clasped his hands under his chin. "Dear Father in Heaven," he called out, "please hear our prayers. We are all miserable sinners and we are deserving of Thy divine wrath. But we beseech Thee not to take John Kennedy from us today! We are like little children. We need our father!"

"Amen," people started to say. A few fell to their knees, hands folded in prayer. All faces were fixed on the charismatic young man kneeling on the bus, his almost-reddish hair glowing like a halo in the sunlight.

Danny had a beautiful voice. It commanded. It persuaded. It made folks change their minds about things. He also had another talent. He could cry.

The tears started to stream down his face now as he belted out his prayer to God. His voice broke in the right places; he sobbed uncontrollably in others. And the crowd cried with him.

The minutes ticked by. No word came from the silent hospital.

Danny jumped back to his feet and gave them his anger. "We have to show the Lord that we don't deserve such punishment. We have to show the Lord how much we love that man lying in that hospital. Brothers and sisters in Christ, let us now offer ourselves up in the place of our fallen president. Let us offer ourselves to God in his place! Let us vow on this very spot to give up a life of sin and Satan worship and promise to return to the path of righteousness—for John Kennedy's sake!"

The crowd went wild. They shouted up to God. They made promises, bargains, anything, so long as He let the President live.

Danny stood with the sun behind him, his arms out-stretched, his slender body shuddering with passion and magnetism. The radio news crew had taken up places close to the bus; his words were at that very minute being broadcast over half of Texas. From a distance away, while they waited for news from inside the hospital, a television crew aimed a camera at Danny and let the film roll.

"I tell you, brothers and sisters," he bellowed. "Make your peace with the Lord right here and now! Promise him on this very spot that you are ready to make sacrifices in order to save our beloved president! Brothers and sisters, ask not what your president can do for you, but what you can do for your president!"

"Hallelujah!" they screamed. "Amen, brother! Praise the Lord!"

Bonner Purvis stood to the side, stupefied. He had seen Danny deliver some rousing sermons, but none compared with this. He looked at the adoring expressions on the faces of the people as they gazed up at Danny. He saw how *his* they were, how ready to be used by him and led over any edge. It made Bonner think of those old news clips he had seen of Hitler.

Bonner suddenly recalled something that happened three years ago, on a day not unlike today. They had pulled their bus into some small town in the Hill Country, and Danny, nervous and agitated, had gone in search of something. That night, while the revival was at its most feverish pitch, Danny disappeared. He came back four hours later looking strangely pale and calm. The next day Bonner heard on the radio about a local physician, Dr. Simon Waddell, who had been found murdered—butchered—in his bed, and the police were questioning everyone in the area. Of course, if asked, a hundred people would have sworn Danny was in the tent that night around eleven o'clock. Danny knew the psychology of crowds, he could hypnotize them into believing any illusion. But Danny hadn't been there, Bonner knew. Not in the flesh, only in the thoughts of a religiously hysterical crowd. And months later the police finally chalked up the murder to a drug addict, whom Dr. Waddell must have surprised in the act of stealing narcotics.

As he thought about that night, and as he watched his best friend manipulate the mob outside the hospital as if they were puppets, and as he heard Danny shout the words—"Kennedy's spirit will live!"—that were going to launch him into instant celebrity, Bonner Purvis suddenly saw the future, and he shivered with excitement.

Carmelita Sanchez heard the news when she went into the nightclub where Manuel and his friends usually spent the day playing cards and arranging drug deals. She didn't make it as far as the back room, where Manuel was waiting for her to take her to the abortionist. The radio was on over the bar. The janitor was standing there like a department-store mannequin, leaning on his broom, staring at the radio, his eyes filling with tears. "At approximately one o'clock P.M. central standard time," the announcer was saying, "President John Fitzgerald Kennedy died at Parkland Hospital of a gunshot wound to the head."

Time suddenly ceased for Carmelita, just as it did for the rest of the nation. While cars were pulling over on freeways and schoolchildren were being sent home and the entire telephone system was jammed with calls, Carmelita came to a halt in the stale darkness of a Dallas strip joint. A voice was coming out of the radio and filling the club. The speaker wasn't identified, and it had been years since she had last heard that voice, so she didn't know who it was who was calling upon everyone to make sacrifices so that Kennedy might live.

Her own tears began to gather and tumble as a grief like none she had ever known overwhelmed her.

She stared at the radio and felt the power of the recorded speech race toward her in waves. It was a speech she would hear over and over again in the weeks to come, as it was replayed on every television and radio station across the country, the famous "Reverend Danny" speech that had been made spontaneously outside the hospital where Kennedy lay dying. The young prostitute was as moved and manipulated by Danny Mackay's powerful oratory as many other people were, and just as many other people were doing, she found herself thinking: Yes, I have to change my ways.

And then it hit her.

God did not want her to be a whore any longer.

Carmelita Sanchez was used to kneeling. She did it in sleazy hotel rooms with nameless customers; she did it in church every Sunday. This was the first time she had knelt on the linoleum floor of a striptease nightclub.

The day clerk behind the front desk of the Bar None Hotel was sobbing softly into her arms. Two old men sat on the Naugahyde sofa, their eyes glassy and staring. Beverly Highland had come to a halt in the middle of the lobby and listened to a familiar voice roll out over the radio waves.

He was here. In Dallas. Just a few miles away.

Like everyone else in America, Beverly was in some way affected by Danny Mackay's moving prayers. But Beverly was affected in a way that was different from the effect on everyone else.

Her body was stiff and rigid. She trembled slightly. Her head moved once or twice.

He was actually here.

She could get into her car and—

But she didn't move. Danny kept her nailed to the spot. He told her she should give up her life of sin and corruption. He told her to accept the love of Jesus Christ. He told her to make sacrifices for John F. Kennedy. He told her, *he* told *her*, to return to the path of righteousness for our president's sake. And while he told her all these things Beverly heard something she had heard in Danny Mackay's voice before, years ago— *power.*

And then she knew beyond a doubt that, as he had promised, Danny Mackay was a man who was going places.

He had foretold it nine years ago when he had thrown her out of his car. And here he was, using people, stepping on them in his maniacal climb to the top. He even used a dying president for a foothold.

As she stood in the middle of that dismal hotel lobby, hearing a car horn honking outside, someone running by in the street, the desk clerk sobbing softly, the voice of Danny Mackay on the radio, Beverly suddenly very much wanted him to become Someone.

Because someday he was going to fall. She was going to make him fall. And she wanted him to fall from the greatest possible height. No matter how long it took, she was going to be patient. She was going to wait and watch and see. And when the moment was right, she was going to return to Danny Mackay and push him over the edge.

"Rachel?" came a tremulous voice.

She turned. Carmelita was standing in the doorway, a carpetbag in her hand. "Rachel," she said, "I'm going with you."

March

22

SHE LANGUISHED IN THE BATH while massage jets shot hard pulsating streams of hot water against her naked body. She felt as if she were floating in a world of pure sensation. There wasn't an inch of her skin that wasn't caressed, warmed, softly lapped by the oily, perfumed water. The air was scented with jasmine, gardenia, and lavender; the ferns and moss and Madonna lilies in the indoor garden that filled a corner of the bathroom were heavy with dew from the mist of the bath. With a lazy hand she reached for a crystal stemmed glass and slowly sipped chilled white wine. Then she tilted the glass and let a little spill on her bare breasts. The sudden cold after so much heat was stimulating.

She closed her eyes and rested her head against the black marble. The sunken bathtub was very large; she could almost swim in it. The fixtures were gold and swan-shaped. Lush plants and tropical flowers grew in green malachite boxes all around the bath; the walls were mirrored with gold veining. At the foot of the black marble steps a carpet of deep llama fleece stretched away over the entire floor of the bathroom. A brass service cart held buckets of ice and a bottle of wine; the silver domes of the covered dishes preserved the freshness of Camembert and Brie, crunchy French bread, chocolate truffles, Italian pastries, slices of papaya, melon, and pineapple. There was even a silver samovar that kept the rich Viennese coffee

245

hot while allowing a little of the cinnamon aroma to escape into the steamy air.

When she felt a slight breeze brush her exposed shoulders, she opened her eyes. He was standing by the door, smiling. He had come in soundlessly. A beautiful young man with a well-muscled body and long blond hair. He wore a white tennis outfit and was perspiring; she thought he looked just like a champion after a victory at Wimbledon.

She watched him as he slowly, teasingly undressed. First the shirt, up over his head, causing him to stretch his torso. Then the shoes and socks. Finally the shorts. He was blond all over; he was perfection.

He climbed the steps up to the sunken bath one by one, deliberately taking his time. She watched his every movement, the ripple of every sinew and line of his body. He stepped into the hot water and stood between her legs, looking down at her. She saw conceit and vanity around his blue eyes and thin-lipped mouth. She felt her breath catch in her throat.

He knelt in the water and, with his hands resting gently on her knees, leaned forward and kissed her. His mouth was sweet.

They kissed for a long time, entwined and floating in the perfumed water, sending trickles over the sides and down to the thick llama rug. Then he stood again, this time straddling her with one leg on either side of her. She reached up and stroked him, bringing him to full erection. The condom had already been placed near the bath. She liked this part, putting it on him. When it was on, she sat up and took him into her mouth. She tasted a pleasant flavor—cherry. That was a nice touch.

The door across the bathroom opened silently again. The man who entered this time, quietly closing the door behind himself, was very dark, nearly black. While her mouth made gentle, intimate love to her tennis player, who stood over her, she watched the second man undress. He, too, was beautiful, perfection.

He stepped up into the enormous bath and slid down behind her, cradling her between his legs, his hands on her breasts, while her blond lover knelt down and entered her in the hot, oily water.

She closed her eyes again and delivered herself up to the delicious sensation of pure pleasure. Her two lovers kissed her, caressed her, left no inch of her body unexplored. Her back rested against a hard, muscled chest, strong arms came around her waist, and rough, callused hands held her breasts, while another strong, hard body moved between her legs, his hands gripping her thighs, his mouth on hers, sucking the breath out of her, his thrusts sending jasmine-scented water lapping over the sides of the bath.

She cried out more than once.

The three moved as one. They drew her up out of the water and led her down the steps onto the soft llama fleece. Her blond lover filled a glass with wine and dipped her nipples in it; then he sucked them clean. He drew her down to the carpet and pressed her onto her back while he knelt at her side and continued to kiss her bruised lips. She held on to him, her fingers tangled in his long platinum hair.

Her second lover retrieved something from under one of the silver domes on the service cart. He fed her a chocolate-dipped strawberry.

The rest of the food was now consumed; they paused in their lovemaking to savor the gourmet excellence of Butterfly's kitchen. The two men fed her, taking morsels from each platter and feeding them to her in erotic ways. They drank the wine and then the coffee and shared the creamy sweet richness of the Italian pastries.

They both entered her one last time, taking turns, going slowly, reserving their own climax so that her pleasure could be prolonged until finally she spoke the first word uttered in over three hours of lovemaking—it came out in a deep, contented sigh: "Enough . . ."

23

Hollywood: 1969

ANN HASTINGS WANTED TO GET LAID more than anything in the world. It was a terrible thing, she decided, to be thirty-one years old and *still a virgin*. Especially in this day and age!

As she pulled her Mustang into the reserved space in the small parking lot behind Tony's Royal Burgers (Eddie kept the sign for sentimental reasons) she thought of all the girls she had just seen up and down Highland Avenue, in embroidered blue jeans, barefoot and long-haired, their hips and thumbs thrust out in hopes of a ride. And a ride was what they usually got!

Ann sometimes found herself bewildered by this new age. She frequently felt as if she had fallen asleep years ago and had only just now awakened, a stranger in an even stranger land. Like a Ms. Van Winkle. There were revolutions going on all around her: racial, antiwar, cultural, sexual. . . .

Sex was definitely on her mind these days.

How could I not help thinking about it? she asked herself as she walked through the rear entrance of the diner, waved to the workers, and headed for the door labeled PRIVATE. With movies out now like *Midnight Cowboy* and *Hair*, and posters for *Oh! Calcutta!* everywhere, displaying flesh, flesh, flesh? TV news casts had shown the kids at Woodstock, naked, making love in the grass, free and happy. Women were now taking the Pill. They were allowed at last to be sexual aggressors. It was an age of free love and liberal sex. For God's sake, *everyone was doing it!*

Well, maybe not everyone, Ann decided as she quietly entered the office and closed the door behind herself. Beverly was at her desk, going through the morning's mail. Carmen was at the other desk, her fingers flying over the adding machine.

They didn't seem to be involved in the sexual revolution.

How many years had Ann known Beverly Highland? Ten, she calculated. They had met in 1959 in that old apartment building on Cherokee. But even though they had worked together for Eddie in the years since, Beverly still remained something of a mystery to Ann.

Amazingly, there wasn't a man in Beverly Highland's life even though she was positively beautiful. Not just in her looks, which were stunning, but in the way she walked, in her manner, in her *soul*, Ann thought. Beverly just seemed to walk right and talk right; she was gentle and poised and soft-spoken. And she looked absolutely perfect in her Mary Quant miniskirt and white patterned tights. She even carried off the old-fashioned French twist in this space age of Sassoon and Nigel Davies hairstyles.

And Beverly was also financially well off. Not exactly rich, but she had made some wise investments out in the Valley, plus she owned part of the Royal Burger chain. She had to be one of the most desirable, the most eligible young women in L.A., and yet, as far as Ann knew, she was not involved with a man. In ten years Beverly had not had a boyfriend. She had not even dated. Beverly's entire life, Ann had come to learn, was devoted to work. In fact, she was so dedicated to work, and put in so many hours running Royal Burgers, that Eddie and Laverne had stepped out of the picture almost altogether.

Why, Ann wondered now as she had wondered many times before, did Beverly avoid men?

And then there was Carmen Sanchez, the company's bookkeeper. On that first day six years ago when Beverly had brought Carmen into the diner and announced that she was going to be working with them, Ann had thought, *Aha!* believing she had her answer at last. Beverly must prefer women, it was that simple. But then Carmen's belly soon swelled and when she went into labor she cursed a man named Manuel.

In the five years since the birth of little Rosa, Carmen led a celibate life. She, too, didn't seem to want anything to do with men.

But at least, Ann thought now, Carmen had known a man, if only once. Ann wasn't so sure about the intensely private

Beverly, who never let anyone get socially or physically close to her. Was it possible, Ann wondered not for the first time, that Beverly was as sexually innocent as herself?

"Where's Debbie?" Ann asked as she threw down her purse, sank into the sofa and put her feet on the ottoman.

Beverly didn't look up from the mail she was reading. "Debbie's left us."

Ann groaned. *Not another one.*

"Where did she go? San Francisco?" That was where the last two secretaries had decided to run off to.

"I don't know. She just came in this morning, announced that she was no longer Debbie Schwartz but Daffodil, and that she was going to go out and find her karma."

Ann shook her head. They were having a hard time keeping good employees.

Beverly finally looked at her. "How did it go?"

"There was a little trouble in the Reseda store, but I cleared it up by firing the manager and putting the assistant manager in his place. I think she'll work out. We should get no more Health Department complaints on that horizon."

"Anything else?"

Ann massaged her feet. She was now the regional manager for Royal Burgers and had to make frequent rounds of the fourteen stores. Her particular responsibility was quality control—she made sure that the same high standards were maintained at all the outlets. "Well, Carmen was right. Sales are falling off in all of them. Ever since McDonald's came out with the Big Mac last year, Royal Burgers has been steadily losing customers. All my managers agreed we should come out with a double burger. I also think we should install the new microwave ovens in all the stores."

Beverly nodded and jotted something on a piece of paper.

Her desk was a mess, which was very unlike Beverly, who was punctiliously tidy in both her person and her home in the Hollywood Hills. Ann had visited the Spanish-style house several times and had never failed to be impressed with the orderliness of it. Beverly insisted upon the same discipline in the Royal Burgers stores. Dirt and untidiness had no place in her life.

But because she couldn't seem to keep a secretary, and because Eddie was no longer interested in being involved in his own company, Beverly had the constant job of keeping from being overwhelmed by paperwork.

Part of which, this morning, had to do with going through the contents of the thick envelope from her clipping service.

This was another mystery about Beverly that Ann often wondered about. Her obsession with Reverend Danny Mackay.

Ann was very familiar with the flamboyant Texas preacher. Anyone who watched the news or read the papers or went into bookstores recognized that famous smile. Ever since his stirring speech outside Parkland Hospital in Dallas back in 1963, Danny Mackay had become something of a celebrity. And now, with his new book, *Why God Took the Kennedys*, on the best-seller list, his fame was growing.

Ann didn't know what Beverly's connection with the charismatic Reverend was, but she suspected Beverly might have actually known Danny Mackay at some time in her past. Whatever the relationship was, Beverly was very private about it. She was also obsessive about it.

Take this clipping service, for example. Beverly had contracted with them six years ago, upon her return from Dallas. "Anything on Danny Mackay," she had told them. It didn't matter how slight the mention, or in what paper, they were to send her the clipping. Beverly spent one morning a week going through that thick envelope and poring over the news items of Danny Mackay's activities. Beverly sat there now at her desk, studying the clippings with an intense look on her face, reading about Danny's tour in Vietnam, where he was preaching to the troops.

Ann got up and went to the small office refrigerator. Taking out a can of Metrecal and slowly pouring it into a glass, she went back to thinking about sex.

It was absurd that she was still a virgin. And Ann couldn't really say why she was, except maybe that she didn't have much opportunity to meet guys who appealed to her. Her job at Royal Burgers kept her pretty busy, and when she did find herself in a social situation, she always seemed to be out of place. After all, she was thirty-one, over the age to be trusted.

She felt old in this suddenly youth-oriented society. Anyone who had gone to high school in the fifties, it seemed, was a dinosaur. With so many nubile and willing young girls around these days, plumpish, thirtyish Ann Hastings didn't stand a chance.

That is, until she met Steve.

Steve Fowler was a professor of political science whom she met at a recent antiwar rally in Century City. They had nearly gotten arrested together and had only just escaped the police batons by jumping into his VW and racing away from the scene. They had gone to a vegetarian restaurant for some meaningful dialogue; one thing led to another, and before she knew it, Ann found herself accepting his invitation to go to his apartment sometime and smoke grass.

And tonight was the night.

She wasn't in love with Steve by any means; she wasn't even particularly attracted to him. But he was bright and intelligent, a man of conscience (he had been reprimanded last year for telling his students to march out of the classroom and not come back until Nixon had called all our troops back from Vietnam), and he had breezily declared that he liked "Rubenesque" women.

He was also older than herself, and hinted at being a very experienced lover.

That was when Ann had decided to take the plunge and find out what it was she was missing. At last certain Mysteries were going to be revealed to her tonight, and she could hardly contain her excitement.

"If you don't need me anymore . . ." she said when she'd finished the Metrecal.

Beverly smiled and said, "Take the day off. You've earned it."

Ann laughed and hurried out. Take the day off! Hardly! She had too many things to do before getting to Steve's place at six: buy a new outfit, get her hair done, splurge on a manicure, and finally get on over to Family Planning for the diaphragm. . . .

The adding machine went clackety-clackety-clack and delivered up its bad news. Carmen pulled the long tape out, tore it off and frowned at the final figures for a minute before turning around and tossing it onto Beverly's desk.

"We're going to be in trouble real soon, *amiga*," she said, "if Eddie doesn't do something and fast."

Beverly didn't need to read the tape. This was a subject they had been discussing for a long time now, ever since harsh reality hit home: that McDonald's and Kentucky Fried Chicken were rapidly taking over areas Royal Burgers had once monopolized.

It was a frustrating situation. Once Eddie had made enough money to provide him and Laverne with expensive new toys and unlimited travel, he had lost all interest in his company. "You run it," he had told Beverly two years ago when he had waltzed out of the diner jingling the keys to his brand-new Lincoln Continental. As far as Eddie was concerned, as long as Royal Burgers kept him in cars and boats and airplane tickets, he wasn't going to bother himself with the company anymore. And he knew he could trust Beverly to see that Royal Burgers continued to turn a profit. She was a hard worker; it was all she did, work. It left him free to play.

The problem was, as long as Royal Burgers was the only place in town that served good, tasty food at cheap prices in clean, reliable surroundings, well, fine. But now the other fast-food chains were moving in and Royal Burgers was starting to lose. Badly.

Beverly had tried last year to talk Eddie into going public. "Put the company on the New York Stock exchange. Franchise it out. We can be just as big as McDonalds."

But for Eddie that only spelled work. And he wasn't interested. "Naw," he said. "Royal Burgers is a family affair. We don't want no strangers involved. We keep close tabs this way. We're doing fine. Folks have been chowing down your spicy burgers and fries too long for them to stop now. They're, like, addicted, right?"

Wrong.

Big burgers and more variety were what the public wanted now. And Royal Burgers, in order to survive, was going to have to change with the times.

"It doesn't look good, Beverly," Carmen said as she opened

the fridge and took out a Fresca. The shelves were packed with
the green-and-blue cans, and in the storeroom there were cases
of the diet soft drink stacked to the ceiling. When the news
broke that cyclamates were going to be banned, Beverly had
ordered as much of a supply of Fresca and Diet-Rite as they
could store. Sugar substitutes, rumor said, were going to be
bitter and unpalatable from now on.

"Where's Eddie?" Carmen said as she took a seat on the
sofa Ann had just vacated.

"Where else? At Santa Monica airfield."

That was their latest toy: a Cessna 172. He and Laverne
were taking flying lessons.

"Are we going to come out with the Crown Burger?"

"We'll have to. And we'll underprice the Big Mac by four
cents."

"What about chicken?"

"If we do decide to introduce chicken, it will have to be
in a different form. Barbecued, maybe."

Beverly's face took on a look of deep involvement, an
expression Carmen knew well.

In fact, unlike Ann Hastings, Carmen knew everything
there was to know about Beverly Highland. She knew what
the clipping service was all about.

Carmen had come a long way since her days as a Dallas
hooker. She had a college degree now, was working on her
CPA, lived in a nice apartment in Westwood, had a bright and
healthy little girl, earned a good salary as Royal Burgers' accountant, and had good friends in Beverly, Ann, and Roy Madison. But she, too, like Beverly, could never let the old hatreds
and angers die. The wounds were too deep, the memories too
painful. She knew that Beverly lived for revenge against Danny,
that every move she made—even running Royal Burgers—was
calculated into her long-range plan to make herself rich and
powerful, and someday to make him pay for what he had done
to her. Carmen sympathized. She, too, had a dream of someday
seeing Manuel get what he deserved.

And, like her best friend, Carmen was done with men
forever.

Back in Dallas, on that fateful November day, a lot of

people had impulsively turned over new leaves. Kennedy's death had suddenly upset the equilibrium of the world. People had felt cut off, abandoned. They sought ways to atone for the sins they were apparently being punished for. Crime dropped in the days following the assassination; church attendance skyrocketed; old grudges were forgiven, debts erased, apologies spoken, rifts mended. Vows and promises were made, to God and to one another. People suddenly examined themselves and weren't pleased with what they saw. Many, like Carmen, experienced an almost religious revelation. They were going to change.

But then, as the shock wore off and the world returned to normal, the oaths and pledges faded from memory and most people reverted to their old ways. But not Carmen Sanchez. The unexpected and untimely death of a man she had loved and respected had made too deep of a mark upon her. She had kept her promise to God. She was going to be pure from now on.

There were times, however, when she felt charitable toward the world—such as when she had received praise from her teachers at Valley College, or the day she had graduated from the UCLA Business School, or the day Rosa had entered kindergarten—and Carmen had softened her judgment against society. And on such infrequent occasions she would look at the intense Beverly and feel sorry for her.

Carmen knew what dragons haunted Beverly Highland. She knew how desperately Beverly loved babies—look at how she smothered Rosa with affection—but could never have children of her own because of what Danny had done to her. And Carmen knew that Beverly had once calculated when her baby would have been born and mourned that never-to-be-birthday privately every year.

Carmen studied the head bent over news clippings of Danny Mackay, the platinum-blond hair shiny beneath the overhead lights, and she wondered what that day was going to be like, when Beverly finally met up once again with Danny.

"You okay for a while?" Carmen asked when her Fresca was finished. "I have to get over to the school and pick up Rosa."

Beverly looked up and smiled. "I'm fine, Carmen. And bring her back here. I have a present for her."

"Again? You're going to spoil her before I get a chance to!" Carmen marched out with the armload of books she was studying for the upcoming CPA exam.

When she was alone in the office, Beverly returned to the news clipping she had been studying. It was a report of an incident that had taken place out in Victorville, in the Mojave Desert.

The small headline read: LOCAL WOMAN BLAMES DANNY MACKAY FOR DEATH OF HUSBAND.

Beverly memorized the name: Mrs. Maggie Kern. Then she opened a drawer and withdrew a map of the State of California.

Ann realized she was scared to death. Which was ridiculous, of course, because, after all, sex was as natural as eating or sleeping. And everyone did it.

She tried very hard to be cool about the whole thing. She sat in Steve's surprisingly messy (and disappointing) apartment, politely listened to Pink Floyd turned up too loud, drank the jug wine, sat cross-legged on the floor even though he had furniture, and nodded through Steve's long-winded discourse on Baba Ram Das and the psychedelic movement. Steve used words like "far-out," "groovy," and "blow your mind." He had Peter Max posters on his walls, candles in the shape of genitals, and a variety of roach clips strewn on the coffee table.

When she was well into her fourth glass of wine and trying not to be deafened by the Grateful Dead, Ann started to realize something. That Steve, with his graying beard and school ring and Bulova watch, was a fake. Still, he was a man. And he *had* promised her some "good sex" after they smoked a couple of joints. And anyway, he was now pawing her, which meant it was time to go into the other room and do something about her diaphragm.

When she had first come into the apartment, she had put her purse and coat in the bedroom. She went in there now and closed the door.

"The closer to the time of intercourse that you insert the

diaphragm," the nurse at Family Planning had instructed, "the better. Of course, you can put it in hours ahead of time, but the spermicide will lose its effectiveness."

Ann was being extra cautious. The last thing she wanted was to get pregnant.

She quickly removed her panties and stuffed them into her purse. She was hurrying. Out in the living room the music had changed to something mellow, which meant Steve was ready and waiting for her. Ann wanted so badly to appear cool and experienced. She would die if he guessed this was her first time.

The diaphragm was like a miniature Frisbee, but soft and rubbery in the center with a rigid rim. Taking out the tube of jelly, she smeared it generously around the rim and added extra in the center. Then she discreetly returned the tube to her purse. She wouldn't want him to come in here and find it. Birth control was uncool. It was square. It took the spontaneity out of sex, which was supposed to be done with a free, un-hampered spirit.

"You fold it like this," the nurse had shown her. "Hold the diaphragm between two fingers, and squeeze the rim to-gether like this. This is for insertion. Once it is inside your vagina, it will spring open and fit snugly over your cervix."

It had looked so easy in the doctor's office. But now Ann's hands were shaking and she had used too much jelly and the damn thing wasn't cooperating.

Finally she got it squeezed together like a taco, and just as she was bending over to insert it the diaphragm shot from her fingers, flew across the room, landed smack against the wall and slid down behind the dresser.

She gazed at the wall in horror.

"Ann?" came Steve's voice from the other side of the door. "You okay?"

"C-coming!"

Hastily smoothing her skirt down, she went to the door and opened it.

He was stark naked and had an erection.

"Um . . ." she said.

Steve took her hand and led her back into the living room,

where Donovan was singing something nice. Ann's heart was pounding. She had never actually seen a penis before. Not in real life. Of course, these days they even showed up on posters. But the last time she had experienced any intimacy with one was during high school gropings fourteen years ago.

Steve drew her down onto the enormous madras cushions and began kissing her.

Ann tried to throw herself into the part. She made all the moves and went through all the motions of making love and tried to get herself sexually aroused (because he certainly wasn't doing it), but all she could think of was that diaphragm behind his dresser and how unprotected she was. Maybe she should stop him, she thought, as his hand went right to the heart of the matter.

But she had come so far, and she was curious, and so desperate not to be a freak anymore, in this age of no more virgins. . . .

"Wait—" she said breathlessly as he was suddenly poking into her. It was too soon. She wasn't ready. Her blouse was still buttoned. He hadn't made a single foray under her bra, which was what she needed.

Steve was on top of her, his eyes closed, trying to get inside her with an urgency that alarmed her.

She reached down to divert him. He mistook her intention, murmured, "Oh baby!" and came in her hand.

Maggie Kern's house stood in a new development where young families were still putting in lawns and where fences had not yet made strangers of neighbors. The news clipping had given out the woman's address, and Beverly found it with no difficulty.

She rang the bell and heard a baby cry.

When the door opened, Beverly found herself looking into a very pretty face framed with frizzy red-gold hair. But the green eyes were sad, very sad, and puffy from crying. Maggie Kern held an infant in her arms. "Yes?" she said.

"Mrs. Kern?"

"Yes."

"My name is Beverly Highland. I was wondering if I could talk to you for a few minutes."

"I'm sorry. Whatever it is you're selling, I'm not interested."

"I'm not selling anything, Mrs. Kern," Beverly said gently. "I read your story in the paper."

Something flared behind the green eyes. Maggie said, "I'm not talking to any more reporters!" and started to close the door.

"Please," Beverly said. "I'm not a reporter. You see, I once knew Danny Mackay. Years ago. I understand what you are going through."

The living room was very neat and clean and furnished with furniture that still smelled of the warehouse. Maggie and her husband, Joe, Beverly was soon to learn, had moved here from San Diego only four months ago. It was their dream house. Joe had even started building a playhouse in the yard for the two children.

Maggie made a pot of coffee and brought out a fresh pecan pie. The baby was wedged safely on the sofa between two cushions, and Beverly couldn't keep her eyes off him.

Maggie, Beverly found, had no difficulty in talking about the incident. In fact, she seemed to want to talk about it.

"Joe had this heart condition, you see. That was why we left San Diego. His doctor told him he was under too much stress. That we should move to an area where the pace was slower. Joe was older than me. He was forty-two and I'm twenty-six." She picked up the baby and held it to her breast. "Joe was a decorated war hero," she said quietly. "In Korea."

She went on to tell the story that Beverly already knew from the clipping. How Joe had gone to specialist after specialist looking for a cure for his problem, only to be frustrated at every turn. And then, two months ago, Danny Mackay had come to Victorville. The famous Danny Mackay who was at this moment over in Vietnam delivering sermons to demoralized troops.

"He set up his tent outside of town," Maggie said. "Everybody went mostly out of curiosity. I'd never been to a tent revival before. Joe and I are Christians. We go to church every Sunday. But this was something new. And besides, we had heard that Danny Mackay had been known to do some healing."

Beverly already knew that also, from her clippings. They were filled with scattered items from newspapers all around the South: Danny Mackay driving devils out of a hysterical woman, making a paralyzed child walk again. He had even made the outrageous claim that he had brought a man back from the dead.

And people were believing it.

People like this poor woman with the baby in her arms. "Joe and I went to Danny's meeting," Maggie said. "I went out of curiosity. But Joe . . ." She sighed and her eyes grew moist. "I know that deep in his soul he was hoping Danny could cure him. We had heard of his miracles. . . ."

Beverly knew the rest. The meeting had been a rousing one, typical of Danny Mackay's frenzied religious revivals, and Joe Kern, in a moment of impulse, had jumped up and run up to the stage, begging to be cured. It was quite a dramatic moment, witnesses had reported, with Danny laying on hands and Joe fainting dead away. But what witnesses did not tell the police or the reporters was that Danny had instructed Joe to throw away his heart medicine. No sir, no one had heard Rev. Danny say that.

But Joe Kern had heard him say it and he'd done it—thrown away his medication because Reverend Danny had told him he no longer needed it and that to continue to take it was a sign of faithlessness before God—and a week later Joe Kern had a massive coronary and was dead.

Maggie had gone wild with grief. She'd gone to the police and the newspapers, accusing Danny Mackay, who was still in town, of murder. But Danny had strong connections with certain officials, and so no investigation was ever organized, and the next day Maggie Kern was fired from her job.

"I know Danny Mackay told them to get rid of me. First he killed my husband, and now he's trying to kill me!"

Beverly brought a linen handkerchief out of her purse and pressed it into Maggie's hand. The young widow cried for a few minutes, then brought herself under control again. "I'm damn good at what I do, Miss Highland. I'm an executive secretary. I type ninety words a minute and take shorthand at a hundred and twenty. I was making good money in San Diego. And I was making decent money here, working for a stock brokerage firm. I'm good at what I do—there was no reason to fire me."

She gazed at Beverly with anger and pain in her eyes. "Miss Highland, I consider myself to be a good Christian. But I say to you now that I would like to see that bastard Danny Mackay hang!"

Then she looked down at the sleeping face of her baby and seemed to collapse inside. "What am I going to do?" she whispered. "Joe had only been on his job for two months. He didn't yet qualify for benefits. His funeral took the last of our savings—"

"Mrs. Kern," Beverly said softly, "I sympathize with what you are going through."

"Why does the world adore that man?" Maggie murmured, wiping tears off her cheeks. "Why can't they see him for what he is?" Her green eyes regarded Beverly again, this time shining with defiance and courage. "It was awful, all those poor people in that tent, putting their money into his collection plates, poor desperate people, crippled and sick and out of hope, giving him their money! Am I the only person who sees Danny Mackay for what he is? A monster!"

"I know him, Mrs. Kern. I've known him for a long time. You see," she looked tenderly at the baby sleeping in his mother's arms, "I would have had a child of my own today, if it hadn't been for Danny Mackay. And he or she would be fourteen years old now. . . ."

The sunlight streaming through the sheer curtains began to cast long golden beams over brand-new furniture that wasn't paid for. Outside, the shouts and laughter of children rang over the young neighborhood. This was a place where couples like Joe and Maggie Kern came to sink their roots deep into the earth, to raise their children among friends and long-term neighbors, and then maybe live here in comfortable retirement, content with what they had done.

Danny Mackay did more than just kill people—he also killed dreams.

"Mrs. Kern," Beverly said softly, "how would you like to come back to Los Angeles and work for me?"

When Beverly walked into the office, prepared to spend the evening doing a full day's work because her trip to Victorville had taken all morning and afternoon, she was surprised to find Carmen and Ann still there. And when she saw that they were crying, her surprise turned to alarm.

"Oh, Beverly!" Ann cried. "It's the most awful news!"

She didn't say anything. She remained by the door, staring at her friends.

"It's Eddie and Laverne," Carmen said. "Their plane went down in the ocean off Malibu. Beverly—they're dead!"

The will was read a week later. Those closest to Eddie were present—even Roy Madison, who had canceled a whole day of shooting on the set of his popular TV spy series. They stared at the attorney as he informed them of Eddie and Laverne's last wishes.

Absolutely everything—Royal Burgers, a miniature golf course on Ventura, a car wash on Wilshire, and a men's clothing shop in Beverly Hills called Eddie Fanelli's—went to Beverly Highland.

24

JAMIE COULDN'T HELP HIMSELF. It was such a turn-on to swim naked in Beverly Highland's pool.

He'd done it seven times now since that first daring time in January, and today was going to be no exception, despite the gray March weather. But he was foiled just as he was starting to unzip his jeans. He was standing there, barefoot and bare-chested, hands on his zipper, already getting a hard-on thinking about the swim for his voyeuristic employer, when all of a sudden someone appeared on the path that came up to the pool.

It was a young man in swimming trunks and wearing a towel around his neck, and he called out, "Hi, there! Can I have a quick dip before you put the chemicals in?"

Nonplussed—he had never before encountered anyone on the grounds of Beverly Highland's estate—Jamie quickly stepped away and said, "Uh, sure. Be my guest."

The young man, who looked to be in his early twenties, said, "Thanks," tossed his towel aside and dived in. He swam a few laps, then emerged at Jamie's end and pulled himself up out of the pool. "Whew! That felt good! I needed to wash out last night's cobwebs!"

Jamie watched the stranger towel off and wondered at his ease to be swimming in Miss Highland's pool. Who on earth was he?

"You know," the young man said, toweling his hair dry, "you look familiar. Have I seen you somewhere before?"

Jamie reached for the pool sweep and guided it into the water. "I don't know. It's possible."

"Hey! Was it at Peppy's?"

"Peppy's! That gay disco on Robertson?" Jamie laughed. "You wouldn't find me there. I don't think my girlfriend would approve."

"How about around the UCLA campus? Are you a student there maybe?"

"Naw. I went to Cal State Northridge. Majored in drama."

"Oh, an actor. What've you been in? Maybe that's where I've seen you."

"Well, I've had a few parts. I was on *All My Children* a couple of months ago."

"Hey, no kidding!"

Jamie watched him do some stretching exercises, a young man definitely not in a hurry and definitely feeling at home here. "So," Jamie said slowly, "are you a friend of Miss Highland or something?"

"You might say that."

"Is she a nice person to work for?"

"I wouldn't know." He touched his toes and then straightened up. "I don't work for her. Why?"

"I was just wondering. You know, like maybe she has contacts in the industry. I sure could use some help, if you know what I mean."

The stranger picked up his towel, draped it around his neck, and paused to take a long look at Jamie. "Yeah," he said slowly. "I know what you mean."

Their eyes met for a moment, then the young man said abruptly, "Well, gotta go! Thanks for holding things up for my swim. Hope I haven't thrown you off schedule." And he disappeared down the path.

Jamie watched him go. Peppy's, he had said. A gay bar. Had the guy been coming on to him?

It made Jamie shudder. That was the trouble with this town. Especially in the movie industry.

Deciding that it was too risky to be pulling down his pants at this point, especially with that guy lurking around, Jamie reluctantly shrugged off his sexy mood, kept his pants on, and got down to the business of cleaning Beverly Highland's pool.

Joe's footsteps could be heard on the marble floor as he neared the solarium. When he appeared in the doorway, snappily dressed in Port Authority and Stubbies, his hair blown dry, his smile dazzling, he said, "Good morning, ladies," and delivered himself into the jungle of ferns and vines.

Beverly and Maggie Kern were enjoying a light brunch of toast and poached eggs and tea and going over the day's business. The New Hampshire primary was coming up and Beverly had pumped a lot of money into the right political pockets to ensure Danny's victory.

Maggie watched Joe as he took a seat and helped himself to a tall glass of orange juice. "Well?" she said. "What did you find out?"

He sat back, a young man confident of his good looks and personality, and gave her his best smile. "He's not gay and he's not married, but he does have a girlfriend. Slightly educated— a drama major. Articulate, doesn't talk like an ape. Looks healthy. His teeth are nice, probably capped. And hungry. *Very* hungry."

Maggie looked at Beverly, who nodded slightly.

"Now," said Joe, leaning forward. "Mind telling me what you wanted to know for?"

"Well," Maggie said, making a thing of tearing open a packet of Sweet 'n Low and stirring it into her tea. "We have to be careful who comes through those gates."

"Why not just have Security check him out, like you usually do?"

"There are some things even a private investigator can't find out, Joe. Thank you for getting the information for us."

"Sure," he said with a shrug and stood up. "He probably thought I was putting the make on him, though."

"Joe!"

He laughed. "Sorry, Mom," he said, bending and kissing Maggie on the forehead. "Aunt Bev, any time you need something done, I'm the man for it. See you later."

Maggie laughed and shook her head. "Young men these days!"

"Yes," Beverly said in a distant voice, thinking of Jamie the pool boy. "Young men . . ."

25

Hollywood, 1971

WHEN BEVERLY CAME IN out of the bright sunlight and followed the hostess across the dark restaurant, she did not see the man at the bar watching her. He was a large man, well dressed, and black. He kept his eyes on her as she was led to a small table in the corner, where she was partially hidden by plants and a single candle illuminated her face. Although white women weren't usually to his taste, he saw that she was quite good-looking, and he wondered if the platinum hair was natural.

The man's name was Jonas Buchanan, and he wore a gun in a holster underneath his jacket.

Buchanan was the only person at the bar. Later, he knew, this place would be packed with people lined up three-deep. But it was just past two; the pickup crowd wouldn't be arriving until four o'clock.

He slowly sipped his drink and kept a surreptitious eye on the young blond woman. She ordered something from the waitress, then pulled a notebook out of her purse and started writing. He saw that she glanced at her watch now and then.

When he finished his drink, Buchanan left money on the bar, buttoned his jacket, making sure the bulge of the gun didn't show, and moved slowly in the direction of the corner table.

Concealed by the profusion of ferns and pothos, he was able to approach her unseen. He studied her, watched the bent head catch white-gold glints of candlelight, saw the hand move rapidly over the notebook. She had a quiet intensity about her, as if she only barely sat on the chair, as if she were coiled to jump and run.

And he wondered if, when she saw him, she would.

Finally he was at the table. Sensing him, she looked up. Their eyes met.

"Miss Highland?" he said.

He hadn't told her on the phone that he was black. He never did. It was a test he put prospective clients through. Frequently, they would take one look at him, at his blackness, and leave.

But there wasn't a single flicker in her eye as she said, "Yes. Are you Jonas Buchanan?"

He nodded.

"Please sit down. Can I order something for you?"

"No, thank you. If we could just get down to business, Miss Highland—"

Beverly produced a large envelope and placed it in front of him. "This is all the information I have. I'm sorry, it isn't much."

"You said on the phone that you have already used the services of three private investigators. Couldn't they come up with anything?"

"This was all they found."

He looked at the envelope. It was disappointingly thin. Then he studied his client. Jonas Buchanan wondered how much she could afford. She looked rich, but he had learned never to go by looks. However, when he had explained his fees to her on the phone, she hadn't balked.

"All right," he said, opening the envelope and spreading out the paltry contents. He was beginning to feel irritated. When he had left the police force to open his own private detective agency, he hadn't dreamed that cases like these— locating the runaway kids of rich white folks or the missing relatives of rich white girls—would make up the bulk of his caseload. He didn't like dealing with white people in general, which was one reason he had quit the force. But unfortunately they were the ones with the troubles and the money. "Tell me what you know."

"The men I hired over the last few years, from three different agencies, found nothing on my mother at all. She disappeared nearly twenty years ago. I've written everything I can remember about her in the letter you have there. Place of birth, maiden name, schools attended and so forth. I believe that when she left New Mexico she might have come back to California."

"But the men you hired before me found no trace of her?"

Beverly shook her head. Her eyes were damp, Buchanan noticed. But he had also learned not to be deceived by tears.

"I have to tell you, Miss Highland," Jonas said, feeling his irritation rise, "I can't promise anything. Especially where three other investigators have failed."

Now he waited for the crumpled look, the tears on the cheeks, the pleading that he just had to find her mother. Instead Jonas was met by a steady gaze and a voice that said quietly, "I understand that, Mr. Buchanan. I will appreciate anything you can do for me."

He tried to categorize her. These days Jonas found it fairly easy to sort out white people and lump them into two groups.

There were the hippie/liberal types who marched for the cause of black people and genuinely believed themselves to be color-blind and were anxious to be his friend to prove it, and then there were the racists who found themselves out of style and adopted a phony liberalism to prove they thought black people were okay. Over the past ten years Jonas had found himself the target of many such, those anxious to be seen with him, to have one of his kind at their parties, or just the curiosity seekers, women mostly, who wanted to know if what they had heard about black men was true. Jonas didn't have a handle on Beverly Highland yet. But he would.

"You said you want me to locate your sister as well," he said, shifting in his chair. Jonas was a big man; he had been a star on his college football team. Ordinary chairs were frequently uncomfortable.

"My twin," Beverly said. "She was adopted when we were born, thirty-three years ago. I believe I actually found the attorney who handled the adoption, a man named Hyman Levi, but at the time I was too young to realize it. Since then, I've gone back, but the offices are no longer there and I found no trace of Hyman Levi Senior or Junior."

Jonas sniffed. Not only was this turning out to be a typical run-of-the-mill case, but it was an impossible one as well. A baby given up thirty-three years ago to persons unknown and the lawyer out of the scene, and an adult woman who walked out on her husband twenty years ago, no doubt having no desire to be found. Well, Jonas figured he could always do with the rent money, and he wasn't particularly busy right now—white folks might want him at their parties, but they didn't rush to do business with him.

"I can't make any guarantees, Miss Highland. Locating your sister could take a long time and a lot of legwork—"

"I'm prepared to pay, Mr. Buchanan."

Rich kid, he thought. Maybe a spoiled Beverly Hills brat who never had to work a day in her life.

"And you must bear in mind that your mother is an adult and might very likely not want to be found."

"I know she doesn't want to be found, Mr. Buchanan. In fact, she will be working very hard at not being found."

"Why is that?"

"She killed a man. That's why she ran away."

He stared at her. "Who?"

"My father. She stabbed him to death. The police never found her."

Suddenly everything was different. And half an hour later, after he had heard all the details of the Dwyer family and Beverly's itinerant childhood in the Southwest and received his first check from her, Jonas Buchanan found himself reassessing this new client.

"I'll do my best," he said as he stood.

Beverly also stood and held out her hand. "I know that, Mr. Buchanan."

He looked down at the slender white hand. He took it. Her grasp was cool and firm. "May I ask," he said, "why you picked me?"

"You were one of several on my list. I liked your ad in the Yellow Pages." She smiled. "I then made a few inquiries about you. I decided that since you're black, maybe you'll try harder."

He looked at her smile. And then, despite himself, Jonas found himself smiling back.

It was a hot day, and nearly three hundred people were packed into the auditorium for the general meeting of the Hollywood Chamber of Commerce. Beverly had never attended before, but she had decided that since she was a member, because of Eddie, and since she continued to pay the annual fees, it was time to come to a meeting and see what it was all about.

Of the nearly three hundred people, Beverly was one of only a dozen or so women present. One of them she recognized as owning a string of beauty parlors in Hollywood. Another, she learned, was a widow who had inherited her husband's business. Still another was a tax preparer who was struggling to make a go of it on Fountain Avenue. All were much older than Beverly. And they had all probably attended these meetings before.

As she sat listening to the opening report being given by the president of the Chamber of Commerce, Beverly thought about her interview with Jonas Buchanan four weeks ago. She had read the look in his eyes: *Hopeless case,* it had said.

In fact, that was what the three previous investigators had concluded. "Give it up, Miss Highland. Your mother doesn't want to be found, and it's impossible, without some sort of lead, to trace your sister."

The first private detective had come up with the most. Naomi Dwyer, he had reported, had changed her name back to Naomi Burgess and lived for a while in a small town in Nevada before moving on, witnesses believed, to California. She spent some time in Redding, working as a cook in a nursing home, and there her trail disappeared. That was fifteen years ago. On the twin sister, all he had been able to learn was that Hyman Levi, Sr., was deceased and that the son was no longer practicing law in California. Presbyterian Hospital had no records and no witnesses who could give any information on the adoption.

The second investigator had done nothing, Beverly suspected, except take her money. She had fired him after two months.

The third had looked promising, but all he had been able to do was duplicate what the first had done. Also taking her money.

And now she had hired Jonas Buchanan. But he had several things going for him that his predecessors did not: he was a former cop, he was a man to be trusted (so a colleague on the force had reported), and he was black.

A hopeless case, his eyes had said a month ago. But Beverly didn't believe that. Nothing was hopeless. Not as long as you kept trying.

And now he had called her, after four weeks of silence. She had gone to her office to find a message from Jonas Buchanan. He was on his way back to L.A. and would meet with her tonight.

He had new information on her mother and sister.

The report being given by the president of the Chamber of Commerce was regarding "Hollywood's most serious problem. A problem we must confront immediately and find solutions for. If not, business will suffer and the city will also suffer as a result."

Beverly watched and listened.

There was a small stage at the front of the auditorium, and several men sat at a long table, facing the large gathering of Hollywood business people. The panel wore expensive-looking suits and had, Beverly thought, impressive titles such as Chief Executive Officer, President and Chairman. Hollywood was a town of name and wealth, albeit now faded from glory under a seedy veneer, and these men were the power in that city. Beverly, who had lived and worked in Hollywood for eighteen years, and who cared very much about its future, paid careful attention to what the president had to say.

He was talking about parking. That, according to his report, was Hollywood's biggest problem. This town was becoming congested and overcrowded, but there were no provisions for expansion of parking facilities. As a result, by day the main boulevards were clogged with business and tourist traffic, by night the streets were filled with teenagers cruising in their cars. There wasn't a person in this room, the president asserted, who could not attest to the fact that the bad traffic and lack of parking were adversely affecting business. He himself, in fact, was hurting.

Beverly knew who this man was. His name was Drummond, and he owned the largest department store in the city; it was located right in the heart of Hollywood's business district. His store owned four parking lots adjacent to the building, but as they had been put in twenty years ago, they could not now accommodate the traffic of the seventies.

Beverly thought about that store and its parking lots. She and Carmen and Maggie sometimes shopped there. The lots were chained off and guarded by attendants. You parked for free if you bought something in the store; if not, or if you went to do business elsewhere on the Boulevard, you paid a steep price. All of which money went into Mr. Drummond's pocket. Since he owned the busiest parking lots in the vicinity, Beverly was wondering how he could be "hurting."

Seeing a few people nod in agreement with him throughout the auditorium, Beverly realized that she was lucky. When the gas station next to the diner had gone out of business, she had been able to buy it, tear it down, and make a parking lot out of it. In the two years since she had inherited Royal Burgers, Beverly had enlarged the diner. The new parking lot accommodated the heavy day and night business the diner brought in.

The president was winding up his report and coming to his proposal—the reason for calling this meeting. "We in the business community have a responsibility to commit funds toward research into the parking problem, and to finance the construction of a parking structure that will solve that problem for years to come."

Beverly consulted the sheet she had been handed at the door. It contained a summary of the president's report and his proposal. The new parking structure was to be a five-level garage that would accommodate two thousand automobiles.

She read the proposed location of that garage: It would stand on the corner directly opposite Drummond's department store.

When the president was finished the audience filled the chamber with applause. Then members were invited to step up to the microphones for comments and suggestions. As Beverly watched a small line form at the microphone in the aisle nearest her seat she thought again about her diner.

It was doing well. Better than ever, in fact. But something was wrong with the rest of the chain. Carmen reported that profits were not as good as they should be, even though Beverly had instigated renovations in certain locations, hired more staff, and brought out the Crown Burger and barbecued chicken. Royal Burgers, according to the accounting sheets, was still falling way behind McDonald's and Kentucky Fried Chicken. So Beverly and Ann, who was in charge of quality control, had gone on a quick driving trip around the Southland to see if they could determine what was wrong.

What they had found was nothing significant. The stores were clean, the food up to standard, the service average. They were in fact just like any other fast-food stores, with young, rather indifferent workers and the usual HELP WANTED sign in the windows. But in the two years since she had inherited the chain and instituted the changes Eddie had refused to make, Beverly had expected the company to be doing much better than it was. What, she wondered, was lacking?

The man at the microphone, a prominent Hollywood realtor, caught her attention. He was saying, "Mr. Drummond, I'm sure I speak for all of us when I commend you on your excellent report. It's a measure we all support every inch of the way." He bent close to the microphone; his voice came too loud over the speakers. "And I also want to take this opportunity, Mr. Drummond, to tell you and the others on the board that I think you guys are doing one hell of a job serving the chamber!"

Beverly looked at the man. He couldn't be serious! Anyone could see that the parking proposal served no one's interest but Drummond's. And then she realized that the way he was kowtowing to the men on the dais, the report could have been about anything and this man would be voicing sycophantic approval.

There was a smattering of halfhearted applause, and a second person stepped up. He was Mr. Mangioni, proprietor of three art galleries on Sunset. He echoed the realtor's praise and voiced his support of the parking-garage project. The third person to speak brought up a new issue—garbage collection—and had it written into the agenda for the next meeting.

The time for taking a vote on the parking structure was drawing near. A few more people waited at the microphones, fanning themselves or mopping their brows, while the men on the dais listened politely to complaints and praise, and the secretary took the minutes.

As Beverly watched and listened, and studied the crowd gathered here today, it occurred to her that everyone in this large room had something in common with everyone else. They were all concerned members of Hollywood's business community. But even though they shared this bond, she detected an absence of cohesiveness. They were like a band of restless people searching for direction. From a couple of rows behind her she heard a muttered comment: ". . . meetings are always the same. . . ." And another, from somewhere in front of her: ". . . won't come next time. . . ."

And she thought, What was the purpose of such a body of people if they couldn't get together and achieve their goals?

She looked at the microphone in her aisle. One person was left. He was raising the issue of the alarming number of X-rated theaters springing up along Santa Monica Boulevard. The president, Mr. Drummond, assured the man, who owned several dress boutiques in Hollywood, that the issue would be taken under advisement and the problem studied. But Beverly saw by the look on the man's face, as he turned away from the microphone, that he didn't feel he had accomplished anything.

Why didn't others speak up? she wondered. She clearly read discontent on many faces. Why didn't they challenge the president's proposal?

And then she thought, *They're afraid of him.*

As Mr. Drummond was about to call for the vote on the funds for the parking structure, Beverly suddenly stood up and went to the microphone. "I would like to say something, please," she said.

Everyone stared at her. Women rarely attended these meetings, much less spoke up at them, and those who did certainly didn't look like this attractive young woman. "I think, Mr. President," Beverly said, "that you haven't looked at Hollywood's problems from the proper perspective."

"How is that?"

"It seems to me that parking is not our most immediate problem."

"I see," he said. "And what is, then?"

"Well—" Beverly had to think. She had stood up impulsively, not really knowing what she was going to say. "We have lots of problems in this town, and parking isn't the most serious."

Mr. Drummond exchanged a look with the chairman, who was seated next to him, then said patiently, "Young lady, the purpose of these meetings is, of course, to give everyone a chance to voice comments and concerns. However, miss, you will have to be more specific. I suggest you get your ideas together and present them at the next meeting. In the meantime, we will get on with the vote on the parking issue."

"But, Mr. Drummond, we're not ready to vote on it!"

"Miss— What is your name?"

"Beverly Highland."

A murmur rolled through the audience. Mr. Drummond looked at her. Beverly Highland? Was the girl aware that she had the same name as two major Hollywood streets? "Well, Miss Highland," he said with an amused look, "I did invite comment from the audience and, as you can see, you are the last to speak. And now if you will please resume your seat—"

"But surely there must be other opinions on this!" She looked around at the crowd. They were watching her, but nobody made a move to join her.

Mr. Drummond and the chairman exchanged another amused look, then the president said in a condescending tone, "We appreciate your concern, Miss Highland, and that's very commendable of you, but, as you can see, there are no other opinions. Now, if you will please sit down we can get on with business."

Beverly's heart was racing. She felt the eyes of three hundred people on her. Why didn't they speak up? Surely they weren't going to pass such a ludicrous measure? "I think that before we take a vote, Mr. President, it should be pointed out that the proposed parking structure is going to be very expensive and is going to come out of the pockets of everyone present."

Drummond's amusement was replaced by annoyance. "You haven't properly identified yourself, young lady. What business do you represent?"

"Eddie's Royal Burgers."

He smiled. He almost snickered. "I see. A hamburger stand. Well, Miss Highland, I'm sure you think you have some very valuable things to say, but I doubt you have had enough experience in business—"

"What I mean to say, Mr. Drummond, is that the proposed parking structure is going to mean a great deal of profit to yourself."

Now the audience stirred. Drummond's tone went cold. "That parking structure is going to profit everyone, Miss Highland."

"And yet it will just happen to be located right across from your store."

She heard a collective gasp around her. Drummond stiffened. His voice carried a hint of warning. "That happens to be the only available land."

Beverly's heart was pounding. She felt all eyes on her, Drummond's most of all. "As I recall," she said, "there are available locations on Cahuenga, Vine, and Sunset, any one of which would be more of a help to those small businesses that have no parking facilities at all."

"Meaning your own, of course."

"I happen to be fortunate enough to have a parking lot for my store. I'm thinking of Mr. Mangioni, over there, and Mr. Peterson, who have to rely on one or two curbside spaces. Your store has four lots of its own, Mr. Drummond—why not locate the garage somewhere else in the business district?"

A few members called out from the audience: "She's right." "Yeah! Why not have it on Fairfax?"

The chairman banged his gavel and said, "Let's have order in here. The discussion is closed, we will now take the vote on—"

"Excuse me," said Beverly, "but I believe I still have the floor."

"You have said what you stood up to say, young lady, now—"

"Let's really think about Hollywood's problems and see what we can do to solve them. Look around you! What do we see in our streets today? Prostitutes, runaway children, drug pushers, people sleeping in doorways! Our neighborhoods have gone downhill. We now have head shops and sex shops, filthy streets!"

More people spoke up, saying, "You said it!" and "You tell him!"

"The name Hollywood is known all over the world. We have over two million tourists a year because they have heard of Hollywood. And what do they see when they get here? A business thoroughfare with ten run-down shops for every decent business. Homeless children who are prey to drug dealers and perverts. Girls *and* boys standing on the curb selling their bodies. People with nowhere to go, living in doorways, panhandling from everyone who passes by. And you're telling us that the problem is *parking?*"

The audience cheered. Suddenly, people were standing up and hurrying to the microphones. The chairman banged his gavel.

Mr. Drummond said, "Miss Highland, you are out of order. If you wish to bring up new business, we will put it on the next meeting's agenda—"

"*New* business! Mr. Drummond, what I'm talking about is *old* business and you know it! I'm talking about something this chamber should have examined and done something about long before now."

"Young lady, you don't know anything about this town—"

"Excuse me, sir, but I was *born* here. And I was born here in a year when Hollywood was in its glory, when the name Hollywood spelled magic and fantasy for millions the world over. How have we let our city come to this? A place where foreign tourists are shocked and scared to come out of their hotels! A place we are ashamed of! We need to do something about it, Mr. President. And we need to do something about it *now!*"

The crowd cheered and applauded. People tried to speak out of turn. The gavel came down again and again.

The president held up his hands for silence, and when order was restored, he said with barely controlled anger, "If you can so easily identify our problems, Miss Highland, then perhaps you have an easy solution for them? Because if you do, I would like to hear them!"

She looked at him. She was trembling. She was furious. A solution? Oh yes, she had a solution. "What is the future of Hollywood?" she asked quietly. Beverly turned and addressed

277

the crowd. "What will the future image of our town be? How do you see it, Mr. Mangioni, or you, Miss Withers? When you look into the years ahead, what do you see? What *is* Hollywood's image?" She turned back to the microphone and said in a rising voice, "This is what we must decide here and now. We must decide which direction we are going to take, and then act upon it. Will our focus be tourism? Shall we emphasize business? Or are we a television and movie town? But however we view the future image of Hollywood, we must accept the challenge today to begin working toward that new future. We must dare to dream of a better place to work and live. We must dare to set high goals for ourselves." She raised an arm and curled a fist. "We must *dare* to make Hollywood great again!"

The crowd was suddenly on their feet, cheering and clapping. The applause was deafening. People came running up to Beverly, to shake her hand, to pat her on the back. Up on the dais the president was scowling and gathering his papers together. The chairman banged his gavel to no avail. All around, the members were pushing to get close to Beverly, to let her know they were on her side, that it was about time someone stood up to those guys, and other things that she couldn't hear because too many people were talking at once, and the auditorium had erupted in pandemonium. Beverly felt dizzy. She felt high. And she suddenly saw everything: her goal, her purpose, her future.

26

HE ROLLED ON TOP OF HER as if he were changing sides for a suntan—five minutes on the front, five minutes on the back. His bottom went up and down a few times and then he collapsed on her.

Pushing away from him and reaching for her Virginia Slims, Trudie gave the guy a look that said, *That's it!*

He didn't see it, however. He was already snoring.

Drawing on her cigarette and inhaling deeply, she got out of bed and walked across the room to the window, from where she could see the lights of UCLA. The campus looked like a small town, and across the street, at a frat house, there was a wild party going on. Good heavens, girl, she silently said to her reflection in the glass, just what do you think you're doing here?

She knew very well what she was doing there, in the apartment of some guy whose name she barely knew, who was only twenty-four years old, she had found out after coming home with him, and whose brains were between his legs. It was Saturday night again. That was why she was here.

Trudie figured that there were three times in a person's life that demanded to be shared, two of which were Saturday nights and Sunday mornings. So she had gotten all dressed up in her best denim and lace, and gone with her cousin Alexis to the Pikme-Up, where they had drunk mai tais in Pic N Save plastic tumblers. There had been the usual bright, preppy crowd in secondhand clothing and tacky jewelry lounging on kitchen chairs on the sidewalk outside, and Trudie and Alexis had been discussing fortune-telling with runes when a young man dressed in summer whites and a leather tie had come smiling up.

She'd liked him at once. Trudie had always had a weakness for men with shoulder-length hair. And he had an intelligent glint in his eye. But what had sold her on him was when he had said, "Runes, wow. The power of Odin and Thor."

They had left the café together, saying good night to Alexis, who had an early-morning surgery schedule, and they drove to Westwood in two cars, Trudie following Miles's VW in her Corvette. Once inside the messy apartment he shared with two other guys, who were away for the weekend, Miles had poured her a glass of red wine from a screw-cap bottle and put Springsteen on the stereo. Five minutes later Trudie realized she had made a mistake.

"Can't we just talk awhile?" she had said when he'd started making the moves.

"What about?"

"Well, like"—a particularly favorite person had popped into her mind—"what do you think of Carl Sagan?"

"Carl Sagan? Oh, the *Cosmos* guy. Caught the show. Great music."

That was when Trudie realized she had been had.

Still, a virile young body was a virile young body, and Miles had shown great bedroom potential. At first. And then that, too, had turned out to be another case of mistaken identity, and so here she was once again, in a strange apartment, sexually frustrated and lonely, wondering what made her do such things.

She found the bathroom on the first try (some apartments were tricky, especially if she was drunk) and took a look at herself in the mirror. The woman with the spiky blond hair and smudged makeup was saying, This has got to stop.

The trouble was, she didn't know how to stop. At least, not until she found the man she was looking for. Where on earth, Trudie wondered as she washed her face, was she going to find a man who had looks, brains, knew how to make love, *and* treated a woman as an equal? Bill the plumber sprang into her mind. He was doing that lately. To her great annoyance, because she definitely did not like him. Oh, he filled out a pair of jeans very nicely, and he knew his business when it came to laying in the steel and plumbing in a pool, but he had that male chauvinist air about him, calling her "honey" and talking to her as if she were an idiot.

Then she thought about "Thomas." What was so unique about her moments with him that she couldn't seem to re-create them outside Butterfly's walls? What was the missing ingredient?

She went to the bedroom doorway and leaned against the jamb, quietly smoking. Miles must have certainly gotten his satisfaction, because now he was sleeping like a baby. Trudie was halfway considering waking him, getting him hard again, and showing him what lovemaking really was all about when he rolled over and farted.

She looked at the digital clock on his nightstand. It was just a little after ten. The evening was still young.

She went to the kitchen, found the phone, dialed a number, and when someone came on the line, she said, "Hi, Butterfly? This is Trudie Stein. Is he available?"

She listened, and then smiled. "Hold on to him for me. I'm ten minutes away!"

27

Houston, Texas: 1972

THERE ARE TIMES when a good meal is better than sex.

That was what Danny Mackay was thinking as he devoured the chicken-fried steak and hash brown potatoes that were crunchy on the outside and tender on the inside, all smothered in spicy country-sausage gravy. A fuck is just a fuck, he thought, wiping the last biscuit around the plate and reaching for his Chivas. But a good meal can't be beat anytime.

Especially a good Texas meal.

"Well, Bon," he said as he stood up from the table and stretched. "It's time we got going. Houston's over two hundred miles away."

Bonner jumped up from the bed, where he had been playing solitaire, and began taking Danny's suits out of the closet.

Danny went to the sliding glass doors of his hotel-room balcony and looked out over the white sands of the south Texas coast. "Corpus Christi," he said with a soft laugh. "The Body of Christ. Hell of a name to give a town." He finished the last of his Chivas and tossed the crystal tumbler down onto the sandy beach.

Danny liked this semitropical town on the Gulf of Mexico. That was why he had come here, to spend a week buying up beachfront property. It was a way of counteracting his Dust Bowl beginnings and childhood in hot waterless places. Corpus Christi made him think of faraway exotic places, of islands where the girls were brown and welcoming, where rum ran like waterfalls, where the days were like butter and the nights like cinnamon. The free and easy life, where you just reached out your hand for sex or food, whichever you had a mind to indulge in at that moment, and it just fell into your palm!

Maybe I'll buy myself a tropical island, Danny thought as he watched Bonner carefully fold Danny's expensive shirts and place them in the calf-hide luggage. Somewhere in the South Pacific. Where the natives will make me their king.

Danny laughed again. He felt so darned good. Thirty-eight years old and riding high!

He was rich, the paperback edition of *Why God Took the Kennedys* was now in its fortieth week on the best-seller list, the crowds that packed into his Houston church every week were big, and he had been on the *Tonight Show* and *Laugh-In*. But the biggest high had come two years before from his Christmas tour of Vietnam, where he had gone, Bob Hope style, with entertainers, celebrities, and his charismatic energies to take the word of God to the homesick troops. Danny had expected his show to be a success, but he had not anticipated such a stunning success. He had stood out alone on that stage and belted out his power and fifty thousand soldiers had cheered.

The sound of so many cheering him . . .

"It might not be wise to go to Vietnam, Danny," Bonner had warned. "After all, Vietnam is a very unpopular subject these days. Folks might turn on you."

But Danny detested antiwar marchers and hippies and bleeding-heart liberals. He wanted to show the world that he believed in America and that America was right. Danny had stood on that stage so many miles from home, held his arms out to embrace the troops, and he had shouted up to the sky, "I know what you are going through, my brothers and sisters! I, too, was once a soldier like yourselves. But I was never given the honor of fighting for freedom and democracy! Don't listen to the voices of the cowards back home. It's easy to sit in your living room and denounce a fight you know nothing about!"

Those in the crowd who were in the war cheered and shouted. Then Danny said, "An ancient noble Roman named Livy once said that a necessary war is a just war, and weapons are holy when there is no hope except in weapons. Brothers and sisters in Christ, this is a just war, and your weapons are holy!"

They had gone wild. Not so much over the words as over the way he said them. Up on that stage in front of so many thousands, Danny might have looked small. But they felt his power come rolling out over their heads, a power that made them feel—for a while, at least—that they were not miserable, forgotten, despised by friends and family back home. And they loved him for it. Fifty thousand troops would have done anything for Danny Mackay at that moment, they would have followed him into any field of fire.

And Danny knew it.

His troupe still traveled about in a bus after all because Danny had found it good politics to go out on a revival circuit now and then to keep his profile high. But he was based in Houston, where he had built a church and had a penthouse on top of the finest hotel. Danny drove a white Lincoln Continental with wire wheels and steer horns on the hood; he dressed in the finest Western-tailored suits and wore a white Stetson. He had acquired expensive tastes and made sure that he was every inch *class*. Politicians and prominent businessmen were now in his social circle. And with each rung of the ladder he ascended, Danny's sights went higher and higher. He had power, but not enough, not yet. . . .

Danny loved this wild and weird city whose veins and arteries ran with black gold and whose name, Houston, was the first word uttered by man when he landed on the moon. The first thing Danny always did upon arrival was to spend some time with the two or three costly mistresses he kept in Houston. Tall, leggy women, all furs and diamonds and knowing every sexual trick imaginable, they would come up to his penthouse to get him revved up for the preaching. Then he would eat an enormous meal and wash it down with Chivas until he could feel the power of the Lord invading his muscles, guts, and lungs. He would spend the next three or four hours in his church using his charisma and sex appeal to remind

folks of sins and demons, of hellfire and eternity, subtly men-
tioning his personal hot line to God, and finally wringing their
dollars out of them with the promise of salvation.

As he pulled off the I-45 and saw the cars already streaming
into the parking areas Danny laughed at the utter simplicity
of it all. The money was literally falling into his hands now.
If he tried to keep people from giving it to him, he couldn't
get them to stop. And it was all because of an idea that had
come to him a few years back, while he was still burning in
the limelight of Kennedy's assassination.

Once people heard the famous Reverend Danny speech,
they wanted to see him in person, to be close to this man who
had prayed for Kennedy right outside the hospital. They poured
into his revival tent with their hopes and their wallets and
prayed for a sign. It was during one such meeting where people
were packed wall to wall that it came to Danny that what
these folks needed was a miracle. So he gave them one. Bonner
died and Danny brought him back to life. He couldn't believe
how easy it had been. A faked death and a staged resurrection.
And they fell for it! Of course, Danny had to admit that it
couldn't be pulled off by just any preacher. Too many had tried
the faith-healing routine and it didn't work. The man himself
had to have the power to make people believe, and once he
had that, then he could make them believe anything.

And Danny Mackay had that power.

He had manipulated that crowd into thinking they saw a
man die and come back to life; another crowd in another town
a year later witnessed a similar episode. But Danny was careful
not to overdo it. Word spread and folks came in the hopes of
witnessing the miracle, but they didn't always get their wish.
Danny was parsimonious with his resurrecting power. In the
past six years he had raised the dead only three times.

But it was enough. He now had the publicity that he
needed. There wasn't a magazine or newspaper in the country
that didn't carry a few words about Danny Mackay at some
time or another. He had been written up even in *Time* magazine, although he had yet to make the cover—but that, too,
would come. And publicity was what he needed in order to
get ahead. Which was why he was careful to cultivate a

smoothness, a classiness that could not be attacked or criticized. Many might doubt his dead-raising abilities, but when they came to throw stones, they found a man who was disarmingly good-looking, full of charm, and gifted with an elegance not normally found in hellfire preachers.

Danny pulled up behind the enormous glass-and-cedar church and listened to the choir belt out a hymn. Then he angled the rearview mirror and made a final check of himself. As always, the look was perfect. His eyes were sly and sexy and they mesmerized. And he knew the power of his smile. He flashed it out over his congregation and they went wild for it, men and women alike. *All men will see what you seem to be*, Machiavelli had written. *A few will know what you really are. The mob is always impressed by appearances, and the world is made up of mobs.*

Danny still read *The Prince*. Even though he practically had it memorized by now, he often took the time to open it to a page and drink up the wisdom of the man who had first inspired him seventeen years ago. In the time since, Danny had read many books. He read anything he could get his hands on—books by or about men of power, their struggles, their formulae for making it to the top. He knew what had made Napoleon and Caesar great; he knew why some men became heroes and some drowned in oblivion. Danny knew what mistakes not to make, the right things to do, and, above all, how to manipulate people.

He was ready for it again tonight as he slipped through a rear door of the church, where seven thousand hopefuls were clapping to the rhythm of a hymn. And waiting to receive the power of Danny Mackay.

Danny always started his sermon slowly, feeling the mood of the audience, sending out feelers to test the waters, adjusting his preaching to suit the crowd. They were good tonight. They were hot and ripe. Houston was entering a financial boom, and folks were coming to the Lord either to expiate their guilt for making too much money too soon or to pray to become the ones to make too much money too soon. Danny just told them what god-awful sinners they were, and they sat there and took it, saying, "Amen," and "Praise the Lord."

He got worked up; he got his audience worked up. He shouted and shook fists; they shouted and shook fists. He shouted hallelujah, they shouted hallelujah. He cried, they cried. They were putty in his hands. He felt good. He felt invincible. He strode across the stage as if he were spanning continents for the Lord and slammed his fist as if he were crushing God's enemies, and the crowd got wilder and the smell of religious zeal and repentance was thick in the humid air, and Danny filled his ears with the sounds of their cheers and cries—he was drunk on their worship.

Under the glass roof he had built to his own design, as the stars of Texas shed a benediction upon his congregation, Danny thought: *Only seven thousand tonight. But someday, they will number more, many more. . . .*

And then, right in the middle of his performance, just as he was about to shift gears and start letting folks in on his little secret about having God's private ear, a shriek came from the back of the church.

Thinking at first that it was an overenthusiastic penitent, Danny didn't break his rhythm. But then, all of a sudden, like the outward ripples in a still pond when a pebble has been tossed in, people started to stand up and cry out in waves until they reached the stage.

"Charlie!" a woman was screaming. "Charlie, get up! Oh God! Oh God, someone help him!"

Chaos erupted as Danny's Brothers ran to the back row, where they found a woman kneeling on the floor with a man's head in her lap.

"He's sick!" she cried. "Something's wrong with him!"

"Hold on there," came another voice from across the church. "I'll take a look at him. Don't move him."

Danny turned to see a balding, heavyset man push his way through the gawking crowd and drop to one knee next to the stricken man. "I'm a doctor," he said to the silent crowd. "This man is probably just suffering from heat exhaustion. Step back, everyone, please. Give him air."

As the people widened the circle Danny came down from the stage and pushed through the onlookers.

The unconscious man looked awful. His face had a queer

grayish cast to it; his lips were blue. Danny watched as the doctor bent and pressed his ear to the man's chest. The enormous church was silent. Seven thousand people watched in eerie stillness as they waited for his verdict.

"What's wrong with my husband, Doctor?" the woman said in a frightened voice.

He straightened at last, gave her a sorrowful look and said softly, "I'm awfully sorry, ma'am. Your husband is dead."

"NO!" She flung herself over the man's body and sobbed hysterically.

Danny felt himself go cold. Had his preaching killed a man?

He glanced over at Bonner, who wasn't looking too pleased. There were a lot of people in the church. And it was an awfully hot night.

As everyone stood watching the woman rock the body of her husband, wailing and keening, a few people started to shuffle nervously and send unreadable looks Danny's way.

He felt the perspiration run down his back. His mouth went dry. And then he saw his opportunity. "My brothers and sisters in Christ!" Danny shouted suddenly.

They all looked at him.

He raised his arms. "Let us pray for the soul of our dear departed brother here who has surely died in God's grace!"

"Amen," someone said. And it was echoed by those around him.

"Let us kneel, brothers and sisters," cried Danny, dropping down to his knees. "Let us praise the Lord, who took our brother from among us on this very night and in the state of grace. Surely this man was blessed to be called so!"

People knelt.

Danny, close to the woman and her dead husband, began to shout out his best, most moving prayer. He felt a new strength surge through him, a strength more delicious and uplifting than any he ever got from Chivas or women or food. It felt like the heat that had raced through his veins that day back in 1963 when he had done his best preaching and people had turned to him in desperation. Danny fed on people's need. Their hunger gave him fuel.

"As surely as I live and breathe, my brothers and sisters, this dear man's death is a true sign from God that we are here all blessed tonight! This is His sign that He is here in this very tent with us and that He sheds his blessing on us all. Let us lift our hearts up now and receive that goodness from God." Danny stretched out his arms and laid a hand on the weeping woman's head. "Let us pray for our grieving sister here. Let us show her our love. Let us reassure her that she has not been forgotten by God. Indeed, she has been blessed by God!"

"Amen! Hallelujah!"

He then laid his hand on the dead man's shoulder. "And let us pray for the hasty flight of this fallen brother's soul so that he might the sooner enjoy God's precious nearness and—"

The shoulder trembled.

"Nearness and—"

The shoulder jerked.

Danny looked down.

The dead man coughed.

The woman straightened up and stared down.

Suddenly, the church was silent again. Every eye turned to the face that just moments before had been pale and ashen with the shadow of death but was now pink in the cheeks with lips that were no longer blue.

The man coughed again, his eyes fluttered open, he gazed up at his wife and said, "What happened?"

"Lord God," whispered the doctor. "That man was dead! I would stake my reputation on it!" He ran a nervous hand over his bald head. "I've been practicin' medicine for forty years, and I know a dead man when I see one!"

Eyes moved from the doctor down to the revived man, back to the doctor, and finally . . . to Danny.

He was still kneeling. He found himself looking up into faces white with shock. For an instant he was confused. And then someone said, "Praise the Lord, Reverend Danny has raised a brother from the dead!"

Pandemonium broke loose. Women fainted, men dropped to their knees. People began to weep in earnest now, not in sorrow but in joy. They had witnessed the miracle they had always prayed they someday would, the living proof that God really was there and listening, concrete evidence that religion wasn't just a false hope but a real, living, and breathing entity that they could find hope and salvation in, and Danny Mackay had been the one to give them that proof.

People started to grab for him, to touch the cuffs of his pants, to kiss the hem of his white jacket. Bonner had to push through the mob, signaling to the other Brothers, and they managed to cluster around Danny and somehow get him back up to the stage.

He was stunned. He was electrified.

The dead man.

It hadn't been an act this time. It had really happened.

Danny fell to his knees, clasped his fingers under his chin and began a fervent prayer to God. He didn't shout it, he didn't use flamboyant gestures or shake a finger heavenward. His voice came out in a whisper. Everyone fell silent, in order to hear him. And what they heard was the sweetest prayer of thanksgiving spoken in the sweetest voice they had ever heard.

"I don't believe it!" Bonner said as he came into Danny's penthouse with the church's bookkeeping log. "This was your biggest take ever!"

Danny was sitting silently in a chair by the window, looking out at the soft Houston night, his gaze deep and intense. He didn't say anything when Bonner came in. He was concentrating on the Houston lights, and upon visions only he himself could see.

Bonner looked at his friend. The two boys from San Antonio had come a long way these past seventeen years—all because of Danny. Bonner didn't mind being Danny's employee instead of a partner. Bonner conceded that Danny was much smarter than he; he was proud, in fact, to be Danny Mackay's closest confidant. Bonner had recognized his friend's power long ago, and knew he was no match for it. But what happened tonight, well, that was something else.

"What do you suppose happened, Danny?" he asked softly. "Do you reckon that old doctor made a mistake?"

Danny's hands were in motion. His fingers turned a

matchbook around and around. Although he was slouched in an easy chair, his feet couldn't keep still on the ottoman. He was charged; he was on fire. "You heard those two reporters, Bon. You heard them interviewing people who vouched for that doctor. They all knew him, they all trusted and respected him. And the doctor had said that man was dead."

Danny shifted his eyes to his friend; he looked at Bonner from under half-closed lids. "Do you believe I raised him from the dead?"

Bonner swallowed. To tell the truth, he didn't like thinking about what happened tonight. And there were times when he was afraid of Danny. Like now, with all that tension just coiling up and Danny turning his head this way and that, and that matchbook going around and around in his fingers. Bonner recognized the signs: it was times like this when Danny was most dangerous. This was how he had looked that night years ago when he had gone after that poor old doctor in the Hill Country, and then later, just before Danny had taken off for a quick trip to California, Fort Ord, where he had a score to settle with a certain sergeant. Danny was on edge now, and unpredictable. And Bonner decided Danny was filled with a kind of evil energy that sometimes burned inside him. "Well, I . . . uh, don't know, Danny. I mean, *something* raised him from the dead, didn't it?"

Danny inspected the large gold ring on his left hand. He held it up to the light, watched it shine and glint. Then his mouth lifted in a slow smile and he said, "Yes . . ."

When a knock came at the door, Bonner looked at it for a long moment before getting up and answering it. If it was another reporter, well, he'd just politely tell him or her to get on his or her way—

"Reverend Mackay?" the flashy man standing in the hall said. "Reverend Danny Mackay?"

Bonner eyed him with suspicion. There was something a bit cornball about the stranger's appearance. He was fifty years old if he was a day, but he was wearing bright pink bell-bottoms and a tight lavender shirt with gold chains in his chest hairs. An enormous peace symbol dangled down on the end of a leather thong. "Frank Hallstead," he said, thrusting out a hand that had too many rings on it.

After they shook hands, he said, "Mind if I come in and talk a li'l bidness with your boss?"

"What sort of business?"

Hallstead pulled out a card and handed it to Bonner. "I manage Good News Productions. We own WBET out of Austin? Get it? Double You Bet! I think we might could use someone like Reverend Danny on our Sunday programs. Think he'd be interested in preaching weekly to three hundred thousand people through a television camera?"

Bonner looked over his shoulder at Danny, who was still staring out the window, ominously silent.

"Danny?" Bonner said.

"What's his deal?"

Hallstead tried to peer past Bonner into the elegant penthouse. He could just glimpse Mackay by the window, looking out. "Well, uh, can I come in?"

Danny made a gesture and Bonner said, "State your deal first."

"Well, ah, what the Reverend did tonight, it's made a lot of folks interested in seeing him. And he can't go driving all over the South, and his church only holds seven thousand. But now my television stations reach hundreds of thousands of people just thirsting to hear the Word preached by Danny Mackay. What do you say, Reverend?"

Danny looked down at his hands. He pictured the face of the dead man, all ashen and blue around the lips. The wailing wife, the seven thousand stunned into silence.

Then he thought of the people in their living rooms, the millions of TV sets in the country, and his face, his voice, his power reaching out to every one of them. . . .

"Let him in," Danny said. "We'll talk."

Beverly was by the window looking out at the otherworldly lights of Houston's oil-processing plants. She had stood there all evening, silent and pensive. She hadn't touched the food room service had brought up, not even the carrot sticks and black tea. There was too much to think about. One thing on her mind was the business deal she had come to Houston to close—the establishing of twenty Royal Burgers franchises in Texas. Another was Jonas Buchanan's latest report.

A year ago, just before she had gone to the meeting of the Hollywood Chamber of Commerce, Jonas Buchanan had called to tell her he had his first new information on her mother and sister.

"You were right about the old lawyer," the private investigator told her that night when he came to her office. "Hyman Levi Senior died a few years ago. His son left California and, according to the Bar Association, is retired and is no longer practicing law. I found him through the Internal Revenue Service; I have a friend who works in the Hollywood branch office. Hyman Levi now lives in a cabin about a hundred miles east of Seattle. He writes detective stories under a pen name."

Jonas Buchanan had been able to persuade Mr. Levi to take his father's old records out of storage and go through them. It had been a tedious process, but Buchanan had found what he was looking for: that the second twin baby born to Naomi Burgess at Hollywood Presbyterian had been adopted by a couple named Singleton. And they had named the baby Christine.

That was as far as Jonas had gotten at that time. He was back in Hollywood and would follow that lead right away.

On the mother, he also learned new information. He went north and visited the nursing home where the previous investigators said she had once worked as a cook. As luck would have it, the elderly black woman who cooked there now had been Naomi's assistant eighteen years ago. But she was very protective of Naomi, for whom she had a great fondness. She wouldn't speak to the other investigators, but as she was black, she opened up to Jonas.

"She said your mother went down to Fresno, where she said a cousin lived, a Miss Ann Burgess. I went to Fresno and found Miss Burgess. She wouldn't talk to me, but a neighbor was helpful. He said Miss Burgess's cousin had moved on to Sacramento when some police came to the door one day. My investigations in Sacramento have turned up nothing so far, but I have friends working on it."

That was a year ago.

Since then, Jonas had made periodic reports to Beverly, none of them amounting to anything of great value. The Singletons also seemed to have been people who moved a lot. Jonas had to travel quite a bit, speak to many people and hunt through stacks of old records. And that took time. But then, this morning he had telephoned Beverly here in her Houston hotel room to inform her that although, unfortunately, he had lost the trail of the Singletons because of a divorce twenty years ago, he had a tip on someone who might have some concrete information on the current whereabouts of Naomi Burgess.

"Thank you," Beverly had said to him. "Please follow through. I anxiously await your next report."

Christine Singleton, Beverly thought now as she looked out at Houston's lights. *My sister, my twin, Christine. Where are you now, at this very moment?*

Maggie Kern, who was picking at the food on the room service cart, watched her employer at the window. Since their arrival in Texas four days ago, Beverly had grown tense and restless. Maggie knew it was the old memories that were haunting her, plus the knowledge that Danny Mackay was here, in this same city. In fact, Beverly had not wanted to come to Houston at all, but the business transaction involving twenty old hamburger stands and gas stations, and turning them into Royal Burger stores, was too important to Beverly to leave to others to handle. It was typical of Beverly's growing financial acumen to oversee each phase and detail personally.

And with astounding results.

Maggie recalled that day a year ago when Beverly had returned from the Chamber of Commerce meeting. She had burst into the office as if something were chasing her. "I have it!" she had said breathlessly to Maggie and Carmen. "I know now what it is we need." What they needed to bolster the lagging profits of the Royal Burger chain. Beverly had gone to the meeting out of curiosity; she had returned charged with her own inspiration. She had given a speech, she said, and the speech not only had stirred the others in the audience but had stirred her as well.

"We need a spirit!" she had said as she sat down and proceeded to draft a plan on paper. "That's what our problem was. The company lacks spirit!"

Well, Maggie recalled, Beverly had indeed come home from that meeting with spirit, and she had struck off at once to inject that very same spirit into the lukewarm stores of Royal Burgers.

Off they had gone in Ann Hastings's car—Maggie and Carmen and Ann and Beverly, taking to the roads of California armed with slogans and pep talks and appointment books waiting to be filled. With unexpected energy and enthusiasm Beverly had visited every Royal Burger outlet, met with every employee, learned their names, wrote down their birthdays, shook hands and gave them her "spirit speech": "We have to be better than everyone else, because we *are* better! You don't want to work for a mediocre company, you want to be proud of your company, as proud as if it were your own, as if it were your family! We don't want our employees going through a daily grind and just earning a paycheck. We want you to strive, we want you to have goals, we want you to dare to dream."

And to back up her passionate speech, to prove to them it wasn't just talk, Beverly established incentive plans within the company. She sketched out a hierarchy, from the lowliest floor washer and beginning trainee cook to the manager, and promised her several hundred employees that each of them was not just a number but a person and that they would be recognized individually for their performance and would be rewarded for loyalty and excellence in their work, and that there was room for advancement and promotion within the company—"All the way up to the corporate headquarters in Hollywood, if that is your goal."

The campaign had been a success. Absenteeism and tardiness dropped as employees started showing up on time and working harder. They received cards and a small bonus on their birthdays, they received a letter of congratulations from Miss Highland herself when a promotion was made or when store profits exceeded a set goal. Contests were held among the stores; the Employee of the Month Award was created; a periodic employee evaluation and pay-raise schedule was established; Beverly welcomed suggestions from her workers and strove to answer them personally. Gradually the face and nature of the Royal Burger company began to change. It became known as a company that cared for its employees, whether you filled ketchup bottles or signed the paychecks. You weren't forgotten, and incentive and creativity were rewarded. Soon the HELP WANTED signs disappeared from the windows of the Royal Burger stands; waiting lists grew as young people sought employment with a company that promised a future. As a consequence the food and service got better, profits rose, and new Royal Burger stands began to spring up all over the West. Next month, Maggie and Carmen and Beverly were going to New York, to start up the East Coast Division of Royal Burgers.

All because Beverly Highland had found the "spirit."

And that wasn't all that that remarkable day at the Chamber of Commerce meeting had generated. Exactly fourteen days after Beverly's speech, the president and chairman of the chamber had approached her with a proposition: they were going to set up a study committee on what Hollywood was going to be like in the next decade, the eighties, and they wanted Beverly to serve as chairman of that committee. All three friends— Beverly, Maggie, and Carmen—had recognized the significance of that gesture immediately. Beverly Highland suddenly had her identity within the business community; she had credibility and now was being given power.

It was, Maggie Kern knew, only the beginning.

A soft knock on the door of the hotel room brought Beverly and Maggie out of their thoughts. They turned to see two men and a woman come in quietly and close the door behind themselves.

"It went like a charm," Ann Hastings said, kicking off her shoes and heading for the food service table. "He bought it hook, line, and sinker."

Beverly looked at the two men, one of whom was peeling a false bald head off his skull and fluffing out his long sandy hair. Now that Roy Madison was a popular TV personality it took a lot of makeup to disguise his looks. But not one of the seven thousand in Danny's church tonight had recognized the actor beneath the doctor's guise. "God damn if I don't deserve an Oscar for that!" he said, and let out a whoop.

Beverly looked at the second man, an actor named Paul who was trying to get into the movies and who was Roy's current lover. "Are you all right?" she asked.

He smiled shyly and said, "Yes, ma'am. I'm fine. I've had training in falling down and holding my breath."

"Not to mention," Ann said, "how good you were with the makeup. That weak little wipe of your hand across your lips took the blue right off."

Roy let out another whoop, pulled the paunch out of his shirt and threw it down. "Damn, this was hot!"

"Tell me what happened," Beverly said.

Ann Hastings, who had played the grieving wife, recounted the episode as she picked Gulf shrimp out of a salad and popped them in her mouth. She ended it with "Everyone in that church, including Danny himself, believes he actually brought Paul here back from the dead. The people were so worked up, you should have seen it! There were a couple of reporters asking questions outside. And do you know what? People actually vouched for 'Doc Chandler'! They swore they'd gone to him for years!"

Beverly turned to gaze out at the lights. "They just wanted to authenticate a miracle that they desperately wanted to be real. You can't blame them for lying."

Beverly wasn't proud of the trick they had played on Danny tonight, but it had been necessary. Danny Mackay had boasted of restoring three people to life. Investigations into each incident had failed to prove otherwise. Those involved had vowed firmly that a miracle had indeed occurred. Beverly didn't like that. She didn't like the idea that innocent people were being duped into believing Danny's fakery and giving him their money. He was giving them false hope, and that was cruel. The only way to stop him from further hurting people was to expose the three miracles for the frauds that they were. And the only way to do that, she had realized, was to stage a fourth, this time with people who would be willing to confess that it was all a hoax.

If Danny tried it again, he was going to wish he hadn't.

28

WHEN THE DOOR to Barry Greene's office suddenly burst open, he spilled his coffee and jumped up in time to prevent it from staining his pants.

"Barry!" said Ariel Dubois, striding in just one step ahead of his secretary.

"I'm sorry, Mr. Greene," the secretary said, flustered. "Miss Dubois just walked right past me."

"It's okay, Fran." He waved her out and continued to mop the spilled coffee off his desk top. The magnificent Ariel, one of the studio's biggest stars, liked to make dramatic entrances.

"Well," he said, throwing the handkerchief away and resuming his seat. "This *is* a surprise, Ariel. To what do I owe this honor?"

She settled into the velour easy chair and crossed one long magnificent leg over the other. "Barry darling, I want you to do something for me."

"When don't you?" he sighed. "What is it this time?"

"I want that bitch Latricia off the show."

He wasn't surprised. In fact, Barry had been expecting this thunderclap for quite some time, ever since the plump Latricia had lost forty pounds and started receiving fan mail and the writers of the show began giving her more lines.

"Do you know what they're planning for the episode of sweeps week?" Ariel asked, venom dripping from her tone.

Barry already knew. Nurse Washington (Latricia Brown) was going to be spotlighted. She was suddenly going to find romance with one of the show's doctors, experience tragedy and then a dramatic brave comeback, all at the expense of Ariel Dubois's air time. Well, he couldn't blame the writers. After going on a health kick and losing weight, Latricia Brown had turned out to be quite a good-looking woman. The letters had started pouring in from viewers wanting to see more of her. And that last show, in which Nurse Washington did an emergency tracheotomy on a baby and saved its life, had shot them up into the next ratings slot.

Barry would, in fact, have liked to see Latricia's role expanded—for two years her part had been a very small one, and in some episodes she had never appeared at all—but he wasn't going to risk Ariel's wrath. He could tell by the way she swung one gorgeous leg and kept tossing back her mane of ash-blond hair that she was out for blood.

Well, this wasn't the first time a star had gotten jealous over a bit player and had him or her canned. And Latricia Brown wasn't worth getting into a fight with Ariel. The number one rule of Barry Greene's life was "Avoid trouble. At all costs."

"Okay, Ariel. I'll find another show to put her in."

One month later Barry Greene had trouble.

"And how is John, dear? Jessica?"

Jessica looked at her mother. "I beg your pardon?"

"You weren't listening."

"I'm sorry. I was thinking about the latest case I've taken on." Jessica gave her mother an apologetic smile. They were sitting in the glass-and-marble dining room, with a view of the golf course and snow-capped Mt. San Jacinto in the background, of the Mulligans' Palm Springs home, where they were eating tender steaks and baked potatoes. The food was perfect, just as the million-dollar house was perfect. Jessica's sixty-five-year-old mother wore an impeccable jogging outfit of lemon-yellow velour, and her father a pale pink rugby shirt and pleated canvas pants. They both looked trim, tanned, and rich.

"A pity John couldn't come with you tonight, Jess," her father said as he carved his steak.

"He's in San Francisco. His company is—"

"I wanted his advice on an investment I'm thinking of making."

"Yes, well"—Jessica moved her untouched steak around her plate—"he'll be home tomorrow."

While they spoke her father didn't look at her once. In

fact, he rarely looked at his daughter when talking to her. Jessica once figured she'd seen the top of his head or the back of his neck more times than she had actually seen his face. Which was just as well, because when he did skewer her with those hard, judgmental eyes of his, she always found herself suddenly at a loss for words.

The three ate in silence for a while. Every now and then Jessica looked out at the spectacular view and wished she had such a view from her own house. All she and John looked out on was Sunset Boulevard.

"What's your new case about, dear?" Mrs. Mulligan asked.

"Well, have you ever watched *Five North*—"

Her father looked up. "*Five North*. Isn't that that TV hospital show? Silliest piece of nonsense I ever saw. Who on earth wants to watch shows about sick people? It's aimed at morons I have no doubt."

"I rather like the show," Mrs. Mulligan said softly.

"You would. Women are obsessed with illness and death."

"In fact, Mother," Jessica said, "have you read about the actress on the show who is suing the producer and the studio for breach of contract?"

Mrs. Mulligan opened her mouth, but it was her husband who answered for her. "I don't see what the woman is all worked up about. I understand they offered her a part in another show—a better part, mind you, and at a higher salary. She flung it in their faces, I hear."

"It's the principle of the thing, Dad. She's being persecuted because the star of the show has taken a dislike to—"

"Pass the sour cream, will you, Jess?"

"I think she looks rather pretty," Mrs. Mulligan said, "now that she's lost all that weight. Sort of like an African princess."

"It's the producer's show," said Mr. Mulligan. "It's his money. If he wants her out, then he has the right to throw her out. After all, she broke their agreement by changing her looks."

"Dad, there's nothing in her contract that says she has to be fat."

Mr. Mulligan mashed the sour cream into his baked potato

and frowned. "Helen? How long did you cook these potatoes?"

Jessica gave her mother an exasperated look and returned to picking at her food.

There weren't any walls to speak of in the Mulligan house. The living room became the dining room, which sort of segued into the family room. Designed for gracious desert living, the golf course "estate" had polished marble floors, stark white walls, sparse furniture in soft pastels, and a few pieces of rare, expensive sculpture. Jim Mulligan was a retired businessman who spent all his time on the golf course, while his wife busied herself with card clubs, flower arranging, and Weight Watchers meetings. The three now took their coffee into the sunken conversation pit; it was too cold outside to sit on the patio and listen to the trickle of the Spanish fountain.

While Jim settled down into the best seat in the pit and reached for the television schedule, Mrs. Mulligan turned to her daughter and said, "You seem awfully preoccupied tonight, dear."

"It's this case I'm handling. I just don't know . . ."

Mr. Mulligan regarded Jessica over the top of his bifocals. He had been fiercely proud when his youngest daughter had graduated with honors from Stanford Law School. He had had visions of setting her up in a substantial practice here in Palm Springs. He had even discussed it with John Franklin, Jessica's new husband, and John had found the idea appealing. But then Jessica had surprised them both by announcing that she was going into practice somewhere in Hollywood with a classmate, and that they were going to go into entertainment law. To Jim Mulligan's way of thinking, that was no better than being an agent.

"What is the case?" Mrs. Mulligan asked, aware of her husband's disapproving stare.

"I'm representing Latricia Brown."

"The one on the medical show?"

"She knows Mickey Shannon. He referred her to me."

"She doesn't have a leg to stand on," said her father. "One two-bit actress against a powerful studio and one of the hottest producers in Hollywood? Why doesn't the stupid girl accept their offer? I think they're being damned generous by half."

"Because, Dad," Jessica said slowly, "it's as I said earlier. It's the principle of the thing. She decided to fight them and she asked me to represent her."

"What are you going to do, dear?"

"I'm not really sure, Mother. We're meeting with Barry Greene at the studio in the morning."

Jessica glanced at her father. He was scowling into the television schedule.

They continued to sip their coffee in silence. Jessica dreaded these perfunctory visits with her parents—she did it mainly to please her mother. They had nothing in common; she and her father invariably disagreed, and her mother never let a visit go by without some mention of Jessica's childlessness. The evening usually wound down with Jessica watching the clock and counting the minutes until she could leave.

She was more than preoccupied with the Latricia Brown case, she was downright worried about it. Jessica had tried to talk about it with John before he left for San Francisco, but he hadn't listened.

Jessica didn't see what was wrong with the specialty she had chosen. There certainly was a need for experts in creative properties. Jessica and her partner dealt not only with contracts but also with copyrights, plagiarism, artists' rights, and anything to do with books, television, or the movies. But, she supposed now as she drank her coffee and looked at the clock, because she mingled on a daily basis with Industry people, neither John nor her father approved.

She thought about the meeting tomorrow morning. She had been losing sleep over it. In the four weeks since she had agreed to take on the case and had been advising Ms. Brown, Jessica had not come up with ammunition to fight Barry Greene and the studio. Although there was nothing in the contract that said Latricia had to stay fat, it was nonetheless implied that she could not drastically alter her looks without the studio's approval. After all, her weight loss had not been part of the show. It wasn't written into the script.

To make matters worse, the press had reported Latricia Brown as having been offered a generous settlement by Barry Greene and the studio. She had turned it down, and as a consequence public sympathy for her was waning. A raise and a new car looked good to a lot of the people who read the Los Angeles *Times*. But Latricia was sticking to her fight because it was about time, she declared, that someone showed the studio moguls that actors weren't pieces of property to be used and discarded on a whim.

Jessica had spent nearly every hour of the past month worrying over the case and trying to find a loophole with which to hang Mr. Barry Greene. But he had the money and the power behind him, while Latricia was black, a woman, and wouldn't even be able to pay her attorney.

Jessica felt like David going against Goliath, and was worried because she didn't even have a good slingshot for the meeting tomorrow morning.

Well, it was really what she had expected. She had known from the start that it would be a no-win case for her client. According to Latricia's contract, the studio literally owned her and could do anything they wanted with her. She was technically an unknown actress; they could even kill off her character if they wanted to. There was no fight, then, so why had Jessica agreed to take on the case, knowing that there was no guarantee of a cash settlement?

Because, as Latricia had so passionately said to her, there comes a time when someone's just got to stop and turn around and fight. And Jessica just couldn't resist the challenge.

When her father picked up the remote control and turned on the forty-one-inch Sony TV, Jessica looked at him. Yes, she thought, there comes a time when you have to stand up for what is right. Had she sat down and really examined her motives for helping Latricia Brown without the expectation of being paid, Jessica might have seen something significant in her siege against Barry Greene and the studio. She might also have expanded her vision and seen why she so enjoyed litigation and a good courtroom fight. It was because that was the one arena in which she could stand up and be heard, and maybe even win. Opposing counselors were surrogates for father and priests and a husband she had never been able to stand up to.

She looked away from her father and was surprised to see the handsome face of Danny Mackay fill the TV screen. His

Gospel singers were belting out an energetic hymn while he smiled beneficently at America.

She turned to her mother. "Since when have you two been watching Danny Mackay?"

"We started about—"

"He's a good man," Jim Mulligan said. "The Reverend stands for honesty and decency in this country, and I'm all for him."

"But, Dad. He claims he talks to God!"

"So did Jimmy Carter. And so did Franklin Roosevelt, for that matter."

"Good grief, Dad. This man is dangerous! Pretending that Danny Mackay is just following an old tradition in politics is pure sophistry. It's one thing to turn to prayerful or meditative thought when in doubt about something, but quite something else to claim certain knowledge of God's desires—"

"Helen, the picture still isn't coming in clear. Did you call the cable company today like I told you to?"

Jessica looked at her mother. Mrs. Mulligan avoided her daughter's eye.

The three settled back into silk-screened Navajo pillows to watch Danny Mackay shout out his sermon. Jessica didn't care for the man. She couldn't put her finger on it, but there was something about him she didn't like. His smile looked genuine enough, and he spoke with heart. But he wore very expensive suits and surrounded himself with big men with crew cuts who looked more like bodyguards than religious disciples.

On his evening show, which differed from his daily morning *Good News Hour*, Rev. Danny always had a guest, a personality whose life had in some way been changed by the Lord. Tonight it was a well-known fashion designer from New York. In front of two and a half million people the man confessed his sin of homosexuality and said that Jesus had straightened him out. It was a very dramatic witnessing, ending up with the Gospel singers clustering protectively around the poor man while he and Reverend Danny sobbed on each other's shoulders.

Jessica had never watched Danny Mackay's evening show,

but she had heard of it because it was the first of its kind to be broadcast during prime time and because it was steadily climbing in the ratings. She wouldn't have thought that such a Christian Fundamentalist program would find so large an audience. And yet . . .

She looked at her parents, who were staring intently at the screen. Catholics, both of them.

Jessica looked back at Rev. Danny. There was no doubt about it, he possessed a certain charisma. She leaned forward, cradling her coffee cup between her hands, and gazed at the spectacle on the TV screen. It was incredibly theatrical, but there was a basic human pathos in those embraces and tears that touched even Jessica's skeptical heart. It was no wonder, she decided, that the man was doing unexpectedly well in the polls. She wouldn't be surprised if he won the New Hampshire primary next week.

As the telephone number of Rev. Danny's Houston headquarters was being flashed on the screen, Jessica stood up abruptly and said, "I have to leave now."

Her mother looked stricken. "But we haven't had dessert yet, dear."

"Don't force her," Jim Mulligan said, clicking off the TV set. "Jessica, you need to exercise more. Why don't you ever go jogging with John?"

Her mother walked her out to the Cadillac. The desert night was freezing; the stars were like ice splashed across the sky, as if snowy Mt. Jacinto had erupted. "We don't see enough of you," Mrs. Mulligan said as she offered a cheek to be kissed. "Now, your sister Bridget, she and those kids are here almost every week. And do they exhaust me!"

Jessica got into her car and started the engine. "Drive carefully, dear," Helen Mulligan said. "One last thing. Do you think you could get Ariel Dubois's autograph for me?"

As she turned off Bob Hope Drive and onto the highway, Jessica pressed the accelerator. She was suddenly anxious to get home. She gripped the steering wheel and urged the car to go faster, faster. Because she had suddenly come up with an idea, a weapon for tomorrow morning. If it worked, Barry Greene was going to be in for the surprise of his life.

. . .

Latricia Brown was gorgeous. Her new thinness made her look taller than before, and now that she was cornrowing her hair, she did indeed look like an African princess. She walked with a certain pride; there was a new crispness to her step that hadn't been visible in the old "Nurse Washington" of a few months ago. It was no wonder that she was starting to receive fan mail and the writers of the show wanted to create more of her part. She was damned if she was going to let that bitch Ariel have her swept under the carpet, as had happened with so many other unknown actresses. Latricia was fighting this fight not only for herself but for exploited actors and actresses everywhere, and for her own black race.

She just hoped Jessica Franklin could find a way to win the case for her. But the odds were definitely not in her favor. Neither was the law.

"Let me see your contract," Jessica had said to Latricia on their first meeting a month ago. "If we can, we'll fight them on the basis of termination without cause." Jessica had used other legal phrases—wrongful discharge, sex discrimination, "good faith" clauses, adhesion terms—in explaining to Latricia the different ways the case might go. And then, two days later, when Latricia had brought in her contract and Jessica had studied it, the legal terms changed to boilerplate clauses, tenuous cause of action, words that summed up one phrase: Latricia didn't have a leg to stand on.

And yet, to Latricia's enormous surprise, Jessica Franklin had agreed to take on the case. "Listen," she had said in all honesty, "I don't think we'll win. But you may profit from the publicity, and so will my firm." The first thing they had done was issue a press statement. "Public sentiment is going to go with *you*," Jessica had told Latricia. "We might not have any bargaining power legally, but it's possible we could get the studio to back down because of the bad press this is going to bring them."

It hadn't worked. The very first dialogue between Jessica and Barry Greene had shown the two women how the fight was going to go—totally in his favor.

The reception area of Jessica's office was quiet and subdued. Once the heavy doors swung closed on the noisy Strip, somber silence greeted the visitor. The carpet was thick, the furniture deep and dark, the brass well polished, the wood oiled and lemony. The receptionist, a young man in his early twenties who kept his nose in law books when not filing or typing, rose to meet Ms. Brown and escort her into Jessica's office.

The two shook hands, and then Jessica looked anxiously at the young man. "Any phone calls yet?"

He shook his head. "I'm guarding that phone with my life, Jess. Trust me."

"I trust you, Ken. But I'm afraid"—she frowned down at her watch—"that Latricia and I have to get over to Barry Greene's office. Now listen, think of that phone call as a matter of life and death. You call me the minute you get it. I'll be in a meeting, but have them pull me out."

Ken gave her an encouraging smile. "Don't worry, Jess. I want that phone call to come through as badly as you do."

She winked. She had promised him a job in the firm after graduation from law school in three months.

Barry Greene's office was at the studio in, of course, Studio City. A light March rain fell as Jessica took her Cadillac over Sepulveda Pass; she explained on the way to Latricia what the phone call could mean. Latricia noticed that her attorney seemed agitated this morning, not her usual quiet, conservative self, but nervous, her hands working the leather steering wheel. She talked fast, almost breathlessly, and laid her foot a bit too heavily on the accelerator. But as she explained this new situation Latricia felt herself become excited as well. She had to admit it was a stroke of genius, and if they could pull it off, if that phone call would come through in time . . .

They rode the elevator fifteen flights and found themselves in the outrageously glamorous reception area of Greene Productions. Jessica and Latricia were, of course, expected and on time—they had set up this appointment over a week ago—but they were asked to wait nonetheless. They sank into the deep velour chairs and declined offers of something to drink by the secretary. They waited in tension-filled silence as the secretary worked quietly at her desk, as the clocked ticked relentlessly, and as the phone never rang.

Behind the enormous doors with the brass nameplate, Barry was sitting in his spacious office going through travel brochures and trying to think of a way of persuading Dr. Linda Markus to go away somewhere with him. He was sure she was interested in him, that she was just playing hard to get. Barry Greene never had trouble having his way with women, either because they were after his money, or wanted a part in one of his shows, or simply to be able to say they had been to bed with a TV producer. Linda, so far, had not succumbed. And that made her all the more desirable.

Greene's secretary had informed him that Mrs. Franklin and her client were in the waiting room. "Let them wait," he said.

Barry figured he would let them stew for a bit, then allow them to air their complaints, and finally deliver the blow. Either Brown accepts his terms or she's out of television all together. It was within Barry's power to see to it that she never worked in front of a TV camera again.

In the outer office, Jessica kept looking at her watch. She couldn't help the tremor in her knee. Latricia at her side, looking cool and in control, was so nervous she was beginning to feel sick. Four weeks ago she had been so angry to be told she was off the show that she had acted on her first impulse: fury. She had gotten a lawyer and begun the fight. But now, after four weeks of being strung along by the television moguls and seeing their threats become more and more real, she found herself being nipped at the heels by the dogs of doubt and insecurity.

God, maybe she *should* take their offer, if it was still open, to appear on another series.

She glanced at Jessica. The phone call was such a long shot. *If* it came at all, and *if* it delivered what Jessica was hoping for. Two mighty big ifs for a person to base her whole career on.

Barry Greene had gone through Hong Kong, Cancún, the Great Barrier Reef, and Aspen when he finally scooped up all the brochures and slid them into a drawer. He looked at the clock on the wall, which was lost among awards, plaques, letters of commendation, and photographs of himself with famous people, and saw that he had kept them waiting for twenty minutes.

He called his secretary and told her to send them in.

"Look, ladies," Barry was saying a few minutes later, "it's all here in black and white. According to the contract, *which you signed*, Latricia, I have the authority to remove you from the show." He turned to Jessica. "And if you knew anything about contract law, you would know that your client doesn't have a legal leg to stand on. What mystifies me is why you are wasting your time on this case!"

Jessica spoke calmly and slowly, trying to drag out the time. "What mystifies me, Mr. Greene, is why you would fire an actress when it is not in the best interest of your show. She has brought up the ratings, which in turn will increase advertising revenues."

"There were creative problems with the role. We simply decided her character was no longer necessary."

"Ariel Dubois decided that, you mean," Latricia broke in.

Jessica cast her a cautioning look. "You see, Mr. Greene, I regard this as a matter of wrongful discharge—"

"Look, honey, you yourself know that we have an unconditional right to do with Latricia whatever we want. The contract that she signed gives us total discretion as to whether we use her or not. This should be obvious even to you. So why are we sitting here and wasting my time?"

Jessica managed a discreet glance at her watch. Damn it, where was that phone call! "Mr. Greene, I intend to take this case to trial, and I can assure you that the jury will be sympathetic with my client."

He laughed. "Juries don't frighten me, Jessica."

"Excuse me, Mr. Greene, I didn't know we were on a first-name basis."

His smile faded. "Listen, honey, Latricia doesn't have a case and that's all there is to it." They were getting to him. They were annoying him, and just when he was feeling so good. He had Linda Markus romantically on his mind, and if that didn't pan out there was that blonde in wardrobe who was itching to sign just such a contract as this ungrateful bitch had once signed. Latricia Brown! Whose idea was it anyway that they needed a Negro on the show?

Jessica licked her lips with a dry tongue. It didn't look as if the call was going to come through. "Nonetheless, we intend to pursue this, and I am sure a great deal of negative publicity, for you and for the studio, will result."

He laughed again and sat back in his executive chair. Threats, that was all she could come up with.

"Television ratings, Mr. Greene, are affected by public opinion, whether you choose to accept that or not. If we go to trial, my client will be talking to the newspapers and appearing on television, and certain—shall we say, *private*—aspects of your life might be revealed?"

He chuckled and shook his head. "Where did you go to law school anyway? People *love* to read about my private affairs. Go ahead. Tell the L.A. *Times*. Tell the *National Enquirer*. Tell *Reader's Digest*. Go on Phil Donahue and tell it to the world! I have nothing to hide."

Jessica bit her lower lip and glanced at Latricia. She needed to hang on, just a little longer. . . .

"Now, if you'll excuse me," Barry said, starting to rise. Then his phone rang, and it was his secretary telling him that Ms. Franklin had an urgent call.

"I'll take it in the other room," Jessica said, jumping up and hurrying out.

Barry strummed his fingers on his immaculate desk top while Latricia gazed about the sumptuous office that was bigger than her whole apartment. She was beginning to hate the man behind that desk, not only for what he was doing to her, but now for the way he was treating Jessica.

Jessica came in then and sat down without looking at Latricia. "Very well, Mr. Greene," she said in a strong voice, "you've stated your position quite clearly. Now I shall state ours. The phone call I just received is one that I have been waiting for. It came from Houston." She paused for dramatic effect. "My client here has just been scheduled to appear one week from tonight on Danny Mackay's evening program. And what she is going to tell his nationwide audience, Mr. Greene, on the same network, by the way, which airs your own show, is that she lost weight because the Lord commanded her to respect and revere her body, His temple, and that you and this studio are persecuting her for it."

He stared at her. Then he looked at Latricia. She was a good actress, a damn good one. She'd have two and a half million people saying amen and crying for her and lusting for the blood of Barry Greene.

And the ratings would go down the toilet.

He thought about Ariel. Well, what could she do? Nothing that a fur coat from Barry wouldn't remedy. All Barry Greene wanted to do was avoid trouble at all costs.

When Jessica pulled into the driveway she was glad to see John's BMW parked there. That meant he was home from San Francisco. *We'll celebrate*, she thought as she hurried into the house, handed her coat and briefcase to the maid, and flew up the stairs to the master bedroom. *I'll call Spago for a reservation. We'll drink champagne till it comes out of our ears! We'll order a duck pizza and amaretto hot fudge sundaes and—* She found her husband standing in front of the mirror buttoning the cuffs of a new shirt.

"We won!" she cried, putting her arms around him and kissing his cheek. "We won the case, John!"

"What case is that?"

"Latricia Brown. I had Barry Greene backed against a wall! Damn, I'm smart!"

He regarded her in the mirror. "I hope this isn't going to result in more negative publicity for us."

Jessica sighed. "Latricia didn't kiss me, if that's what you're worried about. But wait till you hear how I managed to beat the studio!"

"You can tell me in the car on our way to Ray and Bonnie's."

"Ray and Bonnie's?"

"They've invited us over for dinner." He turned and looked at her. "Have you been drinking, Jessica?"

"Just some champagne. Fred always keeps a bottle on ice for when we win a—"

"How long will it take you to get ready?" he asked, looking at his watch. "We're due there in ten minutes."

Jessica blinked. "I thought we would celebrate our winning the case."

"Please don't say *our*. I certainly don't want my name attached to your scandals."

"They're not scandals—"

"Anyway"—he sat down to put on his shoes—"we can celebrate with Ray and Bonnie."

But I don't like Ray and Bonnie!

"Bonnie loves to hear all about your movie-star friends. God knows why! Must have something to do with being a sixth-grade teacher. Get dressed, Jessica."

She gave him an exasperated look.

"Come on now," he said, touching her arm. "Get dressed. And wear your black slacks. They flatter your thighs."

"But I wanted to celebrate alone, just the two of us."

His tone grew impatient. "We can have a perfectly fine celebration with Bonnie and Ray. He's my friend and my partner, Jessica. I wish you wouldn't just think about what *you* want all the time."

"I don't want to fight with you, John," she said softly.

"We're not fighting, Jessica. Just do like I say and get dressed. They'll wonder what's taking us so long."

She stared down at the carpet.

"Hey," he said, coming up to her and putting his hands on her shoulders. "You'll have your celebration, don't worry. And you can tell us all about how you managed to twist Barry Greene around your little finger. I'll bet he couldn't resist a pretty face! Go get dressed now, okay?"

"Okay," she said softly, and suddenly it was all wrong and Jessica didn't know how to make it right.

29

Paris: 1974

*"Hello, Beverly. I'm Christine. Christine Singleton, your
sister."*

Beverly stared. Christine! My sister! Is it really you!

"You've found me at last, Beverly."

*"Oh thank God!" Beverly ran to embrace her. But her
arms closed on empty air.*

*"Christine!" she cried. "Where are you! Please don't leave
me again—"*

Beverly's eyes flew open.

She found herself staring up at an ornate ceiling, curiously
painted in rococo festoons of ribbons and flowers and guarded
at each corner by plaster cherubs. For an instant she didn't
know where she was. She lay listening to her thumping heart;
she felt the damp, twisted sheets beneath her.

Then she remembered. She was in a hotel. In Paris.

Beverly sighed deeply. The dream again. It was because of
Jonas Buchanan's phone call the night before. After two years
of following leads on the divorced Singletons and reaching only
dead ends, he had finally broken through. "I came across an
old newspaper story," he had said last night on the transat-
lantic call, "about a rather bizarre kidnapping case that occurred back in 1947. The family involved was named
Singleton. The couple was going through a nasty divorce, and
the father ran off with the little girl, who was nine years old.
They were never found. But I decided to look into it."

Jonas told Beverly how he had done some research and
learned the name of the father's hometown. On a hunch, thinking the father might have gone there with the child, Jonas went
to investigate. "There were no Singletons listed, but I spent a
day looking at school records. I found that a Christine Singleton had been placed with an order of nuns in a small convent

when she was twelve. I tried to get more information on her, but so far the Mother Superior won't grant me access to the records. I'll keep trying, though."

"What about the father?" Beverly had asked. "What happened to Singleton?"

"I haven't been able to find out. I assume he's dead."

Beverly had only one other question: "Do you know yet what my sister looked like? Have you found any pictures of her?"

Jonas was sorry to report that he was still unable to come up with any photographs of Christine Singleton.

Beverly did not as a rule allow herself to savor luxury; a quick morning shower was her usual daily bath. But on this cold, snowy morning on the Rue de la Madeleine, in the elegant Hotel Papillon, where the Empress Josephine had once stayed, Beverly soaked for a long time in a hot, steamy bubble bath. She had a critical day ahead of her; she needed to have her mind alert and her body invigorated.

By the time she was out and wrapped in a plush terrycloth robe the telephone was ringing.

Carmen's voice came over the long-distance wire, ebbing and flowing like a tide. She had been reporting to Beverly every day during Beverly's three-month buying tour of Europe, keeping her up to date on her various financial holdings and receiving orders.

"I investigated Monument Publications like you asked, Bev," she had to practically shout over the crackling wire. "You were right. Their textbook line is losing money and they're about to let half their staff go. But the magazine is doing well. In fact, *Sex Kittens* is what's kept Monument above water for the past five years. But now even that isn't enough. They're about to file Chapter Eleven."

Beverly made notes while Carmen spoke. Maggie would transcribe them later and add them to the growing file on Monument Publications.

"Did you tell them my offer?"

"They jumped at it."

"Then buy it."

Beverly was still on the phone when Maggie came quietly

313

into the room, the ever-present briefcase and steno pad in her hands.

"How are the children?" Beverly asked Carmen in the end. It was always the last thing she said before ringing off.

"They're fine, Bev. They want to know when you and Maggie are coming home."

Maggie's two children, Arthur and Joe Jr., were staying with Carmen in her split-level ranch house out in Chatsworth. The boys were now eight and six years old, and were the constant playmates of ten-year-old Rosa.

"Can you put them on the phone? We'd like to say hello."

When Carmen said, "It's the middle of the night here, Bev. I don't want to wake them," Beverly felt a pang of disappointment. The one thing she had missed the most during her three-month absence from Los Angeles was the three children. "Tell them we'll be home next week. And tell them I have presents for them."

"Presents!" Maggie said as she opened the door for the room service waiter. "You're going to have to charter a special plane just to get all that stuff home."

"Christmas is coming," Beverly said after she hung up. "I'm just bringing them a few toys, that's all."

Maggie laughed and shook her head. It was a constant fight to keep her boys from being spoiled by Beverly.

They discussed the day's agenda over *brioches* and *café américain*. Beverly only nibbled at one of the buns while Maggie helped herself to two, generously buttering them. She had put on weight since coming to work for Beverly Highland five years ago.

This was their morning ritual, going over business before starting the day. They made quite a team. Maggie had come into Beverly's employ with seven years of experience working in a stock brokerage house, and with a keen mind for investment strategies. Beverly now had money, thanks to the astonishing success of Royal Burgers.

Upon Maggie's advice, Beverly had gone public with her company, offering shares and bringing in revenue from venture capitalists. With that money she had expanded the chain into a hundred more locations in fourteen new states. The Crown

Burger (a double burger with Bermuda onion and jack cheese) and the grated parmesan added to the jalapeño fries, plus the lower prices and beautifully upgraded decor of the restaurants, caused Royal Burgers to be an overnight success. The four friends were rapidly realizing their dreams: Carmen Sanchez, who had once dreamed of working in a respectable office, was now a CPA and the corporate accountant for Royal Burgers; Ann Hastings, who had gained self-confidence and boyfriends and a Porsche, was in charge of quality control for the nearly five hundred outlets; and Beverly Highland was chairman of the board of the largest hamburger franchise in the United States, a fast-food chain that brought in millions of dollars annually.

Now Beverly was starting to diversify. With the help of Maggie's investment background and the benefit of Carmen's excellent business education, Beverly's money was being carefully turned around and invested in other enterprises. This was all being gathered under the recently formed Highland Enterprises, a fast-growing corporation whose motto was *Dare. . . .*

"Dare to accept the challenge to make Hollywood great again!" Beverly had cried at the Chamber of Commerce meeting three years ago. And from that auditorium Beverly had carried her newly born "spirit" out into the world, into everything she did. That day had also given birth to something else: Beverly's identity within the business community. She had accepted the offer to serve as chairman on the new committee, and soon she was recognized by her colleagues as a woman of strength, ideas, and ambition. Beverly now went around to business schools, to clubs and various other groups, and gave speeches. And the auditorium was always full. "Dare to make it happen," she would tell her audience. "Dare to set high goals. Dare to take a chance. Dare to live your dreams!" Few went away unmoved by her spirit and energy.

And now Beverly had brought that spirit to Europe. She had come for two purposes: to locate sites for Royal Burger restaurants and to gain some suggestions as to what might be done with the men's store in Beverly Hills that she had inherited from Eddie.

The Royal Burger deal was now sealed: Beverly was going

315

to open take-out stands on Piccadilly Circus in London, on the Via Veneto in Rome, and on the Champs-Elysées here in Paris. All that remained was solving the mystery of how on earth to save the store on Rodeo Drive.

By the time Bob Manning joined them in Beverly's suite their business meeting was finished and the two women were perusing the English-language newspapers that had been delivered with breakfast.

As usual, the first thing Beverly looked for was any international news about Danny Mackay.

As yet, he was not globally known. But his fame in the United States was expanding in dynamic proportions. Ever since he had signed up with Hallstead back in Houston to appear on evangelical TV, Danny's reputation had skyrocketed. He was a natural showman. If he was good on a stage in a tent, he was dynamite in front of a camera. In his first year of electronic preaching, he had doubled the audience of WBET. By the end of the second year he had bought Hallstead out and was the sole owner of a string of religious stations. By the third year he was calling himself the head of Good News Ministries. And by the end of last year his weekly religious hour was finally being broadcast coast to coast.

He was getting there. And someday, when the moment was right, Beverly was going to have her revenge.

Eddie Fanelli's Men's Store in Beverly Hills came under the Highland Enterprises umbrella, but because Beverly had been so busy the past few years with building up her corporation, she had paid little attention to the store. It had not been a money-maker when she inherited it, but now Carmen was reporting regular losses—the store was becoming a financial drain. That was due to the fashion line it carried: old-fashioned clothes, no doubt picked out by Eddie and Laverne themselves, that were once in style but were now hopelessly outdated. When Maggie and Beverly had first set foot in the store and saw the bright lights, the Peter Max posters, the racks of bell-bottoms and Nehru jackets and fake-hippie, fake-counterculture rags, they had been speechless. The young long-haired, gum-chewing sales clerks, slouched and bejeaned, had stunned the two women even further. What had Eddie been thinking?

But now Beverly wanted to do something with the store, and so they were in Paris with Bob Manning, winding down their buying trip.

Bob came into the hotel room as they were going through the newspapers—a distinguished-looking man of short, squarish build, conservatively dressed, and walking with the aid of a jacaranda wood cane. He was sixty-one years old and had spent sixteen years of his life in a hospital. The toll of his long-term illness showed in his limp.

Bob Manning had been working for Beverly for two years now, and he was desperately in love with her.

Pouring himself a cup of coffee from the silver samovar, he said, "It's starting to snow again."

Beverly raised her eyes and, for the first time since awaking from the nightmare, looked at the window. The Paris sky was ominously dark; white flakes drifted down. It reminded Beverly of the last time she had seen snow—twenty-two years ago, in New Mexico. And recalling the nightmare, hearing again her sister's voice calling to her, Beverly prayed that Jonas Buchanan would be successful.

The limousine inched slowly along the icy narrow streets, carefully avoiding the heavier traffic that swung maniacally around the Arc de Triomphe. The three Americans sat in the back in spacious comfort, with thick alpaca blankets over their knees and sipping hot chocolate from small china cups. Beverly had papers spread out in her lap and was studying them. Maggie was looking out at the beauty of Paris and wishing her Joe were still alive to share this with her. And Bob Manning was reviewing the advance press kit he had received from the three couturier houses they were going to visit today.

He didn't hold out much hope for success.

When Beverly brought Bob Manning into the Highland Enterprises family two years ago, he hadn't had a lot to offer. He was slightly lame, he had no connections, and his education had not gone too far. But, to his surprise, Beverly had a place for him—as manager of a men's clothing store.

His duties hadn't amounted to much, it was really just his presence that was required. But he had liked it, having a place to go to every day, knowing that he even *had* a place, and people he had to watch over and a cash register to guard. Then, over the two years, Miss Highland had started visiting the store more and more often, coming in unexpectedly off the street and walking around deep in thought. Once in a while she went upstairs, where they rented offices to small companies—a travel agency, an interior decorator, three insurance salesmen who shared a desk and a phone—people who wanted a Beverly Hills address. Miss Highland would chat politely with the sales clerks and with Bob, nod vaguely, and then leave. It was as though she came there to search for something— possibly, he thought, for a reason for holding on to the store at all. After all, Eddie Fanelli's was now losing money.

And then, just this last summer, she had arrived in her Rolls-Royce Silver Cloud, marched into the store with a purposeful step, and had told Bob to close it down and dismiss all the employees with six months' salary. She was going to go to Europe, she had said, and come back with new stock. The store was going to be done over completely and reopened in six months.

He had been excited at first, landing in London and rubbing his hands in anticipation of the buying the three of them were going to do. He and Maggie had gone out to dinner, in places like Soho and King's Road, leaving Beverly in the hotel, where she preferred to stay when not out actually attending fashion shows. And the two of them had talked animatedly about their ideas. But then the excitement had begun to wear off when they realized that Beverly didn't share their enthusiasm and optimism. In fact, the more they looked into the fashion world, the more somber she became.

There was nothing new, she said in London and Rome, there was absolutely nothing new or exciting that would make their store different from all the rest.

And the unfortunate thing was, Bob had to agree with her.

As the limousine pulled up in front of the couturier house of famed designer Henri Gapin, Bob looked at his employer. God, but she was beautiful. Her face was flawless. How could anyone be born with such perfection? And she dressed to enhance her grace and beauty—the white Dr. Zhivago fur hat set off her chiseled jaw and long neck; the maxi-coat of soft white fur and white boots gave her the illusion of being tall; underneath the coat, Bob knew, Beverly wore a tailored suit with a gold cameo brooch at her throat. She was always impeccably attired, never flashy or trendy but conservative, dressing in styles that were classic and timeless, and her platinum hair was meticulously swept back in a French twist. Beverly Highland gave the impression of being a woman very much in control, of others, and of herself.

Heads turned when Beverly walked through the doors. And this was an impressive gathering. The wife of France's prime minister was present for the showing, as was the Countess de Bossuite, Lady Margaret Hathaway, the senior vice president and fashion director of Bloomingdale's, Manhattan disco owner Sally Will, and an Oscar-winning Italian movie star known for being a fashion trendsetter. All were here to look at Gapin's latest line of men's wear.

The show turned out exactly as Bob Manning had feared it would: just more of the same.

So far, in their eleven weeks in Europe, they had seen the London look, the Italian look, and now the French look, all with little variation. The Continental influence was widely in evidence: checked jackets with bow ties and narrow trousers; flannel suits in outrageous colors; folding hats of Afghanistan lamb fur. Sport shirts came out in bold prints and were allowed to be left outside the belt. Open collars were in, jewelry was expected to be worn, and men's heels had finally gotten as high as women's. Worse, unisex was still around.

As she sat in the brocaded chair and sipped her champagne Beverly watched the handsome male models on the runway and felt her frustration deepen. Three years of success, with Royal Burgers and her more recent secondary enterprises, had conditioned her to expect success in everything she touched.

Was Eddie Fanelli's Men's Store going to be the one exception?

How was she going to make it different from all the other men's shops in Beverly Hills?

She gazed down at the champagne sparkling in her glass and remembered the first time she had tasted *good* champagne—it had been back in 1961, when Roy Madison had landed his first regular part in a TV series. He had come running into the diner with a bottle of Dom Perignon and had begun pouring for everyone. It was all Beverly's doing, he had declared magnanimously as the bubbly wine had frothed all over the counter. Because she had spoken so honestly about his image, and because he had taken her advice and changed it, and because he had escorted Ann to her cousin's Christmas dance, and because he had met that director there who had liked his looks, Roy had started getting small parts on a regular basis. His agent had told him to keep the new look and had gradually gotten him bigger and bigger roles until now he had his own series. All because of Beverly "Bless her" Highland.

That was the day, Beverly recalled now, when Roy had sworn never to forget what she had done for him.

Of course, she had tasted a lot of champagne since those long-ago days of Spartan living. When Beverly had inherited Eddie's wealth and realized what her true potential was, she had decided it was in the best interests of her future to change her life-style. Wealth was what she aspired to, and power. Those things could not be gotten by living in a vacuum, by keeping oneself hidden and cut off from society. To aspire to both she required friends in powerful and influential places. She needed to build a solid reputation; she needed to construct a stature that would be recognized by figures who held key positions. After careful study, Beverly had sold her small Spanish-style house in the Hollywood hills and bought a small Spanish-style house in Beverly Hills at five times the cost. She had exchanged her Chevrolet for a Cadillac, and that for a Mercedes. She hired a maid, then a gardener, and then a cook. She made friends with her neighbors: lawyers and doctors, judges and politicians, writers and movie-industry types—people around whom the universe revolved. She tasted more champagne. She gave parties and served caviar. She entertained people who could open doors for her; she made her name known. She was active in the Chamber of Commerce and served on several cultural committees in Los Angeles. She kept a high profile. She was on her way.

A murmur ran through the audience and Beverly looked up. "*Mesdames et messieurs*, 'brief' is the byword for today's sports-minded, competitive male," Henri Gapin declared as a sleek, tanned model came out onto the runway. "And *Bref* is what we call our newest in men's beach wear. The bikini need no longer remain solely the province of *les femmes*, as Pierre here so dramatically demonstrates for us. . . ."

Dramatic was right, Beverly thought as the shapely and muscular Pierre strutted before astonished/admiring/envious eyes. The bikini barely covered him.

"It's indecent," Maggie murmured next to Beverly. "I love it."

Beverly stared up at the model. When he walked past her, he looked back over his shoulder and winked at her.

"Did you see that?" Maggie whispered.

Beverly had seen it. And, in spite of herself, she had felt a reaction.

"This summer's outfit will be seen at all the right events," Henri continued as another Gallic male beauty came out wearing a beige wool sport jacket and light flannel trousers.

But Beverly watched this model in something close to boredom. She could swear that she had seen the same outfit in Chelsea and Rome. Cotton print shirt, broad silk tie and matching handkerchief, tan leather shoes with crepe soles. Men's fashion, it had turned out, was the same no matter where she went. This wasn't going to help her Beverly Hills store. How could she compete with the established shops that already carried these lines? Bringing Gapin and Courrèges into Eddie Fanelli's wasn't going to make the customers come rushing in. Which was probably what Eddie had realized and tried to correct by going the other way—offering something downmarket.

"Hey," Maggie said quietly. "Check this one out."

"For the younger man," Henri said, when a model came out wearing low-slung jeans and a leather jacket, his long hair messy, his chest seductively bare. It was the old Mick Jagger look, and it never failed to get one kind of reaction or another.

"I don't care for it," Beverly murmured.

"Not the outfit, the guy!"

So Beverly focused on the model and discovered that underneath the tousled, raunchy look there was a very captivating young man. He had a way to his walk, a saucy step that made his hips do nice things. And that smile! Strangely, Beverly found herself warming to the clothes that she had just seconds before disliked.

"What a marketing gimmick," Maggie said, tilting her head toward Beverly. "Look at the faces on some of these women. They don't really like the clothes, but they like *him*."

Beverly watched the model sashay off the stage and give the spotlight to a young man in a tennis outfit.

"Great legs," Maggie muttered, and Beverly glanced around at the faces of the women around her. Like Maggie, they weren't really looking at the clothes.

Maggie said, "You can't tell me those shorts look one tenth that good in their plastic wrap." And Beverly turned abruptly to look at her.

From then on Beverly was no longer bored. She paid close attention to the men modeling the clothes and to the various reactions of the audience, noticing that the actual fashions were inconsequential. And while she watched and studied, an idea began to take shape in Beverly's mind.

She took a careful look around the showroom, took in the refinement and chicness of it. It was strange, but she hadn't thought of it until now—that these fashion houses that revolved around men, catered to men, and designed and manufactured men's clothing were all curiously feminine. And this large affluent audience, although here to look at men's clothing, was by far predominantly female.

Beverly now caught subtle interchanges between models and certain buyers. Those men up on the runway knew they were good; they were con artists. It didn't matter what they wore, they sold their goods with a smile, a wink, a turn of the well-shaped buttocks. Little gold pens jotted things down in little leather notebooks. Heads nodded in appreciation; signals were made to Henri Gapin. A million dollars' worth of sales was going on all around her, and all because Henri Gapin had a special knack—not for designing clothes but for knowing how to sell them.

Beverly Highland had just discovered his secret. He knew his market.

She settled back in her chair and folded her hands. She was anxious to get home now. There was nothing more for them to do here. She knew now what she had to do to make Eddie Fanelli's the busiest men's clothing store in Beverly Hills.

And it was going to work.

The opening of Fanelli of Beverly Hills, on a balmy May evening in 1975, was catered by Richard, the "in" caterer of the moment. Those fortunate enough to have received engraved invitations to attend the opening found themselves confronting a buffet that, even for this jaded social set, was something to talk about: small cooked-in-a-flash pizzas smothered in prosciutto, feta, and mozzarella; black-bean-and-chorizo quesadillas; almond deviled eggs; baked Brie; Latin-style clams; Greek meatballs; and the expected guacamole. For the sweet tooth, strawberries Bavarian, orange ambrosia, individual crystal cups of English trifle, and old-fashioned fudge brownies. All served on elegant black Bennington plates. Waiters passed among the crowd with fluted glasses of champagne, mimosas, or Perrier. There were three types of coffee, an herbal tea as well as Earl Grey, and spicy after-dinner mints from Blum's.

A great deal of the success of the turnout was due to Roy Madison. Not only had he passed the word among his Industry friends, gently hinting that this was going to be one of *the* occasions of the year, but advance press kits announced that he would be present at the opening of Fanelli, and Roy Madison was a man a lot of people wanted to get a look at.

He appeared in his trademark "look": jeans and blue work shirt, cowboy boots and Western belt. His sandy hair was still worn long; his handsome, once-Fabian face was etched with suntan lines and character. And he was now one of the highest-paid stars on television.

Ann Hastings and Carmen and Maggie had all arrived early, turning their cars over to the parking attendants of Fanelli's private lot. Beverly arrived at the last minute in her Rolls, and she spent the hectic afternoon and evening acting as the friendly but aloof and mysterious hostess. Not a few people went back to their homes in the hills that night wondering for the first time about the beautiful, elusive Miss Highland.

Roy Madison gave out autographs to those who asked for it; Ann Hastings saw to the smooth execution of the fashion show; Maggie played hostess, greeting luminaries and answering questions; Carmen stayed behind the scenes, overseeing the caterers and keeping a close eye on the new sales clerks; and Bob Manning remained in the back changing room, supervising the models.

The models, of course, were the hit of the evening.

This was something no one had expected: a constant show of Fanelli's fashions and accessories on models who were handsome and sexy (Roy Madison had personally recruited them for Beverly), and who strolled among the partyers as if they were guests themselves, smiling and confident, with no annoying narration over a microphone telling people what they were looking at.

Well, there was no need to tell these people what they were looking at—the guests at Fanelli's opening were well acquainted with Cardin and Lauren, with Courrèges and Gapin, with Mr. Harry and Bohan. These people already knew fashion and style; the idea was to get them to *buy*. And buy they did. Under the influence of excellent and plentiful food and champagne, the crowded company of tuxedoed and evening-gowned aristocracy became drunk with materialism. They started spending. When Paul, Roy's old friend who had acted the part of the man Danny Mackay had raised from the dead, strolled through the store in a black wool Cardin sportcoat and glen plaid pants, and smiled and winked intimately at some of the female guests, six orders for the outfit were placed at once. When he reappeared fifteen minutes later in a red velvet smoking jacket over gray silk pajamas—looking so startlingly out of place among all the "dressed" people—eight women placed their orders.

And so it went all afternoon and evening. The big cars pulled up in front of the store, the valets whisked them away, and the women came in, many of them unescorted. They demurely accepted the champagne, eyed the sumptuous buffet, thought about their diets, accepted small plates, and slowly walked around the new store, casually inspecting the merchandise while casually inspecting the crowd to see who else was there.

No one was disappointed in the evening. They came out of curiosity and found a very pleasing atmosphere in Fanelli: there was a somber elegance to the decor—it was a men's store definitely, but it was not a *man's* store. The elegance was feminine; there were hints of masculinity in the dark wood walls and brass coatracks and red leather chairs, but there were flowers everywhere, and the boudoir-style powder room came as a pleasant surprise.

From her place near Accessories, where glass counters displayed matching ties and socks—a novel idea of Ann's that seemed to be well received—Beverly greeted her guests with graceful reserve and watched the robust, healthy birth of her newest child. From the moment she had conceived the idea, in Henri Gapin's house in Paris, Beverly had not had a moment's doubt that she would be successful. To design a men's clothing store for women. A store where women went to buy gifts for their husbands, boyfriends, brothers, and fathers. They would come to be catered to—a flyer in the press kit stated that free refreshments would be available at Fanelli—and they would come to see the male models, a unique feature of Fanelli that, the press kit assured, would not be reserved just for special occasions but would be a regular store feature. Women could look at handsome models and imagine those outfits on their own boyfriends and husbands, or they could imagine that such beautiful men *were* their boyfriends and husbands.

Beverly watched her guests with pleasure. She saw how they enjoyed her buffet, her champagne, her store, and themselves. They would go away with a positive impression of Fanelli. They would tell their friends. They would come back and purchase her Cardins and Mr. Harrys. Fanelli was going to be *the* men's clothing store in Beverly Hills. Because Fanelli was fantasy.

Shortly after the sun went down and the spring twilight lapsed into evening, the guests were invited outside to witness the first lighting up of Fanelli's sign. And once again they were not disappointed. No ordinary sign for this store—its name wasn't even displayed. There was just a single simple symbol, a logo, expertly crafted in wrought iron and painted white gold. A lone floodlight illuminated it, and when the switch was hit and the logo glowed softly on the plain wall, everyone murmured in appreciation and curiosity.

It was a butterfly.

30

HE WAS FALLING IN LOVE, damn it.

He wasn't supposed to, not with one of the members; it was against the rules. "Don't let yourself become emotionally involved with the club members," the director had told him when he had been recruited to work upstairs at Butterfly. "Keep in mind that most of our members are married. They aren't looking for real or permanent relationships. Some of them might want to tell you their problems. By all means, listen, but don't give advice, and don't get involved. Give them love, that's what they're paying for. If it will help, think about the money you're earning. Think about getting a good tip. It helps keep the emotions at bay."

Well, he *had* thought about the money and the tips and the occasional expensive gifts, and it hadn't helped. He was falling in love with one of the members and he couldn't help himself.

It was a gray March day, and when he arrived at Venice

Beach he found deserted sand dunes and a ferocious surf pounding the shore. Locking his car, he zipped his nylon windbreaker up to his neck and headed into the cold wind.

Who was she? What was her name? Where did she live?

He knew so little about her, how could he possibly be falling in love with her? Was he really in love with her, he asked himself now as he committed himself to the salty spray of the Pacific, or with just an illusion? Was he in fact in love with *her* or with the idea of her? Was it the woman who had insinuated herself into his heart, or was it just a phantom, a ghost, someone unreal, untouchable, and nonexistent except in his own imagination?

She had been on his mind so much these past few days that he was afraid it was turning into an obsession. It was getting so that he looked forward to her visits at Butterfly, and anxiously awaited the call from the director with the familiar instructions. He was beginning to dislike time spent with other members, time that was not with her, that should be with her only.

And that was not why he had been hired. To love just one woman. He was expected to love them all.

Some kids had set up a barrel and a ramp on the Speedway and were trying to break their necks on skateboards. He paused to watch them.

And then, on the other hand, what did she feel about him? He thought he knew women, thought he knew how to read them. Was he really seeing love in her eyes when she lay in his arms? Was he sensing real tenderness and devotion when they made love? Or was she merely making love to her own particular phantom and not the flesh-and-blood man?

Illusion. That was what Butterfly was. Nothing but an illusion.

But his love for her was real. He knew that. He could feel it as surely as he now felt the biting March wind against his face. When his phone rang and it was the director asking him to come to Butterfly, and she spoke the words he so wanted to hear—to get himself ready for that fantasy—he felt his heart leap in a way it hadn't in a long time. Not since a painful episode in his past when he had decided that love was no longer

327

written in his stars. And yet here it was again, knocking on his door. He would enter that familiar room and see her, and he would be consumed with joy and passion and the outrageous desire to keep her there with him forever.

She seemed so vulnerable at times. At others, she came across as a tough lady. He didn't know what she did in the real world, but he suspected she was a career woman in the sort of profession a female might have to prove herself in. There were just a few clues here and there, nothing to go on really.

She was such a mystery. Was that what he was in love with? A mystery? If she did one day reveal her identity to him, if she exposed all there was to expose about herself, would the "love" vanish? Was the very enigma that seemed to surround her the thing that kept his love alive?

He thrust his hands into his pockets and watched the kids fly up the ramp and land miraculously upright, the way kids and cats do.

No. He wasn't in love with any enigmas or mysteries or phantoms. She was a flesh-and-blood woman and even though he didn't know her name, he knew her and that was what he was in love with.

But the problem was, where to go from here?

The March cold got to him and made him shiver. It also made him realize he was hungry. There was a hamburger stand down the Speedway, nestled in between the old synagogue and a roller-skate-rental place. Most places were closed at this time of year. The elderly residents stayed indoors, the beach was left to itself. But because a few hardies did venture down to Venice in the winter, and because someone had to take their money, Sylvia's Burgers was open and Sylvia was glad to see a customer. He ordered a chili cheese dog with onions and a cup of coffee, and ate standing up at the counter, catching the greasy drippings with inadequate little paper napkins.

Feeling a little warmer and a little fuller, he said good-bye to Sylvia and continued on his walk.

"Our members come to Butterfly because it's *safe*," the director had told him. "We promise safety from violence, from disease, and from anyone finding out who they are. Break one of those rules, and you will answer for it."

But that was exactly what he was thinking of doing— breaking one of those rules. He wanted to ask her who she was.

But dare he risk it? Suppose he risked asking her and she ran from him? Suppose she never came back to Butterfly? How would he find her, in this vast Los Angeles sprawl? He wouldn't have a clue about where to start looking.

He felt so helpless. Something he hadn't felt in a long time. He wasn't used to it; it made him angry. As a man used to being in control of things, he resented having to wait for the phone call. It made him frustrated and perplexed. Everything seemed topsy-turvy. Nothing was going according to set rules. She would ask for him, he would hurry to be with her, they would spend an afternoon, an evening in perfect intimacy and lovemaking, then she would vanish and he would be left with only a memory of what she had felt like in his arms.

I'll tell her I'm in love with her, he thought.

He stopped and turned to gaze out at the gray, angry ocean. A lone sea gull swooped overhead. It gave out a single cry and disappeared over the rooftops.

He suddenly saw the futility in his plan. Butterfly companions were expected to tell the members what they wanted to hear. It was part of the fantasy. If I tell her I'm in love with her, she'll think it's part of the role I'm playing, she'll think I'm reciting a rehearsed line.

But what if . . .

His gaze traveled to the pier where a few old men and some Mexican kids were hanging fishing lines over the side.

What if she feels the same way about me?

His heart began to race. Was it possible? After all, she asked for him over and over again. As far as he knew, she wasn't seeing other companions. Could that be it? That she was falling in love with him?

But . . . how to find out? How to make sure? And how to go about doing it without risking losing her altogether?

If I'm wrong. If I reveal my feelings to her and she runs . . .

His shoulders slumped slightly. There was no safe solution to the problem. He saw that now in the metallic ocean and fine sand skimming over the beach. Dark clouds were rolling down from Santa Monica. The kids were dismantling their launching pad and Sylvia was boarding up her burger stand. And he realized that he was trapped in a conundrum that had no exit.

All he could do, he finally conceded as he pushed into the wind back to his car, was wait for her next phone call. And pray that there would not be a day when it would be the last one.

31

LINDA HAD JUST FINISHED tying her black velvet mask when she heard the door handle move.

Her heart racing, she looked in the mirror, at the room behind her.

It was all Louis XVI confection, a lady's boudoir lifted right out of the palace at Versailles: small gilt chairs with satin upholstery, cabinets of polished tulipwood and bronze fittings, a delicate writing table mounted with Sèvres porcelain, a bed covered in creamy white satin with gold tassels and fringe, its four posts ornamented with tiny gold bellflowers, the canopy rising to an ornate gold crown guarded by winged sphinxes. There were wine and goblets on a table, and plates of sweet breads, cheese, and fruit. The air swirled with the fragrance of crushed roses; a harpsichord played a minuet softly, as if in the next room.

And Linda herself—not a product of the nuclear age but a daughter of a past age of elegance and gentility. Her hair was hidden beneath a white powdered wig, tall and festooned with strings of pearls; three carefully combed curls fell over her bare shoulder. The dress of pale blue satin was cut daringly low, lavishly decorated with tiny embroidered bows, and flared out over outrageously wide panniers. Around her neck she wore a white lace choker. And beneath the dress, complicated corsets with an impossible number of bows, each to be slowly untied in its turn.

She kept her eye on the door. No beeper was going to intrude upon tonight's fantasy—she had seen to that. Tonight was too important.

And then he came in.

He took her breath away.

His athletic figure was clothed in the finest black velvet: flared jacket with wide, gold-trimmed cuffs, a tight-fitting black waistcoat, snug black velvet knee breeches, white stockings and shoes with large silver buckles. At his wrists, the frilled cuffs of his white muslin shirt; at his throat, a white lace jabot. And his hair—the beautiful black hair that Linda so liked—was hidden now beneath a silver-white wig drawn back into a ponytail and tied with a large black velvet bow.

He closed the door and remained standing there, looking at her. Linda kept her back to him; their eyes met in the mirror.

Finally, after a long moment in which the two were held frozen in the perfume of bruised roses and the melodies of Mozart, he stepped forward and offered her an extravagant bow. Linda watched him as he theatrically pointed one foot forward, made a swirling gesture with his right hand, bent elegantly at the waist, and said, "Madam, your servant."

She smiled, turned in her seat, and held out a hand to him.

When he came and took it, bending to kiss it, for an instant their eyes met again, framed by two black masks.

"I missed you at court today," he said, spinning out the fantasy.

She rose and swept past him, having to turn sideways because of her wide-hipped skirt, and went to pour sweet red wine into the silver cups. Her hands trembled slightly. "I doubt that, monsieur," she said. "You would have had the attention of every lady in the palace, including the queen herself."

When she turned to hand him the cup, she caught a fleeting look cross his face—a dark, disturbed look, she thought. And then it was gone and he was smiling and she was wondering if she had imagined it.

But she had seen that same look before, in each of their meetings. Did she perplex him? No doubt she did. Linda was probably the one member of Butterfly who would allow him to go only so far and no further.

"Even the blessed Marie Antoinette is a dull star eclipsed by the brilliance of yourself, madam."

He took the cup; their fingers touched. She was trying desperately to give herself up to the fantasy. Every time she walked through Butterfly's doors Linda tried to leave behind reality and the world of medicine and Barry Greene and her fears. She tried to allow herself to become someone else, so that that someone, and not Linda Markus, could have her sexual spirit set free. But it was almost an impossibility. One did not just shuck off eight hours spent in surgery and then rounds on the burn wards, a meeting of the Ethics Committee, and a half-typed article for the *Journal of the American Medical Association* sitting in one's typewriter. Linda had too much authority, was too firmly in control of so many things—even on the set of *Five North*, where she told TV stars what to do—for her to shrug it all off and pretend she was carefree and unencumbered.

She watched her masked companion as he paced the boudoir, speaking magnificently, his lithe body at home in the black velvet coat and breeches. His voice was deep; it carried an interesting quality that Linda had heard once or twice on the stage.

Let me enjoy the fantasy. Let me forget who I am. Let me experience at last what other women experience in their lovers' arms.

"Madam?"

She looked up. He stood close, towering over her, black eyes gazing intently down at her. *Let me forget for just a little while all the committees and patients and medical charts. Let me unburden myself; let me relax and enjoy you as I want to. . . .*

"I—" she began.

And suddenly he had her by the shoulders, was pulling her to her feet and covering her mouth with his. "I want to make love to you," he whispered hoarsely. "Now."

The room seemed to swim around her. He had never done

332

that before—acted impulsively before she gave the signal that she was ready. It made her giddy.

"Yes," she murmured, "now . . ."

He hurriedly removed his jacket and waistcoat. The muslin shirt, with its wide sleeves and ruffled lace, was tucked into the tight black breeches. With the white powdered wig and bow at the back, and the black mask hiding half his face, he looked to Linda like a man about to duel. She imagined him striking the *en garde* pose and fencing with the dash and expertise of a Casanova.

He kissed her while he undid the intricate lacings of her dress, held her with his mouth while his hands worked quickly, urgently. Linda pressed up against the rock-hard erection. Hurry, she urged. Hurry, hurry . . .

The whalebone panniers floated to the floor and he helped Linda step out of them. Then he untied the many bows of her corset, slowly, one by one, lingering over them, heightening her excitement. His mouth was upon hers again; they kissed in a mutual desperation. The corset dropped to the carpet; he slid the straps of the linen chemise off her shoulders, down, over her breasts, until his hands circled her narrow waist and he pulled her against him, hard.

But when he reached for the ties of her final petticoat, she stopped him.

Taking him by the hand, she led him to the bed. There she blew out the candles so that the room was cast in a half-glow. She lay on the bed and pulled him down to her. They kissed for a long time, reveling in each other's body. He squeezed her breasts and sucked her nipples. She reached into his breeches and clasped him tightly. But when his hand strayed to the petticoat, to lift it up, to explore her, Linda took hold of his hand and brought it back up.

"Now," she whispered. "Do it *now*."

"No," he murmured. "You're not ready."

"Yes, I am."

"Let me touch you—"

"No."

He entered her quickly, without touching her down there,

as he knew she preferred, and let her set the pace of his rhythm.

He rocked her gently for a long time, kissing her, his hands on her breasts, looking into her eyes. She tried to give herself up to him, tried to let the magic of the fantasy cast a spell over her so that she could believe, if only for a few moments, that she was someone else and free to feel. But the more she tried, the less she succeeded. All she could think of were episodes from the past, when she had made love with other men, men who had seen her scars. They never came back.

She pushed those thoughts out of her mind and tried to concentrate. Her masked companion was an expert lover; he was trying to please her. But Linda could not shake off her inhibitions. The more he thrust inside her, the more she tightened up. And the less pleasurable the experience became. Finally, she just lay there, trying to analyze what went wrong each time, trying to dissect the act instead of enjoying it, realizing in the end that the fantasy, again, had not worked.

And then it was over.

It's all wrong, she thought. Fantasies and masks aren't going to help my problem. I have to confront my demons in the real world, with a real man.

She thought of Barry Greene.

32

IT WAS HERE AT LAST. The New Hampshire primary.

Today was the day that set the stage and players for the coming presidential election. And Danny Mackay was on the ballot.

It was raining. Beverly looked out at the cold gray storm that was ravaging Southern California. She felt the chill through the closed French windows of her living room, smelled the wet earth, heard the torrent coming down all around her. She felt cut off and alone, as isolated as if she were stranded on an island in the middle of the ocean. She kept her eye on the drive, watching for the Rolls-Royce Silver Cloud that she had sent to fetch Maggie and Carmen. The first results of the primary would start coming in soon; Beverly wanted her two friends to be there with her.

She shivered. She wrapped her arms around herself. Her pulse raced. Was Danny going to win . . . ?

Finally she saw the Silver Cloud emerge through the rain like a ghost. Beverly watched as the chauffeur got out and opened the rear door. The butler came down the steps with an umbrella and escorted the two women into the house. Turning away from the window, Beverly crossed the enormous living room in a whisper of silk as her midnight-blue Galanos caftan swished around her.

Her friends came in shivering and shaking off the cold. Carmen went straight to the fireplace that was taller than herself, and warmed her body in front of its roaring flames. Maggie went to the buffet, where food had been set out with a silver samovar of steaming fresh coffee. "Any news yet?" she asked when she came back with a lemon Danish and sat on the antique rose-and-powder-blue sofa.

Beverly said, "No, not yet," and glanced at the clock over the fireplace. She turned on a Sony that sat on a mahogany credenza and joined Maggie on the sofa.

The three of them watched the TV screen.

Their faces were tense. The hands that clutched Maggie's coffee cup were white at the knuckles. Carmen, dressed in wool slacks and a silk blouse, stood in front of the fire barely breathing. And Beverly felt her heart beat faster, faster. . . .

Finally, the news came on. "And so, with only fifteen percent of the ballots counted," the anchorman said, "the surprise runaway leader is Danny Mackay with forty-two percent of the votes. . . ."

The rain came down harder. It pelted the windows. Palm trees thrashed against the house. Sparks exploded in the fireplace and flew up the chimney. A kind of low moaning sound seemed to fill the house.

"It would seem that the founder of Good News Ministries," a commentator was saying, "is winning on the sheer power of his personality. As you know, Jeff, Danny Mackay has never held a political office. In fact, he is not yet an officially declared presidential candidate. But the polls indicate that he has strong grass-roots support. . . ."

Somewhere in the distance thunder rumbled. Maggie found herself mentally counting the seconds. The heart of the storm was twelve miles away and getting closer.

The clock over the marble fireplace gently ticked away the hours. Maggie refilled her cup several times; Carmen accepted hot chocolate from the maid and took a seat in a wing chair; but Beverly never moved. Her eyes stayed fixed on the TV.

Danny Mackay was, astonishingly, continuing to take the lead.

"Thirty-six percent of the votes tallied," the anchorman reported, "show Danny Mackay with fifty-five percent of the votes. He is the projected winner in this first presidential primary. . . ."

Beverly and her friends sat without speaking through the long, wet afternoon and listened to what the experts had to say: ". . . is definitely headed for the Republican Convention in June. Danny Mackay is clearly running away with the delegates, which is phenomenal for a man who has never even held a political office. . . ."

"The people are clearly making their choice known. Danny Mackay, the flamboyant television evangelist, is most famous for his vigil outside Parkland Hospital in Dallas back in 1963, and more recently for personally securing the release of missionary Fred Banks from a Middle Eastern prison back in . . ."

The maids cleared the breakfast buffet and set out an early dinner of cold cuts, salad, and fresh fruit. Maggie fixed herself a ham and cheese sandwich, with macaroni salad on the side, while Carmen nibbled on some Gouda and crackers, raw broccoli and cauliflower. Beverly didn't eat.

The day grew dark. Silent maids went through the house and turned on lights. Carmen pulled a sweater over her silk blouse and Maggie withdrew under a hand-crocheted afghan. Beverly didn't seem to feel the cold. She didn't seem to be aware of anything except what was going on on the TV screen.

He was winning. *He was winning. . . .*

And anyone who didn't know Beverly intimately would have thought she must at this moment be celebrating—after all, she was contributing funds to his campaign. But only a close knot of friends knew the real reason why Beverly was supporting Danny Mackay.

Last year, when he had announced that he was going to run for the presidency, Beverly realized the time had come for her moment of revenge. She had read *The Prince*, she knew what a terrible philosophy guided Danny. *A man who strives after goodness in all that he does will come to ruin*, Machiavelli had written. *Therefore a prince who will survive must learn to be other than good.*

When Beverly read those words and others—*A prince must always be ready to take the way of evil*—she knew then what had fueled the strange light she had seen in Danny's eyes those many years ago when she had accidentally come across his school books and Danny had spoken of his ambition to be a great man someday. Over the years she had followed his rise to power, watching him, keeping a careful eye on him. She had known that someday he must be stopped, and that she would have to be the one to do it. It was one of the things Beverly had lived all these years for. And now she had her plan to destroy him at last. When she disclosed to Carmen and Maggie her intention, three months ago, to hold a party to raise money for Danny's campaign, they had been nonplussed. But once they heard about Beverly's plan—that, in order for her to have the power to bring Danny Mackay down, it was crucial that she first supported him—they saw the wisdom in it.

The three women gazed at the TV screen and at the handsome face they knew so well. Danny was smiling victoriously into the cameras, and there was something chilling in the fire that burned in his eyes.

All armed prophets have succeeded, Machiavelli taught. And Beverly knew that this was a tenet Danny lived by. Publicly he spoke of peace with the Russians; privately, she knew, he believed in first strike.

Watching the reporters fight to get near him and seeing the crowd of fanatical supporters behind him, Beverly knew what had to be done.

Danny Mackay had to be stopped.

April

33

Paris to Marseilles. Across the Mediterranean to Ouahran. Then by train or auto or foot across the rim of Africa to Casablanca in French Morocco. Here, the fortunate ones, through money or influence or luck, might obtain exit visas and scurry to Lisbon and from Lisbon to the New World. But . . . the others wait in Casablanca and wait . . . and wait. . . .

She paused before the closed door and checked herself. It had been raining outside and she was afraid her carefully rolled hair might have fallen. But everything was in place, and the little hat and veil over her face weren't even damp. Straightening the smart jacket and smoothing down the skirt, she reached for the doorknob.

She was nervous. It had taken her a week to arrive at this point; her heart was racing so fast she thought she might faint.

The door swung open upon a small café. There weren't any other patrons at the tables or the bar, but there was life here nonetheless, in the slowly revolving ceiling fans, in the giant potted palms and hanging ferns, in the player piano against the far wall playing a familiar tune. She quietly closed the door behind herself and looked around anxiously. Food had been set out: a platter of spiced sausages, a wedge of Brie, Strasbourg liver pâté and toast points, smoked oysters. The champagne cocktails had already been poured; she knew they would be a perfect blend of sugar, bitters, cognac and chilled champagne with a lemon peel.

The setting was exquisite. All it needed was—

The door in the far wall opened and he came in. He didn't see her at first; his look was one of deep preoccupation. The sight of him made her heart jump. And suddenly her mouth ran dry. He was so handsome in his white tropical suit.

Then he looked up and froze.

She tried to speak. "I . . . ah . . ."

He waited, gazing darkly at her.

"Rick, I have to talk to you," she said finally, breathlessly.

He seemed to consider that. He strode to the bar and picked up one of the champagne glasses. "I saved my first drink to have with you," he said. "Why did you have to come to Casablanca? There are other places."

She twisted the strap of her purse. She could hardly breathe, she was so excited. "I wouldn't have come if I'd known that you were here."

"Funny about your voice, how it hasn't changed. I can still hear it." His tone became sarcastic. " 'Richard, I'll go with you anyplace. We'll get on a train together and never stop—' "

"Don't, Rick! I can understand how you feel."

His dark eyes flashed. He put the glass down and walked toward her. "You understand how I feel. How long was it we had, honey?"

"I didn't count the days."

"Well I did. Every one of them. Mostly I remember the last one. . . ."

"Richard," she cried. "I tried to stay away. I thought I would never see you again. That you were out of my life." Tears came to her eyes.

He was standing close now; she could sense his passion, could see how he was straining to control himself. The song on the piano seemed to grow louder—"As Time Goes By." The fans turned slowly overhead; the smoke from his cigarette seemed to fill the room. His eyes were dark and angry and challenging. It was so good, so *perfect*.

She started to cry.

He took her in his arms and she buried her face in his neck. "Oh Richard, the day you left Paris—if you knew what

I went through—if you knew how much I loved you—how much I still love you. . . ."

His kiss cut off her words. Suddenly all anger and bitterness and regrets vanished, and all they were, were two people desperately in love in a world gone mad. They made love urgently, hurriedly, as if their time together were short. When he lowered her to the floor her mind was flooded with dizzying visions—of a French policeman, of men in Gestapo uniforms, of a dreamy-eyed man lighting a cigarette, of a young girl dramatically singing the "Marseillaise." She clung to him and called him Rick. The song repeated itself endlessly on the player piano. The champagne sparkled in the glasses, waiting to be consumed, with the food, in a little while. She was giddy with ecstasy. It was her most treasured dream come true. It was just as had been promised. And when she whispered into his ear, "Say it, Rick, say it," and he said, so perfectly, "Of all the gin joints in all the towns—" she closed her eyes and knew exactly where she was going to be every Thursday night from now on.

Here at Butterfly.

34

Beverly Hills: 1978

THE CORPORATE HEADQUARTERS of Highland Enterprises was housed in a new black-glass building on Wilshire Boulevard. There were red-brick fountains out front, a multilevel parking garage, a spacious lobby with a newsstand, a pharmacy, and security guards, and six elevators that went up thirty flights. Highland Enterprises shared the twentieth floor with only one other tenant—the Kenya Consulate and Tourist Commission.

Ann Hastings breezed through the large double doors and entered the hushed, carpeted reception area. She was greeted by Esther, the black receptionist, who, with her African print dresses and cornrowed hair, looked as if she really belonged in the offices across the hall. Before going to her own office, which had a view of Beverly Hills and Hollywood, Ann stopped by to say hello to Beverly. She was not surprised to find her friend already deeply involved in something with Carmen and Maggie, and she knew why their heads were together. It was Ann who had done the research and provided Carmen with the data they were now going over.

Carmen glanced up, said "Good morning" to Ann, then went back to the list of figures she had been in the process of explaining to Beverly and Maggie.

Beverly looked up and waved. Ann continued on her way to her own spacious office, where, with the help of two secretaries, she oversaw the strict quality control of the vast Royal Burger chain.

It was a crisp, green-blue-golden day in Los Angeles, the rare sort of day that made Southern Californians who worked in buildings like this one unable to concentrate. But Beverly had no trouble concentrating on what Carmen was saying—Beverly never had trouble concentrating on anything. As the cool recirculated air whispered out from vents and wafted over the expensive furniture and fresh cut flowers and Navajo rugs in the large corner office of the chairman of the board of Highland Enterprises, the chairman herself was paying careful attention to what her accountant was telling her.

Beverly had learned a lot from Carmen. Although everyone had been impressed and a little awed by Carmen's rapid progress through school, starting sixteen years ago when she was barely literate and ending up graduating from the UCLA business school with honors, Beverly had not been a bit surprised. She had known what Carmen was capable of. It had been evident back in Hazel's aroma-filled kitchen. All it had taken to set Carmen free was a sense of self-worth and a chance at an education. And the freedom to *dream*. Despite having a baby to take care of and a job to hold down at a Royal Burger stand, Carmen had taken classes full time, studied around the clock, and made harsher demands on herself than even her teachers had. The result was an uncanny business acumen that was one of the mainstays behind Beverly Highland's success. Beverly herself often wondered where she would be right now if she hadn't found Carmen on that fateful day in Dallas.

Today they were working out their strategy for maneuvering certain enterprises into Danny Mackay's personal ownership. Without his knowing it.

"Okay," Carmen said, "now, this is what you are going to need. Ann has broken it down into types of food you will need: so much beef, so many tomatoes, heads of lettuce, and so on to supply each franchise." She pointed to items on the list with the gold Dunhill pen Ann Hastings had given her when she passed her CPA exam. It matched the classy gold chain around her slender wrist. In fact, everything about Carmen Sanchez was classy these days. She wore her rich black hair up on her head and set it off with long, slender earrings; she forsook wearing a dress for very wide Palazzo pants and a slinky silk blouse that was unbuttoned daringly low. She didn't look like the forty-year-old mother of a teenage daughter.

"Now, I've done some research and I've found what I think is the best management company for our needs." Carmen pointed to the name she had written on the fact sheet. "They can tell you how much acreage you will require, and where to buy it. They will run the farms very scientifically, using computers and the latest methods. You can be guaranteed the best possible yield and the best products for your restaurants."

Beverly and Maggie studied the sheets Carmen had drawn up. This was a new kind of venture for them, something altogether different from anything they had gotten involved in before.

Beverly became thoughtful again. Carmen had explained to her all about vertical integration and horizontal integration, and about the difference between them. The example Carmen had used was in the instance of a small appliance manufacturer. If that company wished to buy out another small appliance manufacturer, then that was called horizontal integration. But if that small appliance manufacturer bought the plant that made the metal for those appliances, thus supplying its own firm with the raw materials, then that was called vertical integration. And that was exactly what the three women were planning to do on this technicolored May morning in the twentieth-floor office of Highland Enterprises. They were going to create a company that would be the sole supplier of beef and vegetables to the gigantic Royal Burgers chain.

A company that would be worth millions and that Beverly had no intention of keeping.

She was creating it only to sell it to Danny Mackay.

"He must not touch Royal Burgers," Beverly said very seriously to her friend.

Carmen gravely shook her head. She knew how precious that company was to all of them: it was their future, their security. "Don't worry, *amiga*. He will get the farming company only."

"And all of its holdings?"

Carmen nodded almost sadly. She and Beverly and Maggie didn't like dealing in such things: a porno magazine, a chain of beauty salons that was really a front for illegal massage parlors, and a square block of the most wretched slums in East Los Angeles. But it was necessary for them to own them. They were part of the plan.

They were going to see to it that Danny Mackay, who was acquisition-mad and buying up any properties he could get his hands on, jumped at this choice company and bought it sight unseen.

"And Fanelli?"

"In case Danny Mackay's staff wishes to investigate some of the farming company's investments, we will encourage them to come and take a look at Fanelli. They will look around, see a very profitable, legitimate men's shop, and will go back to Houston satisfied. The rest they will never find out about." Beverly closed the folder and turned to her secretary. "What do you think, Maggie?"

What did she think? Like her two friends, Maggie thought it was a necessary move. Once again, Danny Mackay was up to no good and he had to be stopped. Seven years ago Beverly had staged a resurrection in Danny's church for the sole purpose of exposing him as a fraud. But Danny had attempted no more miracles. The publicity from that night's raising of the dead had not been good; the press had shot salvos at Danny that caused him to drop such theatrics altogether. And besides, Maggie suspected, he must have decided he didn't need to resort to such trickery anymore, not with his new TV show and sudden skyrocketing of fame.

But now he was involved in other dealings, dealings that hurt unsuspecting people and from which Danny was profiting mightily. Such as forcing companies into bankruptcy and buying them for a pittance, or squeezing someone out of his land because Danny wanted to own it. Beverly kept a watchful eye on him. She had her private investigator, Jonas Buchanan, who now worked for no one but Beverly, make regular reports on Danny's financial movements. He was spreading out over America like an octopus, his tentacles reaching out and grasping. His power grew daily; his wealth was multiplying; he now owned people as well as things.

"When?" Maggie often asked Beverly. "When are you going to stop him? When are we going to have our revenge?"

But the time was never right. Beverly was cautious; she wanted to make sure that when she did finally confront him again, face-to-face, the advantage would be all hers. That there was no chance of her losing. And that he would be destroyed.

Now she was building up her arsenal. She had bought Monument Publications because of its pornographic sideline. This, together with some other carefully crafted deals, would be dangled on a hook in front of Danny, and he would grab for it. In his greed, he would take it all, playing right into their hands. And someday Beverly was going to turn his own greed against him.

"I know how we can arrange the sale," Maggie said now. "Through the stockbroker I used to work for. His is a large company. They have offices in Texas."

"Let's get on it, then. Maggie, get ahold of this management firm. I want to talk to them as soon as possible. Carmen, you get together with Ann. I want this new company operating and supplying our restaurants inside of six months. And see if anyone can come up with a name."

Maggie collected the papers, slipped them into her briefcase and said, "How about Royal Farms?"

Beverly looked at Carmen, who nodded. "All right, Royal

Farms it is. By November I want Danny Mackay signing the papers of ownership."

As Carmen was following Maggie through the door she paused and looked back. Beverly was still seated at her desk, settling into a few more hours of work. There was her Chamber of Commerce report to be written, on her proposed plan for the launching of a new eighties image for Hollywood; there were speeches to be prepared and invitations to be accepted or declined; and Beverly had to get ready for her trip next week to Sacramento, where she was going to meet with state lawmakers on the abortion issue, Beverly's latest personal project. She was pro-choice, wanting not only legalization of abortion but also counseling centers for pregnant teenagers, showing them the alternatives.

"Hey, *amiga*," Carmen said softly. "It's your birthday tomorrow. Let's do something. Let us take you out to dinner. I can reserve a private room at Perrino's. A woman shouldn't turn forty alone."

Beverly smiled at her friend. "Thanks, Carmen. But I don't care for birthday parties. I only ever had one in my entire life, and that one was enough for me."

Carmen gazed across the mote-dusted sunlight and, for an instant, shared Beverly's memory of cheap champagne lying flat in paper cups and Hazel's voice saying, "Here's to our favorite girl." And Danny coming to take Rachel out for her birthday and delivering her instead into the hands of a back-alley butcher.

Then Carmen thought of their reunion in Dallas, fifteen years ago, and how Beverly had taught her to dream and to make those dreams come true, and that made Carmen think of all the people Beverly was inspiring today with that same spirit and ambition, going to colleges and clubs and her own stores and companies and telling people of all ages, young and old, to dare to take chances, to dare to live their fantasies.

If only—Carmen wished as she left the office and quietly closed the door behind herself—Beverly's private dream could come true, how perfect her life would be! But Jonas Buchanan, although he still searched and followed leads (now employing other investigators), had come no closer to finding the lost mother and sister. Naomi Burgess's trail went cold in Medford, Oregon, and Christine Singleton, married for a while, Jonas had discovered, to a man named Rutherford back in 1958, had had her marriage annulled, and she, too, had vanished.

Then Carmen thought of Danny Mackay and how it was because of him that Beverly would not allow herself to fall in love, that she lived the solitary life even though there were men, Jonas Buchanan among them, who clearly were devoted to her. And Carmen also knew that Beverly's vow to someday take revenge on Danny still burned steadily in her heart.

Memories flooded back into Maggie's mind, memories of swimming with Joe in Mission Bay, of walks through Balboa Park, of long, romantic days at the zoo, lying on the grass and watching the lazy progress of clouds. But, of course, Maggie realized as she pulled into the parking lot of the Outrigger Restaurant, those days were long gone and San Diego was a different town. In fact, it was a city now.

As she followed the saronged hostess through the dark, wharf-like restaurant, Maggie wondered if Pete had changed much. After all, it had been ten years—

My God, he was exactly the same.

Suddenly self-conscious of her weight, and surprised to realize how good-looking he was and wondering why she hadn't noticed it when she had worked for him, Maggie hugged her former boss with tears in her eyes. He reminded her of the good days, of simpler days, before Danny Mackay and Joe's tragic death.

"I can't tell you how surprised I was when my secretary said you had called!" Pete Forman said. "I said to her, *Maggie Kern*? Are you sure the caller identified herself as Maggie Kern? And then when I dialed the number she gave me and I heard your voice come on the line, sounding just like you did when you used to work for me, I nearly fell over! Maggie, you look great! How's Joe? That's your husband's name, isn't it?"

"Joe died ten years ago, Pete," she said softly as two piña coladas were set before them.

He laid his hand over hers. It was warm and dry and reassuring. "I'm sorry to hear that, Maggie. Why didn't you come right back to San Diego? I meant it when I said you could always have your job back."

She smiled. "I got a better offer."

Pete and Maggie got reacquainted over teriyaki chicken, wild rice, parmesan vegetables, and more piña coladas. To their right the restaurant slowly filled up. Candles in red globes flickered on tables and cast shadows on old fishing nets, Hawaiian tikis, and fake crates marked "Singapore," "Shanghai," and "Cairo," while to their left fabulous Mission Bay stretched in endless blue to meet the endless blue of the smog-free San Diego sky. Maggie began to wonder why she hadn't done this a long time ago.

Over coffee she explained the purpose of her visit.

"As you can see, Pete," she said, spreading sheets out for him on the table. "Royal Farms owns some of the best growing land in the Central Valley. The beef comes from the best herds. And I know you're familiar with the management firm that is running it for us. Look at the profits already, in just five months of operation."

He studied the figures and nodded, impressed. "You say that Royal Farms is the *sole* supplier of food and paper products to the Royal Burger franchise? Why does your boss want to sell?"

"She wants to expand the Royal Burger chain and she needs the cash."

Pete didn't need to be told the significance of that. He'd been in the investment business for too many years. Normally, an agricultural company wasn't a very good investment—he would shy away from it. But this one had a guaranteed market. And what a market! Not only that, but the money from the sale of this company was going to expand the very market that was going to buy its products!

"I can see your mouth watering, Pete."

"Maggie, if you're asking me to find you a buyer, give me five minutes and I'll give you a hundred of them!"

She rubbed her cheek and looked out at the sailboats on the bay. Here came the delicate part.

"Well, I do want you to handle the sale for us, Pete. But we already have a purchaser in mind. You see, my boss is a

350

keen supporter of a certain evangelist and his ministry. Since
Royal Farms is her baby, so to speak, since she created it herself
and has run it herself, she wants to be certain that it passes
into worthy hands. She wants the preacher to buy it."

"Does he want to buy it?"

"We don't know. That will be part of your job."

"How can she be sure he *will* buy it?"

There was no room for doubt there. Carmen's financial
file on Danny Mackay was as thick as a telephone book. Now
that Good News Ministries was pulling in millions of dollars
annually, and now that he was seen coast to coast on television,
Danny Mackay was acquisition-mad. He bought anything he
could lay his hands on, as long as it promised profits.

"Where is this buyer located?"

"In Houston. I thought you might contact someone in your
Galveston office, have him meet with the buyer, conduct the
actual sale, and then split the commission with you."

"It will be my pleasure," he said as he gathered up the
papers and slipped them into their folder. "I'll get on it right
away."

Maggie looked at her watch and was surprised to see how
late it was. The restaurant would soon be serving dinner.

"Surely you're not going to drive back to L.A. now, are
you?" Pete said, folding his arms on the table and leaning
slightly toward her. "The traffic will be murder for the next
few hours."

"I'll find somewhere to stay on Hotel Circle and go back
in the morning."

"How about staying at my place?"

Their eyes met and held for three heartbeats, in which
time Maggie fleetingly pictured Pete Forman's fabulous house
on the bay, with its private beach hidden by trees. Then she
said, "What about your wife?"

"Corinne divorced me five years ago."

She was suddenly afraid. Since Joe's death Maggie had kept
herself busy with raising the two boys and helping Beverly
Highland build her financial empire. Maggie had kept her distance from men. But Pete was close, dangerously close, both
physically and emotionally. She looked into his gray eyes and

was surprised to find herself suddenly wanting very much to be with him.

"That gorgeous red hair of yours," he said softly. "I remember how I used to stare at it when you weren't looking."

"I have a few gray ones now."

"You must be an old lady."

"I'm thirty-five."

"What's wrong, Maggie?"

She stared at her coffee cup. What was wrong? There was no doubt in her mind that she desired Pete. And there was a very nice, comfortable affection between them. It would be so easy—no messy start-ups, no laying down rules, no wondering where it was all leading. And it had been so long since she had been with a man. . . .

"It may sound crazy, Pete," she said quietly, "but I would feel as if I were cheating on Joe."

"It's not crazy at all. But is it realistic?"

"I don't know."

"Would he want you to remain faithful to him?"

"Promise me you'll marry again, Maggie," a voice echoed from the distant past. *"I've got a bad heart. It can go anytime. I don't want you and the boys to go it alone."*

"Let me take you dancing," Pete said suddenly.

"Dancing!"

He took hold of her hand and said in a quieter voice, "Let me seduce you. At least give me a chance."

Maggie left him long enough to make two phone calls, one to Beverly to let her know that Pete was going to handle the sale, the other to her housekeeper to tell her to give the boys their supper and put them to bed. Maggie's heart was racing. For the first time in ten years she wasn't going to be sleeping alone.

The wedding reception was held in the largest honky-tonk in Texas. Nearly eight hundred guests gathered under the vast roof of Mickey Gilley's three acres to congratulate the Reverend Danny Mackay and his bride.

The newlyweds made a handsome couple, everyone thought, with Angelica in her grandmother's antique lace wedding gown and Danny smartly decked out in the best from Cutter Bill. The admiring crowd thought the Reverend was every inch a Texan, from the white Stetson on his head right down to his ostrich-skin boots. At forty-five Danny was still lean and fit; he cut a striking figure in his Western-style jacket and custom-tailored pants. To the ladies there was something romantic about the sexy Reverend who wasn't afraid to cry on nationwide television, and to the gentlemen Danny Mackay was a true man's man.

While a Western band played all the country favorites for couples doing the Texas two-step, and while the food—traditional Texas barbecue with steaks, ribs, corn on the cob and blazing-hot chili—was being served with tall, cool drinks, no one looked at the bride close enough to notice a shadow of fear in her eyes.

"Well, son," said a white-haired gentleman as he clapped Danny on the back. "I wish you the best."

Danny grinned. "Thank you, Senator. Or should I call you Dad?"

"I know you'll take care of my little Bluebonnet over there. She's made me raht proud, catching herself a fine husband like yourself."

Danny was feeling right proud of himself as well. For a wedding gift the senator had deeded to the newlyweds ten thousand acres of the choicest cattle country in Texas.

As the band struck up the "Cotton-Eyed Joe" and dancers linked arms to form wagon-wheel spokes, Danny made his way to where Angelica was standing with her mother. He was congratulated along the way, slapped on the back, had his hand shaken, and told what a blessed day this was, praise the Lord, and when he finally came up to her, Angelica shrank back.

"Are you enjoying yourself, Mother?" Danny said to the senator's wife, who was outfitted in the best from Neiman-Marcus and dripping with diamonds.

"God bless you, Reverend," she said, dabbing her eyes with a lace handkerchief. "You've made me the proudest mother in Texas."

Danny turned to his bride. The band was calling out, "What do you say?" and the dancers were yelling, "Bullshit!"

Danny moved close to Angelica, grinned out over the merry-making guests and said quietly, "Smile for our friends, Angelica."

She was pale. Paler than the lace of her veil. She was thinking about the coming night, in the honeymoon suite of Houston's finest hotel.

Danny reached for her hand, found it cold, and gave it a painful squeeze. "You're my wife now," he said in a voice only she could hear. "You have to do as I say. Now, smile for our guests."

Angelica smiled. She wanted to cry.

Danny felt prouder today than he had in a long time. He'd pulled off a real smart one, marrying the rich senator's only daughter. What a stroke of genius it had been, and what a switch! Getting her pregnant and forcing her to marry him.

"You do as I say," he had warned her four weeks ago, "or I go to your daddy and tell him you're carrying his bastard grandchild."

Angelica had begged and pleaded with him. She had been confused, she hadn't known which way to turn. The Reverend had seduced her on the night of a political barbecue on her daddy's ranch. She hadn't liked it; she discovered she hadn't liked the Reverend Danny Mackay. But then he'd forced her two more times after that—he was a guest in their house, and she hadn't dared cry out. "Who's he going to believe?" Danny had said. "You or me?"

Angelica knew how passionately her father supported Danny Mackay and his Good News Ministries, how he was helping Danny to build a brand-new cathedral outside Houston. Her word against the Reverend's? And so she had let Danny have his way. To her horror she had come up pregnant.

"I go to your daddy," Danny had threatened, "and I tell him that you confessed to me, your spiritual counselor, that you've had it off with some ranch hand. How do you think he would take that?"

Angelica had an idea of how he would take it. Her fundamentalist Christian father would not be beyond throwing her out of his house, penniless and shamed.

In fear and panic she had agreed to marry Danny. But now,

as she watched the thirsty dancers ordering up more "long-necks," as she thought of the honeymoon suite and what Danny was going to make her do, Angelica Mackay knew she had made a mistake.

Danny looked at his watch and scanned the crowd. Bonner was late. What was holding him up?

This deal with Royal Farms was so important to Danny that he had sent his right-hand man off to California on the eve of his wedding. Danny had wanted Bonner to stand with him as his best man, but he wanted Bonner in California even more, checking out this deal that seemed too good to be true.

It was being handled through an Austin stockbroker. Danny couldn't believe his luck. Everyone knew that Royal Burgers brought in billions annually. Hell, there was a several-year waiting list to purchase one of its franchises, and then the price was half a million. And here he was, being offered the very agricultural firm that was the sole supplier of all those restaurants! He would be a fool not to jump at it. But caution was always good practice. Royal Farms' financial statement listed "income from investments." "What investments?" Danny had asked the Austin broker. The man couldn't tell him. So he'd sent Bonner off to Los Angeles to look into Royal Farms' holdings.

"When will you be breaking ground for the cathedral, Reverend?"

Danny turned and found himself looking into the stern face of a Superior Court justice. "Just as soon as I get me a shovel, Hank!"

The judge laughed. Like the senator, he was one of Good News Ministries biggest supporters.

Danny sometimes had to marvel at his meteoric rise in TV evangelism. It all went back to that incredible night when a man had died during his revival and had somehow come back to life again. That incident had brought Hallstead to Danny's hotel room, and from there, well, Danny often thought of himself as having been shot out of a cannon.

The television audiences went crazy for him. The sex appeal and charisma that oozed from him onstage to electrify a live congregation traveled just as easily over television airwaves. Danny wasn't diminished a bit by the small screen; his voice was no less compelling, the magic not the slightest bit weakened. Power was power, he had discovered, whether he used it dominating a woman in bed or belting out the Gospel to half a million people by way of TV antennas.

And it wasn't just that he was handsome, dynamic, and young that made people like him. Some of his appeal lay in the fact that he stayed away from Bible fundamentalism. While Danny was very familiar with Scripture—he had studied and absorbed the Bible the same way he had *Mein Kampf* and *Profiles in Courage*—he preferred to preach a broad moral message, reminding people that they had sinned but that they could find salvation if only they would listen to him. People listened. And they sent in their dollars because they believed that money bought them grace with God.

Even religion can be made into a tool of power.

Machiavelli had first spoken those words to a young Danny twenty-five years ago, and he was speaking to him still. Danny Mackay knew that he was living proof that the plan sketched out in *The Prince* did indeed work. Which was why, back in 1973, Danny had established the Reverend Danny Mackay Award for Achievement. *A prince demonstrates that he admires talent by honoring men of ability.* A bronze plaque was given out annually to the Christian Man or Woman of the Year. Danny's foundation regularly presented awards of money to citizens who performed good deeds, to students who excelled, to companies that served the public good. *Nothing wins more esteem for a prince than distinctive acts in civil matters.* Danny had also set up college scholarships, funded missionary programs overseas, and conducted TV telethons to raise money for recovering drug addicts.

Good News Ministries was now bringing in millions of dollars annually, making it one of the wealthiest churches in the country. And Danny Mackay, its founder and leader, was growing more famous with each passing Sunday.

And rich, too.

Danny got the idea to create a "shell" company to facilitate the building of his personal fortune. "We create a bogus company," he had explained to Bonner, "and through it I borrow money from the Ministries. Of course, there is no company really, so the money goes right into my pocket."

That was how Danny had purchased those two big office buildings in downtown Houston and the yacht charter outfit in Galveston, and now Royal Farms in California. The ministry's money belonged to God, and with it Danny was going to build the biggest, most impressive house of worship the Lord had ever seen. But his own money was his own, and he did with it as he liked.

"Will you please excuse me for a minute?" he said to the judge. Danny made his way through the crowd, receiving congratulations along the way, and pausing once to exchange a few words with the owner of Houston's largest department store.

"How's that little girl of yours doing?" he asked in his sincerest voice.

"Just fine, Reverend. She should be out of the hospital in a few days. And those flowers you sent really perked her up. God bless you."

When he reached the other side, he walked up to two men who were neither eating nor drinking but standing off from the crowd, their faces blank. "Did you find out the name of that reporter?" Danny asked one of them in a low voice so that no one else could hear.

The man produced a small notebook from an inside pocket. He opened it to a page and handed it to his employer. Danny read the information and nodded gravely. It was the name and address of a reporter who had written some damaging remarks about Danny in a nationally syndicated column. Danny looked at the address—the reporter lived in Washington, D.C.—and memorized it.

"Find out where his kid goes to school," Danny said quietly, handing the notebook back. "And where his wife works. Find out where his parents live, too." That might work—his parents.

He took one last look at the name and filed it away on his private list, the list that had once been headed by the unfortunate Dr. Simon Waddell. In twenty-five years, six names had been removed from the list. But eleven had been added. Danny would eventually get around to taking care of all of them.

And then there was Bonner at last, pushing his way through the crowd.

Danny excused himself and went off into a private corner with his friend. "What happened?"

"I'm sorry I missed the ceremony, Danny. I told the pilot I was in a hurry, but there was a storm over Phoenix and we had to reroute through Utah."

Danny wasn't interested in that. He had trouble standing still. He looked this way and that around the large honky-tonk, not missing a thing, and said, "Tell me about your visit. Did you meet this Highland woman?"

"She wasn't available, but I met with the next two in command."

"And?"

Bonner ran a hand through his corn-silk hair. At forty-six he still had his unusual angelic looks. And he photographed well on television. Folks liked to see him up there on the stage, right next to Reverend Danny. "Royal Farms owns some outfit that publishes textbooks, a string of beauty salons, and a men's clothing store in Beverly Hills. Nothing worth the bother of going out to California and looking at."

"Tell them we'll sign the papers first thing tomorrow."

Bonner laughed. "On the first morning of your honeymoon?"

Danny looked over at the frail young woman in white, who seemed to be trying to hide behind her buxom mother. She had shrunk from him when he'd walked up to her. And she had flinched when he touched her. Well, tonight he was going to give her something to flinch about.

"Hell," he murmured, feeling good. "Call Austin right now. Tell them we'll sign the papers this afternoon. Don't want that Highland broad suddenly realizing what a good deal she's giving us and backing out, do we?"

35

THE SMELL OF RAIN had hung over Los Angeles for days, and yet no moisture fell from the metallic sky. Although Southern California never got enough rain and everyone prayed for it now and then because of frequently threatened droughts, Trudie never liked the rain. It ruined her business. You can't dig a pool in mud. So she was keeping her fingers crossed that the deluge would hold off long enough for her to finish this latest contract. The man for whom she was scooping out a pool up on Coldwater Canyon had just won an Academy Award and was one of the hottest items in movies. The stamp of TruePools on his upper step could mean spectacular referrals for Trudie.

She had just spent an afternoon of fantastic sex with "Thomas" at Butterfly and was feeling quite high. Today's few hours had been like all their other times together—an hour or two of intellectual argument followed by vigorous, skyrockets lovemaking. She wondered if she was becoming addicted to it.

Now, if only, she thought in frustration as she guided her Corvette up the winding drive of the star's residence, she could figure out how to work such an arrangement into her real life. For the rest of her life.

When she pulled around the back of the immense Tudor mansion, she braked to a quick stop and couldn't believe her eyes. The tile and coping guys were in the process of leaving— and they hadn't done the work yet!

Flying out of her car without even bothering to close the door, she flagged down the truck that was heading toward her.

"Hey! What are you doing?" she said to the driver. "What's *that* all about?" She swept her arm in the direction of the mounds of tiles and bricks, stacked next to the excavation.

"You tell me, Trudie. You called us too soon. The steel hasn't even been laid yet."

"What!"

She marched over to the big messy hole in the ground and, with her hands on her hips, looked down. There was water in the bottom, and nothing, absolutely nothing had been done on this pool in a week.

Bill.

He was supposed to have laid in the steel and plumbing six days ago. She was really going to give it to him this time.

She reached her office in minutes, flying down out of the hills with her blond hair whipping about her head. She barely let the car roll to a stop before she was out and bursting through the front door. Cathy, her assistant, looked up from her typewriter, startled.

"Get butt-head Bill on the phone for me!" Trudie said as she strode to her desk. "I've had it with him. Totally had it!"

She lit a cigarette and paced.

Trudie's glass-front office was very small, with just enough room for two desks and a fridge. She didn't need a lot of space, all of her work was conducted in backyards. TruePools faced Little Santa Monica Boulevard, wedged in between an antique store and a café that served espresso and Cajun kebabs; the sign on her window was done in the same blue-green color as her eyes—a single arched wave with the lettering of TruePools cascading down the crest.

"His office says he's out on a job," Cathy said.

"Right. But not on one of *my* jobs, I'll bet. Tell them he had better get his ass in—"

"I've already told them. They're going to call him and tell him to stop in here on his way to the next job."

Trudie smoked three more cigarettes. She couldn't recall ever being this angry. She knew why he was doing this. It was to get back at her for the beer-can incident two months ago. For shouting at him in front of the other guys for not putting in three return lines. He knew how important the Coldwater Canyon contract was to her. This was his way of showing her who had the upper hand.

Well, she wasn't going to stand for it. This time he was going to pay, royally. Damnit, he had totally spoiled the beautiful high she had left Butterfly with.

When Bill came through the glass door and started to say, "Hi, True, what's the prob—" she flew at him.

"Why hasn't the steel been laid in the Coldwater job! That goddamn pool has been sitting for a week! My pools don't sit for a week, Bill! This is the second time you've screwed up!"

He stared at her. "What are you talking about?"

"Don't play innocent with me! You just tell me why that steel wasn't laid a week ago like you said it would be."

He shrugged, clearly confused. "You know as well as I do that it takes at least a week to drain a water table."

Now it was her turn to stare. "To drain a *what*?"

"Sanderson hit a water table. Didn't you know?"

She blinked at him. Then she looked at Cathy. "Have we heard from Sanderson?"

"Not a word."

"Get him for me."

While her assistant was dialing the phone Trudie lit another cigarette and leaned against her desk, tapping her foot. She wouldn't look at Bill. Couldn't look at him.

Finally: "Hi, Mr. Sanderson. This is Cathy at TruePools, could you hold the line for—"

But Trudie was snatching it from Cathy and saying, "Joe? What's this about a water table on the Coldwater Canyon job?"

She listened, her free hand playing nervously with an earring.

"So why didn't you tell me!" she shouted into the phone. "No, I didn't get your message! You know I have a thirty-day completion contract on that pool!" She paused. "No, *you* listen to *me*. When you hit a water table on one of my pools, you tell me about it! I don't want to have to hear about it from the tile-and-coping guys! Now listen, I don't care if you *did* leave a message on my machine. You don't just go around assuming that I get the message. You tell me in person, you understand? So help me, Joe, if you've cost me this contract, I'll see that you end up excavating kids' sandboxes. Now get out there and see that that pool is drained by tomorrow. Bill will be there first thing in the morning with his crew. And Joe? No messages this time."

"Unbelievable!" she breathed as she hung up.

Then she looked at Bill.

"Oops," she said.

"Yeah, *oops*."

"I'm sorry, Bill. I mean it. I feel about two inches tall—"

"Listen, honey, I don't know what your problem is but I'd like you to get off my back!"

She stared at him.

"You walk around with a goddamn chip on your shoulder, and I'm telling you right now"— he jabbed the air with his finger—"whatever it is you're trying to prove, prove it with someone else, not me!"

When he turned to stalk out, she said, "Hey, wait a minute! I said I was sorry."

"Look, honey, I don't know what moron gave you a contractor's license, because you sure as hell don't have any brains. I don't appreciate getting called off jobs so you can scold me like some schoolteacher with a burr up her ass. You keep up this kind of attitude and there won't be a subcontractor in the city who'll work for you."

"I've got guys begging to work for me!"

"Then why the hell do you hire me for your jobs? All I seem to do is make you mad."

"Because you're the best in the business, damnit!"

They glared at each other while the traffic whizzed by on Little Santa Monica. When the phone rang, Cathy quickly picked it up and began talking quietly with a customer.

"Lord," said Bill, shaking his head, "what is it with you broads who go into construction?"

"I'm not a broad. I also don't like to be called 'honey.' "

"Well, believe me, I don't use the term out of endearment."

"If I'm such a bitch to work for, why do you? There are plenty of other pool contractors in this town."

"Yeah? Well, to quote a lady, you happen to be the best in the business."

She turned away and searched for a pack of cigarettes on her desk. When she turned back around, lighting up another Virginia Slims, she looked at the way Bill's T-shirt was stretched over his muscular arms and shoulders. She could tell he had just come off a job because his boots were muddy and there was the fresh smell of Lava soap about him. Not at all like her refined "Thomas," who wore French cuffs and silk ties and never had dirt under his fingernails.

"Look," he said quietly, controlling his anger. "Next time one of your jobs gets messed up, don't jump to the conclusion that it was me, all right?"

She tossed her head back and blew smoke up to the ceiling.

"And another thing. I've lost over an hour today because of your little tantrum. On someone else's job. You owe me."

"All I owe you is an apology, and you got one."

He glared at her for a moment longer, then he threw up his hands and marched out. Outside, Trudie heard the tires of his GMC 4x4 squeal as he roared away from the curb.

36

Washington, D.C., 1980

WHEN JONAS BUCHANAN finally found Beverly's mother, Beverly was at that moment in Washington, D.C., testifying before a Senate investigative subcommittee.

The hearing was taking place because of legislation currently pending before Congress that would greatly expand the definition of areas of land set aside under environmental protection legislation. A land developer by the name of Webster wanted to turn some Southern California coastal property into a new yacht harbor, and because of certain discrepancies in the report from the Corps of Engineers, plus outcries of protest from California environmentalist groups, and because Webster might qualify for matching federal funds for public recreation development, the marina project was being investigated at top level.

Beverly had arrived in Washington the day before and had already turned in her report to the committee. Now she sat in the hearing room waiting to be called to testify. All morning others had traipsed before the seven senators on the high bench and representatives of the Sierra Club, Greenpeace, Earth First! and other preservationist groups. Now Webster himself was at the witness table giving his testimony. While she listened and waited her turn, Beverly kept looking at her watch.

As soon as she was through here she was going to fly to Santa Barbara, where Jonas Buchanan was waiting to take her to her mother.

"Mr. Webster," asked the senator from Wisconsin, "just how large a marina do you propose to develop on this land?"

"A relatively small one, sir. As I state in my report, if I used all of my land it would accommodate a two-thousand-slip marina, but as that would be harmful to the environment, I will be scaling it down to under a thousand slips."

The hearing room was crowded, with television cameras, the press, and the public in the gallery. Beverly wasn't nervous about speaking before such a crowd; she had done it many times over the years. She had in fact requested to be allowed to testify before this Senate Subcommittee on the Environment, because they were investigating an issue that involved one of her personal crusades—the preservation of California's coastline.

"Now, Mr. Webster," asked the senator from Wisconsin, "if you will not be developing all of the land for boat slips, what will the rest of it go for?"

"I would like to point out, Mr. Senator, that I own the land, have owned it for a good many years, and am therefore personally concerned with its safe and nonharmful development. To answer your question, sir, I will be giving up forty-five percent of my land to be set aside as a bird sanctuary, as I have outlined in detail in my environmental-impact report. I have taken care to explore all possible future effects that would result from the construction of the marina. I have consulted with scientists and ecologists, and in no way will my project be detrimental to the local environment."

Beverly looked at her watch again.

Because of Jonas's phone call she had had to cancel the rest of her stay in Washington. She was to have attended a ball that evening at the French embassy, and tomorrow she would have met with representatives of the Children's Lobby to establish a national clearinghouse and information and referral service regarding missing children. So she had arranged to meet with all these people at their next regional meeting. Because she had to leave. Jonas Buchanan had found her mother, at last. . . .

When Mr. Webster was finished, gathering up his notes and looking self-satisfied, Beverly was called to the witness table. She took a seat before a microphone as the press photographed her and as one reporter was writing on his notepad: ". . . founder and sole director of Highland Enterprises, a financial empire whose famous motto is *Dare* . . . , the forty-two-year-old Miss Highland appeared confident and in control as she prepared to bring evidence against Irving Webster of Multi-Development Corp. . . ."

The hearing was being chaired by James Chandler, the junior senator from California, a man whose campaign platform was strongly pro-environmentalist, and a man whom Beverly had been instrumental in getting into office. He invited Miss Highland to speak.

"Thank you, Mr. Chandler. I would like to open my testimony with a question. Who owns the coastline? Surely it is human vanity and ignorance to think that it is for the good of all to carve up our planet into little self-serving patches, each operating in purely selfish interest without regard for its impact upon neighbors and the world at large. The issue before us here today is not about a small part of our planet; we are talking about the earth and all of humanity. Mr. Webster wants our coastline. And all we risk in return is our oxygen supply."

Beverly went on to point out that while the developer had indeed investigated the impact of his project upon the environment, he had done so halfheartedly and with incomplete results. "I would like to point out, gentlemen, some essential information that has not appeared in the other reports, and that is that what Mr. Webster is proposing is the destruction of an extensive network of tide pools that are vital in preserving the balance of the earth's oxygen supply."

She spoke clearly and in a strong voice that seemed to ring

throughout the hearing room as the television cameras kept their electronic eyes on her, as reporters and stenographers recorded her every word, as the public in the gallery listened in silence.

"Methane gas, gentlemen, is produced by bacterial fermentation in the muds and sediments of seabeds, wetlands, marshes, and river estuaries. Methane is a vital regulator of the earth's oxygen, in a process that is very delicately balanced. According to Michael McElroy, Jim Lovelock, and other distinguished scientists, the absence of methane production would cause a dangerous and rapid change in the concentration of our oxygen. We humans exist within a self-regulating biosphere that maintains an atmospheric balance vital to life on earth. Mr. Webster's marina would eradicate a very large and necessary part of that delicate mechanism."

The crowd stirred. People murmured up in the gallery. Senator Chandler banged his gavel.

"I would like to further point out, gentlemen," Beverly continued, "that I have looked into the land that Mr. Webster proposes to set aside as a bird sanctuary, and I have learned that Mr. Webster's own developer advised him that the land would be difficult to work with and would not be worth trying to turn into a marina. And I further discovered, gentlemen, as I explain in detail in my written report, that the land in question is totally unsuitable to the birds in the first place!

"The land he proposes to develop is the very wetlands and tide pools the birds and other creatures have adapted to and used for millennia. The land he proposes to 'give' to them is useless to both man and bird, except as a natural barrier to the last remaining essential habitats on the California coast.

"I suggest, gentlemen, that this land be set aside *forever*, that Mr. Webster be equitably compensated for his investment, including interest. And my foundation, working together with other like-minded organizations, is prepared to fund such a buy-out for the good of us all, for the good of our planet!"

Miss Highland had asked Bob Manning to drive up to Santa Barbara in the Rolls-Royce. So that was where Jonas Buchanan now sat, in the backseat, waiting for the arrival of her private jet.

It amazed him to think of what a turn his life had taken since that day nine years ago when he had sat at the bar of that dark restaurant, studying the young blond woman at the corner table. Jonas recalled how he had had doubts about going through with the meeting, how he had looked her over and wondered if he wanted her for a client. And then how he had remembered his overdue rent and had decided to go over and talk to her. What if he had decided the other way? What if he had just gotten up and walked out? It frightened him sometimes to think about it, to think about how close he had come to making the dumbest move of his life.

Instead, he had made the smartest move. He had gone to work for Beverly Highland, and he hadn't looked back since.

When Jonas had left the police force twelve years ago, his only ambition had been to lead a comfortable life. Well, he had that now and then some, this son of an East L.A. mailman! Jonas Buchanan had the good life—he worked hard, was devoted to his employer, and was paid handsomely. It was back in 1976 that he went to work for Highland Enterprises, closing up his place on Melrose, turning his client list over to another investigator, and moving into the fancy black-glass building on Wilshire, where he had a plush office and a private secretary. Since then he had worked solely for Beverly Highland, as chief of security for the company and as head of a security system that he set up around her new estate in Beverly Hills. Jonas also handled both personal and corporate investigations, such as doing research on Irving Webster's proposed yacht harbor or snooping into Danny Mackay's financial affairs. Today Jonas had private investigators working for *him*, and they were placed all around California and the Southwest, in the continued search for Miss Highland's mother and sister. It had, in fact, been his Santa Barbara–based man who finally found Naomi Burgess, but the new tack had been Jonas's idea. Without it, they might never have found her.

Yes, indeed, Jonas marveled as he watched the familiar Learjet touch down on the runway, he had come a long way since those days in the storefront on Melrose struggling to go it on his own, wishing he had never left the force. Now he drove a Mercedes, lived in an expensive house on Coldwater Canyon, had more girlfriends than he could juggle, and was, at last, the man who pulled the strings. Jonas had always held the belief, ever since he was a little boy, that he was going to be somebody someday. He had wit, streetwise know-how, a college education, and savvy picked up during his years on the force. But Jonas didn't take all the credit for his success—Miss Highland deserved more than half of it. When he had taken on her case nine years ago she had given him free rein. She hadn't balked at the money or his methods, so Jonas had finally been free to conduct an investigation the way he wanted. And she stood by him. He wasn't finding the mother and sister, but he was working hard and sticking to their trails, and Miss Highland appreciated that. She never got mad or threatened to fire him if he didn't produce something soon; in fact, she was always grateful for what little he came up with. And at times, over the years, that had been damned little. She was a heck of a woman, Jonas often thought—and he was thinking it with increasing frequency of late. Just as he had been forced to rethink his views on white women. Nine years ago he had conceded that she wasn't bad-looking for a white woman; now he thought she was downright beautiful. And smart, too. Jonas had seen what her new spirit had done to her hamburger company. She had infected him with it too, the challenge to dream big and make those dreams come true. Beverly Highland was, in her own way, he granted, canny and streetwise smart. Jonas often wondered where she had learned to read people so well.

Bob Manning got out of the driver's seat and came around to open the passenger door. Jonas looked out the window and saw Beverly coming toward the car. Maggie, her ever-present companion, went to the airport terminal, no doubt to wait until Beverly was ready to fly home. Jonas wasn't surprised that Miss Highland wanted to make this visit alone. He would, too, if he were in her place.

"Thank you for calling me, Jonas," she said when she got in and Manning closed the door.

God, but she smelled good, Jonas thought. Like a kind of

flower he couldn't put a name to. And she looked so perfect, as usual, with not a hair out of place, not a wrinkle in her clothing. He knew that Beverly Highland was forty-two—he had seen her birth certificate, but otherwise he never would have guessed it.

"How did the hearing go?" he asked.

"It went fine, Jonas. I think we'll win. Thanks to your excellent research." She smiled at him—sadly, he thought. Then she said quietly, "Take me to my mother now, will you please?"

It was a Protestant cemetery. Beverly was not religious, nor had her mother been, but she was glad that someone had cared enough to bury Naomi Burgess in hallowed ground. The grave marker was simple: NAOMI BURGESS, 1916–1975, *May She Rest in Peace.*

Beverly knelt and pulled a weed out of the grassy mound. A tear rolled down her cheek.

1975. I was looking for you then. We were so close. Barely a hundred miles apart. We saw the same sunsets over the same ocean; we felt the same rains and winds; we read the same newspapers and listened to the same music. I'm sorry I found you too late. . . .

Jonas watched her from the car, mentally chastising himself for not having found the woman sooner. He would have given anything to have been able to give Miss Highland at least a few final days with her mother. But Naomi Burgess had been hiding from the police, determined not to be found. And it was only because he had come up with nothing these past two years that Jonas had decided to take a rather radical and drastic tack. First, he had his investigators go through state death records; then, when that proved fruitless, he literally had them search every graveyard in California. It was a hunch, not much to go on, but then there was nothing else to go on either.

And the hunch had come through. When Jonas had gotten the call that there was a Naomi Burgess buried in a Santa Barbara cemetery, he had felt his heart rise in his throat. That was the last thing in the world he had wanted to report to Beverly.

He watched her come back to the car. Years ago he had boasted that a woman's tears didn't move him. That rule still held, with one exception. Now he had to fight the impulse to go out to Beverly and take her in his arms.

Bob Manning drove the stately Rolls down the streets of Santa Barbara, past the mansions of the rich and the apartment complexes of the college students, until he pulled up in front of an old Victorian house that was not unlike the house Hazel ran back in San Antonio. But this house was not brightly painted, nor did it have music pouring out of its windows; no cars were parked out front. It was run-down, with a yellow lawn and a tired fig tree littering the gravel driveway. Washing flapped on the lines out back; some toddlers played in a sandbox while a tired-looking woman watched them.

Beverly didn't get out of the car right away. She sat staring out the window, at this last place her mother had known. There was a faded sign over the front porch. It read: ST. ANN'S SHELTER FOR WOMEN.

She went up the sagging wooden steps. The front door stood open. From inside the house came women's voices. Someone was singing, someone was laughing, someone was crying. A telephone rang unanswered; a baby howled; the TV was tuned to a soap opera. Beverly walked in and looked around. There was a table in the hallway covered with pamphlets and mimeographed sheets, literature about various charity programs and halfway houses and drug and suicide hot lines. There was a bulletin board over the table where notices were tacked, and a daily work schedule, and a sign printed long ago that said, THERE IS NO SUCH THING AS A WORTHLESS HUMAN BEING.

"May I help you?"

Beverly turned around to find a young woman standing in the hallway. She wore jeans and a T-shirt and carried a baby on her hip. She also had a black eye and a bandage on her forehead. "I would like to speak to Reverend Drake, please."

"Sure!" the girl said. "That's the office. You can wait in there."

Beverly went into the small room that was crammed with

an untidy desk, old metal filing cabinets, and an ancient black-and-gold Remington typewriter. Taped to the walls were photographs of women and children of all ages and in all poses, and certificates and letters and other pieces of paper turning yellow and curling at the edges. Over the desk hung a simple crucifix. Next to it was a religious painting of Saint Ann.

Jonas had found this place. He had made some inquiries at the cemetery and discovered that Reverend Drake had buried Naomi Burgess there, and that the Reverend ran a shelter for women. Jonas had also learned that Reverend Drake founded this home fifteen years ago and ran it single-handedly, relying mainly upon local contributions. That it was a very poor house was obvious even without Jonas's research.

But it had sheltered Beverly's mother. Here was where she had come to live the last days of her life.

"Hello," came a voice in the doorway. "I'm Reverend Drake. How can I help you?"

Beverly turned to the woman whom Jonas had described to her. Mary Drake, an officially ordained minister in the Protestant faith, was in her fifties, lean, completely gray, and wore blue jeans and a T-shirt as if they were the uniform of the house. The one variation was the large cross that hung about her neck and rested on her chest.

"I'm Beverly Highland. I believe you were expecting me."

"Oh yes, Miss Highland! Please, sit down!" Mary Drake spoke a little breathlessly, as if she had been running or had been interrupted at some vigorous chore. "When Melanie said there was someone here to see me, and obviously not someone seeking shelter, I prayed that it was someone who had come to make a contribution! Thanksgiving is coming, and we always have open house and a free meal for anyone who comes here. I still have to buy a hundred turkeys and there isn't any money!" Mary smiled broadly and her face broke into a thousand wrinkles. "But then, maybe you'll make a contribution anyway. Now then"—she folded her hands on her desk—"what can I do for you?"

Beverly explained briefly about her long search for her mother and how it had ended at the cemetery.

"Yes. Dear Naomi. It grieved us all when she died. But it came as no surprise. She was very ill when she came to us. Your mother was an alcoholic, did you know that?"

"I guessed as much. She must have been when I was a child, I don't remember."

"Naomi used to talk about you all the time. Although I seem to recall that she said your name was Rachel. Anyway, she was very proud of you and swore that you were going to make a good life for yourself. I often wondered why she didn't try to find you, but we never ask questions here. Many of our women are hiding from abusive husbands or fathers, and don't wish to be found."

"Tell me, Reverend Drake—"

"Please call me Mary! Most people are uncomfortable with the fact that I'm an ordained minister. That's why I don't have a church. The parish where I came from couldn't adjust to my new status. For some reason, female priests disturb people. I can't imagine why, though. Nowhere in the Bible does it say women can't be priests. And they were, too, you know, centuries ago, before the men took over." She smiled again. It was an energetic, infectious smile, and it comforted Beverly to know that her mother had spent her last years in this woman's company.

"Tell me, Mary, about when my mother came here. I'd like to know."

Mary sighed and sat back in her chair. "Naomi was in a bad way. The last man she had taken up with had been pretty hard on her. Your mother had such a capacity for love, and yet she seemed always to link up with men who abused her. But that's a familiar story within these walls. We were crowded to capacity at that time. . . . I believe it was 1972. We had no more beds. Even the sofas were taken. She said she didn't care. She was desperate and tired and just wanted to rest. She slept in the kitchen, in a sleeping bag."

Beverly looked down at her hands.

"She stayed with us for three years," Mary Drake said gently, "and in that time we all came to love her. She was our cook. And what a godsend! I had been the cook, you see, and

I'm not very good at it. Your mother made the most fabulous hamburgers!"

Mary's smile softened. "But Naomi was more than that. It was as if she had always been looking for an outlet for her love. You see, many of our women here show up ill or injured. The worst cases I take to the hospital. But I was a nurse, years ago, and I keep a well-stocked medical kit. Your mother took up the duty of taking care of the sick ones, nursing them back to health, trying to encourage them not to return to the old life—although most of them did, I'm afraid. Anyway, your mother was a loving, positive force within these walls. We still miss her, greatly."

Beverly wiped a tear off her cheek. "Tell me about this house."

Mary Drake told her story of how, having found herself unwanted in a conservative parish, she had turned to the one thing she had always wanted to do—start up a home for battered women. The rent was very low on this house, and she received contributions from local citizens. But there were too many women in need and the house could accommodate only a limited number, and many arrived pregnant or with babies, scared and running, penniless, often without even a change of clothing.

"We receive a lot of cast-off clothing," Mary explained. "I run an ad in the paper, asking people to give us their old clothes. Unfortunately, my little operation can't afford the press that the bigger outfits like the Salvation Army and Goodwill have. When people donate or give money, they think of the more well known institutions first. Nonetheless, we do manage. There is a psychologist in town who donates two evenings a week for counseling. I have a doctor friend who comes by when he has the chance. You see, Miss Highland, donations can come in many forms. We need people's time, money, skills, food, clothing—even diapers!"

The phone rang. Mary picked it up and spoke quickly, making Beverly think that everything this woman did must be done in a hurry. When she hung up, Reverend Drake said, "That was the supermarket with my turkeys! He says he can only donate fifty! And I need a hundred!" She smiled. "When it comes to feeding my girls, Miss Highland, I set aside my pride. So I shall ask you, do you think you could find it in your heart to buy those turkeys for us?"

"Of course I can."

A young woman burst through the door. "Reverend Mary! Cindy's having contractions!"

"Oh dear. Will you excuse me for a moment, please?"

While she waited for Mary Drake to return Beverly took out her checkbook and stared at it. She felt the old house around her, smelled its old smells, sensed its frail hopes and dreams. It was not unlike Hazel's; the women abiding within these walls, Beverly knew, would have similar stories to tell, like those of sisters of long ago. And then she thought of her mother, frightened, hiding from the police, trying to find shelter. What had it been like for her, stabbing the man she loved but no longer able to take his abuse, and then running, alone and scared?

Beverly's throat tightened. Her eyes swam with tears. *If only I had found you! I would have taken you home! I would have made you well! And we could right now be dreaming together, just as we did so long ago. . . .*

When Mary came back into the office she was breathless again. "Poor Cindy! It's her first baby and she's terrified. She isn't having contractions. Just a little stomach upset. She's only fifteen, but she's been on her own since she was eleven. A Good Samaritan brought her here last month when he picked her up hitchhiking on the Coast Highway. She offered him sex in return for food."

She looked at her visitor, who was crying softly into a handkerchief. "Your mother is with God now, Miss Highland," Mary Drake said gently. "And she is blessed, I promise you. She didn't suffer for long; her end was quick. And she was surrounded by people who loved her."

Beverly sniffed back her tears and dabbed her eyes with the handkerchief. "I can never thank you enough for what you did for her." Beverly took a small gold pen out of her purse and uncapped it. "Tell me. Do you have many women coming to your door for help?"

"More than you would imagine. And the numbers are growing. Unfortunately, I have to turn many of them away. There just isn't room. I try to find other shelter for them. There are a few citizens in town who help me out now and then. And I have a reciprocal arrangement with a couple of runaway and halfway houses. We try to take care of each other's overflow."

"How many beds would you need, do you think?"

Mary laughed. "At least ten times what I have! There's a dilapidated old house down the street I've been trying to lay my hands on. It's been for sale for a long time and the owner hasn't had any nibbles. I'm working on him to let us use it in exchange for fixing it up. He's a stubborn old coot, but I think I'm weakening him. He might give us the house just so I'll leave him alone! I can be a very persuasive woman when I put my mind to it!"

"I've made this out to you," Beverly said as she handed the check across. "I didn't know if you had an account in the name of St. Anne's."

"Thank you, Miss Highland. You are an answer to my prayers."

Beverly stood and held out her hand. "I must go now. I thank you for giving up your time to talk to me. After all these years of looking for my mother—"

Mary took her hand and squeezed it. "I know. I understand." She held up the check and smiled. "The good Lord works in mysterious ways. First he brought Naomi Burgess to this house and now her daughter. With this money, Miss Highland, we'll be able to offer a good Thanksgiving dinner to women who otherwise might not—"

She stared at the check.

She slowly sat down and whispered, "Dear God in Heaven!" Then she looked up at Beverly and said, "Am I dreaming or is this check made out for five hundred thousand dollars!"

"I want you to build a new facility. I want you to make it exactly the way you want it to be, modern and clean and full of love, and to be able to shelter as many women as need it. Hire all the staff you require, make it a home where women can find asylum and recover from their abuses. I'll send my attorneys up to help you work it out. Do you think you can do it?"

"Do it!" Mary said, gazing at the check and shaking her head. "Of course I can do it!" Tears rose in her eyes. "Praise God in His mercy. . . ."

As they were walking out to the car a few minutes later, out to the white Rolls-Royce Silver Cloud, where a few children and young women stood shyly staring at it, Beverly said, "Tell me, Mary. How did you get into this? I mean, why did you choose this particular area of need?"

Mary looked up at the sun and squinted. "I was married years ago. My husband beat me up regularly. I don't know why I put up with it, but I did. And then one night he got drunk and hit my son with his fist. I took my boy and ran. I went to a shelter run by a priest. There I found God and my calling."

"And your son?"

"The blow to his head caused irreparable brain damage. He's in an institution now. He's thirty years old and doesn't even know his name."

At the car, Mary turned and took Beverly's hands. Her eyes were moist as she said, "Perhaps I started this house to atone for that sin, I don't know. But I do know that God brought you here today in answer to my prayers. I'm going to call my new shelter the Beverly Highland Shelter for Women."

"No. I want it to be the Naomi Burgess Shelter for Women. My mother was never able to find dignity in life, but at least in death she will have it at last."

37

THE HARSH LIGHTS of the operating room shone down upon an unconscious body covered in green sheets. There was no sound in the room except for the *whoosh* of the anesthetist's ventilator and the steady beep of the cardiac monitor. Four people stood at the operating table; they were dressed in green and wore white paper masks. The tallest of them, the surgeon, was sweating so profusely that the nurse had to wipe his forehead with a cloth. The air was tension-charged. Fear was communicated through the eyes of every member of the surgical team. If this important patient were to die, their faces said, it would mean an international crisis.

"Scalpel," said the surgeon.

The scrub nurse handed it to him. He positioned it, ready to cut through taut flesh.

"Just a minute," said Dr. Markus from her place in the corner. She walked up to the table, snatched the scalpel from the man's hand and said, "That's not the way I showed you to hold a scalpel. You're not about to slice a salami, for God's sake."

"What the fuck difference does it make!" shouted the surgeon. "Who the hell cares?"

"I care!" she shouted back, and threw the scalpel to the floor.

"Cut," came a tired voice. "Cut cut cut cut. Dr. Markus? May I see you for a moment?"

She gave the man in the surgeon's clothes one last glare, turned on her heel, and marched off the set.

"Dr. Markus, my dear," the director said, coming up to her and taking her elbow. "You realize that if you keep interrupting, we'll never get this scene finished."

"That man is an idiot! You don't hold a surgical knife like that. It requires a praying-mantis hand. How many times do I have to tell him that!"

"Dr. Markus, sweetheart," said the director quietly, steering her away from the film crew. "What's the big deal? It's only a TV show."

She gave him an exasperated look. "Look. Barry Greene hired me to be the technical adviser. If you're not going to take my technical advice, then what am I doing here?"

"Now, now. Calm—"

She turned and walked away.

• • •

Linda lived in Malibu in a house built on the side of a cliff, at the edge of the ocean. Whenever the tide came in, she felt the house shake as waves pounded the stilts. A fine spray would spew up over the wooden deck outside and the house would be filled with the salty smell of the sea. It was an old house, small, with just four rooms, and it cost half a million dollars.

The house was shuddering on this drizzly April night as Linda waited for Barry Greene to arrive. The Pacific seemed to have launched a siege against the pilings, as if determined to bring them down. The ocean was alive in its steady, thrusting rhythm; it seemed to be speaking to Linda with its great spumes of water and aftermath whisperings as the tide receded. As she paced the living room, where Beethoven competed with the song of the sea, Linda thought of the watery world down below, where crabs and seaweed swirled around the supports of her house. She thought of the many nights she had lain in bed, listening to the ocean, reflecting upon her loneliness.

Linda had not chosen to lead a solitary life; it had just turned out that way. She had tried to make her two brief marriages work, tried to find someone to whom she could pledge herself, but always that vital part of herself, the giving, wanting, sexual part, froze under a man's touch. And intimate relationships could not survive such a frost.

She looked at the clock over the fireplace. It had been an hour since Barry Greene had called, asking her not to act rashly—she had turned in her resignation on *Five North*—and saying that he would like to talk about it. So she had invited him here, to her expensive shack on the rain-slicked Pacific Coast Highway.

And then she heard the door chimes.

He had parked his Porsche next to her Ferrari and stood in the light April mist with packages in his arms. He had stopped at Vicente Foods and picked up steaks, French bread, and a bottle of champagne; and it was when Linda saw these, as he spread them out on the counter of her tiny kitchen, that she knew the real reason why he had come tonight, and why she had invited him.

The discussion about the TV show took five minutes: he persuaded her to stay. "I'll lay down the law," Barry promised her as they sat by the fire in her living room, watching the rain come down hard on the sun deck. "I'll tell him he has to do exactly what you say. The man can be such a putz."

Then they retreated into small talk while Barry kept their glasses filled.

Linda tried to relax; she forced herself to smile and listen and laugh now and then. And she let the champagne do some of the work. After all, she decided as she kicked off her shoes and drew her legs up under her, Barry Greene was an attractive man. And he was a man at ease with his power. He was never loud or bullyish or arrogant about it; Barry used his power quietly. Which Linda found appealing.

He was also funny. "Did I ever tell you about my cousin Abe?" he said when the champagne was gone and he came back from the kitchen with a bottle of Linda's wine. He joined her on the sofa and refilled their glasses. "Abe was going across the country on Amtrak, and he had one of those pullman sleepers. One night, he was trying to get to sleep in the upper berth, and he kept hearing a woman in the berth below him say over and over again, 'Oy, am I toisty. *Oy*, am I toisty.' Well, Abe couldn't get to sleep because of it. So he climbed down the ladder, went down to the end of the train car to the water fountain, filled a paper cup, brought it back, and thrust it between the curtains of the lower berth. Then he climbed back up, got all comfortable and was just about to doze off when the voice came from below, 'Oy, was I toisty.' "

Linda laughed and picked up her wine. She noticed that she no longer felt like eating; the steaks were going to stay in the fridge.

"So," he said softly, looking around. "Nice place you have here. I'll bet you paid an arm and a leg for it."

"About that. And I felt lucky to get it."

"You could ask a million for it and it'll be snatched up before you can put out your 'For sale' sign."

"The cliff is slowly eroding away. No one seems to care, though. Someday all the houses along here will be floating to Hawaii."

"Have you ever been to Hawaii?"

"I did my internship there, at Great Victoria Hospital in Honolulu."

"No kidding. What made you decide to become a surgeon?"

Visions flashed in Linda's mind—of operating rooms and surgeons and painful skin grafts and experts trying to reconstruct her after the accident when she was a child. "I guess to prove that I could do it, I suppose. My best friend is a pediatrician. She didn't want to be one, she wanted to be a pathologist, but she succumbed to family pressure and to the brainwashing by our medical school staff. Female medical students are strongly guided in the direction of so-called women's specialties—gynecology, dermatology, family practice."

"In this day and age?"

She laughed. "In this day and age. Women doctors still have a tough go of it, despite the consciousness-raising of the past two decades."

"I remember when my son had to go for a summer-camp physical. He was twelve, and when he discovered that the doctor was a woman, he refused to go. My wife informed him that she and his sisters had had to go to male doctors for years without being allowed to complain, now it was the guys' turn." Barry chuckled. "He went, but he didn't like it."

"I didn't know you were married."

"I'm not. We divorced ten years go."

"I'm also divorced."

"What happened?"

"It didn't work out."

They fell silent. Linda stared into the flames in the fireplace, while Barry stared at Linda.

"I can't believe you're alone," he said softly. "A beautiful woman like you."

She turned and looked at him. She liked the way the firelight played on the planes of his face. "I'm not alone now, am I?"

He reached out and touched her. "No. You're not."

Linda smiled. She felt warm and dreamy. The rain was coming down so hard that it sounded like a dull roar on her roof. The ocean was churning, making her house tremble. The world outside was cold and hostile, but Linda's living room was cozy and safe and filled with a golden glow. She felt herself relax.

Barry moved closer. When he started kissing her, it was not in a hurried, sexual way, but slowly, tenderly, as if that were all he wanted to do. But, of course, that was not all he wanted to do. He soon had his hand up under her blouse; her arms went around his neck. It felt good and right to her; she actually *wanted* him.

"Let's go into the bedroom," he whispered.

Linda's daily maid had turned back the bed, as was her habit when Dr. Markus came home after dark. So it looked as if Linda had anticipated this. Barry became excited. Urgency crept into his kisses. His hands moved anxiously and with purpose.

"Wait—" Linda said. She got up from the bed and turned out the overhead light.

He came up behind her, slid his hands up to her breasts and kissed her neck. She felt herself start to tighten up. She pulled away and went to the sliding glass door to close the drapes and block out the light that came from a bulb on the sun deck. The bedroom was plunged into darkness. She went into Barry's arms. She kissed him. She pressed herself against him. She forced a moan.

And then they were hurriedly undressing.

But as her slacks came off and she stood in her panties Linda realized that the bathroom night-light still shed some illumination into the bedroom. She drew away from Barry and closed the door. Now they were in total darkness and Barry couldn't find her.

"Hey," he said softly. "We need a little light, you know."

"I prefer it this way," she said as she went to lie down on the bed. Now she was able to remove her panties, now that he couldn't see her, now that she was completely safe from his eyes. It was the only way she had ever been able to make love, in total darkness. It was something Linda was used to. She knew her bedroom by heart. She knew where everything was—the bed, the armchair, the TV stand.

But Barry didn't.

Linda heard a dull sound, and then Barry: "Ow! Damn! My toe!"

She sat up and reached for him. "Here—"

"Sorry, darling," he said, "but I just have to have a *little* light."

And before Linda could stop him, she heard the click of a lamp and the bedroom was flooded with light.

She cried out and pulled the comforter up over herself.

"There you are," he said, smiling and limping toward the bed. But when he tried to take her into his arms, Linda tightened up. "What's the matter?" he said.

And then she knew: it was no use. She couldn't go on with it. The light, his stubbed toe—it was all wrong. All sexual desire vanished, as it had so many times in the past, at this point or some other point in the lovemaking, against Linda's will, even when she desperately wanted to go through with it. But her body betrayed her. Her mind wanted to make love; her body froze. Now the thought of Barry Greene lying on top of her, pushing himself inside her, filled her with a familiar dread.

He stared at her. "What's wrong, Linda?"

"I'm sorry," she murmured.

"Sorry! About what?"

"I can't."

"Why not?"

"I just can't, that's all."

He put his hand on her bare shoulder. She flinched. "What's wrong, Linda?" he asked gently. "Is it me?"

"No, it's me. I'd rather you left now, Barry."

"Why don't we talk about it? Maybe we can work it out."

She shook her head, unable to speak, angry and hurt and humiliated, and mentally punishing herself for having tried too soon.

38

THE PEOPLE AT THE NEXT TABLE were having a fight.

Jessica tried not to be obvious about it, but she wanted to see what they looked like.

A giant potted palm stood between the two tables; she turned slightly in her chair and glanced through the fronds. A man and a woman, in their early forties, were engaged in a heated argument, and neither seemed to care about being overheard. They were saying terrible things to each other. The woman was on the verge of tears. The man had his hands curled into trembling fists. They were married, Jessica was able to deduce from what they said, with children in their teens and one child still in grammar school. "How can you do this to us?" Jessica heard one of them say. "How can you just pick up and leave after eighteen years of marriage? How will the children and I get along without you?" They were splitting up. They were getting divorced because one of them had fallen in love with someone much younger and wanted, it seemed to Jessica, to start life over. "I'm still young" was the explanation. "But I won't be forty-three forever. And I don't love you anymore." The other said in a dark voice, "You're making a fool of yourself, giving me up for someone who's nearly twenty years younger than you."

"Please don't leave me" was the final plea, and Jessica quickly turned around, upset for them, embarrassed to have overheard, and stunned to realize that it was the *wife* who was leaving the husband for a younger man.

"Jessica? Do you know what you want?"

She looked at John. He was forty and very handsome. The restaurant's candlelight did nice things to his salt-and-pepper hair. "I, uh . . ." she began, opening up her menu.

John turned to the third person at their table, a man whom John was very anxious to impress for business reasons, and said to him, "My wife likes to eavesdrop on private conversations."

"I'm interested in human nature," she said defensively.

John laughed. "Face it, Jess. You're nosy."

The waiter came up, a surfer type in Hawaiian shirt and tight shorts, and flashed Jessica a flirtatious smile. "What'll you folks have?"

He could work at Butterfly, she thought. *He'd be perfect.*

"Jessica?" said John. "We're waiting. What do you want?"

She looked down at the menu. "I'll have the prime rib, please, small cut, rare, with a baked potato."

"Do you want everything on that potato, ma'am? Butter, sour cream, cheese sauce?"

John spoke up and said, "Change that potato to tomato slices for the lady." He smiled at her.

Her face burned. She looked away, pretended to be suddenly interested in the boats out on the water.

Butterfly . . .

She hadn't gone back. Not after her one wild evening with her fantasy cowboy. Part of it had to do with being too busy—since the success of the Latricia Brown case, Jessica and Fred's phones hadn't stop ringing; the firm of Morton and Franklin was signing on more clients than they could handle, so that now they were interviewing attorneys and thinking of expanding their offices. But another part of the reason for her staying away from Butterfly had to do with the way she had felt in the days following her encounter in the Western bar.

The night with "Lonnie" had been fabulous. It had been just like her dream. And for a while afterward she had felt light and airy and positively smug. But then, as the initial euphoria wore off and she was operating in the real world again, she began to feel doubts and uncertainties creep in. She experienced a kind of confusion over her feelings—to have been made love to so fantastically, but by a man whom she did not love!—and also a little fear. The fear, she knew, stemmed from guilt. Her old Catholic conscience, inculcated into her from her earliest childhood by nuns and priests who had frightened her with visions of Hell, suddenly came rushing back. She had done something sinful.

And so Jessica had found herself unable to return to Butterfly, and she decided not to go back until she had sorted out her mind and heart.

"So, you must know a lot of famous people, Mrs. Franklin."

She looked at the man across the table. For an instant she couldn't recall his name. She panicked. John would be furious. He had stressed to her the importance of this dinner, the importance that she make a good impression because this man, who could bring a lot of money into John's firm, insisted that the people he dealt with were stable in their private lives.

His name was Scandinavian. . . . She glanced at John before saying, "I'm afraid most of my clients are what you would call behind-the-scenes people, Mr. . . . "—she picked up her mai tai and sipped it—"Mr. Rasmussen. Script writers, agents, casting people—very few of my clients are known to the public."

The man laughed and said, "My wife is addicted to *Five North*. That Latricia Brown certainly is a good actress. I read all about how you fought for her to stay on the show."

Jessica could feel John's displeasure rising. Although he sat comfortably in his chair and casually stirred his cocktail, she could sense his annoyance. "Anyway," she said, "my job isn't as glamorous as people think it is. Certainly we can talk about something more interesting!"

The two men entered into talk about marathon running, optimum cardiac outputs, and a rival company while Jessica sat in silence doing exactly what was expected of her: being John's gracious and lovely wife.

And she wanted very badly not to be there.

"Tell me, Mrs. Franklin," Mr. Rasmussen said when their dinners arrived, "what do you think of this Danny Mackay? Think he'll make it to the White House?"

"I'd like to see him there," John said, answering for her. "And I think his chances are looking good. We'll certainly be voting for him."

"I don't intend to," Jessica said. "I don't like Danny Mackay."

John gave her a surprised look. "Since when have you been interested in politics?"

I've always been. You just assume that I'm not.

The young waiter came back and John declined dessert for himself and Jessica.

When they were finishing their coffee and John was paying the check, Mr. Rasmussen turned to Jessica and said, "Say, do you think you could get Latricia Brown's autograph for my wife?"

Behind her, the couple who had been fighting abruptly got up and left the restaurant. The wife was crying.

"John," Jessica said as they drove along the Pacific Coast Highway. "John, I think we should talk."

"Sure, honey. What do you want to talk about?"

She looked out the window. A dense fog shrouded the highway; curves were treacherous here, but John handled the BMW with ease. This stretch was particularly known for its bad accidents.

"John, I'd like us to see a marriage counselor."

"What?" He gave her a quick look and then had his eyes on the road again. He laughed. "A marriage counselor! Whatever for?"

"I . . . I don't think things are right between us."

"Of course they are!" He patted her knee. "You're just tired."

"I really want us to go to someone, John. If I make an appointment, will you go with me?"

"No. You're the one who thinks we have a problem. You work it out."

Jessica had known by his tone that the subject was closed. And she hadn't wanted to start a fight on that dangerous road. So they had driven home in silence, and she had gone straight to bed while John sat up doing some paperwork. And now here she was in her office, wondering why on earth she was so capable in this incarnation, so in control among laws and courts and writs, while as John Franklin's wife she was . . . well, *John Franklin's wife.*

Ken, her receptionist, came through with a box of doughnuts. When he offered her one, Jessica put up her hand and said, "Not me!" But when he went away to put the box in the small kitchen/lounge behind their offices, Jessica felt a sudden intense craving for a doughnut.

She tried to work. She forced her mind along logical, legal tracks. She made phone calls, dictated letters, did some research in their library. But those doughnuts kept coming back into her mind.

She was hungry. Last night she had barely touched her dinner. This morning her breakfast had been black coffee. Now it was nearly noon and she was starting to feel light-headed. She went into the rest room, closed the door and bathed her face in the sink. Then she stepped back and inspected herself in the mirror. This was one of her least flattering suits, the one that John said made her look fat. And it did.

But maybe it was because she *was* fat.

Jessica was suddenly alarmed. Was she gaining weight again? When was the last time she had weighed herself? She turned this way and that, scrutinizing her reflection, displeased with what she saw. She thought of the doughnuts, of the apple fritter, in particular, that was large and crunchy and loaded with sugar. Her mouth watered. She was so hungry.

Hurrying out of the bathroom, she went into the tiny kitchen, praying that Fred or one of the secretaries hadn't taken the fritter. Jessica saw the box on the table, standing open. There were crumbs around it. She rushed to it and looked in.

Relief flooded her. The fritter was still there.

Taking a paper towel, she carefully wrapped the doughnut and brought it back to her desk, where it would sit while she worked and anticipated eating it, putting it off until the afternoon, when she would really enjoy it—

Jessica froze.

She stared in horror at the paper-towel bundle.

It was happening again!

Thirteen years ago, as a freshman at UCSB, Jessica Mulligan, starved and skinny, had developed a grotesque ritual around doughnuts. She would go without eating for days, then rush to the Student Union as soon as the fresh doughnuts were out, buy a dozen buttermilk twists, hurry back to the dorm, lock the door, and devour all twelve, quickly, like a criminal afraid of being caught. Then she would dispose of the napkin, clean the crumbs off the floor, wash her hands and face and spend the next few days fasting, punishing herself for the binge.

A year in therapy, after her hospitalization for anorexia—where they had had to force-feed her—had helped Jessica come to terms with her problem and learn how to keep it under control.

Now here she was, years later, suffering a relapse.

She was suddenly very afraid.

"Fred," she said, walking into his office. "Something's come up. I'm going to take the afternoon off. Do you think you can handle it alone?"

"Sure, Jess," he said, giving her a long look. "Are you all right? You don't look well."

"I'll be okay. If anybody should call with something urgent, well . . . I'm going to be unreachable."

She drove faster than was her habit, pulled into the first gas station and dialed Butterfly's number. Her message was brief. "This is Jessica Franklin. I'd like the same as last time. Will an hour from now be okay?"

Then she went to Malibu, where she spent half an hour walking barefoot in the surf, trying to find herself somewhere in the sand and wind and waves.

Intellectually she knew she was not fat. At five feet four inches, Jessica weighed only a hundred and ten pounds. And yet, when she saw herself, in the mirror or in photographs, she saw a fat woman. She was morbidly afraid of getting fat. It was time, she knew as she dug her toes into the wet sand, to come to terms with that fear.

Jessica turned her face to the vast Pacific and squinted at the horizon.

Back at UCSB, her roommate Trudie had devised a kind of game to help draw the phobias out of Jessica and make her see them, confront them, and thereby find a way of putting them to rest.

"What is 'fat'?" Trudie had asked. They had been sitting in their tiny dorm room with the door closed against the sounds of life and laughter in the hallway beyond and rain pelting the window. "Tell me, Jess, how you see 'fat.' What is it to you?"

And Jessica had surprised herself with the litany she had

suddenly recited. "Fat is self-indulgence. Fat is lack of control. Fat is lack of intelligence. Fat is indecent. Fat is failure." She had broken down crying. "Fat is losing someone's respect. Fat is losing their love. Fat is letting your family down. Fat is—"

"Do you really *believe* all that?" Trudie had asked.

"I don't know! My therapist says it's fear of success that makes me do it. But that's backward. I'm scared to death of failure."

Jessica hadn't thought she would go back to Butterfly, had felt too guilty, too sly, and feared John finding out. But now, as she followed the Butterfly attendant down the hall, Jessica thought they would never reach the room at the end. She was incredibly excited and anxious, desperate to be made love to by a man who didn't withhold sex from her as a punishment or give it to her as a reward. A man, in other words, who wasn't John.

Jessica was stunned by her own thoughts as she went into Lonnie's arms and let him guide her around the dance floor. Why hadn't she realized it before? John used sex as a power tool—and now she was doing the same thing. Their fights always ended the same way, with him breaking her down, destroying her, stripping her of identity and self-respect and then, when she was completely voided, and repentant and in his power, he rewarded her with his love. If she did not give in, he turned his back on her in bed. Never, it seemed to Jessica now, in all their years together, had lovemaking had anything to do with caring or giving or binding their souls as well as their bodies.

Her cowboy didn't criticize her or talk down to her or humiliate her in front of others. He made tender love to her on the floor, concerned that she was receiving pleasure, telling her that she was beautiful, restoring dignity and self-esteem where, under the same circumstances, John would be taking it away.

It was then, as her fantasy lover possessed her, that Jessica came to the realization that her life had to change, that things could not go on as they were. She was suddenly no longer confused. Everything came crystal clear. She didn't want to have to rely on a phantom-cowboy to give her what she should find in an honest relationship with her husband. She wanted this to be real. And it was going to have to be up to her to make the first move. It frightened her a little, to think of standing up to John, to imagine the battle that might lie ahead, to think of what she might lose. But it was a risk she was willing to take.

39

FROM AN ALTITUDE of thirty thousand feet Beverly Highland thought the Pacific Ocean looked like a pale blue counterpane spread across a tired world. She was gazing out the window of her private jet and watching the coastline of California appear now and then through the clouds below. She loved to fly; it made her feel as if her soul had wings.

Maggie, deeply immersed in a book, disagreed. She hated flying. Even in Beverly's comfortably appointed Learjet. She kept her wineglass filled and refused to look out the window.

The rest of Beverly's entourage—press secretary, hairdresser, chef, chauffeur, a personal maid, and bodyguards—were scattered throughout the cabin quietly reading and playing cards. They were getting in their relaxation now because once this jet put down at San Francisco International Airport their work would begin. And there would be no rest for any of them until the plane took off again tomorrow.

Maggie looked up from her book and studied her friend. Beverly looked terribly pale. "Are you all right?" she said quietly.

Beverly looked at her and smiled. "I'm okay," she murmured.

"You haven't been sleeping."

"Don't worry, Maggie," she said softly. "I'm all right, really."

But Maggie was worried. Tonight in San Francisco, for the

first time in thirty-five years, Beverly was going to meet Danny Mackay face-to-face.

Power, Danny thought as he adjusted his white Stetson and grinned at himself in the mirror. *I have it at last. After all these years of working for it, studying for it, eating and breathing for it, it's mine.* He felt good tonight. Damned good. He felt as if he stood on top of the world, instead of at the top of San Francisco's tallest hotel. Those night-school dreams of years ago when he had opened Machiavelli for the first time and read words that were speaking directly to him—*A prince need not have virtues, but only seem to have them*—those endless nights sitting in classrooms and the long hours poring over textbooks, the fight to polish himself, to get the hayseed out of the way he spoke, to dress himself in class and turn himself into someone whom people respected and listened to, all that long struggle had been worth it. Soon, he would hold unimaginable power in his hands, the presidency, and once he had that, there would be nothing Danny could not do.

He thought of last night's press conference and exchanged a secretive, knowing smile with his reflection. When questioned by a reporter about his stand on the issue of entering into a nuclear arms reduction agreement with the Russians, Danny had thought, *We have to strike the bastards first before they strike us.* But to the press he had said, "Peace between the United States and the people of the Soviet Union is one of my most fervent prayers."

He and Bonner Purvis were alone in the hotel room. Danny had asked his ever-present entourage to let them be by themselves for these last few minutes before going down to the ballroom. On the other side of the closed door, which was flanked by two bodyguards, a crowd was gathering in the living room of Danny Mackay's penthouse suite. Their boy would not be going down in the elevator alone but would be accompanied by three private secretaries, a speech writer, publicist, political advisers, and various important party members. Tonight was going to be a big night in Danny Mackay's campaign: he was going to meet one of his most important backers for the first time.

Beverly Highland.

Danny looked at himself in the mirror and winked. This ol' San Antonio boy had come a long way since 1955, and he looked mighty good on this foggy April evening. He wore an expensive tailored Western suit, high-heeled cowboy boots and a Stetson that would have done J. R. Ewing proud. And the body beneath was expensively maintained, too. No redneck paunch for Danny Mackay. A private gym in his Houston mansion ensured that, at age fifty-six, Danny could still hold his own with men twenty years his junior.

Danny still cut a striking figure and he knew it. He also knew that his sexy smile and sly, lazy eyes were getting him the votes. He hypnotized people; he had a special magic that few could resist, and he was going to turn it on full blast tonight, in honor of Miss Highland. She would melt, he knew, and be one more of his pawns before the night was over.

"Hey, Danny," Bonner said suddenly. "Remember the road gang?"

Bonner was leaning in the doorway buffing his manicured fingernails. He still had the strange pale blond hair and cherubic looks that had gotten him into so many beds in their days of traveling around with Billy Bob Magdalene. He still got into a lot of beds, but discreetly now, because of his employer.

"Yeah, boy," Bonner said, grinning. "That road gang . . ."

That particular shared episode in their lives had occurred long ago—back in the days when they had provided whores for Hazel's house. For stealing a church's poor box they were given a year at hard labor on a morals charge, while the police chief's kid, who was an accomplice, got off scot-free. After serving only two months of their time, the two had laid down their shovels and, when the fat guard wasn't looking, strolled off the job.

They'd laughed about that one for a long time. They'd lain low for a while, hiding out with a friend of Hazel's, and a year later, when they knew the statute of limitations was up, they'd had a big celebration with a few of Hazel's girls.

But Danny hadn't forgotten that the son of the police chief had beaten the rap while he and Bonner had gone to jail. That boy, Jimmy Briggs, had been put on Danny's secret list, along

392

with Dr. Simon Waddell and others, and one day he found himself being driven out to a lonely, desolate field wishing he'd never met up with Danny and Bonner.

Danny now gave Bonner a long, thoughtful look. They had been together a long time, longer than Danny had been with anyone. Bonner was a bit of a dullard, not well educated, and he lacked imagination. But he was doglike loyal to Danny, and a man in a high position needed at least one person he could rely on and trust. *The man who becomes a prince through the support of the people will stand alone and no one will disobey him*. Danny liked standing alone, and he liked being obeyed, but there were times when it suited his purpose to have Bonner around. Bonner had served his master faithfully for years, and continued to do so. But, like an old dog, when his usefulness came to an end, so would Bonner.

Danny walked to the window and looked out. The Golden Gate Bridge was strung across the fog-shrouded neck of the Bay like a gaudy necklace. That road gang had happened to someone else in another age. It had nothing to do with Danny Mackay, who was one step away from the White House.

He'd reached it at last, the final jumping-off place he had worked so long to arrive at. Once the money and influence had been secured, he had then made his moves into the political arena.

That was six years ago, at a time when his name was near the top of the popularity polls. Danny Mackay had ranked fourth on the Most Favorite American list, and sixth on Most Favorite Person in the World. He'd been approached then by the chairmen of the central organizing committees for both parties and he'd gotten down to the serious business of placing himself in the political limelight. But his real opportunity had occurred only last year, and everyone had declared what a stroke of luck it had been for him. It had to do with a man named Fred Banks.

"Hey, Bon," Danny had asked his friend last year, on the occasion of that luck, "have you ever heard of a man named Carl Jung?"

"No."

"He had a theory called synchronicity. It means things

happening at the same time, things that appear to occur co-incidentally. Like, for example, two totally unrelated phenomena taking place at the same moment resulting in something fantastic. Most people call it luck or coincidence. Do you know what 'serendipity' means?"

Bonner didn't know.

"It means desirable things happening by accident. And this," Danny had said, holding up a newspaper so that Bonner could see the headline, "is what I call a perfect example of serendipitous synchronicity."

The front page was carrying the story of a man named Fred Banks who had gone to the Middle East to spread the Word of God to the heathen Muslims and had gotten a little too enthusiastic one Friday preaching outside a mosque. He was arrested and thrown in jail on a spying charge, and all of a sudden the State Department was involved.

Well, Fred had denied that he was an agent for the CIA, declaring that he was in the Middle East because of Danny Mackay. According to the newspapers, Fred had gotten all worked up while watching the *Good News Hour* one day, had bought himself a Bible and a one-way ticket to a "godless corner of the world." Now he was being persecuted for the Lord's sake, he had claimed. He was a martyr for Jesus and Danny.

It had been an awkward situation for the American consul, who was working hard trying to keep Fred Banks from being imprisoned for life or executed. And so when Fred appealed directly to the Reverend Danny Mackay, a more private appeal was made to Danny as well. The men in the dark blue suits and unmarked car who came to visit him at his Houston headquarters one day assured Danny of absolute safety and immunity if he would please fly over there and negotiate the release of the embarrassing Fred.

Danny told his private staff that it was serendipitous synchronicity—Fred needing to be rescued by Danny at a time when Danny was trying to push his name higher in the polls. And so amid a flurry of publicity and excited media attention, he had flown to the small Middle Eastern country, where he had met with the king's ministers and, through charisma and showmanship, had been able to convince them that Fred was not a spy at all but simply a misguided Christian zealot. Danny publicly apologized for Fred's actions and showed his good faith by presenting the king with a white stretch limo with Texas steer horns on the hood.

His return to the United States with the bedraggled, bearded, grateful missionary had been met by dizzying media attention. Along with the widely published photo of him shaking hands with the king—the captions read, "The cowboy and the sheik"—Danny suddenly found himself in the uppermost echelons of fame. Talk-show hosts clamored to have him on their programs; four major publishers approached him to write a book; he received awards and commendations from organizations all over the country; he had dinner at the White House.

Just as he had predicted, Danny Mackay became a hero overnight.

Except that it hadn't been luck at all, or serendipitous synchronicity. Danny had sent Fred Banks to the Middle East, and together they had played out a scene.

Danny marveled at how easy it had been. So simple to plan and execute. Danny had advertised for the services of a mercenary in *Soldier of Fortune* magazine, and it was agreed that Fred Banks would receive a large sum of money plus a ranch in Mexico in return for playing a role. Dazzled by the payment that was being offered him, and by the celebrity who was hiring him, Fred had been willing and cooperative from the start. His value was familiarity with the Middle East, a smattering of Bible education, and a great deal of knowledge about desert survival, should it come to that. He had assumed his role at once, clearly enjoying the secrecy, the one-man-mission aspect of it, and the promise of media attention afterward. Danny had already paved the way, through various diplomatic contacts and other secret sources, by striking a secret pact with the Muslim king. His small country needed American tanks and machine guns. Danny, through his representatives, promised the Arab everything if he would arrest and then later release a certain missionary named Fred Banks.

The whole thing had gone off without a hitch. Fred had his ranch, the king had his illegal weapons, and Danny was a hero.

And now that he was campaigning and the convention was only two months away, the whole Fred Banks episode was being brought up again, as was also the Parkland vigil on the day of Kennedy's assassination. Danny's staff kept the Kennedy connection constantly in the forefront, and the people ate it up. His slogan, "Return to Camelot," had been Danny's idea. It was written, in fact, on the bright red banner that was draped across the wall behind the dais where Danny Mackay was going to preside over a banquet being given in his honor by Beverly Highland.

"Okay, Bon," Danny said, checking himself one last time in the mirror. "Go get the bitch and we'll be on our way."

"The bitch" was his wife, Angelica.

Beverly would not sit at Danny's table. The reason she gave was that this was his night and she did not want to steal any of his spotlight. Danny, being a consummate egotist, thought this sounded reasonable.

Twelve hundred people rose to their feet when he entered the ballroom. Their applause and cheering nearly drowned out the orchestra, which was playing "The Yellow Rose of Texas." Danny stood before them with his arms raised and his face alight while flashbulbs went off all around him. Then, when the adulation had gone on for a respectable length of time, he lowered his arms and bowed his head. Suddenly the ballroom fell silent as twelve hundred people also bowed their heads for Reverend Danny Mackay's invocation.

When they were all seated, eyes eagerly upon him, Danny treated them all to his roguish grin and began a slow, drawling chat. "Praise the Lord," he said softly, trying to meet the gaze of as many people in the room as possible. They sat at large round tables and wore evening gowns and tuxedos. Champagne glasses glittered, china plates and silverware waited in readiness for the feast. The first thing Danny did was to thank the orchestra for giving him such a grand entrance. "It was my mother's favorite song, God rest her. She's in Heaven with the Father now, but I know she heard every note of that music. Y'know, folks, I'm stone-deaf when it comes to music. Like Ulysses S. Grant, I only know but two songs—one of them is 'The Yellow Rose of Texas,' and the other one isn't."

Laughter rumbled through the crowd.

His voice rang out over their heads. Even though Danny spoke quietly into the microphone, in a casual, conversational tone, his words carried as if he were shouting.

They laughed. They roared. They loved him.

From where she sat, at a table occupied by various political and social hotshots, Beverly watched and listened to Danny with a fixed expression. She sat so still, so erect and rigid, and appeared to be so cool and controlled in her simple but stunning evening gown, that no one would have guessed the turmoil that was going on inside her. She could barely breathe, her pulse was racing so fast.

That night came rushing back. That awful, awful night . . .

"I've been blessed indeed," Danny was saying up on the dais. "The good Lord knows I don't deserve such good fortune. I have sinned. I am still a sinner! But, with God's grace and compassion, I shall continue my fight against the Devil!"

Beverly looked at the faces around her. They were adoring him; they were worshiping him. She began to tremble. The diamonds at her throat shimmered.

"God is on our side!" Danny shouted. "Didn't I prove that only last year when I walked into the lion's den and saved one of the Lord's servants from certain execution? Wasn't Brother Fred Banks about to be martyred for trying to bring the Word into a heathen country? Amen!" Danny cried, and the audience burst into applause.

Beverly closed her eyes. Fred Banks. Carefully and happily tucked away on a ranch deep inside Mexico, doing what he'd always wanted to do, lording it over his own thousand acres and army of peons. Richer than he had ever dreamed, because of a small ad he had placed in a magazine. But about to become a lot richer.

"But here I stand," Danny said, "talking about myself

397

when I should be paying homage to the little lady who is doing honor to me tonight! A fine woman without whom I would not be where I am tonight. Miss Beverly Highland!"

The spotlight swung away from Danny and suddenly washed over Beverly. She didn't rise. She merely smiled graciously at the applauding audience.

While Danny brought the spotlight back to himself so that he could recite a long string of thanks and gratitude to Miss Highland, Beverly thought about Fred Banks.

When the news story had broken last year about Danny Mackay risking life and limb going to an Arab kingdom to negotiate for the release of a certain missionary, Beverly had been suspicious. That didn't sound like Danny. Altruism and sacrifice were not words in his vocabulary. So she had put Jonas Buchanan to work on it, and Jonas had found Banks happily secreted away on an isolated ranch in Mexico. Poor old Fred, having soon tired of his reclusive life and hungry for the company of an American, had invited the lost "tourist" into his home and that night had gotten drunk, telling Jonas everything.

The trouble was, Fred had confessed, that he had liked the media attention so much that it had spoiled him. Life on the ranch was too quiet; he hungered for that spotlight excitement once again. And so Jonas promised it to him.

Someone was installed in Fred's house to watch him and make sure he didn't try to work an even bigger deal with Danny, and at the right moment Beverly was going to arrange for Fred Banks to sell his incredible story to the press.

She looked at Danny. His speech was winding down. She turned in her chair slightly and caught the eye of a woman seated at a table near the back of the room. She was one of eight women at a round table, and all eight of them were dressed in scarlet-and-white cowgirl outfits, with ten-gallon hats on their heads that had bands reading, "Return to Camelot." These were Danny Girls, although most of them were no longer girls.

The Danny Girls had been Danny's own idea. It was just one more reminder of his connection with the late Kennedys:

he had remembered the Kennedy Girls back in the '60 campaign and had decided to establish his own team of such enthusiastic cheerleaders. The Girls were seen everywhere, handing out pamphlets and bumper stickers, going from door to door, convincing folks with their peaches-and-cream smiles to vote for Danny Mackay.

The Danny Girls who sat at the table near the exit of the ballroom, however, had not been recruited by Danny's staff. These had been handpicked by Beverly.

Beverly caught the eye of one of them now and gave her a discreet nod of the head. The woman nodded back, murmured something to her companions, then got up from the table.

The timing was perfect. She reached the dais just as Danny was about to step down.

She was a pretty thing, and shapely, too, in her tight red cowboy pants. The fringe on her red satin blouse swayed below large breasts, and her pearly buttons were undone enough to expose cleavage. She got Danny's attention at once.

"I wish to present a gift to you, Reverend," she said, standing next to him. "From Miss Highland."

"Well, now," he said. "Well, now! Miss Highland? Why don't you come up here and join me?"

Beverly hesitated. The spotlight was on her again and everyone was clapping. She felt Maggie at her side, watching her with concern. Beverly drew in a deep, steadying breath, made a small reassuring gesture to her friend, then rose and went to the dais.

His nearness made her feel faint. She was surrounded by over a thousand people, there were hot lights on her, and cigar smoke filled the air. She had to stay in control. It would take but a minute, and then she could get away.

The Danny Girl handed him a gold box, and when he opened it, he said, "Well, I'll be! If that isn't a handsome thing!"

"Allow me," the Girl said. She lifted the tiny object off its satin cushion, positioned herself right in front of Danny, and took his tie in her hands. Everyone watched for a silent moment, and then, when she stepped away, they all saw the platinum pin she had fastened to his tie.

Danny looked down at it and beamed. "Why," he said into the microphone. "It's a butterfly. And a right pretty one at that!"

Then he turned to Beverly. Their eyes met for the first time in thirty-five years, and Danny thought, She's even better-looking in real life than in her pictures. "I just happen to have a gift for you, too, Miss Highland, that I was going to present to you after dinner. But since you're up here, why, I might as well give it to you now."

He held out his hand and Bonner placed a leather box in it. Danny spoke a few words about what a great moment this was, meeting her at last, and that he hoped this was the start of a wonderful friendship, praise the Lord, and then he handed her the box.

For an instant, their fingertips touched.

Beverly felt light-headed. She teetered briefly, then she fought for control and was steady again. With shaking hands she opened the leather case. She stared down at its contents.

Lying on a velvet bed was a gold necklace. Beverly picked it up so that it glittered on the end of its chain. It swung slowly back and forth in the bright lights.

She saw that it was a religious medal. On one side it bore a cross; on the other, the image of Danny Mackay.

May

40

IT LOOKED LIKE ANY MOTEL ROOM: cheap madras bedspread on the king-size bed, orange drapes, orange shag carpet, fake mahogany end tables and dresser. Stiff white towels in the antiseptic bathroom; a DO NOT DISTURB/PLEASE CLEAN THE ROOM sign hanging on the inside doorknob. It could have been a room in any motel on any highway from L.A to New York. And the sounds of traffic on the other side of the closed window could have come from any street.

When she entered, she flicked on the light, hung DO NOT DISTURB on the outside knob and closed the door. Then she kicked off her shoes and tossed her overnight case on the bed. She felt as if she'd driven thousands of miles. A good hot bath would feel good. She wondered if the TV worked.

While she was running the water she thought she heard keys in the door. Turning off the tap, she came into the room just as the door flew open. She cried out.

"So!" he said, slamming the door shut behind himself. "You didn't think I would find you, did you?"

Her hand went to her mouth.

He took a step toward her and she retreated.

"I can see now that you've got to be taught a lesson," he growled. "Take off your clothes."

She started to shake. "H-how did you find me?"

"I said, 'Strip.' Now!"

"Can't we talk?"

He raised an arm to strike her. She fell back a step, her fingers fumbling with the buttons of her blouse.

An evil smile crept across his face. "Now you've got the idea. Do it slow and nice. Put on a show for me."

She was shaking so badly she could hardly control her hands. The blouse came away and floated to the floor. Then her skirt. She hesitated at the band of her panty hose.

"Everything," he barked. "I want to see you naked."

"Why are you doing this to me?"

"You know why. This is the last time you're going to run away from me." He reached into the pocket of his jacket and withdrew a handful of silk. They were four scarves, bright red and somehow menacing. "No woman makes a fool of me twice. Now take off the rest."

With her wide frightened eyes fixed on the scarves, she pulled the panty hose down, and then, hesitantly, her eyes on his hands as they twisted the delicate silk into ropes, she removed her bra and panties.

When she tried to cover her nakedness with her arms, he got hold of her hands and dragged her over to the bed. Flinging her down onto her back, he proceeded to tie each of her wrists and then her ankles to the head and foot of the bed.

"What are you going to do?" she cried, struggling against the silken bonds.

"Teach you a lesson you'll never forget."

She heard the sound of his zipper. Then the bed dipped and he was suddenly between her legs. "Wait—" she said breathlessly. But he was inside her at once, with one painful, startling thrust.

She screwed her eyes shut tight. Her hands curled into fists beneath his cruel assault. She clenched her teeth together to keep from crying out.

She thought it would last forever, the unrelenting attack. He seemed to be slamming against her, punishing her. He didn't talk. She heard his heavy breathing, the intermittent gasps. She felt herself slowly sink into a spinning whirlpool; she felt herself being drawn to the focus of the attack, to the weapon that was violating her. She could see it in her mind; she concentrated on it. The whirlpool spun faster and faster until nothing existed at all except the fire deep down in her pelvis, the burning hunger in her legs.

Finally, unable to hold it back any longer, she let out a long high-pitched cry. Her body arched, shook, and then fell still.

Very gently he withdrew, still hard, and retreated into the bathroom. He ran cold water in the sink and coaxed his erection down. He hadn't ejaculated; he never did with her. It saved him for the next member.

When he came out a few minutes later, she was stretching and smiling up at him. He untied the scarves without saying a word, and started for the door. "Wait," she said, running after him. "I have something for you."

This time it was a small gold package. He didn't open it now; he would save that for later. But he knew it would be something very expensive. She was one of Butterfly's more generous members.

41

LINDA WAS HURRYING DOWN THE HALL SO fast, and not watching where she was going, that when she collided with José Mendoza, the orthopedic surgeon, she nearly flew off her feet.

But he caught her and said, "Whoa, my friend! Where is the emergency?"

She bent to pick up the files she had dropped. "I'm sorry, José! It's just that I'm late for an appointment in Beverly Hills."

He helped her retrieve the scattered papers and said as he handed them to her, "I have never known anyone to be always in such a hurry as you, Linda. I think it is not good for you, such a pace."

She laughed breathlessly and made sure the files were all in order. Then she tossed her hair back off her face and smiled at José. "You're one to talk! I've seen medical students run down the hall after you while you're lecturing them."

"We all have our unseen phantoms, my friend. Maybe we should run from ours together. Do you have time for a drink?"

"Not tonight, I'm afraid." She looked at her watch. "I'm already late."

"And what is in Beverly Hills?"

Her smile grew wistful. What was in Beverly Hills? Perhaps, she thought, peace of mind at last.

"I'm sorry, José," she said, starting to hurry away. "But I really must run."

"Hey," he called after her. "I hear you quit that television show."

"Yes," she said over her shoulder. "Do you want the job?"

He laughed. "Not on your life, my friend!" And then she was gone.

Linda sped down Wilshire Boulevard, trying to make her Ferrari fly. Once the decision had been made to return to Butterfly and give it another chance, Linda didn't want to waste a single precious minute. She was now a very determined woman.

The disastrous evening in her bedroom with Barry Greene had so upset her that she had visited Dr. Raymond several times in the past three weeks.

"It was too soon," the psychiatrist had said. "You weren't ready for him."

"I thought I wasn't going anywhere at Butterfly. I was getting discouraged, and anxious."

"You haven't given Butterfly a chance, Linda. You never let the companion go far enough. You should avail yourself of the excellent opportunity Butterfly has to offer you."

"I can't seem to help myself, Virginia. As soon as he starts to venture into that area, I freeze up. I just can't let him see me."

"But you have to, Linda. Think of him as a sex therapist."

Virginia was right, and Linda knew it. That was why she had joined Butterfly in the first place. Linda decided she had to go back, be with her masked companion again, and help him to help her.

An attendant met her at the back of Fanelli and escorted her up in the elevator. The room she was admitted into was a familiar one—the canopied bed on the dais, the drapes and bedding all the color of peaches, the champagne carpet. Refreshments had been set out: chilled wine, liver paté and toast points, fresh fruit. But Linda wasn't interested in food. After quickly running a comb through her hair, she tied the mask in place and turned at the sound of the other door opening.

He wore a tuxedo this time. It made him look tall and elegant. Even the mask seemed right, somehow.

They danced for a while, slow and nice, and drank some wine. And then he began to make love to her.

As they lay on the bed together, Linda naked except for her half slip, he moved his hand tentatively down to her waist and held it there, a question in his eyes. Linda held her breath. She wanted to stop him; she had to hold herself back. She let him continue his exploration, beneath the slip, up along her thigh. Then she said, "Wait."

He waited. He lay on his side, one arm under her shoulders, the other over her thighs. His masked eyes watched her.

"I . . ." she began. "I have a problem."

He kissed her and murmured, "Relax. Please . . ."

She couldn't. Her body was rigid as she felt his hand move beneath her slip, move into a place where she had never before allowed a man to touch her, except for her two former husbands. As his fingers explored she closed her eyes. Her heart was pounding. She wanted to stop him, but she was determined to go through with it.

"Let me look," he whispered.

She nodded and felt the silky slip ride up and gather around her waist. The cool air felt strange on her pelvis. He parted her legs slightly. Then he kissed her again, and held his face inches from hers while he stroked her. First, her upper thighs, her pelvis, and abdomen, to relax her, to massage the stiffness out of her body. After a few minutes Linda began to feel sexual desire, she wanted him to enter her. But he kept at his exploration, letting her excitement mount. And then his hand went farther until she felt—nothing.

"I can't feel that," she said, her excitement dissolving, her sexual desire ebbing. *This is the way it always goes. This is when the lovemaking ends.* "It's scar tissue. I have no feeling there."

When he didn't react, when he didn't pull away as the others always did, she opened her eyes and looked at him. There was tenderness in his gaze. "Can you feel that?" he asked.

"No . . ."

"Tell me what happened."

"I was two years old," she said in a faraway voice. "We were in the kitchen, my mother and I. She was ironing and I was sitting in my high chair, near the stove. She said that it happened so quickly she couldn't possibly have stopped me. She said one minute I was sitting there playing with my blocks, and then next I was screaming." Linda looked away. "Apparently I had reached up and pulled a pan of boiling water down onto myself. My lap was scalded. Mother rushed me to the hospital, where they told her I had third-degree burns from the waist down. I had to have skin grafts, a series of them, over a period of years."

"Is that why you never let me touch you there?"

"I was afraid you'd be . . . repulsed."

His look turned to one of puzzlement. "Why would you think that?"

"That's how men react to my scars."

"I didn't."

"No, you didn't."

"If you hadn't told me about the scars, I wouldn't have noticed them. Whoever worked on you did a good job."

She brought her head back to face him again. "But other men—"

"You look almost normal down there. Your only problem is the loss of sensation. But I think—" He moved his hand again. "How about here?"

"No."

"And this?"

She hesitated. Then she felt his finger enter her. "Yes, I can feel that."

He bent his head and kissed her. Then he said, "Look at me."

She met his gaze. His eyes were dark and mesmerizing. They held her fast while his hand moved again, this time in a different rhythm.

And then there was something—pressure. . . .

She rolled her head away.

"Look at me," he said again, softly.

She felt herself grow tense. What was he doing? *It isn't going to work!*

But his caress was compelling. Lost in the depths of his black eyes, Linda felt her tension start to melt. He began to probe deeper, and when he touched a certain spot, she caught her breath.

"There," he whispered. "It's there. . . ."

"What—"

"Relax. Don't fight me. Let me do the work."

And then she felt a sensation she had never felt before. Her eyes widened; she stared up at him. "What are you—"

"Don't talk," he murmured.

He stopped moving. They lay on the bed, as still as a painting. Even his hand had stopped, and yet Linda was beginning to feel something down there. He was pressing on a certain spot, nothing more, just pressing upon a point she hadn't known she had, deep inside herself. And as he pressed, holding her gaze with his eyes, she started to feel a strange warmth spread through her, as if it were radiating out from that center point. She suddenly wanted to move, to ride with him, but he kept her still.

And then it happened. All of a sudden she cried out and arched her back in a wave of overwhelming pleasure.

42

Beverly Hills: 1983

SOMETHING STRANGE was going on at Fanelli.

Bob Manning, the manager of the store, wasn't sure exactly what it was or when his suspicions had been first aroused—it was only a feeling he had, a sense that something wasn't quite right. He wondered if it wasn't his imagination that sometimes the male models fell silent when he came into the dressing room, or that he sometimes thought he caught secretive looks passing among them. Whatever it was, imagined or real, he decided on a particular rainy morning in early February, when L.A. was held in a gray and wet thrall and the store was more crowded than usual, to leave his office and take a casual stroll among the customers.

For a man who was just about to turn seventy, and who had spent sixteen years of his life in a hospital, Bob Manning was remarkably fit. Of course, he kept himself that way, partly because it was expected of him, being a man who had to deal with Beverly Hills' upper crust on a daily basis, but mostly because he wanted to make up for those lost years. He dressed extremely well in silk blazers and wool slacks, with a fresh rose in his lapel every morning, and whenever he walked where he could be seen he concentrated on minimizing his limp, using his silver-tipped cane with dignity.

Fanelli's regular customers knew him well. Many addressed him on a first-name basis and frequently went directly to him with their requests. He was often called upon for an opinion—"Would you say this scarf goes with this overcoat, or should I take the maroon one?"—or for a special order when a customer thought that going directly to the manager of the store would speed things up.

As he walked through the store on this rainy morning, nodding and smiling to the customers, passing gracefully through the wet raincoats and umbrellas poking this way and that, Bob kept his eye out for anything unusual.

His vigilance was only for his own sake and because he cared about the store he had managed for eleven years. Bob Manning didn't give a damn about Royal Farms, the new owner of Fanelli—ever since Reverend Danny Mackay had bought the company a few years back, no one from Houston had come to inspect the store. Danny Mackay and his ministry now owned so many enterprises, from high-rise office buildings to an airline to a supermarket chain, that the famous Reverend couldn't be bothered with one small men's clothing store. When Danny Mackay had taken over Royal Farms and therefore Fanelli, nothing had changed. Existing management and staff had been kept on and the store was left to continue to operate as before. All Bob Manning had to do was see to it that regular statements were sent to the Good News headquarters in Houston, where someone, he had no doubt, made sure Fanelli was bringing in a regular profit.

This was not to say, however, that because Beverly Highland had sold the store she was no longer interested in it. She had asked Bob Manning to report to her if Danny or anyone from Good News Ministries ever came by to inspect. It was implied that he do this in secret, and of course Bob willingly complied. There was nothing he would not do for Beverly; he was ferociously loyal to her. She had rescued him when he had reached the very rock bottom of his life. She had looked at the human wreck he had become and she had seen a man. She had counted him as having worth; she had given him a job and a reason to live. Now he worshiped her.

He paused near a glass counter displaying velvet smoking jackets and surveyed the busy store with a sharp eye. If there was anything even slightly amiss, Bob Manning would catch it.

He frowned. Was it his imagination or did he just see Michael, one of Fanelli's best models, furtively accept something from Mrs. Carpenter, one of the store's wealthier patrons, and slip it into the pocket of the coat he was modeling?

But there was more to it than that, Bob realized as he stared at them. The exchange had been brief—she had brushed past Michael, pressed something into his palm, and hurried on. But in that fleeting instant when their hands had touched, there had also been an exchanged look. Michael and Mrs. Carpenter had glanced at each other for a moment, and their look had been—conspiratorial.

Worse, Bob realized to his shock. The look had been one of *intimacy*.

He watched Mrs. Carpenter leave the store and step into the Rolls waiting at the curb. Then he went over to Michael and murmured, "I want to see you in my office in five minutes."

The young man came in wearing the polo shirt, Bermuda shorts, and knee socks that he was modeling next. He closed the door quietly behind himself and came to stand before Bob Manning's desk.

"What did Mrs. Carpenter give to you?" Bob asked.

"Sir?"

"I saw Mrs. Carpenter give you something a few minutes ago. What was it?"

Michael shifted his weight and thrust his hands into his pockets. "It was, uh, nothing, Mr. Manning."

"It was *something*, I saw it. Now, what was it?"

Michael nervously cleared his throat. "It was, uh, her address."

Bob's eyebrows arched. "Her address?"

"Yes, sir."

"Why did she give you her address?"

The young man looked down at his running shoes.

"Come, come," said Bob. "Why did Mrs. Carpenter give you her address?"

"Because I'm going to her house tonight."

Bob's eyebrows shot higher. "What do you mean?"

"She asked me to go visit her—"

"*Visit* her?"

Michael avoided Bob's eye and nodded.

"Why?"

"Well"—he cleared his throat again—"I imagine she wants company."

"Has she invited you to a party?"

"Well, no."

"Has she invited anyone else?"

A pause, and then: "No, just me."

"What for?"

Michael laughed a little and finally looked at Bob. "Well, sir. *You* know."

"No, I don't know. Why are you going to Mrs. Carpenter's house? Are you a friend of hers?"

"Not exactly."

"What does that mean?"

"Well, I mean, I guess we're going to be friends. For tonight, at least."

Bob Manning stared at his model for a long moment. And then, when understanding began to dawn, he whispered, "You mean, for *sex*?"

Michael nodded again and shifted self-consciously.

"But, good God, boy," Bob said in disbelief, "Mrs. Carpenter must be three times your age! Don't you find that a bit unconventional?"

"Well," Michael said defensively, "it's not like we're going to get married or anything. I mean, it's purely physical. She doesn't pretend she's in love with me."

Bob continued to stare at the young man in the sports outfit. Michael was nineteen years old, tanned even in winter, and well built. He was an aspiring actor waiting to be discovered. "I don't understand," Bob said. "You can have your pick of any girls. Mrs. Carpenter is, well, she doesn't strike me as being your type."

"Oh, it's not for me, Mr. Manning. It's purely for her. She's paying me to visit her."

Bob fell back in his chair, his mouth open. "She's *paying* you?"

Michael gave a nervous toss of the head. "Well, uh, yes—"

"Good God, boy! Do you know what that makes you?"

"I don't see anything wrong with—"

Bob slammed his hand on the desk. "You work for Fanelli, the finest men's store in this city! You are a representative of this company! By extension, you represent the woman who

413

created this company, Miss Beverly Highland! Don't you know that by prostituting yourself to its customers you sully *her* name!" Bob shot to his feet and Michael suddenly turned pale. "How dare you bring your filthy practices into this store!"

"Hey, wait a min—"

"You're fired, boy. And I'm just sorry that's all I can do to you!"

"But, Mr. Manning! That's not fair! I'm not the only one who's doing it!"

Bob fell silent, his body trembling. "What do you mean . . . you're not the only one?"

"Well," Michael coughed. "There's a few of us. Ron Sheffield is the one who started it." He spoke quickly, desperate to save himself. "You know Misty Carlisle, the actress? She asked him to come to her house one day to model some clothes privately. They ended up in bed and she gave him a hundred-dollar bill. That was about a year ago, and since then—"

Bob sat back down in his chair, stunned. "Who are they? Give me their names."

Michael ended up naming three co-workers in the hope of saving his own neck. It didn't work. The four of them were fired on the spot and let go without severance pay.

Sex.
It was on her mind.
Again.
Still.

As Ann Hastings steered her BMW through the enormous wrought-iron gates that guarded Beverly Highland's new palatial estate, she tried not to think about the fiasco that last night had been. But she couldn't help it. Roger had shown such promise in the bar where they met. He had talked intelligently, seemed like a warm human being, and gave off interesting sexual signals. But then she had gone home with him and he had turned out to be an egotistical, ill-mannered, boorish dud. He had also been thirty-six—nine years younger than herself. With each passing year Ann got older while the guys seemed to get younger.

It was tough being forty-five in a youth-oriented society. Tougher still to be forty-five and fat. Not much of a threat to the competition, she decided.

Well, she wasn't really fat. Not anymore. Ann had started the weight battle ten years ago when she'd hit thirty-five. She'd sweated and starved and bumped and grinded the extra thirty pounds off her frame and had managed through grudging discipline to keep them off. Now she wore the same chic little tennis outfits that Beverly and Carmen wore and modestly picked her way through salads at lunch and dinner. She no longer cringed when she glimpsed herself in the mirror, and scales didn't frighten her. Still, she felt fat *inside*. And that was a weight problem no amount of dieting could get rid of.

She envied Maggie Kern who ate what she wanted, wore beautifully tailored caftans to disguise her plumpness, and enjoyed a good, healthy relationship of sex and affection with Pete Forman, the stockbroker she had once worked for. But Maggie was one of those lucky rare exceptions. For Ann Hastings and the millions of others like her on the prowl for a little fun, a little male attention, and some good sex, the rules of the game revolved around thinness and youth.

Ever since the night back in 1969, when Ann had finally, after two more disappointing romps on his floor, lost her virginity to that fake hippie Steve, she had discovered that she really liked sex. But the problem was getting it.

When her job as the head of quality control for the Royal Burger chain had taken her on frequent trips around the country, Ann had had little trouble in finding accommodating men. But when the job had gotten too big and she became more and more tied to her office while assistants went out in the field in her place, and as she got older and the unmarried men got younger, her prospects began to pale, so that she was now finding herself more frequently in situations like last night, picking up some jerk at a bar and later worrying about herpes and other horrors.

As she parked her car by the garages and went around to the back of the enormous Italian-villa-style house Beverly had recently bought, where everyone was gathered at the tennis court, Ann wondered not for the first time about her enigmatic employer. As far as Ann knew, Beverly had never been with a man in her life. How could she stand it?

Not all women are alley cats, my dear, Ann chided herself as she waved to her friends seated at an umbrella-shaded table. There are those who can do quite nicely without it.

Look at Beverly and Carmen, those two cool cucumbers in stylish tennis dresses. Ann decided that the total of their combined sexual experience with men probably amounted to no more than fifteen minutes.

"Yoo-hoo," she called, putting down her tennis racket and joining the two women at the table. "Sorry I'm late. There was a tie-up on the Ventura." Ann was glad to see that lunch had just been served. Her smile dropped, however, when she saw the salad without dressing, the dry Melba rounds, the sugarless iced tea with lemon. As she sat down at a place setting Ann briefly wondered if sex was worth starvation. Deciding that it was, she picked up a fork and dug in.

"How did it go last night?" Carmen asked.

"You don't want to know."

"Hello, Aunt Ann!"

Ann looked up to see Carmen's olive-skinned daughter running toward her, tennis racket swinging. Rosa, at nineteen, was a knockout. She certainly had no trouble getting her share of men.

"Hello, Rosa, dear. How's the new semester going?"

Rosa poured herself a glass of lemonade from the crystal pitcher and drank it all down. "It's super, Aunt Ann. I have the most fantastic professor for economics!"

"Who won?" Carmen said, looking around for Joe Jr., Maggie's seventeen-year-old son.

"I did. Joe's gone into the clubhouse to play video games with Arthur. Aunt Ann, you'll play me, won't you?"

Ann nodded and put down her fork. This salad would not be missed.

"Go easy, Rosa," Carmen called after them. "Your aunt isn't a spring chicken anymore!"

Ann and Rosa laughed as they ran down to the tennis court.

Beverly watched them go, a faint smile on her lips. Then she looked at Carmen and said quietly, "Rosa is certainly something to be proud of."

The two friends regarded each other for a long moment, listening to the distant drone of lawn mowers over Beverly's vast estate, the sounds of garden clippers trimming hedges, and finally the rhythmic thock of the tennis ball on the court down below. They were both thinking that, come November, it would be twenty years since Beverly found Carmen in Dallas.

"Hi, there!" came a familiar voice.

The two turned to see Maggie coming down the garden path, her bright lemon-yellow caftan shimmering in the February sunshine. Maggie now tamed her frizzy red hair into a knot on top of her head, a style that Pete Forman said he liked. When she stepped into the shade of the umbrella and saw the salad plates on the table, she motioned to a white-jacketed servant who was standing by the beverage cart. "Bring me a sandwich, please," she said. "Any kind, so long as it has lots of mayo. And a glass of white wine."

Maggie cleared away a place setting, set her briefcase down and took a seat. "What a beautiful day!" she said, looking out over Beverly's newly acquired estate. The grounds seemed to go on forever; they gave the impression of isolation.

"I take it Pete's in town," Carmen said with a smile.

Maggie winked and opened her briefcase. "From the clipping service," she said, handing a thick envelope to Beverly.

Using a silver letter opener, Beverly slit the envelope and carefully withdrew the contents. Danny Mackay was so frequently in the news nowadays that she had to set aside a full hour each day to keep current.

"His wife had her baby on Sunday," Maggie said. "It's another boy."

Beverly picked up one of the clippings and studied it. "Good News Ministries has announced that the Houston Cathedral has brought in six million dollars in its first year of operation, and that Danny's TV audience has now reached two million."

"Beverly," Carmen said after some thought, "isn't it time

417

now? He's so popular. So wealthy and powerful. We could move in on him now."

But Beverly said, "No. He hasn't gone high enough. He's known in America; I want his destruction to be witnessed by the *world.*"

Maggie pulled more papers out of her briefcase. "Here's the speech you'll be giving before the Performing Arts Council next week, Bev. And this is your itinerary for next week's tour of the East Coast. I had to extend your stay in Washington by two more days—" Maggie spread the items out on the table. "The lobbyists for two environmental groups are anxious to meet with you, and Senator Davidson insisted on a private conference with you regarding the new abortion bill he's going to try to put through. Oh, and Stanford University is asking you to come and talk again."

A shout from the tennis court caused Beverly to turn and watch Ann and Rosa exchange friendly rivalry. Rosa was tall and beautiful, a dusky young woman who could be mistaken for a princess out of the Arabian Nights. It made Beverly think of her last conversation with Jonas Buchanan. He was just getting ready to depart for Saudi Arabia.

After exhaustive digging, Jonas had picked up Christine Singleton's trail again and learned that, back in 1971, she had gone to Saudi Arabia with a man named Eric Sullivan.

"Your sister went by the name of Rutherford," Jonas had informed Beverly at their last meeting. "That was the name of the guy she married and then divorced. The man she traveled to Arabia with was a consultant for Aramco. Apparently she went along as his secretary. But there's something strange about the arrangement. I couldn't get any information on Sullivan. No one would talk to me about him. It makes me wonder if the consultant business was a cover-up for something else."

"Such as what?" Beverly had asked, alarmed.

"I don't know. It happened twelve years ago."

Since there was nothing further Jonas could find here in the United States—there seemed to be no records of Christine's return to this country—Beverly decided to send him to the Middle East to continue the search. She prayed he would be lucky.

Maggie, tucking into her roast beef sandwich, said, "By the way. Do you want to hear something funny? I had lunch with Bob Manning the other day, and he told me the most amazing thing! It seems that four of Fanelli's models have been going to bed with customers, and getting paid for it!"

Carmen and Beverly looked at her.

"What do you mean?" Beverly said.

Maggie told them what Bob had told her, about Michael and Ron Sheffield and two others visiting the homes of wealthy Beverly Hills women, and when she ended with "Isn't that a laugh?" she was met only with grave expressions.

"Selling one's body is never a matter of humor," Carmen said quietly.

"No," Maggie said, suddenly remembering. "It's not. I'm sorry."

Of their intimate circle, Maggie was the only one who knew about Beverly's and Carmen's past. They had confided in her because she was, in their eyes, a sister: she had been abused by Danny Mackay, as they had. The others—Ann Hastings and Roy Madison—knew nothing of the secret past of their two friends.

"All I meant was," Maggie said, "that the shoe is now on the other foot. I mean, *women* paying for sex. It's a phenomenon of our new liberation, ever since the Pill gave us sexual freedom. Who would have thought, twenty or thirty years ago, that there would be a skin magazine for women, like *Playgirl*, or strip joints for women, like Chippendale's? It just goes to prove what we've been screaming about all along, that women want sex just as much as men want it."

The ball went *thwack* and laughter drifted up from the tennis court. The three women sitting under the striped umbrella enjoying a relaxing lunch watched the two down on the court, playfully chiding each other. A breeze came up, sending the palm trees swaying, rippling the blue-green surface of the Italianate pool. The fragrance of gardenias in early bloom briefly touched the three friends and then went on its itinerant way.

Beverly stared off into the distance. She was thinking of the handsome young models at Fanelli, and the women who had turned to them for . . .

For what? she asked herself. What were those women paying for?

"Listen, kid," Hazel's voice came echoing down through the years. "You've got to do more than just lie there. These guys come here with their hard-earned money looking for a little escape. They come here to buy a fantasy, and you've got to give it to them."

"Fantasy," Beverly murmured.

Carmen looked at her. "What did you say, Beverly?"

"I said 'fantasy.' That's what those women are buying."

"What women?" said Maggie. "You mean the customers at Fanelli? Bev, they're buying sex."

"Perhaps," Beverly said slowly, thinking. "But there's more to it than that. After all, you yourself just said that this was a different age, that the Pill has liberated women from the old-fashioned puritanism and double standard of sex. It's more readily available these days. So why pay for it?"

Maggie shrugged. "To be guaranteed of a good time, I would guess. If the guy wants to get paid, he'd better deliver."

Beverly shook her head. "I think there's more to it than that. I think those women are looking for a dream, they're trying to buy a few minutes of happiness, companionship, maybe even a little flattery."

She fell silent again. Why *would* a woman pay for male companionship? To receive a little of the attention her husband or boyfriend didn't give her? To stave off unbearable loneliness? To seek some meaning in her life? To believe, if only for an hour, that she was beautiful and desirable? Or quite simply to have a good time?

All of which reasons, Beverly decided, were valid. We all want to be loved and told we're beautiful. We all, at one time or another, look for meaning in our lives or try to discover what our dreams are. We all have fears and the need for arms to hold us and a warm body to protect us against the night.

"What did Bob do?" she asked suddenly.

"Do?" said Maggie. "He fired the models. Why?"

"Carmen, Bob Manning says that in the five years Danny Mackay has owned Royal Farms he hasn't bothered to inspect the company's subsidiary holdings. Is that true?"

"As far as I know. He's too busy buying airline companies and baseball stadiums to bother with one little store a thousand miles away."

"And the offices above Fanelli. Are the same tenants still there? The mail order company, the interior decorator?"

"Everybody wants a Beverly Hills address, you know that. There are people renting cubbyholes above Fanelli. Why?"

Beverly looked down at the tennis court again, at the sprightly Ann, who she knew starved to look good in a tennis outfit, and she was remembering when she first met Ann twenty-three years ago, how unhappy Ann had been at having to attend a Christmas party alone, humiliated. And how Beverly had arranged for Roy Madison to escort her, and therefore, by filling Ann with self-confidence and pride, the incident had turned her life around.

"Fantasy," Beverly said again, quietly, deep in thought. It had been only a fantasy, a scene acted out, but look at what it had done for Ann.

Carmen said, "What are you thinking, *amiga?*"

Beverly looked at her friends. "I want Bob to rehire those models."

"What?"

"And then I want the tenants above the store removed. Maggie, you find new locations for them. Help them make the move."

"But why?"

"I have a better use for the rooms above Fanelli."

Beverly asked her chauffeur to pull up to the curb and park. She waited in the air-conditioned comfort of her Rolls-Royce and watched the modest group of people through the smoky glass of her window. There were maybe twelve, fifteen people attending the private funeral. Most of them were crying. Beverly, too, felt like crying.

When the graveside service was over and everyone began to head back to the limousines, Beverly got out of her car and approached a small woman in black, supported between two people.

"Mrs. Wiseman?" Beverly said.

421

The gray-haired woman looked at her with desolate eyes.

"I knew your husband," Beverly said softly. "He did a favor for me many years ago. I promised that I would never forget him. He was a great man."

"Yes—"

"Please, take this."

Mrs. Wiseman blinked at the envelope held out in the gloved hand. One of the two supporting her, a man in his forties, took the envelope and said, "I'm sorry. My mother isn't well."

"I understand. I didn't mean to intrude upon your private grief. I just wanted to give you this, in memory of your husband."

They watched her go, a tall blond woman in an ankle-length mink coat stepping into a white Rolls-Royce. In the backseat of their rented limo, Dr. Walter Wiseman opened the envelope and withdrew the contents. He said, "My God," and turned abruptly just in time to see the white Rolls disappear around the bend.

In his later years, Dr. Seymour Wiseman, plastic surgeon, had espoused the cause of helping Jews escape from Russia. The strange woman, whose name the Wisemans would never know, had established a million-dollar foundation in his name for the saving of Soviet Jewry.

Ann Hastings couldn't believe her ears. She stared at her old friend Roy Madison in such disbelief that he had to laugh. "You're not serious!" she cried.

"Check it out for yourself, if you don't believe me."

They were having lunch in a grimy little diner at Venice Beach, a place not yet "discovered" and therefore safe for Roy. Because of his fame he didn't dare venture into places where he might be recognized, unless, of course, he was in the mood to be recognized. Now that he was up for an Academy Award for his latest movie, there were few places the ruggedly handsome Roy Madison could go without being molested. Except for this grimy diner on Venice Beach where a curious mix of winos, teenage runaways, and elderly Jews on fixed incomes ate corned beef hash and french fries.

Ever since their "date" twenty-three years ago, when a very young and unemployed Roy Madison had changed his image and taken a very young and unhappy Ann to her cousin's Christmas dance, the two had been close friends. They tried to get together at least once a month for the kind of relaxed, shared-secret conversation they couldn't think of having with anyone else. Ann usually complained about her sex life and the nerds she was finding in bars, and Roy usually complained about his sex life and the nerds he was finding in bars. But today was different, today he had something new and deliciously shocking to tell.

"For real?" she whispered, leaning across the table. "They're actually going to have rooms upstairs and everything? I don't believe it."

"I've known Michael for a couple of years. He isn't gay, we're just friends. Anyway, I was the one who got him the job at Fanelli. He's telling the truth." Roy grinned and popped a greasy french fry into his mouth while Ann sat there just not believing her ears.

"But," she said, "why would Bob Manning do it? Start up a bordello, I mean."

"Well, according to Michael, he and some of the guys had already been doing it on the side, for a bit of extra dough. He said that when Manning found out about it, they all got fired. And then, three days later they were rehired, and told that they were going to continue with their sideline, but under Manning's supervision. I guess old Bob figured that if the customers were willing to pay for it, well then what the hell, let them have their fun."

Roy took a long drink of diet cola, and added, "Manning also said something about controlling the standards of the operation. He said they couldn't just have the guys doing whatever and going wherever. It's going to be conducted under one roof with some kind of supervision. They have to think about herpes and VD and all that."

"I just can't believe it!" Ann said again, her eyes alight with excitement. "I mean, Bob Manning is such a stuffed shirt! And what if Beverly found out about it! My God, Roy, she started Fanelli!"

"Now, that's an interesting point. Michael says he's seen Beverly going upstairs with Bob on three different occasions, and that they were talking mighty privately. It would seem to me that Beverly must already know about it."

Now she really gave him an incredulous look. "Oh come now, Roy! I'm talking about Beverly Highland, our old friend who is so straitlaced and prudish that she hasn't been on a date with a man in the twenty-four years we've known her! She wouldn't condone such a thing!"

"Michael said there were two women with her—a redhead and a Chicana. Sounds like Maggie and Carmen to me."

"This is impossible!" Ann whispered. Then she fell silent, suddenly remembering something. Actually, remembering several things. Various occasions, over the years, when she had come upon Beverly and Maggie and Carmen with their heads together, discussing something secret, and falling silent when they saw Ann. She had always known that she was something of an outsider, that she wasn't really one of them. There was something about those three that bound them together more tightly than Ann could ever be bound to Beverly, even though they had been friends for two dozen years. But, the question was, what was the secret they shared?

Fifteen minutes later, having said good-bye to Roy and now speeding along the Santa Monica Freeway in her BMW, Ann digested and finally came to accept what Roy had told her—that Fanelli was going to run a secret bordello upstairs and that, somehow, Beverly was involved. And once she was used to the idea, another idea came into Ann Hastings's mind. It was so boggling and breathtaking that she excitedly pressed her foot down until the car was going ninety and she got stopped by a cop, making her late getting to Beverly Highland's office.

Bob Manning thought it was a brilliant idea—he thought all of Beverly's ideas were brilliant ideas—and was anxious to get started. But they had to be careful.

"No one," Beverly stressed as she faced Bob and Maggie and Carmen across her desk, "absolutely no one must find out about this. We must be very cautious about whom we hire for the upstairs work, and about the clients we accept. What we are embarking upon is highly illegal and could backfire on us. And, more than anything, we have to be careful that no hint of this change gets back to Danny's headquarters. We can't risk snoopers from Royal Farms."

They had argued over where to establish Beverly's "fantasy factory," as Maggie called it. Carmen wasn't so sure that the floor above Fanelli was such a good idea. But Bob had insisted that that was the only way he could maintain strict control over the models and their customers. It was the safest way, he said, and the simplest. And why would anyone find out? he asked. As far as the accountants at Good News Ministries knew, those rooms were being rented by legitimate enterprises. They would still be receiving their rent, they just wouldn't know about the change of tenants.

"Secrecy is so vital," Beverly said. "I want the women to be protected. I'm sure the models will want to keep the secret safe in order to protect such choice jobs. One leak, and they're all out on the street. And as for the clients, they will naturally want the operation kept a secret. Most of them will be married. And I insist upon careful screening of both the models and the customers. We must set the absolute highest standards for both. I'll entrust that aspect of the operation to Jonas when he gets back from Arabia."

The others nodded and then got down to work.

Carmen was the first to report. She had done some research on various "escort" services that were operating in and around the L.A. area. "The most lucrative and longest-running of them don't consider their escorts as employees. There's no payroll, no Social Security withheld, no insurance, and so forth. The escorts actually work as independent contractors. If we set up our establishment along those lines, and deal strictly in cash, we would save ourselves a lot of paperwork and eliminate much of the risk of discovery."

Beverly agreed and turned to the others for input.

"I think we should restrict the membership," Maggie said. "An idea like this, well, if word got around we could literally be overwhelmed with customers. Women would line up around the block! We'll have to keep it small and discreet, with limitations."

"We can establish a charge for membership," Carmen said. "Like a country club. And new members are brought in by members in good standing."

Beverly turned to Manning. "Bob, I'm putting you in charge of the men. We have to have certain guidelines for them to follow. We don't want our clients coming down with herpes or venereal diseases."

This surprised him. Beverly Highland had always struck him as being such a lady. How could she possibly know so much about the running of a brothel? "I'll have a talk with them," he said. Once again he was amazed at her ability to know exactly what it was people wanted. He knew the secret operation was going to be a success.

"Maggie, you see to the refurbishing of the empty offices over the store. The bedrooms and private dining room must be perfect. Don't skimp on cost. The rooms must be beautiful; the environment must be conducive to every woman's fantasy. Finally, Bob, I want you to counsel the men. These women will be buying precious dreams. I don't want them hurt or disappointed."

"What do I tell the guys?"

"You tell them to give good sex, is what you tell them," came a voice from the doorway.

They all turned to see Ann Hastings standing there with her hands on her hips, a big smile on her face. She came in and closed the door. "You tell the guys to forget about pleasing themselves and just concentrate on giving the clients pleasure. You tell them not to rush, not to slobber, not to use dirty language. You tell them to take their time and to be loving and caring and to act as though the woman he is with is the only woman in the whole world. You warn them about bad breath and beard stubble and rough hands." She turned an apologetic smile to Beverly. "I was eavesdropping, I'm sorry."

"How much did you hear?"

"Don't worry, I didn't hear a thing. I got the story from Roy, who got it from his good friend Michael."

When Maggie cast a worried glance toward Beverly, Ann came around to face them and say hastily, "Don't worry about me. I'm not going to tell anyone! I just want to be in on it."

"In on it!" said Carmen. "Doing what?"

"Just what I've been doing for Royal Burgers all these years. Quality control. Making sure we maintain high standards and that each customer benefits from those standards. After all, sex is a commodity like anything else. It can be dynamite or it can be lousy."

They looked at one another.

"Look," Ann said. "Someone's got to tell those guys what works. Someone has to clue them in on how to really make love to a woman. Otherwise, you'll have inconsistency in your products. Some of them might be good, others could be real turn-offs."

"And I suppose," Carmen said slowly, "that you would personally train them and see to it that they are all up to standard?"

Ann grinned. "It works for hamburgers, doesn't it?"

43

JAMIE HAD TO DRIVE around the block six times before he found a parking space. And then he had to beat out a bitch in a white Lincoln Continental, who darned near creamed his VW with her big shiny fender. Dropping coins into the meter, Jamie paused to look across the street, at the men's store with the butterfly logo over its door.

He knew guys who actually shopped here.

Better, he knew guys who had sugar mammas shop for them here.

They were the lucky ones, the fortunate stiffs who, between acting jobs, had managed to find some rich lady to take care of them. Jamie, he hadn't been that lucky.

Strangely, his weekly swims in Beverly Highland's pool

had panned out to exactly zilch. She had even stopped watching him. What had he done wrong?

"You should have made a move," Gary, his roommate, told him. "She's got her reputation to protect, you know. She's Reverend Danny's number one supporter. She can't very well come on to her pool-boy, can she?"

"Make a move how?" Jamie had asked, really wanting the advice. Man, to just step foot in that house. . . .

"I don't know. *You're* the stud."

But Jamie felt he had too much common sense to go making any overt sexual passes at a woman like Beverly Highland, and, as a result, he'd blown his chance.

Anyway, it looked as if opportunity was knocking again. And in a most unexpected way.

He'd gotten a phone call a few days ago, from the director of this very store. Would he be interested in interviewing for a job as one of their models? The work was easy and pleasant, the pay very good. How did she know of him? he had asked. How did she get his name and number? But all she would reveal was that someone had recommended him.

He ran across the street, dodging traffic, and stopped in front of the window to check himself a last time.

Jamie knew he was one good-looking dude, and he worked hard to maintain the image. Regular workouts, proper diet, lots of sun, and a perfected Jeff Bridges kind of look: wrinkled Hawaiian silk shirt unbuttoned down to the navel, khaki pleated pants with no belt, the waistband button left carelessly, teasingly undone.

He entered a little self-consciously, this store being way out of his league, and sort of browsed his way to the back, where the director had said she would meet him. There he found customers—women dressed to the hilt and reeking of money—sitting in brocaded chairs, drinking tea, and watching men strut their stuff in the best of Ralph Lauren and Hugo Boss. Looking at the models, Jamie decided that he could hold his own against any of them; it was a cinch he'd get the job.

A young woman in a black skirt and white blouse with a butterfly embroidered in gold on the pocket came up to him and asked him to go with her. They stepped into a small elevator and rode up one flight. Upstairs she led him to the first door on the right; as they entered he glanced down the hallway and saw two rows of closed doors. Offices, he figured.

A nicely dressed, average-looking woman rose to greet him. She held out her hand and invited him to sit. When they were alone, she introduced herself as the director, not giving him her name, and got on familiar terms at once by calling him Jamie.

"What do you think of our store?" she asked.

"Classy place."

"Did you see our models? Do you think you would like to do that kind of work?"

"Sure," he said with a shrug. "But who gave you my name? I mean, I'd like to thank him or her."

"Let me tell you a bit about the job."

He listened in all seriousness, nodding with a poker face when she mentioned the too-good-to-be-believed salary, and said when she was through, "Yes . . . Yes, I think I could work here."

She smiled. "I should tell you right off that I will be interviewing several other men for the job. We only have the one opening and I've received several recommendations. I won't be able to give you my decision today."

He nearly shouted, "What!" but managed to keep his head. "Yes, I understand. Of course," he said.

"Now, may I please see how you walk?"

"Walk?"

"It's important how you carry yourself, to show off our clothes to their best advantage."

Walk? He got up and marched woodenly across the room.

"Please try to relax, Jamie. Don't force it."

He gave her an exasperated smile. "I've never thought about my walk before. Now that I'm conscious of it, I can't do it!"

"I understand. I tell you what. Why don't you pretend you've just come into a—oh, a bar, let's say. And you see me sitting at this table. And you want to come over and join me. Just start over there and come toward me."

He went to the door, turned, gave her a long look, then

approached her with his best Don Johnson come-on saunter.

She seemed pleased.

"Would you mind taking off your shirt?"

His eyebrows rose.

"You will be modeling bathing suits."

"Oh yeah." He took off the shirt and flexed a little here and there.

She frowned slightly.

"What's wrong?"

"Ah . . . nothing. Nothing at all. That's okay. You can put your shirt back on now."

That rankled him. No woman had ever asked him to put his shirt *on*.

She rose from the sofa and held out her hand. "I'll call you within a few days."

"That's it? You mean the interview is over? Don't I have to fill out an application or something?"

"I don't think that will be necessary."

What the hell—?

He tried to smile as he shook her hand, but found himself too pissed off. What was it about him that she decided she didn't like? Jamie had been on enough job interviews to know when he hadn't made it.

"Say, listen," he began. "I want you to know that I would really like this job. I mean, I'd give your customers a Class A performance. They'll be buying clothes right and left."

"I'm sure you would, Jamie—"

"But?"

"As I told you, I have a number of other men to interview."

"But I ask you in all honesty," he said, giving her his most winning smile, "what could they possibly have that I don't?"

"Well . . ."

He weighed the situation in a split second. The job paid more than anything he could even dream of earning elsewhere, it was cushy work, and he'd be exposed daily to lonely, horny rich broads. He decided he would take the gamble.

"Listen," he said, stepping closer to her. Jamie figured she was in her early fifties. Just the age to be susceptible to a little soft talk. "I really want this job."

She looked up at him.

"I mean," he said quietly, his smile intimate, "I'd do anything to get it."

"You would?"

God, but his heart was pounding. Well, what was the worst she could do? He figured he already wasn't getting the job, he had nothing to lose.

"What would you do?" she asked, also quietly.

She was falling for it!

"You name it."

"Are you offering me a bribe, Jamie?" she said a little coyly.

"All I can say is, once you hire me you'll be glad you did. I'll outshine all those other pretty boys down there. I'll make your customers very happy."

"And what about me?"

He didn't miss a beat. "I could make you happy, too."

"How?"

He hesitated for only a fraction of a second, then bent his head and kissed her on the lips.

When he drew back, he saw to his relief and boundless joy that she was smiling.

"That was nice," she murmured.

"Can I have the job?"

"You're not done bribing me."

And then he had his arms around her and was smothering her with his mouth.

"Hey," she said with a laugh, pushing away from him. "Slow down! We have all day."

He reached for her. "I just want to show you how grateful I can be."

"Not in five minutes, you won't." She took his hand and led him to the sofa. "Now," she said, curling her arms around his neck. "Show me what you can do."

He did, vigorously and hurriedly, thinking: Jesus! Easiest way in the world to get a job!

When she stopped him the first time and magically produced a Trojan, he was stunned, but he put it on as she requested. But when she stopped him a second time and insisted again that he slow down, he felt his annoyance rise. It was hard to do it slowly, he was anxious to slip it to her, to give her, as he would put it, "the fuck of her life." But when they soon got to that stage, and they were on the floor and he had her panties off and he was going away at her between her legs, she stopped him again and said, a little impatiently, "I said slow down. What are you, in a hurry to catch a plane?"

He lifted up slightly and gave her an indignant look. "I've never had any complaints before."

"Oh, I'm sure you haven't, Jamie. Women rarely criticize a man for his lovemaking. They're too frightened of hurting that delicate ego. But I'm not afraid to say it, Jamie. Quite honestly, you're not very good."

His erection deflated.

When he started to get up, she drew him back down and said, "Now don't go getting all steamed up. If you get it right, you've got the job. How's that?"

"If I get it right! Lady, I've fucked more—"

She put her hand on his mouth. "Please don't use that word."

"What do you want from me? Do you want me to f—, make love to you or what?"

"Yes, I do. But in a way that pleases *me*, not yourself."

He frowned genuinely at this. Didn't fucking please both parties?

"Listen, Jamie," she said gently, stroking the back of his beautiful golden hair, "I'm sure you would be very good, but you're going too fast and trying too hard. No woman likes to have a panting, slobbering beast on top of her. For one thing, while you were inside me you never even looked at me. As though you weren't even aware of me."

"How can you say that? Jesus, I've got my pecker up your—"

"And another thing, Jamie. The language. Before you make love to a woman, be certain that she wants to hear words like that. Otherwise, they're a turn-off."

He heaved an exasperated sigh.

"Jamie," she murmured. "Let's try again."

She reached down for him, to coax him back into hardness. But when he took her wrist and said, "That won't be necessary.

I'll be there in a second or two," she realized what one of Jamie's problems was. He had a small penis.

When she voiced this, he looked plainly uncomfortable. "Well, you know what they say! It's not the size that counts but what you do with it."

"And that's true. Not all women like a big penis, Jamie. Many don't even care what the size is, just so long as the man knows how to give pleasure."

This was what she had discovered about Jamie: that, in order to compensate for what he thought was an inadequacy, he made love with too much ardor and physical exertion. The result, however, was not a compensation at all, but a compounding of the problem.

"When you want to make love to a woman in the future," she said softly, caressing him, bringing him back to arousal. "Don't open her legs as wide as they will go, as you did with me. Bring them together, almost touching. Like this. You see? You can still enter me, but now I *feel* it. And it feels good, Jamie."

He was starting to relax. Forgetting his hurt pride, he let her guide him, realizing that he was in fact deriving more pleasure from what she was teaching him than from his usual sexual performance. He could feel her better, it was a tighter fit, and there was something new in it—a warmth, a kind of closeness he hadn't felt before.

"Slowly," she murmured as her hips rocked with his. "Slowly and gently. A woman is most sensitive right at the opening. Bring yourself almost all the way out, let me feel it, and then in again. Oh . . ." she breathed. "Like that. Yes . . . Yes . . ."

He took longer than he ever had in his life, and he enjoyed it more than he ever had. When they were done, picking themselves up and straightening their clothing, he said with a sly grin, "Well? Do I have the job?"

She gave him a long, considering look. "I wonder," she said, as if entertaining a new thought. "Would you like to work upstairs?"

Upstairs? In management? Jesus, if he'd known before what banging a lady employer could bring—

433

Now came the tricky part, revealing to him the true purpose of the interview, the true nature of what went on behind the butterfly logo.

"I must have your absolute trust, Jamie. I mean it. Not a word of this can be breathed outside this office."

"You can trust me."

Yes, she was sure she could. Especially once she told him what the upstairs work paid. It never failed—the prospective companion wanted the job too badly to spout off about it to friends. No sense in risking the golden-egg-laying goose, they invariably thought; no sense in stirring up competition for the job.

At first, he listened and stared at her in amazement. And then, as it started to sink in and he came to accept the idea, all sorts of lights lit up behind handsome Jamie's blue eyes.

"You say I'll get that kind of salary, plus big tips"—and he had no doubt the tips would be big—"*and* all the pussy I want?"

"Our members are women of high class. If they wish to hear language like that, they'll let you know. Otherwise, breasts are breasts and not tits, and so on."

"Yeah, gotcha."

"Now, only I and my assistant will know your true identity. There are no written records, you will be paid in cash."

"Wow. Does the Mafia run this or what?"

She gave him a tolerant smile. "You will never see anyone else who is involved with the operation of Butterfly. You will only ever be contacted by me or my assistant. And I will trust your discretion when you are with the other companions. No crude comparing of notes, please."

"Yeah, I got it. My lips are sealed. Hell, for that kind of money—"

"Now, there are a few things we have to get established ahead of time. First of all, you will use a condom at all times. At *all* times. Do you have an objection to a blood test?"

"I guess not."

"Now then. Our operation is run slightly differently from those that cater to male clients. For instance, our busiest hours are during the day, not at night, for obvious reasons. Many of our members are married. They can only get away during the day. You are never to ask a member her name or where she lives, or anything at all personal about her. It is the anonymity of Butterfly that makes our members feel safe. Women come here for something that would be impossible to find, and too dangerous to look for anywhere else. Again, I must stress the secrecy of what we do here. To somehow let the truth leak out would invite, shall we say, certain snoopers that we cannot afford to have know about us?"

Snoopers! thought Jamie with a laugh. A police raid on this place would no doubt read like a regular *Who's Who*.

"No drugs, Jamie. That is a number one rule. And keep your alcohol intake to a minimum. Don't drink with a member at all, if possible. If you wear a regular after-shave or cologne, go very lightly on it. Our members can't afford to go back to their husbands smelling like Brut. You must act like a gentleman at all times. Our members are ladies, never forget that. Your first few assignments will be with members of long standing and whose sexual preferences are rather simple and straightforward. As for the sex itself, remember always to go by what the woman wants, not what you want or what you think she wants. Look for signals. I'm sure you've heard that some women are above-the-waist women, others are below-the-waist women. Find out which your lady is and move accordingly. And for goodness sake, Jamie, go slowly. These women are paying a lot of money for your lovemaking. Make it good. And learn to be fast with the condom. Don't be obvious about putting it on. During intercourse, *look* at the woman you're with. Eye contact during the sex act is a big turn-on. She'll also know that you are making love to *her*, and not fantasizing about someone else."

She smiled and said, "So. Do you have any questions?"

"Only one. How's the money handled?"

"Very tastefully and discreetly. Don't be obvious about it. And if she gives you a tip, be sure to show your gratitude. Chances are, it will be bigger next time. Any other questions?"

"Yeah. When do I start!"

And that was how Ann Hastings recruited companions for Butterfly.

44

TRUDIE SIGHED as she felt the hard penis enter her. She locked her legs around his waist, closed her eyes and whispered, "Faster. *Faster.*"

His name was John or Mike or Steve. She had met him the night before in the cantina of the Red Onion restaurant and had gone home with him. They had decided to enjoy a morning quickie before they both had to get themselves off to work. She didn't know what he did. And she didn't care. She had no intention of ever seeing him again.

This has definitely got to stop, she thought as he climaxed before she did and therefore withdrew before she was finished.

Later, as she guided her Corvette down the winding, hilly streets of Bel Air, Trudie did some serious thinking about her life. And what she saw did not please her. The game of anonymous sex with revolving partners was just too dangerous to be played anymore. And besides, pickups in bars were no panacea for loneliness. In fact, she decided, they made the loneliness sharper and more unbearable.

She wanted someone permanent. Someone to love and share her life with.

But who? Besides the Saturday-night pickups, who were the men in her life?

Bill came into her mind. He was doing that a lot lately; they ran into each other on jobsites. They never spoke—just a nod to acknowledge each other's presence. He was still mad at her, she supposed. Even though she had apologized to him. It annoyed Trudie that it should cross her mind on such occasions to wonder what kind of a lover he was. She decided just by looking at Bill that he was a three-minute egg: one of those on-again-off-again macho lovers who invariably ask you afterward if it was as good for you as it was for them. In Trudie's experience, the lousy lovers always asked that timeworn question after sex, whereas expert lovers knew they were good and never had to ask. Like "Thomas" at Butterfly. He never asked.

Thomas . . .

There it was again, the enigma that surrounded her relationship with the Butterfly companion. Every time she was with him Trudie tried to figure out what it was about her encounters with Thomas that made them so special. She had decided that it wasn't the anonymity of them, because that was what some of her Saturday-night pickups were: totally without identity. And it couldn't be as simple as the fact that he was a good lover. Some of her Saturday-night men were excellent lovers, but the skyrockets were missing. What, then? What was it about what she did inside Butterfly, with her paid companion, that made those evenings so spectacular?

She couldn't shake the unpleasant aftertaste her night with John or Mike or Steve had left her with. There had been something so animalistic, so soulless about their lovemaking, that it had almost felt like a perversion. How could a rational, intelligent woman like herself do something so tacky as getting naked with a strange man and doing things with him that really should be reserved for times when deep love needed to be expressed?

Lovemaking? That was hardly what she could call her activities of last night and this morning!

Her luncheon with Jessica was at two o'clock and now it was only just eleven. Trudie decided to check up on a couple of pools in progress before heading for the restaurant.

The glorious May sunshine shed its benediction over a washed-clean Los Angeles and upon Trudie's blond shag as she sped down Sunset Boulevard. When she came to the corner where the pink buildings of the Beverly Hills Hotel peeked from behind palm trees on her left, Trudie thought of the job TruePools was doing up the hill on this same street.

She had inspected it only yesterday. Sanderson had done a good job on the excavation (he was on perfect behavior after the water-table fiasco last month), and Bill had been alerted to bring in his crew. That was the next stage in pool building: after the hole was dug, the steel was laid and the plumbing put in.

This job was the first referral from her movie star up on Coldwater Canyon. The house had just been bought by a TV producer, Barry Greene, whose hit medical show, *Five North*, was putting him in bigger bucks than ever. Trudie had spent two intensive weeks with him designing an elaborate pool area that would have combination redwood and brick decking, waterfalls, three spas, boulders, tropical ferns—just like a movie set. What she loved about it was that he had given her free artistic rein and a practically unlimited budget.

On an impulse she turned left, away from the business district and shopping center of Beverly Hills, telling herself that because this was such an important job, she really should keep close tabs on it. Even if Bill would be there with his crew.

And, of course, his GMC 4×4 was parked by the excavation . . .

She put her sunglasses on as she got out of her car and walked over the gravelly construction site. The house was not yet occupied—Greene was having it massively overhauled. And the backyard was a mess with heavy equipment, tools, mounds of dirt, and men sweating shirtlessly in and around the newly dug crater. Bill was going over blueprints and giving orders to his crew.

Trudie hung back by his 4×4. She suspected Bill might take her surprise visit as a personal insult, thinking that she was making sure he wouldn't botch this job. But that wasn't it at all. Trudie trusted him; she had meant it when she had told him he was the best in the business.

Lighting up a Virginia Slims, she glanced inside Bill's car. The front seat was cluttered with contracts, audio tapes, a baseball hat, and a book.

The latter caught her interest. She reached inside, brought it out, and read the title: *Holy Blood, Holy Grail.*

Right! she thought. I can just see Bill reading *this*. What did he do, carry it around to impress the chicks?

"Hey, boss-lady!"

She looked up. Bill was walking toward her. When had he taken his shirt off?

"You were here only yesterday," he said. "Checking up on me?"

438

"I see you've been doing a little heavy reading." She held up the book.

He took it from her and tossed it back onto the seat. "I'll thank you to keep your hands out of my car."

"I'll bet you impress a lot of women with that book. Do you actually tell them you're reading it?"

He picked a towel off the dashboard and wiped his sweating face and neck. "I've already read it, if it's any business of yours."

"Oh?" She walked a few steps away from him, casually smoking, surveying the busy construction scene.

"*You've* read it, of course," he said, reaching into the back-seat for a chilled can of Pepsi.

"I enjoyed it."

Trudie heard Bill pop open the can and mutter, "I'll bet."

"And I think their argument is a good one," she said, turning around.

He took a long drink, ran his hand over his mouth and said, "Well, I don't."

Trudie regarded him from behind her large sunglasses. "Why not?"

Bill didn't look at her. He leaned against his car and watched his crew working in and around the big hole in the ground. "It's too pat. Too simplistic. And it reads like a revenge thing. What have the authors got against the Masons, anyway?"

"So you really read the book. I suppose it was condensed in *Motor Trend*."

"Hasn't anyone told you that sexism is passé?"

Trudie stared at him. The noon sun shone on tanned muscles and longish hair that was damp at the ends. His jeans were slung low on his hips, and a single trickle of perspiration was making a track down his breastbone. He was right, damn him— she had lumped him in with the species of beer-drinking types she usually encountered on jobs; it would never have occurred to her that he would be reading books like that.

"Well," she said quietly, tossing down her cigarette. "I can see I was wrong about you. You're not just another pretty face, after all."

Bill stared at her. He watched how the May breeze stirred the curls on top of her head, the way the bangs fell just over her eyes. And the dress was something new. He had never seen her in a dress or skirt before. "Well then, I guess you had me fooled, too."

They looked at each other for a long moment, then Trudie said, "I'd like to debate the theory of that book with you sometime."

He considered it. "You're on," he said. "But it's only fair to warn you that I'm damn good at it."

"And I was on the debating team in school."

"What school is that?"

"UC Santa Barbara."

"So, she's college-educated yet." He bent his head back and drank down the rest of the cola.

Trudie watched his neck, the way the tendons stood out. When he carelessly tossed the can into the backseat of his car, she said, "And I suppose you have a Ph D?"

"Only a bachelor's."

"In what?"

He walked past her and headed for the excavation. "Oriental philosophy," he said, then shouted, "Hey, Frank! Tell the guys to break for lunch." He turned and faced Trudie, folding his arms and standing with his weight on one hip. "Except that by the time I got my degree I discovered there wasn't anywhere I could go with it. So I went back to what I had been doing to support myself through college. Construction work. Why are you in the pool business, Miss Debating Champion?"

"Tell me what I can do with a degree in English lit besides office work or teaching. My dad was in construction. He taught me everything he knew."

"Your dad must have been a smart guy."

One of the workers had turned on a radio. The Pointer Sisters did "Neutron Dance" while thermoses and sandwiches were produced from lunch pails.

"So," he said, pointing to the book lying on the front seat. "Have you seen their latest, *The Messianic Legacy*? This time they raise the question whether or not Jesus really founded

Christianity. I've only just started it, but I'll be glad to lend it to you when I'm done."

"Thanks, I would like that."

"Would you consider it an insult from a male chauvinist pig," Bill said, "if I told you you look pretty today?"

Trudie squinted up at the sky. "Only if I can tell you you have a cute ass."

"Are you married?" Bill asked.

"Who would have a bossy broad like me? And you?"

A smile slowly lifted his mouth. "I'm married to a Catalina 27 that's moored down at the marina."

"Hey, Bill!" called one of the crewmen. The guy strode over and engaged Bill in a few minutes of shoptalk while Trudie stood and watched them. And as she did, as she saw Bill shift his weight from one hip to the other and run his hand through his hair, she was surprised to find herself suddenly turned on.

Really turned on.

This wasn't just the casual curiosity about what kind of a lover he would be; Trudie was experiencing sudden, surprising and genuine sexual desire for the man. And the more she thought about it and tried to understand it, the more she discovered that she very much wanted to see him again, alone.

Puzzled over this sudden and unexpected turn, she walked away from Bill and his assistant, and paced beside his 4×4.

Why? she wondered. Why these feelings for him now? He certainly didn't look any different from the way he usually looked on jobs: dusty and sweaty, often without a shirt. She'd liked his looks, but she had never been turned on by them. Why now?

She took a cigarette out of her purse and held it in her hand, unlit.

As a matter of fact, she began to realize as she watched him get down on his knees with a piece of machinery and use some tools on it, this new feeling wasn't all that new. It had a familiar flavor to it, as though she had felt this way before. But not with him. With someone else. A feeling that rarely came over her—an intense sexual urge for a particular man.

And then she knew: Thomas.

This was the way she felt when she was with her Butterfly

441

companion; this was how Thomas affected her. It was the same turn-on, the same electricity. Trudie's silver-haired lover had made her feel the way no other man ever had, and, she had feared, the way no man ever would. And yet, surprisingly, here she was suddenly experiencing the same hunger for Bill.

Having finished whatever it was he needed to trouble-shoot, Bill was now walking back toward her, pausing once to turn around and shout something to his foreman. And the way he turned, the way his arms swung, the way the muscles of his back knotted, made Trudie's heart rise to her throat.

"I put in three return lines this time," he said with a smile. "Want to count them? Or would you rather debate the merits of *Holy Blood, Holy Grail*?"

And then she knew. There it was, the reason for this strange, wonderful feeling—why she experienced it with Thomas, why Bill should now trigger it—the mystery of her fabulous evenings at Butterfly and why she couldn't seem to re-create them in the real world. It was the way intellectual argument turned her on. Trudie loved challenging, mental stimulation with a sexy man. It was a kind of foreplay; clashing wits and a test of brain power eventually turned into sexual energy that was more intense and exciting than any kind of ordinary physical foreplay. And she had had her answer to the mystery of Thomas long before she had tried to puzzle it out: she had told the director of Butterfly that she wanted to be with a man who was bright, educated, and would engage her in serious, intellectual debate.

Trudie shifted her purse from one shoulder to the other, suddenly feeling self-conscious. "So," she said, craving a cigarette but fighting it, "Oriental philosophy, huh? You had me fooled."

"It's mutual."

She reached into her purse, pulled out her lighter and hastily lit up. Her newfound knowledge inexplicably made her ill at ease. It had taken her by surprise; she needed to think about it, to sort it all out and find out from herself where to go from here.

Bill! she thought in amazement. Butt-head Bill!

"You shouldn't smoke," he said.

"I suppose now you have a degree in medicine?"

"No," he said quietly. "I'd just hate to see you die young."

Trudie studied the palm trees that bordered Greene's estate. They swayed beautifully in the May breeze. Finally she said offhandedly, "I still owe you."

His eyebrows rose. "For what?"

"In my office, last month. Remember? You lost an hour's work because I called you on the carpet and you said I owe you for it. So lunch is on me today. Maury's, on Roxbury?"

He slowly rubbed his hands and looked around. "I don't want to leave these guys. Got some problems to iron out. Besides, I brought my lunch."

She tossed down her cigarette, ground it out with her foot, and said, "Okay! See ya!"

She quickly got into her car and was just starting the engine when Bill came up and said, "What are you doing Sunday? How about going sailing with me?"

She looked up at him as he stood silhouetted against the noon sun, and she suddenly wanted very much to be out on the open sea with him, alone, arguing, matching wits, making fantastic love.

But then she remembered the disastrous night with a certain masonry subcontractor—"Some of the guys have a bet going that you're a lesbian"—and she thought of the endless string of Saturday-night disappointments and the guys who were after her money, or who only wanted to get into her pants, and she suddenly didn't trust these new feelings for Bill.

"Sorry," she said, throwing the car into gear and backing away. "Let's just consider the debt canceled."

Bill, perplexed, watched the Corvette disappear in a rain of dust and gravel.

45

THE BLACK KNIGHT galloped across the jousting field, the hooves of his charger thundering and sending dirt flying. He held his lance level and sure; when he came abreast of the Red Knight, his aim was true and the lance knocked his opponent to the ground. The spectators cheered as the Black Knight rode up to the stands where his lady was sitting, dismounted, and returned to her her veil, which he had carried into the fight.

The crowd went wild. Jessica clapped and waved to the Knight, who she thought had played the part so perfectly. The illusion had been complete. The Renaissance Fair—she loved it.

She and John and their two friends turned away and continued their stroll through the fairgrounds. It was an event that was held once a year, in the hills behind Calabasas, and Jessica never missed it. This time John had invited Ray and Bonnie to join them. But none of them had come in costume, as so many other fairgoers did. Jessica had wanted to, but John had dismissed the idea as undignified. And so now, as they walked among the crowds, Jessica envied the women in their elaborate Elizabethan gowns and simple wench dresses. They were so *into* the spirit of the fair.

The rules were strict: everything had to fit within the years of the Renaissance—clothing, speech, even the food sold in the stands could not predate or postdate that era. Which was why the fair closed at dusk: it could not be lit up with electricity. A few concessions to the modern age had to be made, by the order of the Health Department. Food stands had refrigerators and ice; milk, beer, and wine were pasteurized. But otherwise all was authentic, and to such a degree and in such detail that it was possible, for a while at least, to lose oneself in an age long past.

Which was what Jessica did every time she came here.

She and John would prowl the lanes and gullies of the vast pleasure fair and inspect handmade goods sold in the hundreds of booths: pewter, felt hats, masks, quilts, a variety of arts and crafts limited only by the human imagination. Street brawls broke out here and there—staged affairs between costumed men with "wenches" looking on and cheering. A juggler might suddenly stop and set up a little show, earning coins in his upturned hat. A man dressed as Copernicus could be overheard arguing with another scholar whether or not the earth revolved around the sun. The fair was a place to come and shuck off the present and plunge wholeheartedly into the past, and to indulge in the romance of fantasy.

It was like Butterfly, Jessica thought when they stopped to purchase four steaks-on-a-stake. This was all fantasy and illusion. You left reality at the main entrance and bought yourself a flagon of sweet wine and watched the pageant of Queen Elizabeth and her court. And it was a beautiful day to enjoy it all: the sun was hot, it was Memorial Day weekend, and Southern California baked in a presummer haze.

"Look, honey," John said to Jessica when they came upon a pottery booth. "Here are those wine goblets you admired last time. Why don't we get them now?"

She remembered the goblets; last year she had thought they were hideous and had been secretly pleased when she and John had returned to the booth at the end of the day to find them gone. As John now signaled to the proprietor of the booth, a man in velvet doublet and tights, Jessica picked up one of the cups and examined it. The stem was supposed to be the figure of a wizard. It didn't quite work.

"How many shall we get?" John asked as he drew out his wallet. "Six or eight?"

Jessica turned the cup around and around in her hands, staring at it.

The goblets were expensive at forty dollars apiece, and she couldn't imagine ever using them.

"Jess? The man is waiting. How many shall we get?"

She looked at her husband. "Well," she said, putting the cup down. "I . . . don't really care for them, John. I mean, they're not really our style, are they?"

445

John arched his eyebrows. "You were crazy about them last year."

No. You were *crazy about them. I never said anything.*

He turned to the seller and said, "We'll take six."

As the shelf was cleared of the ugly maroon-and-gray goblets, which Jessica knew would go into a cupboard at home never to appear again, and John wrote a check for nearly three hundred dollars, she turned away and pretended to be interested in a ceramic soup tureen with a dragon on the lid.

They stopped next for beers, at a crowded intersection of two lanes where hundreds of hot and tired fairgoers sat on bales of hay, quenching their thirst. "Well?" said John to Bonnie and Ray. "Where to next?"

"What else is there to see?" asked Bonnie, this being her first visit to the fair.

"We haven't seen half of it yet. There's archery and games of skill over that way." He pointed down the lane. "And back there, a stage where performances are going on all day long."

"There's the fortune-tellers' gulch," Jessica ventured to say. "They have a whole string of palm readers, Tarot readers, crystal balls—"

"Archery it is, then!" said John, tossing his plastic cup into a trash can. "Let's see who can hit the first bull's-eye."

They followed him down the congested lane to the archery field, where a line of people stood in the hot sun awaiting their turns. Jessica and Bonnie watched while John and Ray competed for the most points, then the four continued on their way along the row of games of skill.

When they came upon the ringtoss, Jessica stopped and said, "Let's give this one a try!"

John looked at the booth and laughed. "Why?"

"Look at the prizes. Medieval puppets. I'd love to have one."

"Okay, honey," he said, walking up to the counter where wooden rings were stacked, ready to be tossed onto a board with posts at the back of the booth.

"Now, here be a fine gentleman," said the woman who ran the game. She was dressed like a dairymaid, the neckline of her blouse cut daringly low. "Spend a penny and win your lady a prize!"

It cost more than a penny. It was a dollar for six rings, and John paid her. As he picked up the first ring Jessica said, "Please let me try."

He smiled at her. "You know you're not very good at things like this, honey. Leave it to me."

But that was why I stopped here—so I could play!

He threw the first one and missed. He threw the second, and missed with that one, too.

Ray laughed and slapped his business partner on the back. "Face it, John," he said. "You're over the hill! The eyesight is always the first to go."

John shifted his stance, steadied himself, took aim, and missed.

"I guess it's not as easy as it looks," said Bonnie.

"Please let me try, John," Jessica said again.

"You want that puppet, don't you, honey?"

"Well, yes, but—"

"Then leave it up to me."

Bonnie was looking them over—the puppets were hand-made out of various kinds of fabric and were hanging on one wall of the booth. "They sure are nice," she said. "I wouldn't mind having one in my classroom."

John missed again.

"The game's fixed," he said good-naturedly, tossing the fifth and missing by a wide margin. "I'd swear those posts are moving!"

The last he threw over his shoulder, Annie Oakley style, and he and Bonnie and Ray laughed.

But Jessica, who thought one puppet in particular would look good on the wall in her office, was reaching into her purse. "Wait a minute," she said as her companions started to walk away. "I'm going to give it a try."

"Don't waste your money, Jess," said John. "It's not worth a dollar."

Neither are your damn goblets.

He and their two friends walked away while Jessica stayed at the booth and bought six rings.

447

Between tosses she kept looking through the crowd, trying to keep track of her companions' whereabouts. It was easy to get separated and lost in this vast fair. Finally, she couldn't concentrate enough to take good aim. She hurried and lost all six tosses.

A few minutes later, after searching for them, Jessica found John and Bonnie and Ray sitting under a giant oak tree, eating strawberries and cream out of cantaloupe shells.

"Did you win?" John asked when she came up, hot and tired.

She sank down next to him, thankful for the shade. "No."

"Told you so."

Jessica looked at the three outrageous desserts. The strawberries were as big as plums and the cream was the old-fashioned clotted kind. You could practically spread it with a knife.

"Want some?" said John.

"You know I do!"

He scooped a strawberry and some cream onto his spoon and lifted it to her mouth. Jessica ate it, and wasn't offered anymore.

"What next?" said Ray when their cantaloupes were scraped clean and thrown away.

"Why don't we get our fortunes told?" said Jessica. "The Gulch of the Seers is only down that way—"

"The Queen's Pageant is going to be soon, honey," said John. "We don't want to miss that."

But Bonnie said, "I think it would be fun to have our fortunes told."

John shook his head. "Don't tell me *you* go in for that nonsense, too? I thought Jess was the only gullible one among us!"

"No one takes it seriously, for God's sake!" Bonnie said. "It's just for fun."

"Okay, if it'll make you girls happy."

As they struck off down the dusty lane Jessica watched John and Ray in front of them—two athletically fit men in their forties, wearing well-cut clothes, their hair expensively styled, their stride and manner fairly shouting success. They owned the world, Jessica thought. Men like John and Ray ran things, they were who counted, and they knew it. As she followed behind them, only half listening to Bonnie talk about her sixth-grade class, Jessica watched her husband move through the crowd with ease and confidence. Occasionally he and Ray would laugh. They flirted with "wenches." They paused now and then to study something, to point and comment, and then move on. And as Jessica watched John stroll through the world with such supreme self-assurance, she felt the day grow dark and her happiness at being at the fair start to slip away.

It had been three weeks since her panicked flight to Butterfly. It had been that long since her vow to stand up to John. She had come home from her interlude with her fantasy cowboy to find John packing for an emergency trip to London. Problems in the UK office had suddenly cropped up, he had explained. And then he had been gone for nearly two weeks. Upon his return, he had been warm and loving toward her, as he always was after a long absence, and the days that followed had been filled with work, court appearances, and more work. This weekend was the first they really had alone together, to relax a little and have some fun.

But the joy Jessica had felt that morning, when they had pulled up next to Bonnie and Ray in the parking field outside the fair, had trickled away over the hours, like a bag of sand microscopically punctured. It seemed to Jessica now, as she looked back over the morning, that with each step she had taken, each booth they had visited, she had left a little of her happiness behind.

She knew now that things between her and John were never going to change. As pleasant and harmonious as his homecomings were, brief spells when Jessica felt she truly loved him, there invariably followed the days of criticism, the gender game-playing, with sex the reward or punishment, the need for John to keep her down and himself dominant. Jessica looked ahead down the long, crowded Renaissance lane, through which her husband sauntered like some lord of the manor, and saw their years together, in which they grew older and older, the roles never changing, Jessica stifled, like her mother in that million-dollar Palm Springs home, the ornamental wife of John Mulligan, a man who counted. And it suddenly frightened her.

A sword fight broke out just then, between two men who might have been Robin Hood and the Sheriff of Nottingham. One wore a leather jerkin and green hose, the other a padded doublet and fancy velvet hat, and they dueled expertly, calling each other "knave" and "villain." The crowd formed a circle around them and goaded them on. Jessica and Bonnie came to stand next to their husbands, who, instantly taking sides, cheered for their chosen champions, exchanging friendly insults as they did at football games.

Jessica watched the fight and felt herself become excited. The duelists were both young and handsome. Their tights covered well-muscled legs and firm, round buttocks. And they played their parts well. No doubt, she thought, they were drama majors in college, and thrilled over this opportunity to display their skills.

When the fight was ended and the two went their separate ways, the crowd cheered and headed for the food stalls, the clash of blades having suddenly made them ravenous. As the four resumed their walk toward the Gulch of Seers Bonnie said, "This is great! I'm so glad you asked us to join you. I had no idea what the Renaissance Fair was like." She turned to Jessica. "Wouldn't you like to have two men fight over you like that?"

Yes. Yes, I would.

"You realize, of course," John said as they rounded the corner and headed down the sloping path toward the wooded gulley, "what was wrong with that duel?"

"What?"

"The one in black, his costume was from the wrong era. Men didn't wear tall hats like that in the Renaissance. And his jacket was seventeenth-century."

"I thought someone made sure everything was authentic here," said Ray.

"The people who work here undergo a training course before the fair opens," John explained, leading his three companions over a small footbridge. "And their costumes are inspected. That one got in through the back door, I'll bet."

"Well, actually, John," Jessica said. "I don't think that's right. His costume was right in keeping with the Renaissance."

"I'm afraid you're wrong, honey. He was a hundred years out of date."

But I know I'm right.

"All right, everybody," John said expansively, looking up and down the gulley lined with tents and booths. "What'll it be? Cards? Tea leaves? Cranial bumps?"

"John," Jessica said quietly, "that man wore a costume very similar to what Sir Walter Raleigh wore. And he lived in the Renaissance."

"Honey, face it, you're mistaken. You're not an expert on history, you know. Now then, it looks like we have about fifty fortune-tellers to choose from—"

"I do know something about history, John. After all, at UCSB I had a history minor."

He patted her arm and smiled. "Yes, very minor." He turned to Bonnie and Ray. "Okay, which fortune-teller shall we go to?"

"I want an optimistic one," Ray said. "One who's going to tell me there's a Lamborghini in my future!"

When the others started off in the direction of the fortune-tellers, Jessica stayed where she was and said, "John, I don't deserve to be treated like that."

He turned and looked at her. "Like what? What's the matter, Jess?"

"You treat me like an idiot. As if everything I say is silly and not worth listening to."

He sighed and came up to her. "Jessica, what are you making a big deal out of this for? Who cares if that guy was in the right costume or not?"

"It has nothing to do with the costume, John," she said quietly. Her heart started to race. "I don't like the way you put me down."

"Put you down!" He laughed. "Honey, you were wrong, plain and simple. What am I supposed to do, go along with you when you are clearly mistaken?"

"It's the way you do it, John."

He gave Ray and Bonnie a look, then said to Jessica, "Look,

451

I don't know what I did wrong, but if it'll make you feel better—
okay, the guy was in the proper costume. Satisfied?"

As he turned once again to walk away, Jessica stood her
ground. "No, I'm not satisfied."

Now he stopped and gave her an annoyed look. "Listen,
Jessica. I don't know what put you in this mood, but I'd like
you to snap out of it. I've already conceded the argument to
you. What more do you want?"

Her heart pounded. "I want an apology."

"You want a *what?*"

"I want you to apologize for the way you spoke to me."

"Jessica, listen. I don't know what got into you today—"

"John, I just want to be treated with some respect. You
insulted me in front of our friends. I don't think that's fair."

John stared at her as Bonnie and Ray pretended to be interested in something else, and people had to walk around
them at the end of the little bridge. Finally John said, quietly,
in a tone she knew too well, "All right, Jess. That's enough.
Whatever is bugging you, get rid of it right now. You can be
as miserable as you want, but you're not going to ruin the day
for the rest of us."

"You're the one who's ruining it, John," she said evenly,
surprised at how controlled she was. "I've tolerated your put-
downs and patronizing attitude for eight years. I'm tired of it."

His eyes widened. Then he threw up his hands and
marched away. Jessica didn't follow him; she stayed where she
was while Bonnie and Ray exchanged an uncertain look. When
John had gone several yards, Jessica called after him, "Turning
your back on me won't work this time."

He spun around. "Jessica, get over here right now."

"Stop treating me like a child."

He glanced at the people walking by; then he came back
to Jessica and said in a low voice, "You're making a spectacle
of yourself."

"I don't care."

"No, I know you don't. That's why you defend clowns in
a public courtroom."

"Don't change the subject, John. I want to have this out
right here and now."

"I will not get into an argument with you in front of strangers, Jessica."

"You won't talk to me in private when I try to bring it up. So why not in front of the whole world?"

"I give up," he said, turning away again. "I can't talk to you when you're hysterical."

She watched him march away, the way she had seen him walk away from her so many times before, when she wanted to talk and he wanted the subject dropped. At home, she would have been punished with his silence and then he would have made love to her as if nothing had happened. This time she watched him go, and then she turned around and headed off in the opposite direction.

It was some minutes before John realized what had happened, and he caught up with her. Grabbing her arm, he said, "What the hell do you think you're doing?"

"I'm going home." She pulled her arm free and continued down the lane.

He ran after her and took her arm again, painfully this time. "Don't you dare walk away from me!"

"Why not? You do it to me all the time. I think it's my turn, don't you?"

He frowned at her. "Jess, what's this all about? Are you having your period?"

She freed her arm again and walked quickly away.

Jessica got as far as the entrance, which was a considerable distance from the little footbridge, when John caught up with her again. Just as she was about to go through the gate he took her arm and spun her around. "Snap out of it right now, Jessica!"

"If you want to get back into the fair, John, you'd better have your hand stamped."

She hurried through the gate and he stared after her. Then he pushed through and stopped her on the other side. "I won't stand for this, Jessica. Let's go back inside right now, and then *you* apologize to our friends."

"They're not *our* friends, John. I don't even like Bonnie and Ray."

"This is a great time to tell me!"

"I've told you before, you just haven't listened. Let go of my arm. I'm going home."

"No, you're not."

"You didn't get your hand stamped, John. Now you're going to have to pay to get in again, just to retrieve your ugly goblets."

"I bought them for you!"

"You did not buy them for me!"

The color rose in his face. His grip on her arm tightened. "I swear, Jessica, if you don't go back in there with me right now, you'll be sorry."

"I've been sorry for eight years, John. Right now is the first time I'm not."

"What the hell is the matter with you!"

"I just reached the end of it, John. That's all. I'm tired of your treating me like a child, telling me what to do, what to wear, what to eat. You humiliate me every day in a hundred little ways. I can never have an opinion unless it matches yours. You put me down in front of other people. You make fun of my career—"

"So you're just going to drive off, is that it? Leaving me here?"

"Bonnie and Ray can give you a ride. Unless, of course, you want to come with me and talk this out."

"I'm not going anywhere with you, damn it! You're going to stop acting like a spoiled brat and grow up."

"I find that an ironic twist." She pulled free of his hold and started to walk away again, quickly this time, nearly running.

He ran after her and blocked her way. "I will not let you do this."

"I don't need your permission to go. I'm quite capable of driving myself home. I'm quite capable of doing a lot of things that would surprise you, John."

"You don't surprise anyone, Jess. You are the most unimaginitive, predictable woman I have ever met! Christ, but you're boring!"

She gazed at him, finding herself suddenly close to tears.

454

They had had arguments before, but she had never seen such contempt in his eyes, had never heard him speak such words.

"I think you've made me a boring woman, John," she said quietly. She heard a tremor in her voice and hoped she wouldn't start to cry. "You haven't allowed me to grow."

"Grow!" He spun away, thrusting his hands in his pockets. "You dumb bitch! Where would you be if I hadn't married you? What would you do without me telling you every single day what to wear, what to order in a restaurant, for God's sake? You don't have a mind of your own, Jess."

"That's because you never let me have one!" she cried.

People walking by, heading from the parked cars toward the entrance gate, cast surreptitious looks at the couple. John, for once, didn't seem to care. "Okay," he said, his face flushed with anger. "You want to go home? All right, we'll go home." He seized her arm and dragged her toward where their car was parked.

"You're hurting me!"

He walked close by her side, his fingers digging into her arm, forcing her to stumble over the uneven ground. When they reached the BMW he pushed her against it and reached into his pocket for the keys.

"I won't get in," she said.

"You wanted to go home, we're going home. Get in!"

"No. I'll get home by myself."

"You can't find your way around a supermarket by yourself." He flung the door open. *Now get in!*"

Jessica fought back the tears that threatened to come. "I can get along by myself," she said in a tight voice. "I'm capable of doing a lot of things by myself, John."

His voice was full of scorn, "Name one thing, besides demeaning yourself in a courtroom."

The sound of her heartbeat thundered in her ears. Her mouth was so dry she was having difficulty talking. "For one thing," she said quietly, "I'm capable of going to bed with another man."

He laughed contemptuously. "And when do you plan to do that?"

"I've already done it."

His mouth lifted in a mocking smile. "Am I supposed to feel threatened?"

"In fact I went to bed with him twice."

John's eyes flickered. A small crack appeared in his façade. "Who?"

"I don't know his name. He was a total stranger. I went to bed with a man I don't even know."

"I don't believe you."

"And I paid him money for it!"

His hand flew out so quickly and he hit her across the face so hard that Jessica was knocked off her feet. As she fell to the dirt both she and John were stunned.

Putting a hand on her cheek, she looked up at him and said, "I hope that made you feel better."

"You had it coming—" he began. He was shaking; his hands were fists at his sides.

Jessica pulled herself up and leaned against the car. "I concede your physical superiority to me, John. You outweigh me by eighty pounds. If it makes you feel more like a man to beat me up, then do it."

He turned away, his eyes filled with pain and anger.

She waited for him to say something. Her cheek throbbed; her palms were scraped and stinging. She stared at John's rigid back, expecting him to speak, to make the next move. But he stayed turned away from her, his gaze fixed on the rows and rows of cars stretching away to the hills. A hot summer silence descended upon the scene. This area of the parking lot had been filled early in the morning—there were no merry fairgoers passing among the cars; only flies and bees droned in the heat. In the distance, sounds from the fair drifted up to the sun-washed sky.

Jessica waited.

Finally, taking in a deep breath and squaring his shoulders, John slammed the car door shut, thrust the keys back into his pocket, said, "You can do whatever you want. I don't give a damn," and he walked away, back in the direction of the fair.

46

IT WAS TIME TO START the countdown. With the California primary only four days away, and the Republican Convention just one week after that, the hour had come for Beverly Highland to put the final phase of her plan into motion. This was the moment she had spent thirty-five years working toward.

The destruction of Danny Mackay.

She hadn't slept for the past few nights, and now she paced the carpet of her imposing library, frequently glancing at her watch and listening for the front-door chimes. She had actually begun the preliminary work two weeks ago, after her return from San Francisco. Beverly had given Maggie and Carmen their instructions, and had sent Jonas Buchanan to Texas. In the ensuing days they had reported their progress to her, and now, on this last sunny morning of May, they were going to gather in this silent house for their final secret meeting.

Beverly felt charged. Her body was electrified—with passion, with excitement, and with fear. It *had* to work. The revenge she had sworn against Danny thirty-five years ago *had* to be a success.

Ghosts paced the Persian carpet with her: the tortured spirit of her mother, driven to murder, who had found a haven at last in Reverend Mary Drake's home; the soft and tender little specter of the unborn, unformed baby that Danny had made Rachel give up; and finally a phantom named Christine Singleton, Beverly's twin sister whose trail ended mysteriously in Saudi Arabia and whom Jonas Buchanan had, ultimately, not been able to find. And finally there was the ghost of Maggie's dead Joe and the unhappy spirits of people whom Danny had ruined. It was for them, and for the safety of everyone else, that Beverly was now going to set the final machinery into motion.

The chimes sounded, and the maid opened the library door

for Carmen. For a moment she and Beverly stared at each other across the enormous room, two women standing among walls of leather-bound books with sunshine streaming through the diamond-paned windows, illuminating the red, gold, and black intricacies of the carpet.

Carmen seemed to hold her breath for a second, then she said, "It's done."

Beverly turned away, her hands tightly clasped. So . . . it had already begun.

There was no turning back now.

"I went to the Century Plaza," Carmen said quietly. "Danny will be checking in day after tomorrow. He's reserved two suites and six rooms. His wife will be with him."

Beverly's back was straight and rigid as she gazed out at the giant tree ferns framing a window. Beyond them, golden marigolds and red roses made a paradise of her garden. A Chinese vase on her ornate mahogany desk held freshly cut butterfly lilies. They were so fragile that their blossoms lasted only a day.

Beverly had not seen Danny since the night of the banquet in San Francisco. She had not seen him, in fact, after the brief, dizzying moment when she had shared the dais and spotlight with him. She had looked at the gold religious medallion he had presented to her, then she had quietly thanked him and returned to her table. She had successfully avoided his company after that, leaving as soon as the banquet was over and hurrying away. But since that night her name had been linked with his. Just as she had planned.

"When will the Los Angeles *Times* receive the package?" she asked softly.

"Three days from now. That will get everything started."

"Did you take care of things at Butterfly?"

"Everything is ready, Bev."

"Fred Banks?"

"Jonas has left for Mexico. He'll be helping Fred with his statement to the press."

"What about Ann?"

"Maggie has gone to get her. They should be here soon. When will Bob arrive?"

"He telephoned from Dallas this morning. He should be getting into LAX any minute now."

"Was he successful?"

Dear God, Beverly thought. "Yes," she said. "He was successful."

Beverly turned around. "Do you remember, Carmen? Do you remember my first night at Hazel's and how you took care of me?"

"And the night you took care of me, when I tried to commit suicide. And how you taught me to dream." Carmen came up to her and said, "These things will never be forgotten, *amiga*. We have traveled a long road, you and I."

"Yes."

"And the end is almost here."

Beverly closed her eyes. *The end. . . .*

The chimes sounded again and Maggie came into the library with a perplexed-looking Ann.

"Beverly," she said, "what's this all about? Maggie just told me you're closing Butterfly down. Why?"

Beverly looked at Carmen and Maggie, then she walked up to Ann and said, "Take a walk in the garden with me. I have something to tell you."

Bob Manning said a hasty good-bye to the pilot of Beverly's private jet and hurried into the waiting Rolls. "Take me straight to Miss Highland's home, please," he said to the chauffeur, and clutched his briefcase tightly to himself.

His heart was thumping. He was scared, he was excited, he was just plain nervous as hell. He felt as if he were carrying a ticking time bomb in the leather case. *Hurry*, he mentally urged the driver. *Hurry, hurry. . . .*

They stood in an arbor of breathtaking bougainvillea named, ironically, Texas Dawn. Its silvery lavender petals fluttered down on the heads of the two women as Ann, her face slightly pale, said, "My God, Beverly."

"I'm sorry to have to drop it on you like this. There was no other way."

"You know," Ann said as they turned and started walking

459

back toward the house, "I've suspected something for a long time. I had a feeling that you and Carmen and Maggie shared a secret. Beverly, you could have told me! You know you can trust me! We've known each other for thirty years."

"It wasn't a matter of trust, Ann. It was, well—very personal. But now you have a right to know because of what is going to happen in the next few days, and you need to be prepared."

Ann gazed down at the flagstones she and Beverly followed. It was all so overwhelming—the strange and sordid tale of a runaway girl back in Texas, her transformation in Hollywood, the surgery, the change of name, and the subsequent years of plotting revenge against the man who had done it to her. Ann knew it would take a while for her to adjust to it, to Beverly's past and to what Beverly was about to do. But Ann would keep those secrets safe. Beverly was the only true friend she had had all these years, a woman who had made a certain Christmas dance the highlight of an unhappy girl's life, and who had included her in a spectacular rise to fame and fortune. For Beverly, Ann Hastings would do anything.

"I'll talk to Roy," she said as they neared the house. "He'll understand. He'll keep your secret safe. Roy owes you as much as I do, Bev. No one will ever know the truth about Butterfly."

They found a very agitated Bob Manning in the library, showing the contents of his briefcase to Maggie and Carmen. When he turned and saw Beverly come in, he said, "You won't believe what I've brought back—" He stopped when he saw Ann also come in.

"It's all right, Bob," Beverly said. "I've told Ann everything. You can speak freely in front of her."

He handed the briefcase to Beverly. "It's all here. And more."

"Let's get started," Beverly said.

June

47

THE HEADLINE on the morning after the voting read: MACKAY WINS CALIFORNIA PRIMARY.

The accompanying article on page one described the sweeping but, at this late stage, rather expected victory of Reverend Danny Mackay over his Republican opponents in this "kingmaker" primary. Having won all the California delegates, these being more delegates than any other state had, the founder of Good News Ministries was now just eighty votes shy of getting the presidential nomination. Experts were predicting that he would have no trouble in getting the "swing" votes at the convention, which was six days away. The text included a photograph of a smiling Danny, the trademark Stetson on his head. Parties were going on around the clock at the Century Plaza Hotel, his temporary Los Angeles residence.

Quite a different and very unexpected headline appeared, however, on the next day's front page: MACKAY'S NAME LINKED TO BEVERLY HILLS BROTHEL.

"Jesus Christ!" Danny muttered when he saw the morning paper. He had a hangover from his victory party the night before and was trying to nurse himself out of it with tomato juice and Tabasco. He hadn't slept well, not after the call he'd received shortly after 2:00 A.M. from the newspaper.

The *Times* people had called to inform him of information they had received from the police, information they were going

463

to print. Considering who he was, they had said, they thought it only fair to warn him.

And there it was.

Danny threw the paper down and looked at Bonner. In the outer room he could hear the phones ringing and a steady knocking at the door. In his private bedroom Danny had turned on his TV set. And now he saw his face on the screen—a publicity photo from his own files. A voice-over was saying, ". . . raided shortly after midnight. The police, responding to an anonymous tip, searched the rooms above the clothing store and found what they describe as premises set up for the purpose of illicit sexual activity. Fanelli, a posh men's store on Rodeo Drive, it has just been learned, is owned by Royal Farms, which in turn is owned directly by Danny Mackay, presidential hopeful. So far, no direct connection has been made between Reverend Mackay and the operation upstairs, but the police are examining certain evidence that was found in what appears to be the office of that illegal operation."

While his staff in the outer room took care of reporters and phone calls Danny just stood in his pajamas and silk dressing gown, staring in disbelief.

His press secretary had sat up all night writing a statement to the effect that the Reverend denied any knowledge of the establishment over the men's shop, and that as Fanelli was such a small part of his many holdings, Danny Mackay had never once, in his years of owning Fanelli, set foot inside the store.

"Damn it, Bon," he said as he sat down to a breakfast of chicken-fried steak and hash browns. "How could something like that happen? I thought you checked the place out."

"I did, but that was eleven years ago! I inspected the place myself. It was just an ordinary men's clothing store. And upstairs there were offices rented out to various legitimate enterprises."

Danny kicked the newspaper that lay on the floor. "Offices! Did you read what they found up there? Whips and chains, rubbers, sex devices! Where in hell is Duane?"

"He's still down at police headquarters, Danny." They were referring to Duane Chadwick, Danny's attorney.

Danny picked up his Bloody Mary and tossed it down. Outside, in the hallway beyond his doors, bodyguards were keeping reporters and curiosity seekers away. His two phone lines were being kept busy by his secretaries, who were explaining the mistake to the necessary parties—his senator father-in-law and various powerful political supporters—while the Century Plaza was preparing a room from which Danny could televise a public denial of the preposterous allegations.

"Don't worry," Bonner said a little nervously, trying to calm his boss. "Ain't no one in this world gonna believe you knew about that whorehouse. Look, it's happened before, right? People suddenly finding themselves responsible for something they knew nothing about. Shoot, like as not, it was some moron's idea of making a fast buck. The police find the manager of the store, he spills his guts out and you're off the hook."

"They'd better find him, and fast."

Danny glanced up to see Angelica standing in the doorway. She had her usual pained expression on her face.

Christ, she made him sick. Ever since the night of their honeymoon he'd never seen anything but that suffering martyr's look on her face. The only time she smiled was in public, when she was forced to play the good-wife role. They hadn't even slept together since the honeymoon, eleven years ago. The only reason Cary, their younger son, got conceived was that Danny had gotten so mad and drunk one night that he'd tied her up and given her what she deserved. "Go back to your room," he growled at her now. "This isn't any of your affair."

Angelica retreated like a wraith to the elegant bedroom off their suite where she spent all of her time reading and making lace, when not needed to pose with Danny for the cameras.

By early evening Danny had made a public statement about his innocence. He vaguely hinted that this was the work of someone out to slander him but that he forgave him as certainly the Lord did. And he did such a good job of making himself look like a victim that public sympathy for him ran high. By the next morning Danny was still at the top of the popularity polls and was able to laugh about the whole thing as he put away fried ham steak and biscuits with gravy.

And then a Lieutenant O'Malley came to the hotel, and Danny couldn't refuse to see him. He was a detective lieutenant with a detective sergeant in tow.

The man was clearly uncomfortable. He apologized profusely for disturbing the Reverend and assured Danny that this wouldn't take long, that it was just a matter of formality, and that, in the investigation of the secret bordello above Fanelli, all parties even remotely involved were being questioned.

"Believe me, sir," the lieutenant said as he took a seat, "I discussed this with my superiors. We debated all day yesterday whether or not to bother you with this. We finally decided that we had no choice, considering what, er"—he cleared his throat—"we found in the office upstairs."

Danny stared at O'Malley. The man didn't look like a detective. For one thing, he appeared to be too short. For another, he struck Danny as being too nicely dressed. He also looked to be a meticulously neat man—his shirt collar was immaculate and pressed, his hair carefully slicked down, his hands pink and clean. Even the little notebook he pulled out of his pocket looked too tidy, and Danny glimpsed neat, cramped handwriting.

"When we investigated the premises above the men's store," O'Malley began, not looking Danny in the eye, "we found what was clearly the center of operations. It was a room with a desk and telephones and a wall safe, which, when we opened it, was found to contain a great deal of cash. Now, there were no written records or anything that could give us a clue as to who worked there or who might have been customers there, but we *did* find a letter." Now he raised his head and looked directly at Danny. "From you, sir."

Danny blinked. "From me? What kind of letter, Lieutenant?"

"A letter of congratulations."

"*Congratulations!*"

"Praising one, er"—he consulted his notebook—"'Bob Manning for his efficiency and for raising profits considerably. The letter has been verified as being authentic, Reverend. It was written on Good News letterhead and signed by yourself."

Danny frowned and said, "We must have sent out hundreds of those letters, Lieutenant. Whenever we receive good reports from one of our investments we reward them with praise and encouragement. That letter was referring to the men's shop, Lieutenant, not to whatever Devil's work was going on upstairs!"

"Yes, well." O'Malley cleared his throat again. "There was a photograph with the letter. I have a copy of it here." He reached inside his jacket. "We have the original at headquarters, of course, but as you can see, sir, this is a picture of you."

Danny stared down at it, dumbfounded. There he was, against a backdrop of beach and palm trees, sitting with a bikini-clad young beauty in his lap. He brought his head up sharply and said, "Get Duane in here. Fast."

Ten minutes later Danny Mackay's attorney was assuring an apologetic Detective O'Malley that the photograph was a fake and that "serious reprisals" would occur should the picture somehow make it to the press.

"Would you have any idea who would create such a photograph of yourself, sir?" O'Malley asked.

Danny was fighting for self-control. "Well, Lieutenant," he said with the unhappy smile of a martyr, "it's hard to believe, but I guess I've got a few enemies. Anyone doing the Lord's work has Satan and his minions as his enemies. And whoever put that piece of filth together, well, I intend to pray for that man's soul. Because he is in serious danger of eternal hellfire."

"Lieutenant," Duane said, "what about this Bob Manning person? Why haven't the police found him?"

"We haven't found him yet, but we have his home under surveillance, Mr. Chadwick, and we're interrogating anyone who might be able to tell us of his whereabouts. We've questioned the employees of the men's store, but they all claim not to have known about the operation upstairs, and none of them knew Manning socially. But please rest assured that we will find the perpetrator behind all this."

As he was leaving, O'Malley paused at the door to say, "I just wanted you to know, Mr. Mackay, that the wife and I voted for you, and that you have our votes come November."

"You have the Lord's blessing, Lieutenant," Danny said magnanimously. And then when the detective and his silent assistant were gone, he turned around and growled, "Whoever's behind this, I aim to have his balls."

48

TRUDIE WAS SCARED. Of herself, of her feelings for Bill.

As she sat at her desk sifting through the morning's mail, she felt her mind return to the squirrel cage it had been running on ever since her last encounter with Bill in Barry Greene's backyard. Should she take the chance, she had been asking herself over and over; should she pursue the man as her feelings were telling her to, or should she play it safe and let him go? For the first time since she could remember, Trudie was suddenly very much concerned about a man's opinion of her. The Saturday-night pickups, well, who cared what they thought? She loved them and left them. And Thomas—he was paid to pretend to like her. Whether or not he did wasn't a question Trudie was troubled with. But Bill . . . all of a sudden, here was a man whose view of her was very important to Trudie.

And she had no idea how he felt about her.

She was afraid of getting burned again. It frightened her to think of going to him, of letting him know how she felt, only to be turned down, to be told that all he wanted to be was friends. Which was worse, she wondered, making a fool of herself and wishing she'd kept silent, or keeping silent and therefore never finding out how he felt about her? And the most maddening thing about it all was that Trudie Stein, normally unafraid of risks and challenges, was suddenly scared to death to put it to the test.

Cathy, her assistant, came through the door carrying two white paper sacks. "They were out of chicken curry," she said. "So I got the scrambled eggs with chorizo. Is that okay?"

Trudie didn't care; she wasn't very hungry.

"Have you seen the paper today?" Cathy asked as she opened a carton of milk. "I just can't believe it! And I voted for Danny Mackay on Tuesday."

Trudie looked up. She said, "What?" then remembered: yesterday's shocker headline about Mackay being linked to Butterfly! As soon as she'd seen it she had called Jessica. Could it be true? they wondered. Was Good News Ministries behind the secret operation above Fanelli? Jessica had briefly considered stepping forward and offering information to the baffled police. But then sanity had overridden her Catholic conscience. "Let's just keep our mouths shut," she said and Trudie had agreed.

Now Trudie looked at the headline and her coffee cup stopped at her lips. MACKAY OWNER OF PORNO MAGAZINE.

"What on earth—?" she said, reaching for the paper.

"It's positively amazing!" Cathy said. "Now they've found out that Danny Mackay owns a girlie magazine, a string of illegal massage parlors, and the Hot Pink adult movie theater chain. And he claims he knew nothing about it!"

"This is going to hurt him at the Republican Convention," Trudie murmured, her mind on something else.

"He's madly denying it all and insisting it's the work of the Devil. Read what he says there. 'Attacking a man of God is an attack on God Himself.' And can you believe them finding a whorehouse right in the middle of Beverly Hills? I must have gone into Fanelli a dozen times, and I never knew about the establishment upstairs! I'll bet they had some pretty explosive names on their client list!"

When the news had broken yesterday about the secret operation above Fanelli, Trudie had decided that the people who ran Butterfly must have known they were going to be raided. A few days ago she and Jessica had received notices of the closedown and refunds on their membership money; all the other members must have, too. But what about the companions? What about her precious Thomas? Where was he now? Would he think of her, she wondered, in the future?

Trudie laid the newspaper aside and looked at her watch. It was two o'clock. Then she picked up the contract of the latest job she had taken on. Swimming pool and spa in Brentwood. A tricky one this time—they wanted the pool to extend into the house. "I'd better give Bill a call," she murmured. "See if he can fit this one in."

Cathy looked at her employer. Trudie *never* made the calls to the subcontractors.

As Trudie dialed the phone the silver bangles on her wrist clinked and glittered in the hot June sunlight pouring through the plate-glass window. Cathy noticed a new one among them. A chain with a tiny butterfly charm. Not Trudie's usual taste, she thought.

"Hi, this is Trudie Stein," she said into the phone. "Is Bill there? Oh, I see. Out on a job?" She listened. "Oh? Uh, no. Don't tell him I called. I'll try again tomorrow."

Trudie hung up and reached for her cigarettes.

"He's out on a job?" Cathy said.

"No. Playing hooky. Down at the marina, working on his boat."

Trudie moved papers around on her desk. She called Jessica's house and left a message with the housekeeper. She called her manicurist and made an appointment to have her nails filled in. She looked at the papers for the new job again— the pool was going to wrap halfway around the house with the shallow end in the entertainment room. Underwater barstools, barbecue pit, volcanic rock waterfall. . . .

Trudie looked at her watch again.

She put out her cigarette and lit another.

They wanted flagstone decking and a small arched bridge over the deep end. Spanish tile, a fountain in the center. . . .

"Listen," she said suddenly, closing the folder and reaching for her purse. "I'm going to take the rest of the day off. I don't think there's anything that will come up that you can't handle."

Cathy stared at Trudie. "No problem," she said, trying to recall the last time Trudie had taken *any* time off. "Where can I reach you if I need to?"

"You won't be able to. I'm going to do some shopping. I'll check in with you before you close."

The way Trudie breezed out through the front door, Cathy would not have guessed how fast her employer's heart was beating.

He's down at the marina working on his boat, Bill's office had said.

But the marina was a big place with hundreds of boats. So Trudie went about her search methodically, slowly driving up and down, first A Basin, then B Basin, scanning the rows of parked cars, looking for him.

She kept telling herself this was ridiculous. They had barely spoken in the past four weeks since they met at the Greene excavation and made discoveries about each other. Bill had asked her to go sailing and Trudie had said no. She'd rudely driven off and left him standing there in a cloud of dust and gravel. In the days that followed, she had made a point of avoiding him, of communicating with him through his office, of making sure he was never around when she inspected a site. And now here she was, driving up and down, looking for his car, as if she were an adolescent, not stopping to think that this wasn't fair to him, that he might have someone on the boat with him.

There it was. The brown and gold GMC 4×4.

She pulled into the space next to it, killed her engine, and sat in the marina silence.

As this was a weekday, few people were working on their boats. Even those who lived here on boats were away at their jobs or schools or wherever. With the exception of the rhythmic clank of rigging, the groan of masts, the lapping kiss of water against hulls, a kind of sea-silence hung over the many gently bobbing craft. Trudie rolled down her window and took in the salty smell, felt the crisp breeze go through her hair. There wasn't a cloud in the sky. The day felt as if it were eternal.

She got out and walked to the security gate that led down to the dock. She scanned the two rows of boats—sailing vessels on the right, cabin cruisers on the left. Down on the dock she saw an Igloo ice chest, buckets and mops, a pile of rags. All heaped next to a blue-and-white Catalina 27. Trudie tried to see if there was anyone else aboard. If he had a woman with him—

She tested the gate and found it unlocked. Swinging it open, she launched herself down the steep ramp that rose and fell with the water.

What on earth did she think she was doing? she wondered as she headed straight for the Catalina, her heart racing.

Trudie knew very well what she was doing.

"Hi!" she called when she reached the boat.

He was down in the cockpit, bent over and coiling a rope line. Startled, he turned around and looked up, shading his eyes.

Good grief, she thought. Didn't this guy have a shirt to his name?

"Well, hi," he said, surprised.

She stood on the dock and looked at him with her hands on her hips. All he did was gaze at her—warily, she thought.

"Well?" she said. "You did invite me to go sailing, didn't you?"

He stared at her for an instant longer, then said slowly, "Sure. Come on aboard."

When he held out a hand, she took it; he hoisted her up onto the deck and over the safety rail. As she jumped down into the cockpit he said, "Do you know anything about sailing?"

"Of course! I'm an expert."

"If I told you to cast off the bow line, do you think you could?"

"Easy," she said, looking over the boat. "The bow. Is that the pointy end or the flat end?"

They looked at each other for a moment, then Bill laughed and said, "Come on, I'll show you around."

He touched her elbow as he followed her down into the cabin below, and when she reached the bottom step, Trudie was pleasantly surprised.

This little Catalina was clearly a second home to Bill the pool plumber. The rectangular windows were covered with curtains made of chintz; the bit of wall space was hung with pictures of square-riggers; nautical-motif pillows were strewn over the padded bench-type seating; the tiny galley shone and sparkled and had a maplewood rack of spices over the sink. Bookshelves were built into the walls and were crammed with paperbacks, best sellers, and magazines. There was even a small portable TV bolted up in the corner where the wall met the low ceiling. The cabin looked lived in and smelled clean, and Trudie found herself wondering if the fridge and cupboards were stocked for a long trip.

"So, to what do I owe this honor?" he said, standing close to her in the dim, cramped space.

She avoided looking at him. "Well, you did invite me," she said, scanning the spines of the books. "*African Genesis*," she said as she reached up for a battered paperback. "I read this in high school. It's very good. Have you read *The Hunting Hypothesis*?"

"Yes."

"What did you think of it?"

"I don't agree with him."

"You know," Trudie said as she reached up and replaced the book, her arm accidentally brushing his. "There's a woman up at Berkeley, Rebecca Cann, who believes that by studying mitochondrial DNA we can trace the ancestry of humankind all the way back to a single woman—"

"The Children of Eve," Bill said. "I saw the show on *Nova*. A farfetched theory if I ever heard one. But I suppose you agree with her."

Trudie finally turned to face him. He was standing so close that she could see flecks of gold in his brown irises, the suncreases at the corners of his eyes. "I guess we disagree on just about everything," she said quietly. "Don't we?"

He looked down at her. Those blue-green eyes got to him every time. "Why you?" he said softly. "Why is it that you get to me when no one else does? Why do I have to think about you all the time, even though it only makes me mad?"

"Well, you bug the hell out of me. All you male chauvinists are alike—"

473

And then he was kissing her and she was kissing him back and they were suddenly saying things with their bodies that no words could have expressed.

While a man from Marina Security was placing a parking ticket on her windshield because her bumper didn't have the required parking-permit sticker, and while Bill's office beeper beeped ignored in the pocket of his pants that lay crumpled in a heap on the floor, Trudie received a big shock.

Bill was an expert lover.

He took his time, slowly and lovingly, knew where to touch, where to touch again; where to kiss and how; he read her subtle signals; he didn't try to push or force or hurry, but he moved in harmony with her until she was breathless with passion and wanted to tell him she loved him. When he produced a condom and slipped it on quickly and discreetly, the way the guys at Butterfly did, Trudie was surprised. And then she wasn't surprised, because it was so in keeping with his being such a considerate lover.

They wound up on the small couch, panting and sweaty, entwined in each other's arms saying all the things they both suddenly realized they had wanted to say for a long time. Bill wanted to know everything about Trudie from the moment she was born, and she wanted to tell him. They talked about the construction business and how maybe they could combine their two companies and expand their radius, and about sailing to Catalina next weekend just as soon as that Pacific Palisades job was done, and about the exhibit of pre-Columbian art that was opening at the L.A. County Museum next week, which they agreed to attend together, and then he started making love to her again, while the boat gently rose and fell on the tide.

Trudie closed her eyes and held on to him tightly and thought: This is it. I've found the real thing. I don't need Butterfly anymore. . . .

49

AS THE SENATOR CAME THROUGH the arrival gate at LAX he was immediately surrounded by reporters and TV cameras. "What are Danny Mackay's chances now, Senator?" they all asked.

The old man smiled beneath his cowboy hat and said, "Ah have every confidence in mah son-in-law. You boys know that Danny Mackay is a man of the Lord. We'll get this straightened out in no time so we can get on with the business of puttin' him in the Oval Office!" He climbed into the limousine and rode off, smiling and waving.

As soon as he was alone in the hotel room with Danny, the old man shouted, "Just what in *hell* is going on here!"

Danny didn't look his usual handsome, confident self. It was three days now since the initial breaking news, and instead of dying down and blowing over, things were only getting hotter. He hadn't slept the past two nights and it showed.

"Damned if I know, sir. I'd swear the Democrats were behind all this."

"Don't blame the goddamned Democrats, boy! I want to know how you happen to come up owning bawdy houses and X-rated theaters! And now *slums*, for God's sake!"

Newspapers were strewn all over the hotel suite. The front page of every one of them carried the latest dirt dug up about Danny Mackay: through Royal Farms, his privately owned company, he owned a large block of slums in downtown Los Angeles. Wire photos of dangerous, dilapidated tenements accompanied a story about pimps, whores, and junkies living in rat- and cockroach-infested buildings.

"I'm telling you, sir," Danny said wearily. "I just couldn't go all over the country and examine every little pissant investment I had. I bought Royal Farms from Beverly Highland. Now, you know her reputation, sir. She couldn't have known about these things. And she certainly wouldn't have passed the company on to me if she had known."

The old man took out a cigar, slowly undid the wrapper, clipped off the end and took his time lighting it. "Well, you're just damned lucky that I've come to rescue you, son," he said after his first few puffs. "We can still save your ass in time for the convention. You'll go on TV tonight and tell America that you had no knowledge of these evils, that you are very sorry to have been a part of them, and that you intend to do something about them at once. We gotta get you as pure as the driven snow come the weekend."

Danny closed his eyes and nodded. He didn't like his father-in-law, but the man was powerful. His sudden flight to his son-in-law's troubled side was taken by the party as a good sign. Danny still had supporters, albeit nervous ones. Tonight, on TV, he was going to give his best performance ever. He was going to ask the country for forgiveness. And he had no doubt they would forgive him.

Lieutenant O'Malley wished for the hundredth time that he wasn't on this case. It was a messy business; it was starting to aggravate his ulcer.

And now with this new development—this second photograph that, unlike the one found in the bordello, was beyond a doubt genuine—the waters were only going to get muddier.

The woman said she had come to the police because she believed Danny Mackay should be punished. And she sat there now, in the outer office with a Styrofoam cup of coffee in her hand, a faded, dried-up Texas farm wife who lived a lonely widowed life and no doubt hoped to get a bit of excitement for telling her story.

About Danny Mackay and Bonner Purvis.

Jesus!

The detective went into the men's room, where he carefully washed his face, cleaned his fingernails, and combed his hair down flat and shiny. The morning had been going downhill as it was, what with pressure from above to drop the bordello case and close the file, but now this woman in her cotton print dress and broken-down shoes had dropped a time bomb in his lap.

The photograph was genuine, all right. She said she had taken it herself, back in 1955, when a revival bus had come through her town and she'd volunteered to put up two of the troupe's members in her own home. Out of Christian charity, she declared, she had taken in the young Danny and Bonner, only to be rewarded with a curse from Satan himself. "It wasn't natural, what them boys did," she had told O'Malley. "And I saw them at it, right there in the bedroom."

Actually, the snapshot appeared to be innocent enough: two smiling young men sitting naked in a tin tub out in some backyard, clearly trying to get cool and goofing off. They held beers and had an arm up on each other's shoulders. Just a couple of good-time boys passing the time of day.

But not so innocent when accompanied by this woman's story of witnessing an act of homosexuality. That changed the picture entirely.

It also changed everything else.

Because, O'Malley knew, once this got out, people would start asking themselves: If Danny Mackay once engaged in indecent acts with another man, then it was just possible that he *could* own a whorehouse and a porno magazine and all the rest.

The photograph and the woman's testimony could hang him.

Lieutenant O'Malley had a problem. Simply, he liked Danny Mackay and wanted to vote for him in November. But he was also a man of conscience. The woman and her photograph could not be ignored.

There was a flurry of activity in the Mackay suite of the Century Plaza. While his personal makeup man got him ready for the television cameras Danny's aides and advisers prompted him in his hastily written speech. Off to the side the senator stood with a dark expression on his face, with his daughter, Angelica, hovering close behind him.

Danny felt good. The Jack Daniel's had warmed him and

infused him with power, just as in the old days, and the speech was a damn good one. He'd have America begging him to become president when he was through with them tonight. There was even a clever bit of insinuation in the speech that even the great John Kennedy's name was sullied by detractors.

One of Danny's secretaries came up and said, "There's a Detective O'Malley outside, sir. He says he wants to have a word with you."

Danny waved a hand. "Later. After my speech."

"What do you suppose he wants?" Bonner asked.

"He's probably selling tickets to the policemen's ball!"

But when the other secretary came hurrying in and told Danny that Miss Highland was on the phone, Danny jumped up, yanked the towel from around his neck and dashed into the bedroom to take her call. Of all his financial backers, Beverly Highland was one of the most important. Her silence these past three days had been killing him. He prayed now, as he picked up the receiver, that she had something good to say.

His prayer was answered.

Not only did she believe him to be innocent of all these sordid things, but she was going to make a public statement tomorrow morning announcing her continued support of his candidacy. "I have no fear, Reverend," she said in her quiet way, "that this will all pass and that soon, very soon, you shall have your just reward."

50

LINDA MARKUS leaned against the frame of her sliding glass door, watching the last rays of a Pacific sunset paint peachy-orange streaks across the western sky. The ocean smelled hot and salty. It was June, and Malibu was awakening to summer life: down the beach from her house, people were cavorting in the surf; steaks were being seared on hibachis; kids were blackening marshmallows over open fires; teenagers were throwing

Frisbies and volleyballs and engaging in hasty, furtive sex among the dunes. Behind her, a commentator was saying over the radio: "Two more people have come forward claiming to have known Danny Mackay in his early years as a preacher in Texas, one of whom once ran a house of prostitution in San Antonio. A Mrs. Hazel Courtland has signed a sworn statement that Danny Mackay and Bonner Purvis once supplied girls for her house. The second person is a retired minister from Austin, Texas, who used to host Mackay's revival meetings in his church. Reverend White claims that at the time, in 1955 and 1956, Danny Mackay worked for a man named Billy Bob Magdalene, who disappeared mysteriously one day and has never been accounted for. Mr. Mackay was questioned by the police this morning regarding that disappearance."

Linda only half listened. When the news broke four days ago about the secret rooms above Fanelli being somehow connected with Good News Ministries, she had understood why she had received the notice informing her that Butterfly was closing down and a refund of her membership money.

Where did he go? she wondered. The masked companion who set me free?

"Who are you?" she had asked on that remarkable night, when he had released her from her prison. "What's your name? Why do you work here?"

But he had only smiled and placed a fingertip on her lips. And then she had realized: she didn't really want to know his name or who he was outside the walls of Butterfly. He would be remembered as the fantasy lover who had broken her bonds.

He had said to her, "The rejection you thought you saw in men was only in your mind. You imagined that they were turned off by your scars. The men were driven away not by your physical flaw but by your sudden coldness toward them. You were defensive. And I doubt they pulled away from you; probably you pushed them away, as you had done with me."

He was right. And Linda had left Butterfly feeling a mixture of awe and newfound courage. She hadn't known her body was capable of such a reaction. And now she was anxious, like a child who has learned to walk, to try it on her own.

A warm breeze came up from the ocean and Linda hugged

herself. She felt like shouting out loud her joy; she wanted to run down the beach and tell everyone how happy she was.

Last night . . . last night!

She turned away from the sun deck and went into the kitchen, where remnants of last night's dinner still lay on the counter. He had brought pizza, of all things, and they had had it for both dinner and breakfast this morning. Now evening was drawing in and they would need to eat again. Linda looked around. What should she cook? What would he like?

She heard the shower running.

He was awake.

And suddenly she didn't want to cook or eat or anything else. Except make love.

She caught sight of herself in the polished window of her oven: a thirty-eight-year-old woman with dancing eyes and flushed cheeks and wearing only a bathrobe.

Butterfly. Had it been real? Had her interludes with Casanova and Zorro and a Confederate officer really taken place? Had she really found herself in those incredible dream-rooms? If only she knew whom to thank.

But she didn't know who had run Butterfly, except maybe for Danny Mackay, as was being reported in the papers. But she doubted he had anything to do with the fantasy fulfillment. Linda had not been able to learn the name of her companion, nor the identity of anyone else behind Butterfly's operation. Only Alexis, her friend the pediatrician, had managed to get some information. Alexis's companion had fallen in love with her—he had told her who he was and his feelings for her—and now they were living together, in a cabin in Benedict Canyon. His name was Charlie, and all he had been able to tell Alexis was that the director had interviewed and hired him and told him what to do. Beyond that, Butterfly had been as much a mystery to him and the other companions as to the members.

The real secret of Butterfly, Linda suspected, would probably never be revealed.

She heard footsteps cross the living room floor. And then he was in the kitchen and coming up behind her, sliding his arms around her waist. "Good morning, my friend," he murmured. "Or is it evening? I've lost track."

Linda turned and looked up at José. His hair was still damp from the shower. She put her arms around his neck and kissed him.

"Look what happens when I ask a woman out for a drink," he said. "I fall in love."

"Is that what this is?"

He grew serious. "I mean it, my friend. When I look at you, and remember what you were like last night, I think I don't have to go to parties anymore."

Linda rested her head on his shoulder, and felt at peace.

51

THE TINY BUTTERFLY shimmered in the dying June sunlight and cast golden reflections. It seemed to flutter down into Carmen's open palm, and then it lay still.

"I won't be needing it anymore," Beverly said softly. "I want you to have it."

Carmen gazed down at the delicate butterfly bracelet through tear-filled eyes. There had been something so final in this last gesture. She had sworn she wouldn't cry when this moment came, but now she couldn't help herself.

"I will miss you, *amiga*," she whispered.

"I know. And I'll miss you." Beverly turned away from Carmen and looked at the others gathered in the room.

Maggie, with her frizzy red hair escaping its knot, sat red-eyed and speechless. Ann Hastings shared a love seat with Roy Madison, both grave-faced and silent. And Jonas Buchanan, standing like a sentinel by the closed door. Only Bob Manning was not present. He was out in the car, waiting for Beverly.

The enormous old house, a mansion once owned by a silent movie star, seemed to hover all around them in a kind of expectancy. Dust-filled beams of afternoon sunlight streamed through the diamond-paned windows and cast an otherworldly glow on the silent occupants. Beverly Highland stood wraithlike in the center of the circle of friends, tall and thin, her platinum hair swept neatly up, her cream-colored slacks and white silk blouse emphasizing her paleness. She was pausing to give her friends a final look at her. Everything that had to be done was done; everything was ready and finished.

All that remained was for her to go to the Century Plaza Hotel, where Danny Mackay was waiting.

"It's time," she said at last, and her friends bestirred themselves.

They accompanied her to the white Rolls-Royce Silver Cloud that waited with its motor purring, and one by one they embraced her. Beverly paused to look at them—Carmen, who had once been Carmelita; Ann, who had been lonely and unhappy; Maggie, who had been a new widow with two babies when Beverly found her; and Jonas, the black ex-cop who had found her mother and nearly her sister, who now regarded her with damp eyes. Then she got in and Bob Manning closed the door behind her. Beverly didn't do or say anything as the car snaked its way down Beverly Canyon Drive to Highland Avenue. But finally she had to—there was one last thing to do before she got to the hotel.

Picking up the car telephone, she dialed a number she knew by heart, and asked for Detective O'Malley.

The day had started out badly for the lieutenant, and now, in late afternoon, it was only getting worse. Why did this Danny Mackay business have to happen in his precinct? O'Malley looked at the thick file on his desk and shook his head. What a mess! That Texas farm wife with her photograph had sure started something. The minute that picture was printed in the newspapers, it seemed to O'Malley, all sorts of characters began coming out of the woodwork. It looked as if half the population of Texas had known Danny Mackay in his earlier years and had some dirt on him. They talked to anyone who would listen. In these past two days newspapers all over the country had carried stories of Danny and Bonner's wild, whooping and hollering days as young tent preachers. The supermarket tabloids even published photographs of old barns and fields where orgies and satanic rituals were reported to have taken place. O'Malley had no doubt that 80 or 90 percent of these people had never even *seen* Mackay, much less been fleeced or seduced or abandoned by him. And the thirty-odd women all claiming to have had illegitimate children by Danny only served to point up the ludicrousness of the whole affair.

But these eight Danny Girls in their red cowgirl outfits, coming forward and telling the press that they were prostitutes and admitting to having been in an orgy with Mackay on the night before the primary, well, this was a little too close to home.

Pressure was mounting on the lieutenant to take action. Because of all the dirt that was suddenly coming out about Mackay, public opinion was rapidly shifting. People were beginning to think that not only did Danny know about the Beverly Hills whorehouse but he personally ran it and frequently availed himself of its services. Well, in the eyes of a self-righteous public that had been duped and was angry to find itself so gullible and therefore was looking for revenge and a way to redeem itself, Danny Mackay was guilty of a crime and should be arrested.

By Lieutenant O'Malley.

His phone was ringing and there was a stack of telephone messages he had yet to read. More supposed confessions from Danny Mackay's past. More indignant complaints from decent citizens wanting something done. O'Malley retreated to the relative quiet of the men's room and gave his fingernails a good scrubbing.

How on earth could they arrest Mackay? They had no real proof of any wrongdoing in this city. Sure, what they had on him now would be enough to bring in anybody else, at least for questioning, but not Danny Mackay. My God, O'Malley thought as he lathered and washed and rinsed his hands clean, this was *Reverend* Danny Mackay everyone was talking about, one of the richest men in America, the leader of the Moral Decency movement, a man of powerful connections—a man with one foot in the White House, for God's sake!

O'Malley dried his hands, tossed the paper towel into the trash can, and paused to look at himself in the mirror.

The man who put the cuffs on Danny Mackay had better be damned sure he knew what he was doing. Or he might regret it for the rest of his career.

On his way back to his desk O'Malley was told that Beverly Highland was on the phone asking for him.

He groaned. Beverly Highland was one of Danny Mackay's staunchest supporters. Hadn't she made a statement to the press yesterday about her continued belief in the man? She was one of the people who made this city tick. One word from that woman, O'Malley knew, and she could have his badge.

His hand hovered over the phone. What on earth did she want to talk to him about?

It was going to be an order to lay off Mackay.

With a sinking feeling that not only was this not his day, it hadn't been his week, Detective O'Malley braced himself and picked up the phone.

Things were looking bleak in the Mackay suite of the Century Plaza Hotel. A kind of frantic chaos had Danny's large staff in its grip as they shouted into the phones, received and sent telex messages, talked to the press, and tried to fight off the ultimate doom that seemed to be racing toward them. Tomorrow the Republican Convention was going to open. Already, Danny's political supporters were falling away at an alarming rate. And his financial empire was beginning to crumble. Investors were pulling out, various of his holdings on the New York Stock Exchange were dropping sharply, Christians all over the country were clamoring to get their donations back. And Danny, in the midst of this nightmarish maelstrom, had no idea why all this was happening to him.

That Texas farm wife, for instance. Seeing the photograph in the paper had stopped him cold. Yeah, he remembered the woman and the day she had snapped a picture of him and Bonner in that old tin tub out back. Hell, she had been in it with them! Danny remembered those few good days of eating her hot Texas chili and romping in her bed, the three of them. But what was all this garbage about homosexuality? Why on earth would she appear all of a sudden and tell such an outrageous lie?

"Someone must have put her up to it," a bewildered Bonner had said.

Yes. But who?

And then, all of a sudden, like an avalanche or a gigantic ocean wave, all those others with their incredible stories, swearing that they had known Danny and that he had done this or that to them. A couple of them were actually true—he admitted he had left a few bastards around the South—but the rest—satanic rituals, orgies—where had all that come from?

He was pacing the carpet and frequently looking at his watch. When Beverly Highland had called that morning to say she wanted to meet privately with him, Danny had felt as if the marines were coming to his rescue. She had assured him on the phone that she continued to stand by him and that together they would work this out. She was rich and powerful, and people believed her. There was yet time to save Danny's neck. And Beverly Highland was going to do it.

Danny made the mistake of glancing up at his father-in-law. The senator sat in a chair like some old pasha, puffing on his foul cigars and passing judgment on his son with each hour that ticked away. He had spent the day behind locked doors with party organizers, trying to save the drowning rat that was his son-in-law. For their own sakes they were going to try to rescue him, but it was going to take a miracle to do it.

That all these recent stories were lies and imaginings the old man had no doubt. What infuriated him was that the boy was stupid enough to let it all get started in the first place. Danny Girls turning out to be prostitutes! Of course Mackay was denying knowledge of that. As far as he knew, the girls his staff had recruited were all peaches-and-cream American virgins. Where those eight came from was beyond him. And that business about the missionary, Fred Banks, who was arrested in some Middle Eastern jail—the man himself had come out and announced it had been a hoax engineered by Danny! Danny insisted the man was being paid by someone to tell the story. But who? That was exactly the problem—Danny hadn't a clue as to what was going on. Hell, what kind of a man is that to have in the White House?

The senator was giving his son-in-law one last chance. If

Beverly Highland came through for him, then there was hope of saving his ass yet. If she didn't, then the senator was packing up his daughter and taking her back to Texas. And Good News Ministries, as far as he was concerned, could go to Hell in a handbasket.

"She's here," someone said, and Danny rushed to the window. Even from so high up he could see the commotion down on the street, where reporters were surrounding the Silver Cloud and bulbs were flashing and TV cameras were following Beverly Highland into the lobby.

She glided serenely through the crowd, with Bob Manning carving a path for her, and entered the elevator without having said a word. It was Manning who told the press that Miss Highland would make a formal statement after her meeting with Danny Mackay.

Bob Manning knocked on the door for her, and it was opened almost as soon as his knuckles touched wood. Beverly entered the smoke-filled room and immediately felt the tension in the air, sensed the panic and desperation, smelled the fear. For an instant she was reminded of the dirty smell of Hazel's whorehouse, where men gathered to smoke and drink and sweat their fears away. Danny's staff parted for him like an obedient sea, giving way as he came to greet Beverly like a magnanimous monarch. He came toward her with out-stretched hands, but she merely held on to her flat eel-skin bag and requested that they be left alone.

"Alone" to Danny meant having just eight or nine people around him—it had been years since he had drawn a breath without secretaries, bodyguards, and advisers in his presence. But Beverly meant *alone,* and so he sent his people off to the other suites and closed the door behind them.

The room felt strange, being suddenly so silent. Beverly had allowed "Mr. Purvis" to stay, while she kept her chauffeur with her, explaining that he was also her secretary and body-guard. Three of them sat down while Manning remained standing by the closed door.

"Miss Highland," Danny said, leaning forward with his elbows on his knees, "you don't know how much I appreciate your standing by me and continuing to believe in me during this awful nightmare. Surely the Lord has blessed me to have given me a friend like yourself."

A faint smile lifted her lips. "It must be awful for you, Mr. Mackay."

"It's been terrible. The curses which Moses visited upon Pharaoh couldn't compare to what I've gone through in this past week!"

She watched him. Although he had clearly fixed himself up to look his best for her visit, the toll was showing on Danny's face. "Has it been torture for you?" she said softly.

"Yes, ma'am."

"Has it caused you great pain and anguish?"

He blinked. "It certainly has."

"Do you feel alone and abandoned?"

Perplexity briefly flickered across his handsome face. Then he said quietly, "That is exactly how I feel, Miss Highland. It's remarkable how well you understand my situation."

"I am not a stranger to those afflictions myself, Mr. Mackay. And surely you must feel confused and bewildered by everything that has happened. You must think that your whole world has suddenly come apart for no reason."

"Well, I'll tell you, Miss Highland"—he cleared his throat—"or may I call you Beverly?"

She nodded slightly. "You may call me anything you wish, Mr. Mackay. There was a time when you called me Rachel."

He stared at her. "How's that again?"

"You know, Rachel. Don't you remember a girl named Rachel, Mr. Mackay? Rachel Dwyer?"

"I, uh . . ." He glanced at Bonner, who shrugged. "I'm afraid I don't, Miss Highland. Who is she?"

Beverly spoke in a gentle, almost detached way. "Rachel Dwyer was a young girl you picked up in El Paso thirty-seven years ago, Mr. Mackay. You took her to San Antonio and put her in a whorehouse run by a woman named Hazel. Then you forced her to have an abortion and made Hazel throw her out. Surely you remember her now, Mr. Mackay?"

Memory suddenly dawned behind his eyes. Danny licked

his lips and said, "Well, no, I can't say I do. Is she another one of these sensation seekers who have climbed on the scandal wagon?"

"No, Mr. Mackay. I told you, you used to call *me* Rachel. I am Rachel Dwyer."

His eyes widened, and then narrowed. "You can't be. Rachel was—"

"Ugly? Yes, I was. But plastic surgery took care of that. I used to have brown hair, too."

He stared at her with his mouth open.

"Do you still not remember me? I have a tattoo on the inside of my thigh. You put it there. It's a small butterfly. . . ."

"I—" His voice caught. He looked again at Bonner, who now had a strange look on his face. "I don't understand, Miss Highland. What is this all ab—"

"Please call me Rachel. I want to hear it. For old times' sake."

"I don't understand."

"It's very simple, Danny. After I left Texas I came to California. I changed my name and my looks. And now here we are, together again."

Beverly could see the pulse throb in his neck. Color drained from his face as comprehension finally dawned. "You?" he whispered. *"You're Rachel?"*

"Yes, Danny. After all these years. Did you think I was dead?"

"Well, I. . . ." He shifted in his chair.

"You hadn't thought about me at all, had you?" she said softly.

"Well, it was so long ago, and all. Well. . . ." He swallowed. "I'll be. Rachel Dwyer." He laughed nervously. "Well, what a reunion this is! Why didn't you tell me before? I mean, why keep it a secret? What with all the money you've put into my ministry and the political support, you could have told me. Rachel!" he said too loudly. "This is a happy moment!"

"Is it?"

"Well, yes. I mean, we're a team again, just like we were all those years ago. To think that you've come here tonight to

help me. Praise the Lord for his miracles, Rachel. He caused
your heart to forgive me. I know I did wrong, making you have
that abortion. And, believe me, I got down on my knees afterward and repented. I went to Hazel's house and she said
you'd gone and I went looking for you."

"You did? Why didn't you look in New Mexico, where I
came from? Or in Hollywood, where I'd always talked about
searching for my sister."

"Well, uh, I. . . ."

"It's all right, Danny," she said gently. "It happened so
long ago and we've come so far since then."

"Yes we have, praise the Lord. And what a good Christian
woman you are, Rachel, to let bygones be bygones and come
to my aid in this hour of need."

"Oh," she said with a small frown, "I'm afraid you mis-
understand, Danny. I never forgave you for what you did. And
I haven't come here tonight to rescue you."

He stared at her.

"I came here to tell you a few things that I think you need
to know."

Beverly sat in the wing chair, the picture of relaxed confidence. She held her flat eel-skin purse in her lap and spoke
softly. There was no anger in her voice, no coldness, no hate.
She was just a woman quietly telling a story.

"On the night you kicked me out of your car and left me
to bleed to death, Danny, you told me to remember the name
Danny Mackay. Well, I did. And I made a vow that someday
I would have my revenge. I have lived these past thirty-five
years with no other thought in my head except to see you pay
for what you did to me."

He squirmed a little. Perspiration broke out on his forehead. "You can't be serious."

"I am dead serious, Danny. Every breath I took brought
me one breath closer to seeing you destroyed."

"Why wait so long?" he said in a tight voice. "You had
plenty of opportunities in the past to strike at me."

"That's true. But I wanted you to fall from a great height,
Danny. I also didn't want you to be able to slither out of this
one, and go on to hurt more people. I had to be certain, I had

to be positive that I had enough on you to hang you." She leaned forward, clutching the purse. "So I allowed you to continue your pursuit of power until I decided the time was right."

"What are you talking about? You *allowed* me? You didn't allow me anything! Where I got, I got on my own!"

"Oh yes, you made it this far on your own, Danny, but only because *I let you.*"

"You're crazy."

"Am I? Think back to 1972. In your Houston church. A man died and you thought you'd brought him back to life. That was my doing, Danny. I staged the whole thing."

Danny looked at Bonner.

"I was in Houston that night, Danny," she went on. "The man who died was an actor friend of mine. He's very good at death scenes. Another actor played the doctor and a friend of mine played the wife. We staged the whole thing, Danny, and you fell for it."

His hands gripped the arms of his chair; his knuckles were white. "For what purpose?"

"To have the ammunition to stop you if you should try that stunt again. Fooling all those innocent people with your tricks! So I staged one more, with people who would be willing to admit it was all a fraud, if it became necessary to do so."

"I don't believe you."

"And Fred Banks. I bought him off a month after you brought him back to the United States. He told me how you had worked it all, how you had deceived the American people with your charade, how you gave illegal arms to an Arab king. And, finally, Royal Farms, Danny. I created Royal Farms just for you to buy. I loaded it with such secondary holdings as a men's clothing store, a dirty magazine, and massage parlors, counting on the fact that you would be too greedy and too busy and too wrapped up in yourself to sufficiently investigate the company you had just bought. And you never let me down, Danny."

The air conditioner clicked on just then and a low hum filled the silence. Cold air wafted through the wall vents, gently stirring the drapes and chilling the occupants of the room. Outside, Los Angeles sweltered on this sultry June evening; in the lobby below, reporters loosened their ties and mopped their brows, waiting for Beverly Highland.

"You're mad," Danny growled. "I don't have to listen to any of this."

He started to rise, but sat back down when she said, "You do have to listen, Danny, because what happens next is up to you."

"What do you mean?"

"Everything that has gone on in this room is known only by the four of us. It can stay that way, and I can continue to be your avid supporter, if you'll do one thing."

"What's that?"

She clutched the purse to herself; her heart was racing so fast she was nearly breathless. "You have to beg me," she said softly. "Beg me to help you, Danny."

He shot to his feet. "Go fuck yourself."

"That won't save you, will it? Think about it, Danny. When I walk out of this room, the press is going to want a statement from me. It's up to you what that statement will be. You see, Danny, I can clear your name. I have proof in this purse that you have been framed, that everything that has come out this past week was designed to destroy you. If I hand it over to the press, you'll be a hero, Danny. People will see you as an innocent victim and they'll worship you as a martyr. You'll go even higher from here, Danny. There will be no stopping you then. But . . ." She paused. "It is also in my power to ruin you completely. One word from me, and the world will turn its back on you, Danny, and you'll be left to rot. Which will it be?"

He looked at Bonner, whose face mirrored his own fear. Then he looked at the chauffeur standing by the door. An old man. Guarding a frail woman.

"Don't even think of it, Danny," she said. "Violence will not save you now. Do as I ask and you walk out of here an exonerated man."

"Go to Hell."

"I suggest you comply with the lady's request," the chauffeur suddenly said, surprising Danny.

"You keep out of this."

"I don't think so," Manning said as he walked slowly toward Danny. "Now, I know what's going through your head right now, boy. I can read you like a child's book. You're thinking that she's making all this up and that you can sweet-talk your way out of it. You think she's insane and that she can't hurt you. Well, boy, not only can she hurt you, but *I* can as well."

Danny snorted. "You! What could you possibly do to hurt me?"

"Well," Manning said quietly, "I can tell those reporters out there the answer to the question they've been asking you. Which is, whatever became of Billy Bob Magdalene?"

Danny narrowed his eyes. The police had already harassed him with that one, and he'd told them about how he had bought the bus honestly and legally from Billy Bob and had left the drunken old preacher in a town where Billy Bob had decided to retire. And the police had believed him—no reason not to. "You don't know anything about Billy Bob," he said.

"You thought Billy Bob Magdalene was old when you knew him," Beverly's chauffeur said. "But he was only forty-three years old when you linked up with him. That was thirty-four years ago, which would make him about seventy-seven today. And his real name wasn't Magdalene, it was Manning. Come now, don't you two pudknockers recognize me?"

A shocked silence filled the room. Bonner slowly got to his feet, his mouth hanging open. Danny stared at the old man with wide eyes.

"You boys left me for dead," Billy Bob went on. "And I darned near did die out in that desert. But some tourists who had lost their way came by and got me just in time. They put me in a hospital in Odessa, and there I remained for sixteen years, crippled and demented from too much sun and no water. And then one day, just like that"—he snapped his fingers—"my memory came back, and the first sane words I uttered were 'Danny Mackay.' By chance my little story appeared in a small newspaper, and Miss Highland here got wind of it because of a clipping service she uses. She drove out to that hospital and had a long talk with me. She rescued me from that prison and gave me a reason to live. To last long enough to see the day when you pay for what you did."

Thunderstruck, Danny stumbled back and fell into his chair.

"You see," Billy Bob said as he went to stand behind Beverly, "it's all true. Every word of it. She has watched you all your life, boy, followed your every slimy move. Son, you didn't even fart without her knowing it!"

The air conditioner went on and off; sounds in the next room came through the closed door in a muffled roar; telephones rang in the distance; a siren wailed down Wilshire Boulevard. Beverly sat patiently in the wing chair, her purse and its precious contents hugged to her breast. She was in no hurry; she had waited long enough, she could wait a few minutes more.

Finally, dry-mouthed and white-faced, Danny said, "Rachel, don't do this to me."

"You'll have to do better than that, Danny."

"Christ, do you really want me to beg?"

"Yes, Danny," she said, her voice growing cold and hard now. "As I once begged you. Think of that innocent girl lying on the abortionist's table. Picture her terrified face, hear her voice pleading with you to let her keep her baby. And then you do the same for me. Let me see your fear, let me hear you beg to spare your life."

Danny's hand shot out for the phone by his chair.

"Do that," she said, "and you'll be destroyed before you leave this room!"

His hand fell away. "Please, Rachel," he whispered. "Please don't do this to me."

"That's not enough, Danny."

"Oh God," he cried. "Don't do this to me!"

She slowly rose and looked down at him. "I've waited thirty-five years for this moment. I've sacrificed and denied myself just for this moment. I won't be cheated, Danny."

He clutched his hands together and slid to his knees. "Please, Rachel. Please save me."

"Let me see the tears you're so famous for. You produce them well enough for the TV cameras. Now produce them for me."

"Jesus, you can't do this to me! Please, Rachel. *Please!*"

"God," she said softly. "You make me sick."

He was crying in earnest now. "I'll do anything, Rachel. Anything. Just get me out of this. Don't let them crucify me! I couldn't bear it. Not after all these years! I couldn't bear the disgrace. I couldn't live with it!"

She gazed down at him for a moment longer, then she walked toward the door. As she put her hand on the knob she said, "I'm afraid you're going to have to live with it, Danny."

"*What do you want from me?* I'm begging you, isn't that enough?"

"No, Danny, it isn't. I never intended to save you. I only wanted to see how low you would sink. The papers in this purse are my final statement to the press, denouncing you and everything you have stood for. If it had been only me that you had hurt, I might be able to forgive you. But you have hurt so many others, and you murdered my baby. For that there is no forgiveness."

"CHRIST!"

"And one more thing, Danny. A Detective O'Malley is on his way here to arrest you."

He reached for the chair and pulled himself up to his feet. "What are you talking about? He wouldn't dare arrest me!"

"I'm afraid he will, Danny. He has to. Do you remember the time you came to see me at Hazel's and you got drunk and bragged about getting arrested on a morals charge and then escaping from the road gang?"

He and Bonner stared at her.

"You thought the statute of limitations was up and you were free. Well, you were wrong, Danny. I sent Billy Bob to Texas to look into it, and do you know what he found? That there is an outstanding warrant on you, a felony escape warrant, Danny, for which there is no statute of limitations and no bail. In just a few minutes, Danny, you will be taken out of here in handcuffs. And that"—she turned the knob and the door opened—"is what I have lived thirty-five years to see at last."

He flew at her. But Beverly pulled the door open just as he reached her, screaming, "You fucking bitch!" causing the roomful of people to turn around and fall silent.

She entered the suite as Detective O'Malley came in with a couple of uniformed policemen. Having seen the detective, the newspaper reporters and television people had followed him up from the lobby and were now crowded in the corridor outside Danny Mackay's suite. They had heard Danny's shouts and now clamored around Beverly, firing questions and taking her picture. She held up her hand for silence, then handed the eel-skin purse to Billy Bob. "Everything I have to say to the press is in this written statement. I am hereby withdrawing my support, financial and political and personal, from Danny Mackay."

The media people created a roar in the hallway and blocked her progress to the elevator. As she reached the double doors she heard Danny's voice screaming above all the others: "You bitch! You filthy bitch! You won't get away with this! I'll get you! You'll see! I'LL GET YOU—"

She stepped into the elevator and turned around in time to see Danny struggling with the policemen, his wrists hand-cuffed. Then the doors closed and she was engulfed by silence.

The Rolls-Royce Silver Cloud sped along the deserted Pacific Coast Highway. Bob Manning was driving, Beverly sat in the backseat. To her left, sheer cliffs dropped down hundreds of feet to the Pacific Ocean, which was splashed with silvery moonlight. To her right, hills rose up like dark giants to touch the stars. The Rolls raced like a silver bullet through the night, silent and in a hurry.

Beverly was aware of the headlights behind her. They had appeared shortly after she and Billy Bob had left the Century Plaza, and had stayed with them ever since. Once, she turned and looked back. It was a brown sedan, the driver a silhouette in the glare. When Billy Bob sped up, the brown car sped up. When he slowed down, it slowed down. And now they snaked as a pair, bumpers too close, along the winding, treacherous coast highway.

Billy Bob, also aware of the car behind, glanced frequently

in the rearview mirror. At the same time he tried to keep his eyes on the dangerous curves. He was acutely aware of the sheer drop down to rocks and breakers below.

Then the headlights moved and Beverly turned in time to see the brown car pull up alongside the Rolls. She reached for the hand strap. She braced herself and said, "Bob—"

His foot moved for the brakes.

Moments later the Silver Cloud was flying through the air in a beautiful silver arc and plunging to the rocks and churning ocean below.

52

IT WAS ALL OVER.

Butterfly was finished; "Lonnie," the fantasy cowboy, no longer existed.

Jessica stood on the balcony that opened off the master bedroom of her Sunset Boulevard home. It was a warm June evening, and she was staring down at the white dry hole of their swimming pool. It had developed serious cracks, so now it had been drained and was going to be inspected tomorrow. When the Franklins had had the pool put in, Jessica had begged John to let Trudie do it. She had assured him that Trudie was good at what she did and that they would get a quality swimming pool from her. But John did not like Trudie Stein, thought of her as just another inconsequential airhead, and so he had hired another company to install it, headed by a man he'd met in a bar. Now, just three years later, they had problems.

But Jessica didn't care. She gazed down into the empty crater in their back garden and thought about the step she was about to take.

Eight years ago Jessica had walked from her father's house straight into her husband's house without once having gone outside. It was time now to go outside and see what was there.

She turned away from the pool and went into the bedroom,

where all that was left to do was snap down the clasps of her suitcase. As she did she paused to look at the king-size bed she had slept in so many nights alone, even when John was lying next to her. Then she picked up the case, her sweater, and her purse and walked out of the bedroom.

"I need a vacation," she had told her partner, Fred Morton. And he had agreed. In their years of struggling to build a practice Jessica had never taken any time off. "I'm going to go away for a while. You can manage without me."

He could, for a short time, now that they had added three junior attorneys and a paralegal to their growing firm.

Jessica had told Fred first, then Trudie, who was at this moment sailing around the Channel Islands with her love, Bill. Finally she had informed her parents that she was going away for a while to do some thinking. In response to their question about John—was he going with her?—Jessica had said nothing. Now only one person remained to be told.

She and John had not spoken to each other since Memorial Day, when she had driven away from the Renaissance Fair, leaving him behind. The days that followed had been cold ones, despite the Los Angeles heat wave, with John and Jessica sleeping apart, taking meals separately, never touching or acknowledging the other's presence, like two phantoms haunting a house on two different planes. On that day in the parking lot outside the fair a decisive threshold had been crossed. Too much had been said, too much laid bare. Things would never be the same again, nor was there any hope of their ever getting better. Jessica knew that, in John's eyes, she had committed an unforgivable crime: she had provoked him into an undignified act—striking a woman. For the rest of their lives he would cling to the belief that it was her fault, hers alone, and that any steps for reconciliation or forgiveness had to be taken by her.

Well, she was taking steps at last.

John was in his study, watching the TV news. All the stations were covering the sensational death of Beverly Highland. "A witness at the scene, identified as Ms. Ann Hastings," the anchorwoman reported, "says she saw a brown four-door sedan force Miss Highland's Rolls-Royce over the edge of the cliff and then drive off. Rescue efforts are still going on, but because of ocean currents and the fact that the car, when dredged up, was found with its doors open, there is little hope of recovering the bodies of Beverly Highland and her chauffeur, Bob Manning. The accident occurred shortly after Miss Highland left the Century Plaza Hotel, where she had met privately with Danny Mackay."

Jessica came and stood in the doorway and gazed at the man she had once vowed to love, honor, and obey.

"John," she said.

He either didn't hear her or chose to ignore her.

"John?" she said a little louder. "I have something to say to you."

Finally he looked up. His face was cold and hard. He saw the suitcase in her hand.

"I'm leaving you," Jessica said.

And then she was in her dark blue Cadillac on the Pacific Coast Highway, speeding into the sunset, free at last.

Epilogue

ON THE ISLAND that could have been any island in any green sea in the world, the woman lay back on plush velour towels and watched the news that was being broadcast from the other side of the world. While the camera recorded for posterity the stately burial of a famous Houston personality, the commentator was saying: ". . . Danny Mackay, who hanged himself in jail three days after his arrest on an old morals charge. It is believed that he was driven to suicide by grief over the total disintegration of his political and evangelical empire."

The woman on the chaise longue picked up the remote control and clicked the television set into silence. Then she smiled at the young man kneeling at her side.

He didn't know what it was all about, and he didn't care. She had approached him at Butterfly one day with an offer he couldn't refuse—that she would take care of him if he took care of her and not ask any questions.

He watched her smile in contentment and stretch under the deliciously hot sun. Clearly, the news on the TV had been good. It was also a signal that he resume his lovemaking.

He drew himself up and kissed her long and lingeringly on the lips. She moaned softly. Then he drove his hands through her dark brown hair and kissed her more passionately, with the urgency that he knew she liked. He moved slowly down her body, untying the strings of her bathing suit, brushing his lips over her oiled, coconut-scented skin.

When his mouth reached her thighs, she sighed deeply, relishing his sensual touch, his gentle, artful way of making love. Opening her eyes slightly, she squinted in the dazzling sunshine at the things that surrounded her: a tray of rich, creamy chocolate truffles; a stack of novels as delicious as the bonbons, waiting to be read; the golden head of the young man who was feasting on her body.

She felt content and languid and filled with a peace deeper than she had ever known. It had all gone so well, the staged accident to "kill" Beverly Highland—Maggie and Carmen in the brown car; the Rolls going over the cliff; the hasty, secret drive to the airport; the funeral with an empty coffin because Beverly Highland's body was never found. And now the friends were separated forever, wealthy and secure, living the lives they had mapped out for themselves. Carmen in the Beverly Hills mansion, Ann Hastings in Hawaii, Maggie with her lover in San Diego, Jonas Buchanan opening a nationwide detective agency, and Billy Bob living out his last years in the tropical decadence of Rio—

The young man looked up and said, "What's this mark inside your thigh? It looks like an old tattoo."

She laughed and said, "It used to be a butterfly." Then, not knowing which to indulge in first—the chocolates or the boy—because it had been such a long time, Rachel finally reached out for Jamie, who used to swim naked in her pool.

ABOUT THE AUTHOR

KATHRYN HARVEY lives with her husband in California, and is at work on her next novel.